# Echo of the Evercry

E. J. Dawson

Literary Wanderlust | Denver, Colorado

# Dedication

To every girl who felt like she never belonged,
and every woman who wore a mask to cope.
I see you.

*Run little runtling*
*Flee with all your fears*
*Mother's gone a-hunting*
*Won't be back for years*

*Sigh little weakling*
*With a pocket full of tears*
*Hear the wolf howling*
*When the orb appears*

*Die little darkkin*
*After the echo clears*
*Debts will be a-settling*
*When the Evercry nears*

# Prologue

*I*n the heart of the mountains, beneath the city of Lathore, lies an ancient grave enfolded in rock, dusted with ash, swathed in steam, and lit with a slumbering fire. The Descent marks the place where an evil god once fell: the Evercry.

Rather than allow its existence to remain a blight on the world, the Fair Lady sacrificed herself to silence the chaos of the Evercry. Her actions saved the world from the Evercry's darkness, marking her as the guardian of its death for all time. But she could not banish its power completely. Tendrils of its essence still permeate the world, taint souls with chaos. Foremost are those who use magic: the manipulation of earth, air, water, and fire.

Any who apply themselves can learn to bend the world to their will, but magic holds within its heart the same darkness and chaos as the Evercry once did. Power begets power, and through these human vessels, slivers of the Evercry find a home. Insinuating itself like weeds through farmland, the Evercry's appearances are subtle, but infect the unwary fields *of humanity until the blight is too well rooted to be removed with anything other than death. A stain in the mind, a door that once open cannot be closed, the Evercry goads the magic user to reckless abandonment. All compassion and empathy lost, the user becomes the used. The Evercry takes possession and turns its host to chaotic zeal, leaving behind a shell vacant of everything that once made it human.*

*A madness of malicious intent and lust for power poisons the mind until the host becomes an evercry. For a thousand years, our sisters have followed the Fair Lady's grace, guarding the crypt of the Evercry and slaying all who become tainted by its power. But first, the Fair Lady must deem a sister worthy, pure enough of purpose, body, and soul. Those who pass her trial will one day be called upon to slay an evercry. A sound, a calling within the soul, will guide them to their foe. A foe only they can kill.*

*The song changes from knight to knight: some hear a piece of music, others nothing more than a vibration over the skin. A deep urge to hunt down its source, to slay those corrupted until there are none. One evercry, one song, one knight.*

*All distant, all different, all deadly.*

*And now…it is my time…*

"That's what you can hear now?" Larissa asked when her mother's voice trailed off.

Larissa had questions. She always had questions. She ever sought for knowledge, reading all she could, to ensure she would one day be worthy. She tugged her jerkin tighter against the cold of the stone room, sitting so close to the fire that the wool almost smoldered. Words curled on her tongue, but she pressed her lips together.

The scrape of stone on metal was her only answer for a time. Her mother's focus was on the weapon in her lap. A great sword, its handle embossed in gold, it had been passed down to each matriarch of swords, one of the three leaders at the Fair Lady's city of Lathore. To Larissa it carried more weight than the metal of its components: it was a symbol of all the Lady's knights.

"Yes," her mother said. "My time to answer the Fair Lady's call has come. I must track it throughout the land until I find its source, and kill it, as I am the only one who can."

Larissa shivered. "What does it sound like?"

"It is unique to every knight, but one thing remains the same. We cannot deny the call. We must answer, seek our prey, and destroy it. Or die in the attempt." Back and forth scraped the steel and the stone, sharp as her mother's words.

Larissa fell silent. She was not strong, she was not brave, she was not ready.

"Do you have to go?"

Her mother stopped her laborious task, setting aside cloth and stone. When she stared down at Larissa, something inside Larissa clenched, the affection other mothers showed their daughters absent between them. Her mother nevertheless stroked Larissa's hair from her face.

"I must." She drew away. "As far as the evercry takes me. One day, you may understand. But that day is very far away. Until then, you must learn how to become a knight. As my daughter, it is your duty. Can you do this while I'm gone?"

Larissa swallowed past the truth of her self-doubt, and lied. "I can. I will."

# Chapter 1

Larissa was going to fail.

The day of the Empirical was here, her final graduation test, but for all her training and scars, she wasn't ready. Even the relief at her mother's absence couldn't remove her dread.

After six years, there was still no word of her mother's quest. Guilt nibbled on the sliver of relief that she wouldn't witness Larissa's lack of strength—not of body but of character. As the only daughter of the matriarch of swords, the expectation set on Larissa was clear. Undergo years of training, a daily regime to be flawless in battle, all so that, one day, she could become a knight. A perfect plan, except for one inescapable shortcoming.

Larissa couldn't kill.

Instead, she found other ways to subvert conflict, through discourse or diplomacy, adding to her intellect through the consumption of books.

One was on her lap even now.

She sat on a narrow bench in a corner of the preparation room, studying before the final exam. The girls around her prepared for combat, the perfume of their metal polish mingling with the salt of sweat and fear. The Empirical would decide their fate among the sisters, and Larissa was not alone in her anxiety. While they sharpened swords, she honed her mind, squinting at the text.

Frowned upon in the arms of a student, this book taught of the elements, their forms and constructs, and how one could use magic to manipulate them through ritual and rune, breath and blood. The lie she told herself to peruse such an illicit tome was that it would help prepare for the Empirical. That it wasn't about the growing whispers of magic within her mind.

Reading did not make her unaware of her surroundings.

A prickle over her skin, the rush of air her only warning. She snatched the book above her head just as a splash of water spilled over her lap. Harmless enough to her cotton underthings and armored leather, it would have spelled destruction for the book. As it was, raindrop kisses laved their spatter marks across the pages. Larissa cringed.

"Careful there, bookkeeper."

She ignored the taunt and brushed aside the water droplets.

"I don't know why you're bothering," the voice continued. "The time for ink scribbling is over. You may be first in all other classes, but you will always be last in the one that counts."

Larissa's cheeks warmed, her hands perspiring. She'd spent years not retaliating to the barbs, ignoring pettiness and rivalry, but on this last day, she couldn't contain her scorn. Valare's taunting would not go unanswered, not if Larissa had a chance to bite back before they parted ways forever.

She rose from her seat, book in hand. Better than a blade, because to her it was an equal weapon to the broadsword across Valare's back. "I've never been able to tell, Valare, what it is you're angrier about."

A susurrus rippled through the long low room, a sudden pause, as though a stray dog had done an interesting trick.

"It speaks!"

Larissa flinched at Valare's ridicule She tossed thin blonde braids over her back and glared in defiance at the other acolyte.

Hands on her hips, Valare stood bedecked in her accustomed fighting garb, cream armor that marked her family lineage. Her mother was Atticus, defender of the realm, matriarch of shields. Valare's armor glinted near gold in the low flickering torchlight, extra polished for the momentous occasion of the Empirical.

Her tawny, sun-tanned skin gleamed, thick muscles evidence of her training. Hair black as a raven's wing shorn short, her dark eyes narrowed on Larissa in condescending amusement. "Go on now, lamb-tongued one. Let's see what you'll bleat for me."

Valare's companions grinned at one another, enjoying the culmination of a years-long rivalry.

All knew the cause. Larissa should be strong like Valare, like her mother, and she was...not.

The only similarities between she and her mother were the same caramel hue in their eyes, the same blonde hair. But Larissa lacked a knight's stature, held softness at her waist and hips from hours spent reading when she slipped away from training. It made her armor pinch, and she avoided it whenever possible.

In short, Larissa was soft, hesitant, girlish. She'd spent six years dodging either Valare's viper tongue or not-so-subtle attacks. They were meant to be a match, one a shield, the other a sword, just like their mothers. Only the flaws of Larissa's character intervened. Valare was as easy to violence as blood to a blade, but Larissa cowered every time. Conflict churned her stomach, sent tremors through her hands. Years of training gradually steadied them but could not take away Larissa's revulsion. Much to Valare's disgust and contempt.

Larissa's face burned, but she squeezed the book, grounding herself in its worth. Valare would never understand the content within. Could never appreciate the delicate phrasing of dark magics. Never taste knowledge from forgotten corridors of the world.

Larissa did, and often, but kept it secret out of necessity. And while she wasn't the warrior Valare was, she could fight with words.

"Is it because you're afraid brawn won't carry you to victory?" She tilted her head, glaring up at Valare. "Or is it because you're so dreadful at everything else that without knighthood you hold no purpose?"

"Oh, I see." Valare stroked her chin in faux contemplation. "You want me to beat you to a pulp *before* the Empirical, so you have a chance to...what? Cry foul?"

There were hisses among the throng, Valare's words an insult to any of the Fair Lady's acolytes. Especially to Larissa. Who had taken every beating Valare had ever given her, and not once given in.

Larissa hefted the book in her hand, teeth grinding as she readied to say something she'd regret.

"Leaving your rear exposed again, Valare?" The newcomer's voice lilted with a Lysonese accent, the harder consonants smooth. "Your bitches are no better at guarding your arse. You'd think they would have learned by now."

Valare raised her arms in the air.

A sliver of metal caught the low lights, pressed to Valare's exposed neck. Jyan had emerged from the throng and gotten close enough for the advantage. Her nonchalant handling of the weapon would only fool those who hadn't seen her pin a fly to a wall at fifty paces.

"Do you always have to backstab to win a confrontation, Jyan?" Valare chuckled, dark and mocking. "Because it won't serve you well today."

The preparation room cleared to form a ring about the three, even Valare's entourage stepping away. They had suffered wounds more than once at Jyan's hand.

"Today of all days you had to prove yourself a royal bitch again." Jyan circled Valare, a wary eye on her companions.

She tugged off the hood of her cowl, short brown curls falling rakishly over her face. Though several heads shorter than Valare, in combat she made up for it with agility, her lithe form honed to an enviable sleekness.

"Today is the only day to prove it." Valare's glare switched to Larissa. "It's for the best your mother isn't here to witness your impending dishonor."

It was as though Valare had read her thoughts. Larissa's hand curled into a fist, words of magic building in her mind until she tasted the taint.

Copper hot on her tongue, she reminded herself she couldn't use magic before Valare. She swallowed the power, forcing it to the back of her throat. To use it would bring not only shame but, worse, expulsion from the order and disgrace to her name and her mother's legacy.

Yet pressing it down became harder every day.

Valare's lip curled in a sneer at Larissa's silence, and she stalked to the room's far end. Around her, the other acolytes dispersed, snickering at two of their class fighting like a pair of cats—all yowling and no real action, but amusing nevertheless.

Jyan's hand brushed Larissa's arm in reassurance. "This is not the time for false bravado."

Larissa masked her irritation by slipping the book back in her waterproof leather satchel. This was not the first day she'd been victim to such a prank. "Valare pushed me, and I swear, after today she will never do it again."

"Or what?" Jyan snorted. "You'll strike back with a glib tongue? You aren't very good at banter, and you positively suck at non-defensive combat. Those are the only battles you can have with Valare."

"It doesn't matter what I say to her anymore." She was swamped with bitterness over her years of study, learning to use her head rather than resorting to brute force. For nothing. "Violence shouldn't be the answer to all of life's battles."

"They are today, dear friend." Jyan sheathed her blades.

"And the time is nigh."

True to Jyan's words, a sister called for them to make ready; the hour was at hand.

"Do you need help?" Jyan offered, fetching her weapons of choice, twin curved swords she wielded as though born to them. The blades were oddly shaped, thick with a dull surface along one edge. Jyan held them in a reverse grip so the flat side could be braced against her outer forearm.

"I'm fine." Larissa grit her teeth against a wince as she strapped on the armor with her mother's emblem.

Another mark of shame.

The steel carapace was white, metallic-edged from peaks at the shoulders across her back and down her spine. The chest piece was emblazoned with a sword wreathed in flames, a hallmark of her mother's title: Maladel Westwyn, matriarch of swords.

The greatest knight of their time.

As her eldest and only daughter, Larissa wore her mother's symbol. She had not earned it. She wasn't even going to use a sword at the Empirical.

Instead she hefted a well-crafted spear, its long-tapered blade shaped like a leaf, and a hard butt on the other end, polished to a shine from her palm. It gave Larissa the reach she needed to keep most enemies at bay. If she couldn't bring herself to attack, she would defend—strike when her opponents tired, trick them into defeat. Her strategies were near impenetrable except for the brute force of Valare's attacks and the subtle acrobatics of Jyan's dual-bladed style.

The acolytes picked up their shields and lined up to take their seats in the atrium beyond the preparation room. Larissa forewent her own; she didn't need the extra weight.

"I'll see you out there." Jyan patted Larissa's shoulder. "Afterwards, we'll drink wine and not care about it anymore. Do what you do best—study the matches before yours. Learn from them."

Larissa attempted to mimic Jyan's parting grin, but her lips tugged into a grimace. Jyan took her place in the queue.

Larissa wrapped her hand around the spear. The solid weight settled against her palm, a reassuring touch. She might not be ready for what came, but she could rely upon her wits and training. This trickle of hope gave her feet the courage to follow the others out the door and into the stadium.

Six grandstands encircled a round table of stone etched with an image of the four elements. Embedded in the outer edge of the arena, mimicking the directions of a compass, were four orbs, each the color of its element. Fire swirled in flames of black and red, sinister with waking for the oncoming battle. Air was a gray smoke, as though trapped in glass, its writhing plumes bashing against the confines of its cage. Water waited as a block of ice, solid white and slickened to a gleam. Earth did not move, its brown dirt holding rocks within that could shatter bone.

Each element would become corporeal once released from its orb, solidifying to a human outline made up of its matter. Only upon receiving a fatal blow would the elemental retreat to its respective stone, to await the next challenger. Black chains of binding held them the rest of the year.

The orbs glimmered under the afternoon sun that shone through a hole in the domed roof, casting a circle of light across the stadium. Trickles of snow crystals dripped from the roof opening, only to vanish on the spell-worked arena, kept clear despite the season. When the sun's beams touched the arena's edge, the testing would begin. It wouldn't end until the winter solstice passed, and the disc was left in darkness once more.

Acolytes who defeated the elementals earned the honor of knighthood. Those who failed joined the caste best fitting from their studies. To fail was not unexpected—many purposefully surrendered, by remaining on bended knee. Their goal to serve the sisterhood, but not in combat.

Yielding was not an option for Larissa.

For those who wished to fight an evercry, they faced the

Empirical to prove themselves worthy to the Fair Lady so they might one day hear the call. The test was to ensure an acolyte's readiness to face the Evercry. It was a harsh trial, not only for the elementals but for the arena itself. Beyond the round platform, the ground fell away to rocks below. Not far enough to cause death, but the ledge's drop had crippled more than one.

The circular disc of the arena was made accessible by a narrow wooden beam. At the other end of the beam, a stone balcony held room for the sixty graduating girls, all anxiously awaiting their turn. As her namesake was last, Larissa sat at the back of the balcony. Jyan's surname placed her in a distant seat, but it was Valare at the front, first in line, who distracted Larissa.

Her face fair glowed in ecstatic anticipation. No one in the class would match her, and she knew it.

As the grandstands filled with civilians and sisters alike, Valare raised a hand, acknowledging many who wished her well. Her bright eyes diminished when she caught Larissa staring. Larissa's gaze darted out into the crowd, to watch the other sisters of their order arrive.

The colored robes of each caste sailed in. Knights wore a startling white, shoulders marked in gold for those who had heard the call and slain an evercry. Blue for the beloved librarians Larissa longed to join. Green for those of the healer's touch. A gay yellow for the olmsyn, those attuned to the seasons, food, celebrations, and accounting—a strange but bountiful combination. Somber gray for those descending from the Tower of Skies, where the stars told a cyclical story. The skyseers believed all light belonged to the Lady. The light that shone on the world was reflected across the night, and the stars were the Lady's light returning. Reading the night sky taught all that passed, and foresaw all to come. Their predictions were right often enough that many gave the sisters the benefit of belief.

The last to enter were the crimson-robed sisters of the Evercry.

The darkkins.

Of all the Fair Lady's castes, the darkkins were the most dangerous. They studied magic, the tool of the Evercry, to better understand and defend against their foe. Sisters warned all acolytes to steer clear of them; they bore taint for their meddling with magic.

The stadium was almost filled now, only one empty place remaining: the throne of the grand matriarch. Oldest of knights. Judge, jury, and when need be, executioner.

A hush fell on the crowd as Grand Matriarch Landra Navus entered. A golden sash across her chest, white robes marking her as a knight, she was imposing as her gaze swept the arena, silencing all within, chin held high before taking her throne. Across her knees she placed the sword with which she would anoint the graduates who passed the test.

The grand matriarch's voice echoed across the stadium.

"May the Fair Lady look justly on you, as she decides who is strong enough to hear the Evercry and slay it in her name."

"*Until there are none.*" The chant reverberated through the dome.

Larissa mumbled along, throat clenching too hard to articulate the words. Not that any would note her stuttering. She was in the very last row, the final acolyte.

"Valare Atticus, I summon you."

The grand matriarch's words were barely spoken before Valare stood. She stepped across the narrow wooden bridge, and attendants pulled the beam back in her wake.

There were only two ways off the stone tablet: success or surrender.

Valare crossed the arena, scanning the crowd, before she drew her broadsword. With a steady hand, she placed the point in the center of the ring. She lowered her head, bowing to the grand matriarch, and the older woman's chin dipped in approval.

With a wave of her hand, the grand matriarch signaled to

begin the Eternal Empirical.

Red-robed darkkins undid the chains that bound the elements and shucked them to the side. Soon as the sun's light fell on the lip of the stone arena, the elementals sprang forth. Four women, made of water, fire, earth, and air. They surrounded Valare with weapons made of their element: Water a frosty blade, Fire a morning star, Earth a club, and Air a bow.

Air was the first to attack.

A volley of arrows ripped toward Valare's throat. Her shield rose to meet them, but her gaze was set on Fire, who charged across the arena. Valare's broadsword arced to meet Fire's strike, cutting the flaming ball from the morning star.

The head of the weapon flew away and hit the approaching Water on Valare's flank, its impact destroying the elemental in a burst of steam. One opponent vanquished on Valare's first blow.

She did not slow her swing, driving the side of her sword into Fire. The elemental buckled under her strength. It vanished with a shriek, leaving Valare with two opponents, and she'd only struck once.

Air shot another volley of arrows. Valare held aloft her shield and fell to one knee. The arrowheads thudded into her defense, but also struck the cumbersome Earth coming up behind her. The hardened shell of Earth's carapace cracked, and it stumbled. Valare rose and twisted, her sword swinging in a backhanded arc that lopped off Earth's head.

The crowd roared. She didn't spare them a moment.

Form rippling, Air gathered itself to shoot again, but it was too late. Valare, sword raised above her head with both hands, leapt forward and brought the blade down on Air's head, splitting it in two, the elemental knight vanishing in a gust of wind.

The stadium held its breath.

A three-stroke win. Such a small number was unheard of but for the matriarch of swords, Larissa's mother, who had set the record at four.

The crowd erupted.

All but the grand matriarch and Larissa rose from their seats, clapping as Valare crossed the arena. A wooden platform was lowered for her to leave the arena on the far side and climb to the main stadium where the grand matriarch waited.

Matriarch Atticus touched her daughter's shoulder as she passed, the two exchanging a brief embrace before Valare knelt in front of the grand matriarch. Whatever words were said, Larissa could not hear over the thunder of the crowd. Grand Matriarch Navus touched Valare's shoulders with her blade, anointed in the Fair Lady's tears—a sacred pool guarded by the grand matriarch herself.

Larissa stared down at her hateful armor, the sheen blurring through tear-filled eyes. She gritted her teeth. Her spear felt as though it might break under her hands, the wood vibrating with her tremble.

Navus called the next name. Each elemental rose in a new form when the acolyte indicated her willingness by standing in the center of the ring, weapon ready.

One by one, Larissa watched the battles numbly, successes and surrenders, combat whirling by in a blur until the grand matriarch shouted a familiar name.

"Jyan Mahcenae."

Jyan strode out onto the platform, twin curved swords by her side, and she whirled them with a flick of her wrist, as practiced as though they were extensions of her arms. She stood in the center and waited for the elementals' approach.

Water struck first, throwing two icicles Jyan avoided by spinning her blades before her face, shattering them. Fire was fast by her side, long sword held in a double grip. It slashed upward at Jyan's exposed flank. With a tumble, Jyan ducked to one side, missing a staffed strike from Earth and coming up to bring both blades down on Fire's exposed back. It snuffed out in a whirl of smoke.

Jyan grinned when the crowd bellowed their approval. She

danced out of range to give a small bow, before focusing on her remaining foes.

The three elementals circled her. Air spun a chain and long hook over their heads, lightning crackling down its length. When it flung the chain at Jyan, Water attacked from Jyan's other side. Jyan lifted her blade, catching Air's chain, and she spun about to pull Air off balance, using the elemental as a shield from Water's icy projectiles. Air vanished.

Earth ran across the arena, swinging its staff, bearing down over Jyan's head. She lifted one arm to block. With her free arm, she hacked the oncoming Water, who'd stumbled through the remains of Air. Water splashed on the arena floor as it died, spraying about Jyan.

With only one opponent left, Jyan dropped her guard to sweep her leg against Earth's knee, before springing onto Earth's chest and beheading it with both blades. It fell away to nothing but clods of dirt.

Larissa clapped along with the others, harder than for anyone who'd passed before.

Jyan bowed to the cheering crowd and took her place in the stands before the grand matriarch. The older woman gave Jyan a warm smile as she knighted her.

A yearning to be on that side of the arena filled Larissa's chest. Her friend sat on the edge of the knights' circle, exchanging handshakes and embraces with the other new knights. After the next name was called out, Jyan's gaze found Larissa through the throng and she nodded.

Larissa returned the gesture, then focused on the next participant. Before, the battles had rushed by in a haze, but now Larissa quavered with each girl who got to her feet and trotted down to the floor of the arena.

The sun narrowed its path across the tableau's edge, a shrinking crescent moon.

Soon, she was the last acolyte remaining. The girl just before her slew Fire with a stab at close quarters, a desperate bid that won her knighthood but left her flesh burned on one arm. Healers took her away.

Now Larissa was alone, there was no one else left to be called, and there was no escape.

And she did not have a plan.

# Chapter 2

"Larissa Westwyn."

She rose and walked down the empty bleachers, gaze fixed on that last crescent of sun. She'd studied its path stretching overhead for hours, hoping it would pass before she stepped upon the stone floor. If the sun fell from the arena, she need not fight; it would be over before she'd had her chance. But the sun lingered even with her slow steps.

The crowd fidgeted, whispers stirring around the ring. There was no hiding now, as the entire sisterhood watched her approach, to face the test she'd trained for all her life.

She took a deep breath and forced her foot out onto the wooden bridge.

There was a distant thrum through the air, its echo trembling through her. Larissa's chin jerked up, the noise of the crowd drifting away on the drumming of her pulse in her ears. Time slowed down as she stared up at Navus.

Silver eyes returned her gaze with all the compassion of a basilisk. Larissa stilled; her breath caught, held, and would not release. The noise in her ears grew until it became the thundering hooves of a horse, cracking her ribcage with each beat of her heart, her pulse rising on a scream she couldn't unleash.

The bridge swayed under her, and her foot slipped, threatening to topple her into the void.

Larissa's spear tip hit the wood, a quick catch that broke her fall.

Her breath released. The crowd seemed to pick it up as they gasped at her stumble and near plunge. Larissa steadied herself, her cheeks flaming, aware that over a thousand eyes had witnessed her clumsiness.

In a hasty flurry, she crossed the bridge. With one rise and fall of her chest after another, she placed the point of her spear in the center of the arena to signify she was ready. She wore this lie across slumped shoulders, along with all the unfulfilled expectations placed there years before.

Larissa lifted her gaze to meet the grand matriarch's again, ready for her assessing glare. With cool indifference, Navus's hand dropped, and the elements stirred from their prisons.

An awareness of magic prickled over Larissa's skin.

Familiar with its description only from her books, she almost didn't recognize it. Yet it resounded with the beat of her heart like the magic she'd buried within so many times. Now it came from without, seeking a way inside her.

As she scrutinized the platform, understanding rippled along her nerves, sinking into her muscles to take possession of her bones.

The chains were magic. They bound the elements when the sun's rays fell from the disc. The gleaming knife edge of an idea sliced through her thoughts as the elements burst from their orbs and bore down on her. Though only the thinnest thread of hope, Larissa clung to it as she gripped her spear, ready now in a way she had not been before. Now, she had a plan.

The elementals took form around her.

Her spear shot out in a sweeping gesture that had Earth

rolling to the side, its rocky chain crashing into Fire, throwing both out of step but injuring neither.

Larissa spun her spear's haft, wielding it in an arc that forced the elementals back. The spear's length and her dexterous handling forced them to retreat, allowing her to maneuver across the disc, rather than fight in the center. She backed herself to the brink of the arena, closer than any before her.

The other girls were wary of the edge, a lesson drilled into them by many a fall on the practice mats. Larissa was used to navigating the verge, often forced to retreat in combat training; she used this experience to her benefit and adopted the same tactic now.

On steps light as a dancer, she nimbly hooked her foot about one of Earth's chains, sure of the elemental's clumsy nature working to her advantage. All afternoon it had been a lumbering creature, the one easiest to dispatch. Slow, cumbersome, predictable.

The spear twisted between her well-practiced palms. The elementals leapt back, but Larissa left an opening to goad Earth into a lunge. It took the bait. She kicked the chain into the air, winding the end about the butt of her spear and then casting the chain toward Earth. It caught and wrapped around Earth's legs. For a brief moment, the chains sagged, not taking back their captive. Larissa inhaled, panicked that she'd made a mistake. Then the chains shuddered and fastened on Earth's limbs, the sliver of sun left in the arena—growing thinner by the second— narrow enough for the chains' magic to reengage. Earth's attack ceased as it fought the restraints, trembling under the magic's pull to return it to confinement.

Larissa heard a cry, a warning, and spun about. Nimblest of the four, Air had used her distraction to close in, striking out with twin punching daggers.

Larissa dodged the attack, blades whistling past her midsection. Air's flank open, she lashed out with a kick, sending Air scrambling too close to the platform's edge. Fire and Water hung back, hands tight on their weapons. They tested her defenses with sharp jabs, trying to move in. Surrounded, Larissa knew she needed more distance.

She pulled the spear's end back, sliding the wood through her hands before shoving it forward at Water's midsection, a clear movement Water should have been fluid enough to avoid.

It hit.

The blade's tip sank into Water, liquid spilling over the gray stone and turning it black, the elemental pierced but unconquered. Larissa hesitated. The same inky darkness had spilled from the throat of the first rabbit she'd ever been forced to kill, crimson black over snow. The hunting trips used to dull their empathy. To make the evercry nothing but animals. Her controlled breathing rose in rapid gasps.

Transfixed, a wave of warm air startled her into movement. She evaded Fire's strike, spinning out of its path. It rushed by her; she'd barely missed it. But it was close enough for its blade to slice through the ends of her hair, cutting off one of her thinner braids. Her twirl moved her away from the hot elemental, and she left the spear's tip in her wake to discourage a riposte. Fire's broadsword finished its blow and landed on the arena floor, ringing out like a gong, sparks darting into the air. Steam plumed as Fire's sparks rained down and spattered in Water's puddle, rising around Larissa in curls of mist.

Fire's blade had struck so hard it became wedged in the stone.

This was not the same as previous battles. Not anymore. She was not what they had anticipated: small-minded and driven by magic as they were, and her not playing by the conventional rules. Her cheat with the chains invited greater challenge. But she held her ground. Her strategy was working.

Air struck out, and Larissa readied the spear to her defense, but a claw wrapped about her ankle. Tripping, her knee crashed into the stone, a sharp click sending pain through the joint. Earth had freed itself from the bindings enough to wrap its fingers around her ankle, but its grasp wasn't strong.

Her inadvertent dodge made Air's strike fall short, sharp blades skimming where she'd stood. She needed to bind the others; luck was a fool's gambit on the arena floor.

Larissa ignored the stabbing protest of her knee and yanked her ankle free. She vaulted over the crouched Earth, its grasp easily evaded as it was dragged back to its prison. Scanning the battlefield, she had but seconds to plan her next move. Now that she had a chance, she didn't *want* to fail.

A handspan of sun was all that was left on the floor.

Fire freed its sword; Air drew closer. Water lagged behind, clutching its side. In a true mimic of human flesh, a dark liquid trail followed its path, proving she had hurt it but not enough to kill. They were too close, and she wasn't in position for the next binding.

Larissa struck out with the spear, her wide arc anticipating the elementals' trajectory. She was near the chains for Air—had to get it closer—but with Fire on the wrong side of her, she was fast running out of options. Fire only needed to step inside the reach of her spear and its broadsword would cut her down. Air looked ready to make another strike, forcing her to change the elevation of her spear's swing to give it pause. Water hobbled toward them, just visible over Air's shoulder, elongated blade still in its hand.

They were ready for her trick now, but she had no alternatives.

The tip of her spear whistled by Fire, who wasn't swayed by Larissa's sweeping stick and rocked forward. She tugged the spear through her grip with her other hand, shortening its length before she thrust it back into Fire's path, diverting it away. As it dodged her attack, Air moved in. But the maneuver put Larissa in position, the bulbous end of her spear sliding through a loop of chain, spinning it once, twice, and over her head. Air bid a hasty retreat but couldn't get far enough, the chain arching over its form. It fell about the elemental's shoulders and dropped it to the floor. Caught.

Shackles tightened around the flailing Air, stronger than they had been with Earth. Larissa made sure they would hold before she slipped by, not about to fall for the trap of Earth's half-bound form again.

Air's arms stretched out to snatch at her, and Larissa stepped aside, right into Water's staggering path. She barely got a block up in time to stop Water's blade, saved by training and instinct. She stepped closer, forcing it back toward its chains, using her body to shove it tumbling onto the arena floor.

Heat burned the back of her neck. Larissa brought her spear above her head, hoping the hardened wood would take the brunt of Fire's falling broadsword. The weapon struck her staff, the blow reverberating down her arms, through her body, and forcing her to one knee.

It wasn't enough to stop the sword.

The haft of her spear snapped, cracking into two in her hands. The burning blade cut through her armor.

Blades, maces, and clubs were a pain she had become accustomed to, could endure. The heat of the metal cut into her shoulder and didn't stop burning. She bit back a shriek, tumbling away across the stone. Her hasty retreat sent her rolling through a puddle of Water's blood, spilling steam into the air from her melting armor.

She dropped the broken bottom half of the spear, and with deft hands used the bladed end to shove between the straps of her armor. She cut it free from her back as melted metal singed through the leather beneath. With each hack, she moved backward away from Fire, flinging the scorching metal aside.

So focused on her steps, her searing back, and Fire's approach, she forgot the danger of the arena's edge.

Larissa's foot slipped over the verge.

One leg dropped down, and she instinctively curled her body forward, crouching on the platform's brink. She grasped for a handhold, and her fingers found Fire's chains.

But they were too loose. She careened over backward,

hauling with all her might on the chains. Her fall halted as she swayed over the abyss, feet on the lip. Fire rushed in, a charge to push Larissa off the last little toe ledge she had left.

Magic crackled within Larissa's hands, the hunger to trap and recapture Fire echoing up her arms. She couldn't stop the magic's path as the chains awakened under her touch, flinging her forward. She dove under Fire's swinging blade to drop the chains at its feet. The chains coiled up the elemental's legs, cobbling its stride, sending it crashing back into the arena. It collapsed, dropping the broadsword in an attempt to fight off the chains' hold. Larissa rolled away, watching to be sure the angry elemental stayed shackled. The chains groaned but did not release their prey, confining Fire back to its prison.

Panting, she reached for her weapon and rose in time to see the light fade from the edge of the disc. She'd made it.

Cold lanced through her, freezing agony that sent her spiraling into a numbing terror.

Water stood over her, its narrow blade shoved far into Larissa's side. Breathless, she fell to one knee. Water followed her down. There was no mistaking the glee on its face as it wedged the blade deeper, the tip coming out Larissa's back. Larissa dropped her spear, hands wrapping around the slick surface of Water's wrists as she stared up into the icy depths of its eyes. It grinned at her.

Despite the writhing nature of its form, something else twisted behind the translucent body.

Chains writhed like snakes across the arena and wrapped around Water, strangling it. Larissa let go of the sword to pull the chains closer, winding an end about Water's throat. It gave a wordless shriek at its impending confinement. She let go as the chains tightened on its form, the last element unbound.

Its capture sealed her fate.

Water's blade yanked from her side with an agonizing jerk as the elemental was tugged back toward its orb. Agony rushed to her head, tilting the world, and she careened to the arena floor. She lay on the edge, gasping in pain, and watched her blood mingle with Water's, funneling through carvings in the stone, turning the rivulets into tiny crimson rivers.

Larissa fell into oblivion.

# Chapter 3

Larissa wasn't in her own bed.

She wakened to the crackle of a fire, pained murmurings, footsteps scuffing on the floor. Her mattress was narrow, thick blankets softer than that of the dormitories. Slitting her eyes open, she took in the dim light, muted by curtains of cream wool all around her bed, held aloft with blackened iron.

The hospital ward. She hadn't died.

She hadn't run either.

Her mouth tugged in a half smile, cynicism forgetting her chapped lips, which pinched under the gentle pressure. Her throat ached, itching for relief.

She spied a cup of water on the bedside table. Extending one arm for it, a sharp pain in her torso was her reward. Her hand flew to the packed wound on her left side, fingers fluttering like a bird, afraid to touch it, and the intense agony faded on waves as she stilled.

Taking a few shallow breaths, she tried with glacial slowness to grab the cup. Each time her fingertips brushed it, a deep echo of the earlier pain warned her not to, keeping the cup out of reach.

The curtains flickered, twitched aside by Oris, the matriarch of the healers' caste. Larissa's care had fallen into the old woman's hands more than once. Dressed in green, about her shoulders was a silver-edged mantle of threaded cloth, the commendation for saving knights in the field who defeated an evercry.

"Awake?" She raised a brow. "You've been here enough times to have developed a resistance to our balms." Tittering, she came forward to give Larissa the cup.

"How long was I asleep?" she asked after she'd quenched her thirst and wet her lips.

"Two days," Oris said. "Though you should have stayed under for three. It might have been for the best."

The curtains fluttered. Larissa glanced over Oris's shoulder and met eyes with a nurse, who quickly scurried away. Without looking, Oris sighed.

"She's off to tell Deaconess Dunedin you are awake." Oris tugged up the side of Larissa's shirt, taking a quick peek at the wound, before covering Larissa and tucking the blankets around her with care. "And I can't give you anything to send you back to sleep before she gets here."

"Why...why would I need to be asleep?"

"I'd better leave the deaconess to tell you that." Oris refilled the cup with water from a stone jug. "But I'll get you another pillow, and some hare's bane tea to ease what's to come."

Oris patted Larissa's shoulder, then left her alone. Trepidation tried to crawl up her throat in a panicked mewl, but apathy swelled from the ache within. Dunedin managed the city's daily affairs, matters deemed important but not enough for the grand matriarch herself. What did she want with Larissa?

Her actions at the Empirical. Manipulating the magic of the chains to win.

If she'd broken any rules, she hadn't known they existed,

but it would still cost her. Her hand trembled as she rested the empty cup on the bed against her hip. Lifting the collar of her nightshirt, she studied her newest scar.

Beneath her chest was a swaddled wound. They'd wrapped the bandage around the base of her ribs, but a smear of red still showed through white cotton. She risked lifting the cloth to peek at the red gash. Stitches jutted like a badly turned sock, puckering the skin, leaving an ugly scar. Just like the others that covered her torso. Some as light as spider threads, one a nasty gash stretching from hip bone to ribcage. A gift from Valare the last time they'd sparred. Her injury from Water was almost little by comparison, though it had punctured farther through her.

As deep as the blade had dug into her internal organs, a deeper, all-consuming despair took hold as her worst fear came to fruition: her mother would be so disappointed. No matter where in the world Larissa's mother was, fighting her own evercry, Larissa's eyes burned in shame at the thought she might somehow know what had happened.

At Oris's return, Larissa dropped her shirt, biting her lip to stop her vision from blurring.

"Brush those away now." Oris's brisk tone instilled a little spine in Larissa. "This will not be pleasant, but I can at least promise a sweet oblivion by the time you drink this tea. Just don't gulp it or I'll take it off you."

Oris helped her sit up with a spare pillow, in time for Deaconess Dunedin to fling back the curtain. Matriarch Atticus stood behind her, glowering at Larissa over Dunedin's shoulder.

Two of the highest authorities in the Fair Lady's sanctuary.

Larissa leaned back into the pillows, bracing her body as though their words would hit her like physical blows. Though it would not be her first dressing down, it promised to be the most painful.

The noble matriarchs entered the little alcove of her room, Atticus ever haughty in her sneer and intimidating in her size, the same bulk she'd passed on to her daughter. Larissa avoided her penetrating stare and watched Dunedin, who came to stand by the end of the bed, hands clasped before her.

"Are you well, Acolyte Westwyn?" Said with all the care of a hangman to his customer.

"Yes, thank you, Deaconess." Larissa wanted to drop her eyes, but stopped at the sight of several sisters gathered beyond the curtained doorway designed to give her privacy. Come to witness.

Atticus hadn't bothered to close the curtain. Larissa poured her tension into a clenched fist hidden beneath the bedspread.

Dunedin lifted her chin to speak down her nose at Larissa. "Your deficiencies have deemed you unworthy in the eyes of the Fair Lady, and you will never hear the call of the Evercry."

There was a susurrus of whispers from the onlookers. Oris's knuckles turned white. Atticus's top lip curled in disgust.

Larissa did nothing.

Dunedin's brows rose at Larissa's apathy, as though she should have wept at the news. Refusing to give her the satisfaction, Larissa pressed her tongue to the roof of her mouth, bit down on the inside of her cheeks, and remained resilient. She would not cry in front of the brutish woman who looked fit to burst if Larissa didn't say something soon. Possibly apologize for existing. Her mouth was too tight to open. She tasted copper sweetness, but she would not answer, would not acknowledge the shame.

When she didn't speak, Atticus sneered. "Your attempt to belay the elementals by returning them to their imprisonment demonstrates your disrespect to your mother's legacy. It's a disgrace to the Fair Lady's name that the Westwyn line ends with *you.*"

Larissa's mouth fell open, and there were indrawn breaths across the room. Not just dishonor on Larissa, but her whole family line. Proof that any daughter Larissa bore would be shunned. She'd made a mistake, hadn't lived up to expectations, but to cast out any daughters she might bring to the Fair Lady's service?

"Matriarch Atticus," Oris snapped. "I'll not have you speak in such a way in *my* ward."

"Knights only deal in hard truths," Atticus said. "Which is why she'll never be fit to serve the Lady...in any capacity." Atticus swirled away before any could form a response. Even Dunedin appeared taken aback, hand on her chest, but her mouth formed a grim line as she turned back to the bed once more.

"Regardless of the outcome, you were automatically disqualified for your...*ridiculous* tactics." Dunedin paced at the end of Larissa's bed, preaching reform with flushed cheeks and a fierce scowl. A rant about duty. Honor. Tradition. Integrity. None of which Larissa possessed.

As Dunedin droned on, Larissa sipped the concoction Oris handed her, standing silently by her side. Half the ward listened in as one of the highest members of their order tried to reduce her character to dust. Futile—Atticus had already achieved that with far fewer words. She zoned out, chin to her chest, the tea starting its work of easing her pain, but a part of her was already numb.

"Do you understand?" Dunedin said, and Larissa focused.

"Yes, Deaconess."

The subdued answer seemed to satisfy Dunedin. She glared for another moment, but then parted the feeble division between Larissa's privacy and the other sisters, and strode away.

The growing oblivion of the hare's bane tea sank into Larissa's bones. A quarter of a cup left, she downed the remainder, put the cup on the bedside table, and rolled away from Oris and the open curtain so none could see her tears.

"It's...it's a strong dose," Oris said. "Sleep and think no more on it. There are other paths to take." Her hand fell on Larissa's shoulder, who mumbled her thanks.

Oris left, drawing the curtains closed. "What are you all gawking for? Get about your chores or go back to bed if you're injured," she commanded, but Larissa still felt eyes on the wool barrier.

Gathering the thick cotton of the bedcovers, Larissa shoved the cloth between her teeth before the sobs could escape.

—

A week later, a yellow-robed sister placed a box at the end of Larissa's bed.

The box was a death knell.

It contained her possessions from the acolytes' wards, where she'd stayed these last few years. But it wasn't the box itself that aroused an overwhelming dread. It was the lack of a letter. Graduated acolytes received a referral to tell them where they were best suited among the First Lady's castes, should they fail to pass the Empirical. The letter would give Larissa a place among the sisterhood.

Larissa's tentative hand ran over the contents of the box. Books, notes, blade sharpener, armor polish. Nothing with the seal of the teachers' hall.

She'd never felt more the outcast.

What would become of her? With nothing to dispel the whirling turmoil of her thoughts, Larissa spent hours wondering with nail-biting anxiety what she'd do if the sisterhood expelled her.

Despite her peers' ill-spoken words and treatment, she'd never before feared she didn't have a home.

The despair wouldn't fade, swelling in her throat so strongly she couldn't breathe. She needed air, to be somewhere other than wallowing here, waiting to be told she was evicted from the only home she'd ever known.

As afternoon turned to evening, Larissa struggled to put on her boots, uncaring of her personal disarray from a week of not being able to wash properly. She covered it all with a thick coat and took small steps to Oris's office door.

"I'm...I'm going for a walk."

The elderly doctor set aside her spectacles to study Larissa. Half of the small room was a cluttered and paper-strewn office, the other half an immaculate bench to blend healing potions.

"I think that would do you well," Oris said. "You should take it easy, but stretching your legs is a good idea."

"There are some of my things—" Larissa broke off. The concept of all her worldly possessions, of her self-worth, kept in such a small box, choked off any further words.

"It will be in my office when you are ready to collect it." Oris's compassionate gaze began to border on pitying.

Nodding her thanks, Larissa stared at the floor. Dunedin's speech still rang in her ears, sprinkled with Atticus's disgust. She couldn't bring herself to ask the old woman whether she should just take her things and leave. She couldn't even meet Oris's gaze.

Hopelessness urged her feet to escape, to walk out of the stone walls of the ward, down the corridors. Away, from everyone.

Larissa scurried through the labyrinthine corridors of the sisters' city, then up a turret. Her chest compressed, the walls too close around her. She needed the sky. Another set of stairs led to a terrace, and she hurried along it, passing two guards whose eyes narrowed at her presence. Walking the walls for their spectacular view of the valley was common on nice summer days, but not at the height of winter.

Onward and upward, legs burning from the climb, until she found herself on the highest tier, the disused wall surrounding the Descent. Wind whipped her hair and a snowy chill nibbled her exposed skin to goosebumps, but above the sky was clear. Behind her, she could look down on the turrets, walls, and city of Lathore, before the valley opened to the plains beyond.

At the valley's mouth sat Abbidon, on the edge of farmland and the river Diphon, a key trading hub that supplied Lathore with any goods they couldn't grow on the mountainside themselves. Farmland disappeared into the growing gloom of night, hiding places Larissa had long dreamt of visiting. An entire world to explore.

She turned her back on it, not yet ready to face the idea of leaving Lathore.

An orange sunset burned the snow-capped walls of Lathore and turned the ring of mountains around the Descent into a golden halo. The glow too bright for her eyes, Larissa walked along the wall until she saw the snow piled high, the masonry old and broken, where few bothered to walk. A dead end of sorts, it seemed as good a place as any to decide her future.

Across the way, the skyseers' tower observed the emerging wheel of stars. She studied the narrow windows, but no one looked out.

She was alone.

Above her troubled head, warm hues darkened to an indigo shroud. Scraps of cloud sliced across evening sky to spear the deepening night with gold. The cool breeze whistled in her ears, tugged her mangled plaits. She clutched the coat tight about her shoulders and forced her limbs to the wall's edge, to gaze into the heart of the Descent's darkness.

The Descent was a sacred place, an eternal warning. It was the tomb of the Evercry, felled by the Fair Lady's grace. All that remained was the ashen mouth of a dead volcano.

Larissa had never felt more in tune with the most forsaken place in the world. The crumbling wall gave way to bare stone in front of her, hovering over a long plummet to the mouth of the Descent. All she need do was take a single step.

A part of her screamed there was no reason not to take it— she served no purpose here.

The thought pinched inside, trembling over her skin, cracking through the numbness made of lingering hare's bane and shock. Where should she go, if not here? What should she do, if she could not follow in her mother's footsteps? Whether she left for whatever lay outside Lathore or fell over the edge, it mattered not to the sisterhood of the Fair Lady. To Grand

Matriarch Navus, who overlooked all referrals. Who'd stared at Larissa so coldly when her turn came in the arena.

Her thoughts chased themselves, rabbits across the snow, her doubt and fear shooting each one down. Spilling the blood of truths she never wanted.

Larissa lifted her foot to take the final step.

"Acolyte Westwyn?"

Larissa glanced over her shoulder, at first thinking it had just been the breeze, but a shadow flickered out of the dark gathering against the pale stone walls.

A skyseer in charcoal gray, Matriarch Nelasar.

Larissa spun on her heel and inclined her head in respect, retreating from the ledge. "Matriarch, good eve to you."

"You found my view." The matriarch came to stand beside Larissa, but then grimaced. "My knees aren't what they used to be in this cold." She shuffled back with a groan and sat down on a seat of tumbled stone, easing herself onto it. Larissa stood, head lowered, waiting for a scolding.

"Join me?" Nelasar invited, and after a moment of surprise, Larissa sat beside her. She was glad her coat came down to her thighs, long enough to pad her bottom against the cool rock. When the matriarch opened a paper bag and offered it to Larissa, she dug her hand in and took out a few morsels. The scent of salted nuts greeted her nose, potent despite the wind.

"Don't tell Matriarch Oris." Nelasar grinned. "She thinks they're bad for my digestion."

Larissa studied the elderly matriarch, noticing the deep grooves about her face, the washed-out blue eyes, and the whispering white hair escaping the hood of her robe. There was nothing but indulgence, round-cheeked and kind.

"Of course not." Larissa ate one of the salted treats. Smoky flavors coated her tongue, and when she bit into the nut, the taste enhanced. She popped in another.

"Careful now," Nelasar said with a laugh. "That's how I got addicted to them."

Larissa chewed in due consideration before she ate another.

The matriarch said nothing else as they watched the sun set, none of the words of chastisement Larissa waited to hear. After several minutes, the tightness in Larissa's shoulders eased. There was an amicable silence in Nelasar's presence.

Night's skirt turned from its festival's riot of color to the dulcet tones of jeweled infinity. Larissa wanted to stay, to linger, to perhaps finish what she'd started. To be alone with the decision she'd reconciled herself to, now that she'd had more time to think on it.

"Look at that." Nelasar interrupted her thoughts, gesturing to the sky. "This is what I came for. It's the only time of year to catch Phaylinar shooting her arrows."

Larissa studied the sky, ever eager to learn. "Where?"

"See her bow, in those six stars?" Nelasar leaned into Larissa, who ducked her head down to sight along the old woman's arm. "Those three become the arrow, and they say if you see a falling star, to wish upon Phaylinar."

It sounded like the usual poppycock of the skyseers, but when a star fell, Larissa still made a wish—for some other escape than the village or a long fall with a short end.

She'd scant time to be surprised at her own thought before footsteps echoed along the wall, a bright yellow light illuminating the snow and pale stone. A sister in gray robes approached them, and she wasn't alone; Jyan trotted behind her. Larissa swallowed past the sudden tearful joy at seeing her friend.

"Matriarch Nelasar?" the sister said. "Sister Calrian is asking for your presence at the tower."

"Very well, then." Nelasar rose, but gave the packet of nuts to Larissa. "Perhaps Oris is right. They are too rich for me nowadays."

"Thank you," Larissa said, for more than the treat, her head bowed to avoid the matriarch's knowing eyes. Nelasar's hand clutched her own.

"The path you walk lays in the dark between stars," she

whispered. "But that doesn't mean you aren't of the light."

Larissa's gaze darted up. The old woman was beaming at her. A denial hovered on her lips, but it faded under the matriarch's kindness.

"Don't stay up here—go on and find that path." Nelasar let go of her hand with a pat and hobbled beside the other skyseer.

Jyan waited until they passed, then took Nelasar's place beside Larissa. Putting her lantern at their feet, she tugged a bottle from her coat and grinned when Larissa chuckled.

"Now then." Jyan took two cups from her other pocket. "About that post-graduation drink—"

Larissa threw her arms around her friend.

"I've got you." Jyan set aside the bottle before she returned Larissa's embrace. For all her lonely thoughts, Larissa wasn't alone. "And while I want you to know, deeply, that I care for you...you kinda reek."

Larissa lost her breath in a huff of laughter, the dry chuckle tinged with a well of tears. "I know, but what am I supposed to do?"

"Well, that's easy," Jyan said, drawing back. "Let's start with this."

She thrust the cups at Larissa. Picking up the bottle, she then flicked out a wrist blade and popped the cork with a delighted grin, and poured the frothing contents into the two cups.

"What is that?" Larissa asked, distracted from her woeful situation.

"Sparkling wine made of the sweetest apples, given to me by my mother. Who passes on her congratulations for your quick thinking and incredible display."

"She's the only one."

"That's not fair to me." Jyan squinted at Larissa, before setting aside the bottle to take her cup. Sniffling, Larissa fought back the tears and straightened her spine.

"You're right," she said. "Congratulations to us both, but *especially* you for making the knights' caste."

"To you," Jyan returned. "For being braver than all of us. I know how much you didn't want to do it, but you faced the Empirical anyway. That's where true courage lies."

Larissa's hand tightened about the cup, but she bumped it against Jyan's, and they drank. Sparkling effervescence coated Larissa's tongue, and she savored the sweetness combining with the salted nuts. She took another sip and sighed in contentment as Jyan leaned against her shoulder, tilting her head to look up at the sky.

"To answer your question," Jyan said, "I have a solution on hand."

"Become the desert pirate queen of Alaminor?" Larissa waved a hand at the endless sky and far-reaching possibilities. "That's near your homeland, and it's full of bandits who raid desert caravans. Except I'd burn to a crisp inside of a few hours. Still, I'd like to travel. I've always wanted to see the sea…"

"You are always welcome in my homeland," Jyan said. "But why not go where that pale skin suits you and join a different caste altogether?"

She held out a slip of yellowing paper.

"What's that?"

Jyan grinned. "Your referral."

Larissa snatched it out of Jyan's hand, spilling the contents of her cup on her sleeve. The wax seal was broken.

"You peeked," Larissa accused.

Jyan shook her head. "Not I. It was with your things down in the ward. When I retrieved it, the seal was already broken. Oris said they delivered it after you left, so I came looking for you. One of the sky sisters told me where you were."

Confused how they'd known, Larissa tilted the paper in the dying light, eager to see the results of her six years of schooling. What all that work had amounted to, what she could become after failing the Empirical. The assurance that she wasn't forsaken.

Gladness rose in her heart, banishing her despair as she

flicked open the letter. She hoped to see the blue stamp of the librarians, so that she might hide in the depths of the archives and pretend she was nothing more than what Valare had accused her of being: a bookkeeper.

The paper's bloody stamp showed a far more sinister occupation.

Her referral was to become a darkkin.

# Chapter 4

L arissa awoke clutching her head.

Jyan's insistence the night before had led them to her parents' quarters and another bottle of wine. Larissa hadn't regretted it then; it was easier than facing her referral. She'd swaddled herself before the fireplace, drunk and too terrified to go to the darkkins' halls.

In morning's light, the letter lay innocent of any crime on the floor by Larissa's makeshift bed. She eyed it owlishly. The letter was the source of her current discontent, of course, not the fact that she'd supped too much of the fine wine.

A lie, but more bearable than the truth. She needed tea, a bath, and something that wasn't the gruel they served in the hospital ward.

But she couldn't leave the letter. It was proof she had a place here.

With a sigh, Larissa snatched it up and headed past a snoring Jyan for the bathrooms. It was well before dawn, and she took advantage of the early morning emptiness. Dark gray stone of the Lathore mountains gave way to rock pools, water heated far beneath the earth.

On a footstool, with a bucket of scalding water, she scrubbed her skin raw. Undid her plaits to sluice grease from her hair and lathered soap into her scalp. The remains of the tub she dumped over her head, gasping at the cooled water.

Next she combed out the tangles of her waist-length hair, rubbing oil into the wet strands. Her fingers slipped on the shortened braid Fire had cut, memories of the battle stirring within. Her habit was to leave her hair to dry, but today she wrung out the water and braided the locks tight to her scalp, two winding from her crown to meet and become one down her back. Having little to wear, she dried and put on the communal gear used for hunting.

Thoughts of the crimson robe of the darkkins churned her unsettled stomach. Rather than focus on her referral, she sought out sustenance.

In the dining hall, more than one person glanced in her direction, but few were present at the early hour. She ignored them, the letter of her allocation burning in her pocket like a guilty secret.

Taking tea and oats, the one food her stomach didn't rebel at the scent of, she sat in a far corner of the hall. Long tables stretched beside windows that overlooked the valley, sunlight growing brighter off snow-laden mountains. She laid the letter out flat, to read while she ate. A list of her courses and scores.

Valare hadn't exaggerated; Larissa was in first place for all classwork. A black line lay against the Empirical test. Her fingernail scratched against it, as though to rub it away, but her gaze returned to the referral at the bottom. No students were tested for aptitude with magic—what might it mean?

"Have you thought any more about it?"

Larissa flinched at the loud voice, her head still aching from the wine. Jyan thumped down across from her, far too bright and bubbly for this early, a plate of fried meat and eggs in hand.

How Jyan could face such a breakfast after last night, Larissa didn't dwell on.

Lost in study, she'd failed to notice the dining hall's chatter increasing. No one had sat near her, but that wasn't unusual. The hall was full now of other sisters, many faces Larissa recognized from her graduating class, spinning about and laughing in the new robes of their caste. Bright yellows, soft greens, even a few midnight blues. The knights' white was worn with unabashed pride.

There were no crimson robes among the throng, no others newly cast as darkkins.

"I'm just reviewing the referral," Larissa told Jyan. "It isn't the only choice."

Graduated acolytes were free to choose where they went, to a degree. The letter showed that Larissa could have her choice of any caste bar the knights. She could become a medic, administrator, teacher, gardener, metal smith, even an engineer to repair the older parts of the great city.

The darkkin brand on her letter was bright as fresh blood.

None had ever volunteered to join the darkkins. Neither could she recall anyone recommended to them in all her years of study. But it must happen, for the caste existed.

Darkkins studied magic to aid knights against the Evercry. All precautions were taken to ensure the knights' success, even if it meant learning the ways of the enemy—its taint fell not on the knights' hands, but on those of the darkkins. The hope was that the darkkins would die before magic turned them to the path of the Evercry, because that's where all use of magic led.

The more her eyes traced the darkkin symbol, four interlaced circles, the more she sensed some other hand at work. Navus's glare. Atticus's insult and Dunedin's lecture. But Nelasar's words of the previous evening came back to her.

"*To walk between the stars...*"

A path of darkness.

"What's that now?" Jyan said from where she was devouring

her plate of protein and fat. Larissa's tray of oatmeal and berries lay forgotten, her stomach still queasy.

"Why do you think they referred me to the darkkins?"

Jyan shrugged. "You have an interest in magic. You're always reading books about it. Perhaps they're short this year?"

Larissa flushed at Jyan's observation of her reading habits. She'd done what she could to conceal it; she just had to hope she'd fooled everyone else.

When Larissa scanned the hall and saw no darkkins, her chest constricted.

"That's all they think I'm good for," she mumbled. "To use me against the Evercry until I die."

Jyan scoffed. "Knights take the same risk. You won't be stuck here in Lathore for the rest of your life. You get to accompany knights on their quests, study the Lady's greatest foe for weaknesses. That is not an insult but an honor."

Larissa had a hard time accepting the praise, and her silence must have said so.

"Look here." Jyan pointed at the letter. "See the date? Someone stamped this the same day as the Empirical. Someone was *watching* your battle. Admit it, your actions were pretty unorthodox. And you *nearly* did it."

She did.

What would have happened if she'd beaten Water? The grand matriarch would have stared down at her, given her verdict in front of the entire sisterhood. And yet...she had an invitation to join the darkkin ranks despite her failure. It meant that even after she'd lost, they wanted her. But why?

Because she'd used magic in the arena.

The world stilled around her, the noise of the hall dying away as she studied the thought. If she'd done something wrong, they'd have evicted her. Or worse, killed her. Instead they decided to assign her a future she'd been told was a condemnation. A future that wasn't just about studying the theories of magic but how to use it. And if she could use magic, learn to control what was inside her, her best chance was with them.

Before she became exactly what her mother hunted.

"Why did you do it?"

Jyan's question caught Larissa off-guard. "Do what?"

"Use the chains."

Of all the people who could have asked her first, she was relieved it was Jyan.

That question had kept her awake whenever the hare's bane tea hadn't lulled her during her bed rest. What notion had snuck into her head? To use the chains against the elementals rather than just giving an appearance of trying, enduring whatever punishment they dished out. Every sparring session of the last six years had been in practice for that beating, and she'd wasted her chance on a foolish notion of somehow winning.

Larissa shrugged, folding the letter closed, to rest under her palm. "I didn't want to fight them."

"I know that." Jyan rolled her eyes. "But what made you think it'd work?"

Larissa debated lying, but she knew she couldn't tell anyone else. She wanted to share the truth with at least one person. "I sensed the chains, knew they were...magic. But it was more than that. I thought since I was last, if I could recapture the elementals, it would still count as a win without any need for slaughter."

Jyan's scowl deepened, but her eyes had drifted over Larissa's shoulder.

"Any way to victory?" Valare's voice rang out behind her. "Is that why they chose you for this year's darkkin? I can think of no one more...suitable."

Valare. *She* opened Larissa's letter. That's where it had been all this time. Valare got her hands on it and kept it a week before returning it, letting Larissa stew over her failure.

Fury welled up inside, the anger from years of Valare's taunts and punishments bubbling over. Larissa snatched the letter from the table, twisted about on her seat, and stood to flash the paper in Valare's face.

"Did you only have one choice? Because I can go wherever I want. I'm not limited to being a meat shield, unlike you, Valare. I'm not trapped in my mother's ambitions. I, at least, have a choice."

Valare swatted the letter aside, sending it fluttering to the floor. "Except where it matters," she hissed. "Imagine your mother's face when she finds out her daughter isn't just a failure, she's a traitor."

Larissa shoved Valare.

Anger flooding through her, the force she intended should have knocked Valare to the floor. But Valare was bigger, stronger, and better trained. The other girl took a single step back.

Valare's face twisted in a malicious grin. There was only a slight tell from the jerk of her shoulder before a punch came flying, but Larissa dodged it, reaching up to yank Valare's oncoming arm to tip her off balance, trying for an elbow lock. Valare swung under it, her fist aiming for an uppercut to Larissa's exposed flank. Larissa let go to spin out of reach and launched a kick at Valare's wide stance, but Valare stepped inside the attack and punched Larissa's still wounded side.

The fist hurt. The follow-through tore stitches.

Agony radiated from Larissa's wound, lashing through her, squeezing tighter until she could take no more. Breath knocked from her lungs, she fell to her hands and knees, trying to absorb the pain in her gut as nausea rose from the blow and the previous night's debauchery.

A watery mess of oats spilled out of her mouth. Bile burned in her nose, the fetid stink of alcohol making her vomit again. Her body jerked in spasms.

Beyond the drumming pulse in her ears, the hall had fallen silent. Eyes teary, she watched Valare's boots step back, but she couldn't raise her pounding head to look at Valare's face.

"You're pathetic, Larissa," Valare said, walking away. "The Westwyn family name deserved better than you."

Regaining control of her breath, Larissa rose to her knees, fumbling for a cloth napkin to slop up the mess she'd made. Sisters shared glances about the room, but no one came to her aid.

Except Jyan, who fetched a bucket of hot water, and a cloth for Larissa's face.

"Thank you." Larissa wiped away the spittle on her mouth, and then used the same rag to remove the floor stain.

"In all the years I've been here, I never asked why." Jyan's voice was cool and impersonal, soft even—it was far angrier than she'd ever sounded before. She knelt across from Larissa, who didn't want to answer.

"Valare has her reasons."

"She's cruel, Larissa." Jyan pushed off the floor and moved toward a nearby bench, but then leaned over to whisper, "What she does to you should be reported—no other acolyte would have gotten away with it. You've said nothing, not in all this time, not even when she damn near killed you last year. If you think people haven't noticed, you'd be wrong."

Larissa gave a halfhearted shrug. "Our families should serve one another, the shield and the sword." She picked up the sick-stained cloth and tossed it into the bucket. "We were friends... once. Valare was to become my blood-bonded sister at our graduation, but we both had to succeed. I cost her that honor."

"That doesn't excuse her behavior."

Larissa sighed, rising with the bucket in hand. "But now that I've been allocated as a darkkin, I'm not just failing my mother, or even Valare. I'm betraying them both."

Jyan grasped her arm. "Any service to the Lady is valid, and as much as we can see the signs of her everywhere, you do not know her mind, or her plans. Besides, Valare proved before the test that she hated your guts. Her opinion doesn't matter anymore, and even if it did, how could she think worse of you?"

Larissa could see the logic, but it didn't undo years of older women badgering her with their expectations. She shuddered, her aching stomach still queasy. Needing to flee the gaze of her friend, she turned away from Jyan and the letter, picking up the bucket and dirty cloth as she left the hall. When she passed by, those watching returned to their breakfasts with bowed heads and sidelong glances.

She went to the nearest bathroom. Even after she cleaned up as best she could, she couldn't bring herself to go back in the hall where Jyan and the note remained.

Snatching a mint leaf from the dining hall's edge, Larissa chewed it as she walked down the corridor. She was wary of Valare, but remained unmolested as she approached the doors to the library.

Books were Larissa's greatest solace in life. In her darkest hours, she'd sought refuge in their words, a purpose, and research became her strongest skill. The librarians liked her. She wasn't close to any but knew them all by name. As well as she knew the library. Among musty smells and with an itchy nose, she'd wandered the long halls, plucking titles off the shelves that took her fancy. Even to the point of diverting down more than one restricted but unwatched corridor of the catacombs.

Despite all her reading on magic, she'd never felt anything outside herself before the Empirical. But each book she stole fed a thirst for knowledge, each forbidden tome carrying both the anxiety of being caught and delight in newfound information. Her excuse for the quiet thefts was to learn control, to subdue the inclination within her. But in the darkest, deepest recesses of her mind...she knew it was a lie.

She hesitated now before the doors. Her hand hovered above the arched handle, the cold emanating from the library almost a warning to stay away. A shiver curled her outstretched hand into a fist.

Determination overrode doubt, and she snatched the handle to slip inside.

The chill of the city was at its worst here, no hearths or pipes to supply heat, smoke and steam diverted well away from the sacred texts of Lathore's great library. Its entrance encompassed a large hall and a roof that opened but was now shuttered against the end of winter's bite. Instead, glowing lanterns were held within canisters of marbled water, light rippling over the spines of thousands of books. Long corridors of arched ceiling stretched away into the mountain's side, floors were smoothed to a polished gray slab, and the walls held aloft row upon row of tomes.

Before the catacombs of the library's interior sat a large desk of stone with a surface of gleaming cream marble. Behind it, a stern-faced librarian stood on duty, clad in the navy robes of their caste. Larissa found the blue soothing. The color of the evening sky, or the seas she hoped to one day visit.

Matriarch Enyonam lifted her head as the doors creaked at Larissa's entry. No one else was about, and Larissa approached the wide bench counter, nodding at the matriarch, who smiled in kind. It warmed Larissa down to her toes.

"Good morn, Acolyte Westwyn," she said. "Are you recovered from your fight?"

Larissa thought she meant the breakfast hall, but then realized she referred to the Empirical. "I will be, thank you, Matriarch." She'd have to go back to the ward, to check if Valare had done any further damage. But right now she was ignoring the pain with a flicker of hope that she might yet salvage her place in the sisterhood without dishonoring her mother.

"Come to borrow more books?" A friendly question from the matriarch, who had no time for students yet had always been kind to Larissa. Her stomach tightened in knots as she worked up the courage to speak.

"I thought..." She stumbled over her words. "If I may...that I would be very helpful, to you, to-to the library...that I might—"

She faltered as the matriarch's eyes fell, a glimmer of a smile ghosting away.

"Do you have your referral?" Enyonam asked, formality returning as she folded her hands in front of her, straightening her shoulders.

Larissa scrunched her hands by her side. The referral's crimson stain would be stark compared to the comforting blue of the library. After a moment of her fraught silence, the matriarch came around the bench to stand beside her. Larissa met her compassionate hazel eyes and hated herself even more.

The librarians wouldn't take her. No matter that she spent more time there than anywhere else, that they all knew her name and it was where she was safe.

Matriarch Enyonam placed her hands on Larissa's shoulders. "We sometimes find ourselves in situations outside of our control, but it isn't the end, or what defines us. You'll do well with the darkkins. You have the call of magic within you."

Larissa stared at her, aghast that she knew, a private shame made public by someone she respected, even loved.

"But I—" The sob was strangled in her throat by what little remained of her pride. "I don't want to be tainted."

"You poor thing," Enyonam whispered, shaking her head. "It isn't as bad as all the rumors say, or they wouldn't exist within our sisterhood, would they? You can still be of great aid to the Lady."

"I never wanted to help her like this."

"It isn't a mark of shame. It's a measure of trust. Only those who face the darkness can help lead us into the light." The matriarch's words echoed that of the skyseer, and Larissa envisioned a cage coming to wrap itself around her, force her down the darkest of paths.

She had no other place to go but where the matriarchs thought she would serve best: in the halls of those who gave parts of themselves away to magic.

Who could succumb and turn to the Evercry.

# Chapter 5

Larissa stood before the doors of the darkkins' catacombs. Box in hand, torn letter lying on top, she couldn't bring herself to knock. She'd spent three days deliberating over what to do, one day lost in the ward at Matriarch Oris's insistence she rest and the other two in Jyan's private rooms.

Acolytes had another week before they needed to be in the dorms of their chosen caste, but many gathered there straight away. To acquaint themselves with their older sisters and start their duties in the safe and happy knowledge that this was their purpose.

Larissa wasn't sure of anything, but her choice was clear: stay and be a darkkin...or leave.

*"If you could face the Empirical, you can do this."* Jyan's last words to her before she left for a training mission in the mountains.

Setting the box to one side, Larissa knocked on the heavy wooden panels. She fetched the letter off the top and straightened it out as best she could, flushing at the tear left from Valare's actions.

Her head jerked up as the door creaked open, and she stopped fidgeting.

An unfamiliar sister stood there, with rich brown hair and eyes, her wide mouth framed in a welcoming smile. Her robes were edged in silver; she'd assisted in slaying an evercry. "Acolyte Westwyn."

"Good morn to you, Sister." Larissa lowered to a respectful bow.

"Sister Correal." The darkkin beamed, and the warm gesture did much to ease the tension freezing Larissa to the spot. "Would you come in?"

Correal needed both hands to tug the door wide, and it groaned under her pressure, but it allowed enough room for Larissa to enter.

"Thank you, Sister Correal." She collected her box. Fearing a dark and gloomy room, Larissa swallowed and took the last step across the threshold.

Sunlight poured into a sunken stone atrium, three tiers of desks surrounding a central open space. On the fourth wall hung the largest map of the world she'd ever seen. Easily twice her height, many more across, it displayed the continent. Detailed tan ink lines were drawn over its surface, held by elegant borders of curling ferns. The map comprised the mountain range of Lathore, down to the southern farmlands before the deserts of Jyan's home. Then east to the craggy edges of the continent with its many ports bearing ships to foreign lands, and to the west were the many kingdoms, fiefdoms, and clans that comprised Aesethen, a network of diplomatic relationships assisted by the Fair Lady's order. The landscape was dotted with names, provinces outlined, towns marked, geographical features laid out. But littered over its surface were black circles, pox spots on the face of the beautiful world-encompassing map.

Women garbed in dark crimson were bent over their desks working, but when Correal clapped, they all stopped.

"Sisters," she called, and they swiveled about to look at her. "Please welcome our newest member, Darkkin Larissa Westwyn."

The other sisters of the caste came to the stairs, in an array of dress—some in plain robes, others in armor, but all wore crimson and all were...unique. Larissa couldn't quite put her finger on what it was, but each sister she spoke to was different.

"Darkkin Oleth." A girl not much older than Larissa offered her hand, almost tripping in her eagerness to mount the stair. She had mismatched eyes, blue and green, and a streak of white at her temples.

"Darkkin-Thane Goverin." An older woman offered Larissa her left hand to shake; her right ended in a hook. Gray threaded Goverin's blonde hair, and there was a hardness in her eyes that intimidated Larissa.

"Darkkin Farrast." A woman with skin darker than the night sky and eyes yellow as suns nodded to Larissa but did not offer her hand, though her smile was broad.

Half a dozen other names followed, and Larissa started to feel awkward and overwhelmed by their friendly greetings.

"Back to your desks, darkkins," Correal said. "You'll have time with our new sister, don't fret."

"Yes," a stranger's voice called. "Return to work. The new darkkin and I must speak."

The voice came from a distant staircase, half-hidden in the shadows behind the map. Streams of light obscured the ledge the map hung from, part of an enclosed balcony above the central room, lined with windows from which the woman must have watched her meet the others.

Unnaturally crimson lips curled at Larissa, the woman's green eyes bright despite the gloom she lurked in. Not many sisters painted their faces, but there was something enthralling in that smile. Inky hair curled about her face and shoulders, glimmering in the lights around the edge of the world map. Her dress was a red dark enough to be black, and around her neck hung a gold medallion, embedded with a ruby the size of Larissa's eye.

"I am Matriarch Theras of the Darkkins." Her voice was melodious, soft, but carried across the cavernous space as she came down the stairs.

"Good morn to you, Matriarch Theras." Larissa bowed her head over her box.

"Put that down and join me," Theras said. "Thank you, Correal, but I will take over the induction."

Sister Correal didn't bat an eyelid. "What if I were to take Darkkin Westwyn's things to her room?"

"It would be wonderful of you," Theras said.

Thankfulness toward a lesser sister sounded strange coming from the matriarch of a caste. Larissa was confused, and above all, intimidated by how approachable they were being. She opened her mouth to ask a dozen questions, but one spilled out before the others.

"Isn't...there some test to pass to become a full darkkin?" She glanced between the two women. "Or an initiation? That's what the Empirical is for, to test knights. Don't you need to test me to see if I can—" She changed her words at the last second, didn't want to confess how easily magic came to her, even if she was untrained. "...if I can be of use to you?"

Correal gave an indulgent twist of her mouth and took the box from Larissa's unresisting hands. Theras came to Larissa's side, grasping one of her shoulders.

"Turn around."

She did so, confused until the matriarch gestured back the way she'd come.

Symbols were carved in the doorway's heavy wooden frame, even on the back of the door itself. Magic she hadn't registered as she entered. Now that she witnessed its presence, could sense the dormant power slumbering within, she wondered what it would take to wake it.

"To enter these halls is the test," Theras whispered in her

ear. "If you possessed a tainted soul or twisted mind, the magic of those wards would have stayed you from entering. Your hesitation at the door was made of more than your doubts. That they allowed passage shows we can trust you to be pure of heart and intention. All we can ever ask of a darkkin."

"But all the rumors—" Larissa broke off.

Theras laughed. "There is no offense taken—it is an image we cultivate with intent. We walk on a knife's edge and must ever be reminded of our purpose and trust in one another. Our reputation keeps away the conceited, angry, and prideful. There is no room for any but the humblest."

"Not that humble," an older woman said as she approached. She wore a pale pink gown, of all things, silver lapels layered enough to show she'd assisted with the deaths of three evercrys. "Matriarch Theras will have you believe we're all gossiping handmaidens if she carries on like that."

"Sister Larea is our carer," Theras said, with no offense at the old woman's words. "She keeps us grounded, and safe."

There was a whisper to the last word that had Larissa wondering what an old woman was supposed to keep them safe from. But at a pointed glare from Larea, wrinkled eyelids squinting, Theras laughed again and slipped her arm into Larissa's. A ring glimmered on her finger, silver with a moonstone.

"It's her first day, don't frighten her."

"The things you could learn from me as to this one's mischief," Larea said, scowl deepening, though her lips twitched with an echoing grin. Their easy banter belied any discontent, but Larissa wondered at the disrespect Larea showed to someone of such importance.

"You may tell her all your stories later," Theras said. "Our new darkkin has some reservations, and I want to dissuade them. Come."

Arm in arm, Theras tugged Larissa away, past the desks and toward the balcony. Theras let go to mount the stairs, and Larissa took the chance to survey the map up close as she climbed.

A shimmer caught her peripheral vision. There was magic within the map's weave. With no time to linger, Larissa hurried up the last stairs to the enclosed balcony. A single candle on an inscrolled table illuminated the dark space. The long, narrow gallery's windows looked out over the desks. Bookcases lined the walls, tomes aplenty with spines scrawled in languages she had yet to learn, other trinkets hidden by shadow, and across every surface was the tell-tale tingle of magic.

Symbols and objects brushed against her senses. Larissa gasped, turning in a circle to take it all in. She had never been near magical objects, except during the Empirical.

Now she was surrounded by them.

"Have a seat," Theras instructed.

Larissa curtailed her wonder and sat in the chair before an ornate desk. The desk bisected the gallery, an odd position, barely enough room to pass on one side. Theras stood behind it and lit a few more candles. It did little to banish the gloom; they may as well have been in deepest night for all the intimacy of the setting.

"You have doubts." Theras swept aside her skirt to sit in the gnarled chair behind the desk, carved in twisted, meandering shapes. "About the magic you sense, rather strong in the untrained, but that is why we chose you."

"How did you know?" Larissa still clung to some idea that this was all a mistake, that she should be in the library. That as soon as she left the safety of these halls, Valare would be waiting to give her another thrashing and life would continue as normal.

"Larissa." Theras clasped her hands and leaned forward. "I am not lost to your plight, how being assigned here might appear to an outsider, but first I must ask you an important question. Why did you aim for the chains at your Empirical?"

Larissa hadn't liked the question from Jyan, but from Theras, a stranger, she liked it even less.

"Is that why you chose me?" she asked, not daring to ask what she truly wanted: if her designation as a darkkin was a punishment.

"Stop letting your fears tell you why you are here," Theras said. "Start listening to the voice that told you to use those chains to bind the elements. Why did you do it?"

Larissa stared at her a moment, Theras's gaze hard and uncompromising. Surrounded by magic, the casual display of objects laden with power, the confession came with greater ease than she expected. "Because I sensed the magic within."

"That is not the only reason..." Theras hinted. Any reservations Larissa still clung to wilted in the face of Theras's sparkling green eyes. "What? Did you think you were the only one of the Fair Lady's children to try? To avoid the fight using your intellect?"

"But it's wrong to use magic."

"Not so," Theras said. "They have taught it is, and for good reason. Your fears are founded on age-old rumors laid with purpose. We do not want or need girls desiring to test themselves against an enemy they know little about. Who think magic an easy path to glory. How hard did you all fight for the Empirical? You would not have done so if you thought magic could make it easy, but you cannot treat magic in the same manner as you would a sword. Discretion is required, and many who seek it out have already set themselves on the path of the Evercry. It possesses those who *think* they are at their strongest, who covet power. When truly, the soul couldn't be more weakened. In a world where our adversaries use tactics and strengths beyond the knights' abilities, it is up to the darkkins to predict them, to muddy ourselves in magic hoping to understand, and anticipate who the Evercry may strike, and where."

"Did you know my mother would be called?" Larissa asked, unable to stop the sudden question. "Did you see who she needed to hunt? Why hasn't she slain it and returned?"

"No, we didn't know." Theras's gaze dropped to the table.

"We track magical objects and users across the land, looking for those who stray too far down the dark path of chaos. But we cannot predict all who fall to the taint, or which knights will follow. We help where we can, but only in the capacity of information, not all of us combat-inclined. And we don't have to be. That is not our role."

The hard knot of tension in Larissa's chest eased again, slipping away to nothing with Theras's easy and honest manner. "What must I do?"

"Learn." Theras said the word as though it were all that mattered. "The first year here is not dissimilar from your schooling. You study our ways, but so too does it encourage independent thought. You must forge your own path, and we will help guide it. There are many unique branches of magic. Ritual and death, life and potions, artifacts and history. You will find one that calls to you, a piece of a puzzle that fits you with all of us and becomes a lifelong passion. We still train like knights, to ensure we are not a burden in battle, but an evercry's song is not our trial. Each darkkin will find herself tested in a manner far more dangerous, and not unlike a knight facing their evercry. That is what it means when you earn the title of darkkin-thane."

"Sister Goverin." Larissa remembered the odd title.

"Darkkin-Thane Goverin lost her hand rather than fall to the Evercry." Theras pushed some paper to the side, fussing with the documents. "She chose to...remove a curse rather than suffer its fate."

Having seen Goverin's metal arm, Larissa could guess what this meant. "I thought we only traveled with knights who'd heard an evercry?"

"Not always. Though we are charged with finding it, only some manifestations warrant our presence."

"I understand." Larissa didn't know if she had it within her to cut off her own hand. Doubt unfurled inside her once more at the strength of her convictions, her aversion to combat. "But...if what we do is so important, why choose me?"

"We only take one acolyte of every year's class. We always get first choice, and our choice supersedes all other castes, including the knights." Theras's warmth faded, a heaviness in her tone that took Larissa's breath away. "And we chose you, Larissa, for doing what few have dared try. It was bold—near reckless, should it not have worked. Nevertheless, it did, making you very brave, and with what I suspect is a hidden affinity for magic."

Larissa swallowed against the discovery. Theras had turned her world upside down, but it would take far more than a few sentences for Larissa to accept them as truth. She didn't yet feel she belonged here, but the possibility of doing so swelled within her like the oncoming spring.

"I...I still have much I need to learn." Larissa's declaration met with a return of Theras's warmth.

"Yes," she said, "but it wasn't the only reason I chose you, Larissa. You have a thirst for knowledge, and here, we need to know of all the avenues available to us to help defeat the Evercry. Not just those that involve brute force."

Larissa's gaze narrowed, the comment too close to what she'd said to Valare on the day of the Empirical. Theras's enigmatic smile wouldn't have indicated the remark was anything other than an observation, except for the sparkle deep within her eyes.

Larissa suspected the Empirical hadn't been the end of her trials.

—

Theras gave Larissa an overview to the daily routine, less a curriculum than a guideline, and took her on a tour of the place she would now call home.

Larissa got her own desk, and Theras told her she could borrow any books she fancied from the darkkins' private library and reliquary underneath the "Pit"—an unflattering nickname for where they all worked. In another corridor were lounges and a dining hall. No other caste had their own kitchens, and given how insular the darkkins were, despite their friendliness, Larissa began to make sense of why she had seen so little of them over the years.

The darkkins were not only outcasts for their use of magic. They were...odd.

There were many with personality peculiarities. Some didn't speak, others didn't like to be looked at. One scurried through any open space, almost hugging the walls. Others bore their differences in more physical manners: Darkkin-Thane Goverin with her hand, another sister in a wheelchair, and a third disfigured by burn marks. None let their differences stop them performing their duties, and everyone she met treated her as though she belonged there.

It was a foreign concept to Larissa. So much so, she excused herself to the bathroom to cry. Theras asked no questions about her reddened eyes as they resumed the tour.

Despite their differences, Larissa soon learned that the darkkins were all a little alike too. Quiet, studious, but with an easy manner underneath that belied the seriousness of the work. A quirk as much to do with their diverse personalities as it was their aptitude for magic.

Theras showed her the map, explaining each dark mark—symbols of an existing evercry—and what signs indicated the presence of one. Many were assigned to a darkkin, but Larissa wouldn't get one until she'd been there a full year. Even then she'd accompany another darkkin first, to gain experience.

Oleth, the young darkkin about Larissa's age, took over the tour then, bringing her to the immense tunnels of the darkkins' library. Theras had not exaggerated the number of volumes hidden down in these passageways, and if not for Oleth's unfaltering familiarity, Larissa would have gotten lost. As it was, she stacked her desk with books she would read for the next dozen morrows.

Larissa finished her unusual day with a stomach full of curried meat, made with spices from a far-off land. She forgot the name of the sister who made dinner; too many names made her mind an overflowing dam of information.

But every new detail filled her with unfamiliar excitement.

After dinner, Oleth offered to lead her to the darkkins' sleeping quarters. She fidgeted beside Larissa as they tiptoed through the halls, the hour late from studies long into the night.

"I saw the chains were magic too," Oleth confided. "But I'd never have dared do what you did. It was like something out of a fairy story."

She sighed, before taking an imaginary swish with a spear. Larissa found her somewhat childish for a girl a full two years older than her, but it was hard to dislike Oleth's lighthearted nature.

"It didn't seem that way," Larissa said, words broken by a cracking yawn.

"I've already written an account of it. Theras said it was wonderful, and they've added it to the archive."

"What?" Larissa tried to pay attention as she rubbed fatigue from her eyes.

"We record the Empirical for all who are chosen to become darkkins." Oleth raised a brow at Larissa's tiredness. "But don't worry about that now. You need a bath and a good night's sleep."

The thought puzzled Larissa, as though they'd chosen her before the Empirical. But she let it go as they arrived at the bathrooms.

Oleth pushed a heavy wooden door, groaning with the weight until Larissa helped her shove it open. Inside was a cave, where steam wafted over the still surfaces of a series of pools from an underground spring. Tiers of rocks sat one above the other to spill into those below. Across the roof hung dozens of glittering stalactites, water droplets glistening from their tips. It was an unrefined cave compared to the rest of the underground labyrinth that was Lathore.

A foul, heavy smell assaulted Larissa's senses, and her nose wrinkled. "What *is* that?"

"Sulphur," Oleth said. "From the water. It's a mineral spring, but it sure smells like a latrine."

"Worse. Why don't the ones in the acolytes' dorms smell like that?"

"We're closer to the source—smellier but hotter water. Come on." Oleth walked to one side of the pool, where a narrow opening led into a small dressing room with benches. Hooks above for clothes, a cupboard held thick brown towels and thin cotton shifts. Oleth picked up two and thrust one set at Larissa.

"Get changed."

In the student baths, no one wore shifts into the water. Larissa accepted hers nonetheless. Though she was tired enough to prefer bed, a hot soak appealed to her stiff back. She'd carried books all day, few of them small.

"That's nasty," Oleth commented as Larissa lifted her shirt. "From Water's sword?"

Larissa looked down at the mark. The stitches were an angry red thanks to Valare, but the wound was healing. The ache that lingered was much deeper inside. "Yes."

"See this?" Oleth dragged apart her robe and showed her upper thigh. A horrendous burn mark scarred her flesh. "Fire. Bitch sliced off part of my leg during the Empirical. I...I can't go into the field because of it. I can't run. Which is good because I enjoy *telling* stories. Not experiencing them." Pronounced with such vehemence that Larissa believed her, eyes lingering on the mark. Oleth hadn't stumbled on the stairs when Larissa met her earlier that day. It was a limp.

Larissa was unsure what to say. "I'm...so sorry."

"Why?" Oleth shrugged, pulling her hair above her head to tie in a bun, white streak stark against the rich chestnut curls. "I get to do what I love most. That's what you'll discover about Theras. They teach it during school, but Theras embodies it. She finds what you didn't know you always wanted to do, but more than that, the calling is a passion you cannot deny."

Larissa tugged off her clothes and pulled on the shift. "I

wonder what she has in store for me."

"You aren't listening. She'll help *you* figure it out, but the actual reckoning you have to do yourself." Oleth flicked a towel over her shoulder. They walked back out to the caves, Oleth's awkward gait more noticeable without the crimson robes swishing about her legs.

"So, one thing to warn you about is that these get hot," Oleth said as they stood by the green pool's edge. "This one is the most moderate. Start there, with your wound. The higher the tier, the hotter the water. The baths also get smaller. Down the bottom is a cooling tank, if you feel sadistic enough to do that to yourself."

"Cooling tank?"

"Body of cold water, insulated from the rest of the spring." Oleth scowled at the offending water. "Apparently it's good for you to soak in the hot water and then jump in the cold—repeatedly. Because why have an evercry torture you when you can do it to yourself?"

Behind them, someone tutted.

"Until you've tried it, don't underestimate the invigorating effect." Correal walked down the stairs from a higher tier, brown hair tied in a crown above her head, shift damp and clinging to her body. "You can sit in any of these pools, but work your way up to the hottest one. *Then* jump into the cooling tank."

"Says the Matriarch of Sadistic," Oleth said.

"None of your cheek," Correal said without ire. "Have a soak, Larissa. Forego the cooling pool until tomorrow when you need something to startle you awake. You'll sleep like the dead tonight, I promise."

She waved to them both and disappeared into the changing rooms.

"Why is everyone like this?" Larissa whispered, the casual atmosphere and easy compatriotism so far from the strictness of her childhood that she couldn't swallow the question anymore. Oleth didn't pretend not to know what Larissa referred to, giving her a gentle smile.

"What we do is hard enough without pretending we are anything but what we are. No one understands our true selves, or what we go through for the order, better than a fellow darkkin. The knights aren't the true defense against the Evercry. Even without hearing the call, we stop more evercrys from beginning than have ever been slain."

"How?"

Oleth led her to the tepid pool, and they sank beneath the water.

"A lesson for tomorrow," she said. "Isn't your head full already?"

"No," Larissa said, wonder keeping her struggling lids open. "It's only just beginning."

# Chapter 6

arissa's life tumbled from the strict hours of her lessons to the indulgent, fluid days of the darkkins. She could get up early, enthusiastic that no beating awaited her in the training ring, and instead, she could read books all day with guilt-free pleasure. Theras's gentle instruction still prompted Larissa to study as broadly as she could, training included, to be sure she could find a subject she was passionate about. It allowed her insatiable curiosity to feed until stuffed as she came to know the sisters.

Every darkkin in the Pit was happy to share whatever project they were working on, be it translating an old tome, studying magic items, or training for combat. She was recruited for a variety of tasks, such as tending herb gardens along the rocky mountainside, which required her to study the names of odd plants and review those she'd learned in school, and deciphering handwriting in older books, copying the fading prose for rebinding.

She came to learn of her sisters' pasts and about what each

of them did. So much of the knights' information came from the darkkins' reports. From the research done on magical artifacts kept underneath the Pit, to the rumors that poured in on the wings of the Fair Lady's network of birds. Darkkin Farrast looked after the birds of prey from a tower embedded in the mountain's side. The birds let Farrast walk among them, receiving or sending them to deliver waxed scrolls to all corners of the western continent of Aesethen, but especially to the knights, out there, facing the Evercry.

The darkkins funneled every tidbit of information to the world map above the Pit, the great canvas always growing and changing. Dark spots removed or made bigger, new ones added, an ever-shifting pattern of some design Larissa didn't yet understand, but the darkkin hid nothing from her, and she grew bolder in her questions. In her free time, she roamed the catacombs beneath the Pit, discovering how to navigate the narrow, twisting corridors and picking up any book she liked without fear of restriction or having to hide. Though she wasn't yet allowed to examine artifacts unsupervised.

Her only contact with the outside world was letters from Jyan. Larissa hadn't ventured out of the darkkins' halls since arriving, instead keeping to paper and ink to communicate with her friend. At first the messages were lengthy and enthusiastic, but they grew infrequent as Jyan completed her first tour as a knight. Larissa didn't mourn the loss of her friend as she had before, when jealous of Jyan's calling.

Larissa had found her own.

Days morphed into weeks as she studied and worked with the other darkkins. When weeks rolled into months, she began to worry. She had yet to find a specific path to follow among the darkkins.

Theras assured her it came to all in time. For some it was the matter of a month, for others it came not until a full year had passed.

Larissa engrossed herself in studies so as to not dwell on the restlessness that grew within her every day.

The darkkins had their own exercise yard, with training equipment and obstacle courses. Larissa tackled them once a day, not for strength as Valare had done, but for physical health and nimble feet. She also practiced combat with Darkkin-Thane Goverin, who was a master swordswoman despite her handicap, her left hand dominant. Goverin was always willing to spar, but often ran Larissa ragged through the training courses.

Whenever Larissa picked up her favored weapon of the spear, Goverin never criticized her choice but was quick to give instruction.

"Be surer of your footing," she admonished. "Not engaging in combat is admirable, of that there is no question. But you push too far in your enthusiasm to keep an enemy at bay."

None of Larissa's former teachers had even thought her style effective. "How do you mean?"

"All your previous opponents used conventional methods to attack you." Goverin hefted her sword, coming at Larissa in a standard attack as she spoke. "Your movement should be far more dexterous, without compromising your ground."

Sword and spear clashed together, Larissa finding the rhythm in the moves she'd learned so far from the darkkin-thane. Goverin flung a rock she'd had hidden in her hand at Larissa's face. Unprepared, Larissa ducked aside, and this allowed Goverin to move closer. To compensate, Larissa stepped forward, slashing her spear in a defensive arc, but Goverin brought her sword down on Larissa's weapon, breaking the haft with one booted kick. Larissa swung the bulbous end at Goverin's head, but the woman dodged the blow and thrust at Larissa's overextended leg.

The sword stopped a fraction of an inch away from her body. If the blade had bitten into Larissa's skin, it would have severed ligaments behind her knee. Left her crippled and defenseless.

Larissa glanced into Goverin's face, the experienced swordswoman who cut so close. She was just scratching the surface of Goverin's battle history. Goverin withdrew her sword, and Larissa eased her stance.

"Is that what it's like?" she asked. "To fight an evercry?"

"No. Evercrys are much more difficult. But they have their agents."

Larissa nodded. She'd heard stories. Cutthroats, thieves, pirates; those without magic, but who were willing to accept coin from those possessed by an evercry. Willing to sell out their fellow human beings for greed.

"Do they deserve our help?" she asked, voice trembling. She wasn't sure she could kill someone who simply made a bad or ill-informed choice.

Goverin was silent a long moment. "When they come for you, it will be to kill you, to stop you in your duty. It is one of the many reasons they teach you not to hesitate in the Empirical."

Larissa hung her head. The reminder that she hadn't passed churned in her stomach.

"Don't worry so." Goverin's hand landed on her shoulder. "You are clever and quick. But there is no time for honor when you know that one of you will die depending on what transpires within the next few seconds." She sheathed her sword. "You should never engage in combat unless it can't be avoided, and if it can't, don't fight fair, fight to win. There are weapons that can hurt far more than a blade. I lost my hand to such a weapon, imbued with dark magic intent on consuming me. It did not even cut me—I only had to pick it up."

Larissa's eyes darted to Goverin's hook before she could stop herself. "You didn't sense the magic within?"

"Not until it was too late." Goverin glanced down at her hand with a shrug. "I've been shot with poisoned arrows, fought a sorcerer with a blade tainted by the Evercry, and struck down a fallen darkkin."

Larissa swallowed. "Does that happen a lot?"

"No. It would be a lie to say it does not happen at all, but it isn't common. Most darkkins would never allow themselves to tread down that path."

"But the rumors—" Larissa cut herself off. She'd come to learn the truth of the darkkins' rumors for herself; they were there to frighten the shallow and susceptible.

"What about our sisters in the other castes, even the knights?" she asked instead. "Aren't they ever tempted too?"

"Even less likely for them to fall," Goverin said, glancing up at the city's towering shadow that spilled over the yard. "It's hammered into them from school days to hate magic, but by the time a knight's training is done, they abhor the very mention of it, and as such would never wield it."

Larissa thought back on Valare's attitude. Remembered her own mother instilling the same loathing in Larissa from an early age. During her time with the darkkins, much of what Larissa had come to learn undid lessons taught to her by her mother.

"If we both face the Evercry, how are we different?"

Goverin gave an almost bittersweet smile. "The knights are guardians—they can see their opponents coming, and sometimes their enemies know it. The darkkins are investigators, have yet to learn who is a foe, and sometimes their adversaries don't know either."

Larissa absorbed the concept of discovering an unknown enemy, and she shivered despite the warm morning light.

"Come," Goverin said. "Time to practice more with a sword. You already know the spear well enough."

—

Every art Larissa thought she'd mastered turned on its head in the halls of the darkkins, from combat to the subtler arts of potions. Sister Correal was an alchemical wonder, with a fount of knowledge on herbs and ritual Larissa envied. She visited Correal's laboratory many times, the doors never closed to her inquisitive mind.

One night, Correal woke her and told her to wrap up in a cloak, the mountains cold despite the warmer spring weather.

They stole out of the city. Moonlight guided their path across the slopes, the stars' muted glow a pale sister compared to the glaring lunar beams. They rendered the mountainside monochromatic, patches of white snow against the russet grassland and stretches of dark gorse. A chilly wind slunk daggers beneath the flaps of their coats. Larissa was glad for her woven wool underwear; without it, she'd have lost feeling in her legs.

Along with her sword, Larissa carried her bow on her back, a safety against snow leopards, and Correal was armed with a dagger and basket.

"Moonslips and merryweather." Correal snipped the plants from beneath rugged brush.

"They're highland flowers," Larissa said as she trod over the heather. The plant's soporific effects rendered subjects unconscious, as Larissa knew from her own trips to the hospital ward.

"We use both herbs for sleeping potions." Correal bent over a starred white flower smaller than Larissa's thumbnail. "They are most potent when picked at the heart of night during the full moon. It's when they bloom."

"Why do darkkins need sleeping potions? To subdue an enemy?"

"Sometimes. Other times when the things they see are so dark, nightmares keep sleep at bay." Correal moved among the foliage, and Larissa walked in her wake, gaze watchful on the shadows. "The skyseers' use it for their visions, too."

"I thought they read the stars." She glanced upward, as though the twinkling gems could hear her.

Correal chuckled. "Not all the secrets of their order come from the stars alone. We mix a combination of herbs to reach different dream states. The darkkins see the present in faraway lands, though it takes the right mind to do it, and few possess that talent. The skyseers use the images they receive to see what is to come. They believe that time is cyclical, so what has gone before will come again. You know this?"

Larissa nodded as Correal ducked headfirst into a crevasse, scraping moss from the underside of the stone. "Yes, the theory is that if we can see stars, then they can see us too. The light of the sun reflects, over and over, causing the cyclical effect. Studying the stars captures the light that was once here, and allows us to study the mistakes of our past."

Another glance skyward made her doubt that was all there was to the skyseers, given what she had learned of the darkkins.

"They have a mirrored hall where light is cast in rainbow hues." Correal grunted as she kept scraping. "With the right meditation and a trained mind, they make many predictions that are correct. It's an invaluable tool to us when they sense darkness in the land we cannot otherwise reach or know of, and they send us to investigate without waiting for it to become an evercry."

Correal ended her lecture with a cry of delight, holding up a root with an odd quirk of her lips, not quite a smile.

"Gorsen woe."

Larissa frowned. "I've never heard of it. What's it used for?"

"Putting off amorous men." Correal held it out to Larissa. "In the field, they can get the wrong idea, and a little of this goes a long way. You just drop a sliver in their drink, or worse, put it in your own mouth to give to them when they become too impassioned, and *it* doesn't work." She made a gesture at her nether region, the elongation of her hand implying the phallic symbol of the opposite sex.

Larissa was glad darkness concealed her pinkened cheeks.

She had endured the lecture on human biology along with all the other girls during their studies. At the right age and when they were ready, it was common to find a man and carry a daughter for the Fair Lady. Though some left for a time, many sisters returned to the halls with their progeny. Larissa had no interest or inclination to do anything involving a man, let alone allow one to rut between her legs like a hog.

"I'm not going in the field yet," she said, wondering how to decline the gift.

"But you will one day, and it dries into a beautiful powder," Correal said, thrusting the root into Larissa's hand and returning to picking moonslips. Larissa tucked the root in a pocket and tried not to think about it as they returned to the city.

—

She soon learned many uncomfortable truths of the world beyond Lathore's walls, and not all of them were about the opposite sex.

Darkkin Larea taught history, and she skipped none of the more scandalous stories Larissa's previous teachers opted not to tell.

"If the queen knew her son would use magic to kill his father," Larissa speculated to Larea over tea and many tomes, "why didn't she stop him?"

"Ah," Larea said, "but she *wanted* her son to be king, no matter the cost. Her husband was a brute, and she would have done anything to aid her son in his ascent. What she didn't predict was that her son would keep using magic, go insane, and become an evercry. When he was crowned, none could stand in his path, not even his mother. This is what it means to become an evercry, to no longer care for those you once loved. He was a mad king. A bad king. Many died."

In the distant annals of history Larissa had once studied, the son killed the king with magic and it started his descent to the Evercry. But that the queen knew, and allowed it to happen, was news to Larissa, and it was abhorrent.

"How did we ever come to learn of such a thing?" she asked. "The story speaks of the knight sent to slay him. The king's guard gave the knight entry, but by then the king had killed his mother. How do we know the mother's thoughts?"

"It didn't happen quite like that," Larea said. "The dying queen confessed to the darkkin traveling with the knight. The evercry her son became had killed the mother during the battle.

He sacrificed her to get in the knight's way. The knight killed him, while the darkkin assisting the knight took a true account of the events from the last of the queen's breath. It is one reason a knight will often travel with a darkkin. To make these matters clearer so we can be better warned of the evercry's mannerisms and actions."

Larissa struggled to grasp the difference between what they did and the possession of an evercry. "If we can use magic and resist it, then why couldn't the son?"

"It is not one decision that leads to the fall of an evercry. For some it can be as many as hundreds. Little things every day, for years and years. By the time the Lady calls for a knight, the Evercry has already made itself a home inside that person. It takes them over, sits inside them like a toad in a pond. Only when the pond is a dank swamp overrun with toads is it evident what has occurred."

"Surely she would have seen the signs?" Larissa pressed.

"She didn't marry the king by choice," Larea said. Larissa quieted. "He was not good to her, that man, as it happens in some marriages. People who find themselves in circumstances beyond their control will often do anything to get out of it. Even what they consider a lesser evil, rather than endure any more of what has passed."

It painted a far different picture of what Larissa knew from the history books. The more she researched, the more she became aware of her black-and-white view of the world. She needed to widen it to accommodate people who acted without sense or rationality, especially where love and power were concerned.

She hoped it never happened to her, heard the warnings deep within Larea's lessons, but still, she could see what the temptation might be as she began learning magic.

—

At dawn's first light, she was always with Darkkin Farrast,

studying magical artifacts. One of Larissa's first loves in the caste, Farrast was tentative with her teaching but had an extensive and subtle skillset.

"See an ordinary goblet?" Farrast placed a silver chalice in the center of the table, surrounded by a circle of salt. For any magical item not due to be destroyed or locked in protected vaults, salt was a temporary barrier as a matter of precaution.

Larissa sat across the table, used to Farrast placing ordinary objects in front of her and testing whether she could identify its enchantment. Larissa gave the obvious answer so that Farrast wouldn't suspect what little trouble she had on that score. "It's tainted with magic."

"Where?"

Larissa studied it without touching. "There is scroll work in the sides, pictures of flowers. There are no runes there, but the kaltir thorns motif indicates a cup for...persuasion?"

Farrast picked up the cup in thick leather gloves, the same used for hawking. She turned it over, and underneath a single rune was carved into the base.

"*Dendekonai*," Farrast said. The rune activated, turning purple with the power of her voice. Spoken magics were still new to Larissa, and her skin tingled every time. She relished the lessons to come when she could speak them for herself.

"If you were to pour wine in this now," Farrast said, "and drink it, you'd be susceptible to any instruction I give. Do so."

Larissa's mouth fell open. "I beg your pardon?"

Farrast reached to the end of the table, fingers wrapping about a jug. She flipped the chalice the right way up and poured a half cup of wine, before offering it to Larissa.

"It is not a simple matter of knowing it's there," the yellow-eyed woman said. "You must learn to experience it for yourself."

"No." Larissa stood, backing away, wary of the constant tests. Farrast didn't flinch, but her eyes flickered over Larissa's shoulder.

"Go on, Darkkin Westwyn," Correal said from the doorway.

"You're among friends. Though your distrust is not unwarranted, you are safe here to experience the Evercry's subtleties."

Larissa resumed her seat. Farrast gave an encouraging smile as she handed over the cup.

The swirling magic within the metal made Larissa wish she had gloves as it touched her palm. Even as she raised the cool edge of the cup to her lips, a voice inside shrieked at her to throw it to the floor.

She took a sip.

"All of it."

Larissa didn't want to, but she drained the cup. She set it back down in the salt circle, eyeing Farrast.

"Stand up," Farrast told her. Larissa saw no reason not to, so rose to her feet. "Walk with me."

Farrast took Larissa's hand and led her down the corridors. Past the tiered study, where several older darkkins looked up, gave slight grins of amusement, and went back to their work, all while an odd sense of displacement settled on Larissa's shoulders.

Larissa was in no danger; she had Correal's assurance. But even as everything felt fine, the voice in her head repeated over and over that it was not.

Farrast led her down the steps into the bathing room. This early in the morning, steam clung to the walls—except for the last pool, where a thin layer of ice denoted the chilliness of the dipping tank.

Farrast stopped at its edge.

"You need to cool down," she said. "Jump in."

Larissa found her feet shuffling forward, even as a part of her screamed not to move. The warring compulsion tripped her feet, and she fell fully dressed into the pool with a shriek.

Cracking through the ice, the cold enveloped her before she even sensed the water. It stole the breath from her lungs. She clawed out, reaching for an edge, kicking her feet as hard as she could despite the waterlogged robe tangling her limbs. She swallowed a mouthful of water and struck for the surface, hands smashing into the ice and finding no handhold.

Farrast knelt nearby, long arm outstretched, and Larissa lunged for it. Farrast dragged Larissa out of the pool.

"Quick, take your things off." Farrast bent to undo the laces on her boots.

Shivers took her over. Larissa yanked off her robe and undershirt, shucked her breeches, and ran to the closest heated pool. An ungainly lunge splashed water everywhere, but she did not care. Warmth wrapped her in the softest blanket, and she drifted down until the water touched her ears.

Farrast carried her wet things, but she laughed at Larissa too.

"An unpleasant lesson," she said, "but it is easy to see how it can be used for great evil. A simple spell like this in one instance is a harmless joke, while in another it can force a man to walk off a ledge to his death."

"That was terrifying," Larissa sulked from the pool. "Magic isn't a game."

Farrast shook her head. "No, it isn't. But you can see for yourself how dangerous it can be, how easy to fall into the lure. Yet you almost resisted, did you not?"

Larissa sank back beneath the surface. "Not enough."

"No one does their first time." Farrast shrugged. "Or, few do. Most don't have the experience."

Larissa shuddered as the worst of the chill was banished by the heated water. Inside, though, a hotter fire raged, and she climbed out of the pool. "Again."

Farrast grinned, holding out a dry robe.

—

Larissa tried over a dozen more times before being able to say no.

"We can stop there." Farrast took the chalice away. Larissa looked up from where she was sitting.

"Why?" She let go of the table where her hand had clamped down to keep any digits from inserting themselves in her nostril.

Larissa had fast learned Farrast had a sadistic side. Her cheeks were pink where she'd slapped herself. She'd strutted around the workroom, crowing. Passing darkkins had called out encouragement, even though they'd laughed, adding to Larissa's determination to control herself.

"You understand this one," Farrast said. "There are others to learn."

Larissa stared at the chalice. "How is doing this any different from a magic user?"

"Do you mean, why aren't I corrupted by the Evercry?" Farrast clarified, and went on when Larissa nodded. "The path to the Evercry is dark, and though this cup holds its own vileness, it is a small thing. Why use magic when a real poison will do? Because magic holds an unswayable power. With poison you merely kill—and while murder is vicious, would it not be crueler to pretend at peace with an enemy, break bread and drink wine, only to order them to kill the one they love most? To force them to succumb to your will and subjugate their people? Such is powerful magic. But this kind of cruelty cuts the soul until the opening is wide enough for an evercry to enter. Magic users aren't themselves by the time they hurt the ones they love."

Larissa mulled over the words, thinking on her own need for magic, and wanting to change the subject. "Is that why Larea is reteaching me history?"

"Among other things." Farrast handed a dustpan and brush to Larissa for the salt on the table. Farrast herself collected the cup, cleaned it, and put it in a velvet-lined box. Across its surface, wards of binding restricted the magic of the item inside.

"The world is not a stagnant history book." Farrast locked the box. "It changes all the time, with every passing day, and many of us are never aware. No one wants to know that their magic-wielding friend, father, husband, or son could become an evercry. To them it is a protection, a convenience. For those who possess the self-control to manage it, that's all it ever becomes."

Larissa finished sweeping up the salt, taking her time before she asked her next question. "Why does anyone risk using it at all, then? If they knew the truth of history, they wouldn't be tempted."

Farrast gave her a long, slow look, one that bespoke a lifetime of experience.

"The stories of our past come from those that survived," Farrast said. "They are full of actions and consequences not to be believed, and that is for the best. History is not always sung by heroes. It is sometimes written by the villains who told their story first."

# Chapter 7

Larissa's face danced with illumination. Deep in the darkest cellars of the darkkins, she wrested with shadows and light, weaving together simple magic in an attempt to create the perfect illusion. A doppelganger of her figure that could distract an enemy.

Much as trepidation sent nerves skittering over her, and more than one glance over her shoulder, she knew one thing for certain: what she was doing wasn't evil.

She was only creating an image of herself, and not for vanity's sake. Once she'd honed the spell, she planned to create other images, of knights or darkkins—illusions that would allow enough confusion for attack or escape should she come face to face with an evercry. This possibility excited her and drove her to her hidden refuge beneath the Pit to rehearse. To prove she could do it.

The magic that flew between her fingertips she thought little of, except each time she crept away to practice, guilt snuck beneath her validation.

She should tell Theras.

A spell of this nature wasn't forbidden so much as it was supposedly beyond her. But even after three months of becoming acquainted with the darkkins' ways, the baggage of her past schooling kept her from speaking of her aptitude.

Among the books of the darkkin halls, Larissa no longer held back on her studies. From ancient tales to modern magic, from the fabled city of Lisolel to the records of knowledge held at the Library of Aongatha, in Jyan's home city, Larissa devoured it all. But she'd begun chafing against the gentle and restricted manner with which the darkkin sisters taught her to manipulate magic. There was, after all, a vast difference between understanding magic and using it.

The ease at which spell work came to her was startling. She feared knowledge of her innate talent might get her removed from the darkkin order, deemed too dangerous to stay. Or worse, executed. She wasn't willing to risk it, not when she'd found something in these halls she'd not experienced anywhere else.

Belonging.

Sitting cross-legged in a dusty, disused corner, she was in the darkkins' storage room on the pretense of selecting magical items for Farrast to explain to her. A map with a curious marking lay to one side, but her focus had turned elsewhere once she was alone.

A bowl of water sat in front of her, three candles surrounding it. Checking her notebook, Larissa tried a new inflection, mouthing the words soundlessly before looking into the bowl of still water, candlelight glimmering on its surface.

*"Mihni vidi, fasti sunay mihni, quam astra mihni."* The words slid over her tongue with the cool taste of magic. They fell from her lips to curl in the air, crossing to the flame of the candles. The water rippled and frothed. At first she feared she'd botched it, before the movement turned into a whirling vortex.

Delight filled her as the spire rose, growing to a tower the height of her seated head. She climbed to her feet, and the tower rose with her on an ever-thinning pinnacle of water.

Holding her hands out to either side, the column swayed before her, flattening out, changing shape, until it was as though she stood before a mirror.

Except the reflection did not mimic her movements. The manifestation was blank, no nuance of expression—even the eyes didn't blink, nor did the chest rise and fall. But a burble of excitement rose within Larissa at her success, and she breathed animation into the figure.

"*Gradauelaus.*"

Larissa raised her hand, and the figure returned her gesture. Laughing at her own lips twitching in delight, Larissa's reflection did the same, eyes bright, mouth curled but soundless. The reflection swished its arms back and forth, and even performed a deep curtsy. Larissa clapped her hands and the water splashed, but its form remained, held in slivers of dew and light. She held out her hand to command it to move from the bowl.

There came a scrape of stone down the corridor. She flinched.

"*Exilios.*" The muted whisper and her slashing hand dispelled her image. Water splashed over the candles and snuffed them out into pale streams of smoke.

The only light was from a far stairwell, and Larissa watched it grow brighter, wide-eyed with fear. She slid the bowl and candles under a nearby bookcase.

"Darkkin Westwyn?" Correal called from the stairs, and Larissa breathed a sigh of relief.

"Yes?"

"Are you free a moment?"

Larissa left her tools where they were but snatched the scrying map of Lathore from the floor beside her.

"Of course," she said, entering the stairwell's light. Correal gave Larissa a quizzical glance for her emergence from the darkness but waved her hand to make haste.

"It's your turn to cast the breeze," she said. The spell she spoke of created a crosswind that alleviated the heat of summer and still air of the Pit. Larissa quickened her step on the stairs.

"They say a storm is on the way." Correal fanned herself at an intersection while she waited for Larissa. Dressed in crimson pants and a light shirt, sweat gathered in the material about her armpits. Larissa could feel her own shift sticking to her skin. "Should be quite a squall."

"Long as I don't have to clean out the falconry again." The last storm a week earlier had scared the birds into making rather a mess of the falconry's floor.

Correal grinned. "Luck of the draw, I'm afraid."

"Cool weather, at least?"

"According to the skyseers. Though it may flood the valley."

Larissa didn't mind; she wasn't due to leave on a quest for another three months or more. The itch for travel and escape was absent when there was less shame for her true fascination.

"Do you want me to do one first?" Correal asked.

In a rare show of confidence, Larissa shook her head. "No, I've been practicing the incantation. I think I can do it alone."

Correal's brow lifted, but she gave way as they reached the base of the Pit. Several darkkins sat at their desks, drinking pitchers of water and cold tea, all sweltering in the warmth pressing down from the wooden dome above. Slivers of daylight gave illumination through the shutters, but with them came summer's bane.

"About time, Westwyn," Goverin said. "This weather makes my hook chafe."

"Of course, Darkkin-Thane," Larissa called, and setting her artifact to one side, she walked to the center of the Pit.

What goaded her next, she could not say, but rather than use the incantation most often recited, she tweaked it a little based on what she'd learned through her own studies.

"*Sumae per spirtaeum, audaea vocato mea, savitour ventis, et clo mitiae extrulae.*" Between her widening hands, she captured the breeze of her breath, growing in force. As she raised her hands above her head, the swirling winds danced at her command. With a flourish, she flung them up to rattle the Pit's domed roof.

The rafters trembled in the violent wind that burst forth from her grip. The breeze should have circled the room in a constant flow of air, but it was closer to a gale that shook the ceiling.

Startled darkkins grabbed papers sent skipping over desks and across the room, book pages fluttering and the great map itself rippling in the wind. The wind disturbed little else, but several of the sisters shouted warnings and other small chastisements.

Larissa resisted the swell of panic, shouting another command. "*Cadunt voec meam.*"

Her will exerted over the wind and brought the spell to heel, until only a cooling ripple fell about the sisters, relieving the heat. Pleased, Larissa's smile soon wilted under Correal's narrowed gaze.

"Where did you learn that?" she asked.

"In a book." The lame answer was a fumbling cover for her undisclosed research, and when Correal's frown deepened, Larissa expanded. "I was looking into wind and water spellcraft, just trying to understand it better for the...draft." She gestured at the ceiling.

Through the glass of the balcony, she caught Theras's gaze. The matriarch's thoughtful look was both assessing and concerning. Larissa swallowed against her dry throat.

Theras curled her fingers, and Larissa could not mistake the gesture to come. Butterflies swirled in her stomach, worse than the vortex she'd created in the Pit. There was now a soft and steady breeze distilling the humid air, but more than one darkkin gave her an even cooler look as she passed.

"Shut the door," Theras instructed when Larissa entered the matriarch's study.

The curt tone and closed door denoted she was in trouble,

aided by the furrow of confusion on Theras's temple.

"I'm sorry," Larissa began to babble. "I got carried away. I thought if I knew the spell better, I could control it—"

"How did you do that, Larissa?" Theras asked. Something in her tone reminded Larissa of being in trouble with her mother. Old fears banished for months came rushing back, and Larissa flushed a guilty red.

"I—I read something that may have helped," she said, one hand twitching a thin plait between the ends of her fingers. "I've been spending a lot of time learning runes with Farrast and thought I might...bolster the spell."

There was a long silence, Theras's green eyes almost glowing in the low lights of the room, wide pupils drawing Larissa in. But Larissa did not fall into them, too used to the feeling of permanent dread—dread of her affinity for magic, of the Evercry, and of what her mother would think.

Months of inclusion couldn't counteract years of censure.

"I...will try to have more control." Larissa rubbed one arm, folding in on herself. Theras gave a huff of annoyance and came to stand in front of her. Her clenched hand rose between them, palm upward, white-knuckled as though she tried to hold something too great for her fingers. Her silver moonstone ring, which Larissa had never seen her without, shone like starlight.

"I will open my hand," she said, "and I want you to do whatever action comes foremost. If you do not, I will ask you to leave, and I will never allow you to return. Do we understand one another, Darkkin Westwyn?"

Larissa almost swallowed her tongue. Whatever test she would face, this left no room for preparation. Theras was waiting for her answer, so Larissa nodded, sure that hesitation would make matters worse.

The matriarch of the darkkins opened her hand.

Nestled within her palm was a golden cicada—so fine in its design, it took a moment for Larissa to see the cicada wasn't alive but crafted. Wings wrought of gold filigree, body encrusted with rubies, and at its head a black pearl that glistened as the body began to twitch. Music played from inside the carapace.

The scratching noise was nothing more than an irritation to start, but when the cicada's song echoed through the room, Larissa heard a lullaby. The sweet tune sang of hot nights in the desert. Along with the music came the scents of dark wine and sun-dried dates. She sensed on her skin a hidden gaze, seductive and intimate. In her ear, a whisper of a night that would never end...

Larissa's fingers snatched out, plucked the cicada up, and crushed it in her grasp.

The tune cut short, dying in a whine.

Larissa opened her hand to reveal the crushed insect. The wings bent, the song of its body destroyed, but something inside remained. A vial of sorts had broken open. Dark brown liquid spilled onto Larissa's palm, sticky and revolting, as though she'd squeezed a live bug and not one adorned in jewels. Larissa's mouth fell open.

"I'm sorry," she said, instantly contrite. "You said to do the first thing that came to me."

"No." Theras took a sharp breath, one hand going to her throat. "It's fine, I'll take it back now."

She took the crushed metal from Larissa and placed it in her top drawer, not hiding the salted circle the little creature rested within, despite its battered state.

"What did I break?" Larissa stared down at where it lay, fragmented and lame. A fine sheen of the brown slime that still covered her palms glimmered on its body.

"A test of sorts," Theras said, sounding confused herself. "I had not expected you to react with such reflexes or violence."

Both stared at the cicada before exchanging glances. Theras didn't ask her to leave, and the constriction in Larissa's chest eased. On instinct, she stroked the back of the broken insect, mulling over what she thought the test had been for.

"It was filled with an herbal concoction to help infiltrate the subject's mind," she said. "You weren't worried about its song reaching the others in the Pit—the scent and the spell would only affect you and me. But it didn't alter you, because you made it."

When Theras gave a long, slow blink, Larissa knew she was right. But she sensed Theras waited for more, so she continued her assessment.

She lifted a finger to her nose, coated in brown liquid from the cicada. When she inhaled, her herb craft told her how it was made. The last piece was the creature itself, and Larissa flipped it over. Finding no runes on its back, she lifted the delicate gold wings beneath the carapace to see writing engraved where the music had come from.

"Moonslips, mugwort, wormwood," she said. "They induced a hypnotic and suggestive state, combined with the tune and whatever runes the cicada is inscribed with, to produce an effect similar to the Evercry. This seems a dangerous magic to present to someone not past their first year." The reproach slipped from her tongue before she could stop it.

Theras shut the drawer, then poured two glasses of iced tea, adding a dollop of clear liquid Larissa assumed was alcohol to each.

"There's a sink there." Theras gestured to a far wall. "Wash that off your hands and come sit."

Larissa obeyed, sluicing the muck from her hands before taking a place opposite Theras, who drank long of her glass. Larissa wanted to do the same, but she feared what else Theras had in store for her.

"It was a test," Theras repeated, though her tone was far more measured. "It has been some time since a magic user of your strength became one of the darkkins. If you had tried to take it, to keep the cicada, I would have known the Evercry could entice you. But you...didn't use magic to destroy it either." The latter came out with some surprise.

"Why use magic when actions will do?" Larissa tucked a braid behind her ear, heart beating in lingering fear they would still throw her out. "And I study a lot, I work at it—there's little more to it."

Theras was slow to answer. "You've been showing signs of aptitude uncommon for a first-year novice. Power I would expect in someone with years of training."

"I only ever read books."

Theras waved her hand. "It takes more than reading words to do what you have done. I'm just pleased you passed both this and the door."

Larissa glanced toward the runed entryway she'd arrived at so many months ago, recalled Theras's explanation that the magic wouldn't have allowed her past if she was impure.

"Has anyone not passed before?" Larissa put her hand around the glass of her iced tea and let the coolness press upon her palm.

"A few times," Theras said, taking a deep breath. "It isn't usual for a darkkin sister of the Fair Lady to have such control over it as you do. But you've been hiding it very well."

Too well.

It wasn't said aloud, but Larissa heard it in Theras's tone, saw it in her astute gaze, felt the pressure of her past weigh on her. She ducked her head in subservience.

"I meant no harm—"

"No one serving the Evercry *means* harm, and it is half the reason we require the precautions we do."

Her huff of dissatisfaction made Larissa cringe, not sure if she'd passed the test at all. Dread filled her that she would be labeled as tainted, executed as an enemy, before Theras quickly brushed aside her fears.

"You need to train with me," she said. "Or Correal or Farrast, no one else. We need to exercise and hone your magic in the most private of settings."

She gulped her drink, the gesture so far beneath the fastidious woman that Larissa panicked.

"I'm sorry," she said, "I didn't mean to cause problems. I can tone it down, hide it away. I've done it for years."

Theras was already shaking her head. "It will only get worse. Magic is a door that once open cannot be closed. Those that open the door seek access to more, invite the Evercry into the home of their minds."

It mimicked too closely her mother's admonishment of magic. Doors within people that opened to let in the Evercry…

But her mother wasn't here, and Theras was.

Larissa fumbled for the courage to ask what she feared. "How am I different from someone who will eventually succumb to the Evercry?"

"Magic like yours isn't a tool to put aside. The source is not external, it is within. If you try to make it too small, or bind it in chains, one day it will burst out and you'll lose control, hurt those around you. You may even reach through the door in order to regain control. It is one of the many paths to the Evercry."

Larissa's skin grew clammy, the summer heat unable to compete with the chill of Theras's words. She shivered, goosebumps pricking over her body, and she rubbed her arms.

"I don't say this to scare you," Theras said, "but to warn. I will guide you on a path that doesn't risk you succumbing to the Evercry. But promise me one thing."

Larissa didn't hesitate. "Anything."

Theras took a deep breath before she gave her ultimatum. "No magic unless I oversee. No showing off, no experiments, but most of all no hiding down in the archives. Anything you do, you do with me."

Larissa saw then what a fool she'd been, that Theras had guessed her secret projects, or at least suspected what Larissa had been about. She was quick to agree to the matriarch's terms.

"I promise," she said. "Nothing without your guidance."

# Chapter 8

Wolves slunk on padded feet into Larissa's dreams. The beasts came from the mountains, shadows against the snow, slipping over the walls and through the outlying streets, entering the doorways to the sisterhood's secluded fortress. They stalked the halls of Lathore, sniffing each corridor, seeking where she slept. Low growls of frustration became long howls through the city shrouded in night's cowl. Larissa ran, until she was above the city, on the snow, climbing ever higher. Ahead of her, a single wolf leapt out, staring at her. It howled. The lonesome cry echoed in her ears, morphed into her name.

*Westwyn...*

"Darkkin Westwyn."

The voice stirred Larissa from slumber, her nightmare shaken off as she raised her head. There was another hasty knock, an urgent tapping. She slid from her bed, padding barefoot across the carpet of her room to the door.

It creaked open to reveal Theras, face stern and serious. She was dressed in formal robes despite the late hour.

"The grand matriarch calls for you. Your mother sent a message."

Cold washed across Larissa's feet, dimpling her skin with goosebumps. Her night robe fluttered, and stillness crept up her legs to wrap around her torso and steal the breath from her lungs. Fears she'd kept locked in the back of her mind burst from their chains and barreled into her heart.

Theras stirred her from shock. "Get dressed. Navus has ordered your presence."

Larissa slipped on discarded day robes and belted them about her waist. Theras hovered, slender frame tight with tension, and gestured for Larissa to follow.

As they approached the doors of the darkkin halls, Larissa hesitated, the measure of time that she'd not left these halls giving her a brief pause. A full year since she'd first entered. But as Theras strode through, Larissa forewent doubt to stay by her mentor.

The door's magic caressed Larissa as they left, lingering on her skin. As though it would miss her while she was gone.

Through tunnels and disused back passages, they came closer to the heart of the mountains. The pale stone walls darkened and became pockmarked with age, the marble beneath their feet slick with eons of passing feet.

Ahead, a door wreathed in carvings waited for them, certain as death and seemingly as dark. The frame was similar to the one that barred the darkkin halls from the rest of Lathore. Larissa was given no time to ponder or study the deep magic within, as Theras knocked on the door and pushed it aside without waiting for a response. Larissa trailed after her, then stopped abruptly.

At the other end of the room, windows looked out onto the heart of the Descent.

Bathed in darkness, the distant gleam of snowy mountaintops on the Descent's far side looked like teeth in the night's mouth. Navus's expression matched its coldness.

"Come in," she said, though from the dour look on her face,

Larissa felt she was as welcome as a debt collector.

She did as she was bid, crossing a dark carpet wreathed in a pattern of pale vines.

Books lined the wall to one side, but on the other was a map not dissimilar to the one in the Pit, on a smaller scale. Black spots marked the surface, but there were marks in different colors as well. The code was lost on Larissa.

She was startled to see Matriarch Atticus standing by the fireplace. Imposing in her armor, Atticus didn't appear roused from sleep as the others were, but there was a smudge of darkness beneath her narrow, brooding eyes. Lines marked her face in a way Larissa didn't remember.

"As requested, Grand Matriarch," Theras said, "I have brought you Darkkin Westwyn."

Atticus gave a low click of the tongue, barely discernible over the fire's crackle, but Larissa didn't miss it. She found herself less perturbed by Atticus's dislike than she once was, able in her newfound confidence to ignore it.

"Please sit...Daughter." The familiar address given to all beneath her fell from Navus's tongue like icicles. Larissa kept silent as she took a chair before the grand matriarch's desk, glad to hide her shaking knees.

Navus descended to her own chair and plucked a scroll off her desk. Larissa wrapped her hands about themselves in her lap to stop the inclination to snatch it for herself.

"They've found the darkkin that traveled with your mother. She's dead."

Navus's words echoed within her. Relief warred with fear as she heard one of her sister darkkins had died. Her mother might still be alive, but her sister was lost. Any knight would give her life to save her darkkin. For a swordswoman of her mother's prowess to have failed this meant her mission had gone awry.

"But my mother?" She couldn't feel her mouth as she uttered the words.

"The darkkin's corpse was old," Navus went on without

consideration for Larissa's question. "We gather at least a few months, perhaps more. There is some evidence to suggest the darkkin was held captive against her will, but the report is quite garbled. Your mother appears to still be seeking her evercry, or she may have found it and run into…difficulty."

No sister of the Fair Lady faced an evercry without "difficulty," but that Navus admitted to such problems chilled Larissa.

"D-do you think she's…" Larissa couldn't bring herself to finish.

"No," Theras assured, taking the seat beside her, laying a hand on Larissa's forearm. "She sent instruction on what she needs now."

The trio of matriarchs exchanged glances, a silent conversation lingering on the air.

Larissa observed them each in turn, tried to source their hesitation. "What does she need?"

"Nothing that concerns you." Atticus spoke over her shoulder from where she studied the map. "We should dispatch a squadron of knights and leave now."

Theras inhaled, nostrils flaring. "We've already discussed this—"

Atticus slapped the map. "My knights can be at Meggaloth in three days by the river route."

"I will not tell you again." Navus's voice was soft, as if she regretted the words. "It cannot be you—one must stay to defend. There is no other choice, and I've made my decision."

Atticus glared at Larissa as though she were to blame.

Navus poured wine for all, Atticus dragging a chair to sit beside her desk, deferential but superior to Larissa. Navus sipped her wine, considering Larissa with tilted head. "What I am about to impart to you, Larissa, is a secret that must never be told. Pick up the wine."

Larissa feared what was coming but did so without hesitation.

"*Drathrenni*," Navus intoned, her voice a hot breeze over

Larissa's face. Light flared in Larissa's palm. Similar to the cup she'd used in practice with Farrast, she presumed this one also had a glyph etched in its bottom.

She drank the lot.

There was an approving glint in the grand matriarch's eye. "Swear never to speak of what you next hear to another."

*"I swear I will not speak of what I next hear to another. No secret shall leave my lips. To even think upon the spoken words will bring water's curse."* Larissa couldn't stop the speech once she'd started. The words ripped from her throat by magic, slimy and cold, settling on her teeth like hard candy, but with the bitterest of flavors. She sensed it wrapped about her tongue and sinking down her throat. She wanted to poke it, like a sore tooth, but left well enough alone at Navus's assessing gaze. Theras gave Larissa's arm an encouraging pat after Larissa set the cup on the table.

Navus was kind enough to refill it. "For the aftertaste."

"Thank you." Larissa sipped the wine to wash the foulness from her mouth.

"Someone of your skill level should not learn of this for many years to come, if ever." Navus twisted the stem of her goblet, dragging each word out as though loathe to speak it. "But it has become a dangerous necessity."

Larissa swallowed, the wine's sweetness making her stomach churn. "Why?"

"Your mother went out there to slay an evercry, but from what we've been able to gather, this is an evercry that has come before. One that your family has slain. An old and ancient enemy."

"That's not how evercrys come into being," Larissa protested, the metal of the chalice biting into her palm. "We kill one and it dies along with the person it possessed. The host's death causes it to vanish."

"An evercry can return," Atticus said, the words dripping with disdain. "Cutting the head of a weed does not always remove the roots."

"The one your mother hunts has tied itself to your bloodline," Navus said. "It's why your mother has been gone so long. Because it saw her coming and has run from her long enough to gain power, to fight her and perhaps this time...win."

Larissa thought she might be sick on the carpet.

"And now you know that for some sisters such a thing exists," Theras said. "An evercry that won't die."

It was against the code to which they all adhered.

It was against the oath.

It was a lie.

*Slay the Evercry...until there are none.*

The three stared at her, waiting for her comprehension. Larissa understood now the binding placed on her tongue. Only one question formed on her lips.

"*How?*"

The grand matriarch looked to Theras, who folded her hands in her lap.

"The forces of chaos will be present as long as life exists," Theras said. "What is chaos to the prey is natural to the predator. Our battle with the Evercry has never been a war but a matter of balance. At the dawn of time, the Fair Lady and the Evercry were so removed from one another that the world was kept in equilibrium, like a seesaw. Then, legend says the Evercry fell in love with the Fair Lady and moved toward her."

"They weren't always enemies," Larissa said.

"Indeed, they were not. But as the Fair Lady came forward to help balance the world, the Evercry took it as invitation to draw closer, until they faced one another. The Fair Lady knew the Evercry would never be sated, would never retreat, and so bound it within the heart of the Descent, even though it consumed her to do so."

Larissa's eyes drifted to the expansive view behind Navus's shoulders. Her hands tightened on the arms of her chair. "A story we tell children so they understand. But what has this to do with my mother?"

"We are uncertain—"

"There's no point coddling the girl," Atticus interrupted.

"And there's no point scaring her any more than we have to," Theras replied. "The fact of the matter is that none of our histories speak of this. There may be no need to fear this evercry is the one fought by Dothreal."

Larissa recognized her great-grandmother's name, remembered the tale of her ancestor, even as she scrambled to make sense of the new information.

"They're all echoes," she said. "Evercrys are slivers, ghosts, remnants that possess people who open themselves to magic. Chaos infused in a person. They're not thinking, knowledgeable entities with a past beyond those the humans possess. How could it be the same one my great-grandmother defeated?"

Navus stood up, walking to her shelves and retrieving a great tome. "There's more to the role Dothreal played when defeating her evercry than recorded. Your great-grandmother defeated a being of immense power, but it became clear it had not vanished from existence as should happen." She thumped the book on her desk and put on spectacles as she thumbed through the pages. When she found what she was looking for, she swiveled the book around for Larissa.

A stern woman painted in black ink glared from the page, and Larissa recognized the heavy brow and long nose of her mother, but the figure was different in subtle ways, somehow harder. Written beside it was Dothreal's story, but Navus summarized it before Larissa could study its contents.

"Over a hundred years ago, a being calling itself the Evervast rose. Dothreal heard its song, but more than that, she knew it had been here before, though we know not how." Her fingers brushed the page. "The darkkin's account resides in our sister city, Scythia, but it's near useless. Dothreal made her sister darkkin stay behind. She faced the Evervast alone, and it consumed a part of her. She lost an arm and leg, and part of her mind."

Navus sighed and turned the page. On the other side was a depiction of an orb hanging on a chain. About the orb were several rings of metal, as though they formed a round cage.

"One of the reasons Dothreal didn't recover was because when she slew the Evervast, its song did not die. An echo of the song remained in her head, a cry she could never silence." Navus's withered hands caressed the paper, eyes unfocused and lips bent in lines of sorrow. "In her final days, she was...not sane."

The grand matriarch lapsed into silence, and Theras picked up the story. "Dothreal thought if she sealed away the song, the chaos in her mind would end. Through a magic ritual, the echo was trapped inside this artifact and locked in our vaults. When the evercry called to your mother, none of us thought it could be this same creature, but Maladel's message alludes to a need for the echo. But we fear that if the echo is reunited with the Evervast, it will become stronger than the song that originally called to your mother."

"The song is of the Fair Lady," Larissa said. "Why would the echo strengthen the Evervast?"

"A being such as this is clever," Atticus said. "A creature like the Evervast can absorb the echo, part of its former self. If it does, it may become too strong for Maladel to defeat." It was a confession grudgingly made, given the snarl on her lips.

"But you still want me to take it to her," Larissa guessed.

"We *want* the orb and you to stay here, in the mountains," Atticus said. "Safe with all the other novices from such dark and woeful intent. But it may be Maladel can't defeat her evercry without making it whole. Without making it the Evervast once more."

Much as she was afraid, Larissa burned to go. But she knew a respectful attitude was necessary to assure them she understood the danger.

"I've practiced with many artifacts in my time as a darkkin," she said, "and if there's one thing I can do, it's resist them. I can take on this burden, but...why me?"

"Dothreal knew it would come again for her bloodline," Navus said, "and so it is tied to her descendants. Only a relative can carry the orb from the Hall of Songs without risk to the bindings. You have a second cousin, but she is far away, and a child."

The Hall of Songs was the most sacred of vaults, deep within the mountain, where sat an eternal spring made of the Fair Lady's tears. The water of which knighted those who passed the Empirical.

The grand matriarch seemed to age before her, shoulders hunched, proud visage bowed. Her unfocused gaze still lay on Dorthreal's picture. Atticus's frown had deepened to its usual scowl.

Theras cleared her throat. "I have absolute faith in Larissa's ability to carry this orb. And I do not doubt she would do more than many to keep it safe."

"The time will come when she may just need to," Atticus said, gaze shifting to focus on Larissa in a challenge. "And you cannot go alone."

"The party should be small," Theras said. "To avoid detection by any of the Evercry's agents."

"I must give the orb to her first." Navus closed the book. "Atticus, ready horses and supplies, and find this girl some decent armor. Choose one guard you trust to journey with her—one, and only one. They must travel unobserved if we are to stop the Evervast from knowing the orb has left Lathore. Theras, get her things. You know what to pack. Make sure she has what she needs. And you..." Navus turned to Larissa. "Come with me."

Atticus strode to the door, only a sidelong glance denoting her displeasure. Theras squeezed Larissa's shoulder before she vanished after Atticus, calling out to the other matriarch as she left. Whatever else she said was lost as the heavy door swung shut, and they left Larissa alone with the grand matriarch.

An awkward silence filled the space as she studied Larissa, who did her best not to squirm under the cool gaze. Appearing to come to some unspoken conclusion, Navus walked to a nearby cupboard and retrieved a silk scarf.

"Put this over your eyes," she instructed.

Larissa took the scarf. She didn't think the grand matriarch would hurt her, but she hesitated as she touched the cloth. It was embroidered with runes and tingled her hand with magic. Another test.

"It is sometimes necessary to take someone down to the Hall of Songs," Navus said, her tone softening. "But none may see the path, lest the worst happen."

"How much worse could the situation be?"

"Darkness envelops the world when the last bastion of the Lady is breached." It sounded like a promise rather than an observation. She waited for Larissa.

Larissa tied the blindfold over her eyes.

Then the older woman's hand was in Larissa's, her touch cool. "*Archenhiem.*"

The blindfold tightened, and Larissa flinched. With the cloth tied over her ears, sounds were distant, as though underwater. No light penetrated the material. The only sign she'd not sunk into the darkness of a cave was the itching brush of silk on her face. Magic crawled through the blindfold, but she refused to touch it.

Navus said nothing, but guided Larissa forward. Larissa stumbled along, tentative at first, uncertain in her footing, not wishing to lean on the older woman. A breeze rustled past her exposed skin, indicating she was outside, but she didn't ask, didn't even reach out her other hand, just took one step after another. For such thin hands, the grand matriarch held her firmly, leading her through a maze of corridors, up and down stairs, until Larissa was hopelessly lost.

Navus stopped. Larissa stood for several moments, absorbed in the silence around her. After a moment, Navus's muted voice called through the blindfold.

"I cannot reach. Take it off yourself."

Larissa undid the binding and found that she stood in a white stone corridor. Before her was a bridge, the pathway enrapturing as she caught sight of what lay underneath. Within the dark water glimmered the lights of a thousand stars. For a moment she feared it was true night she stared at, that she'd fallen through the earth into the endlessness beyond, but as she drew closer and studied the surface, her own face reflected back.

Matriarch Nelasar's voice echoed within.

*"The path you walk lays in the dark between stars, but it doesn't mean you aren't of the light."*

"What are they?" she asked.

Navus's smile was weak, her affectionate gaze fixed on the pool's depths. "They are the grand matriarchs who have come before."

"What are they doing here?" Larissa knelt to better examine the murky depths.

"Doing what all mothers do. Watching over their daughters. Come now."

Navus walked down the path, and Larissa rose to follow.

Torches lit the walls as they passed, startling Larissa before she spotted the magic glyphs Navus stepped on as she walked. When the bridge ended, more lights flared up on either side of the corridor, revealing a greater pool of dark water. Unlike the still waters before, it burbled, a hint of its distant source, the torchlights illuminating a single stone that jutted out from the center. The stone's gray surface rippled with the water's stain, the stone itself the shape of a tear, as though weeping into the water.

The old woman paused by the pool's edge. "Few who are not grand matriarchs ever bear witness to this."

Larissa knew well where she stood.

If the Descent was the resting place of that once powerful god the Evercry, then here was where its opponent had died to defeat it. The Fair Lady's grave. The Pool of Tears.

Larissa fell to her knees.

The Fair Lady's sacrifice was at the core of their faith—her grace resided within them, and here was the mark of her passing, the last place she was known to have walked. To have fallen. Her tears eternally flowing for being unable to stop the Evercry.

As though the story alone were too much, so too did Larissa weep, tears for every woe spilling down her cheeks from a fount deep within her soul.

Regret for not passing the test of knighthood.

For her decision to become a darkkin, and the secret self inside that loved it.

For turning her back on her mother's teaching, unable to fulfill her mother's, *everyone's* expectations.

But she was ever in the Lady's grace, ever vigilant of the lure, ever humbled and sure of her abstinence from seeking power. She would not succumb now.

A grip she hadn't realized was there let her go. She swayed with a groan, having forgotten where she was. Larissa blinked away crusted tears, revealing Navus standing nearby. Her aching knees told her how long she'd stared at the dark pool, captivated by the Lady's mourning, building her own determination to overcome the Evercry.

Larissa wiped the tears from her eyes. "That...was a test."

"Yes," Navus said. "You passed. Otherwise I could not have given you this."

She held aloft a gold chain.

From the chain hung an orb as big as Larissa's circled thumb and first finger. Intricate symbols were carved across its surface. Around its middle sat three rings of differing sizes. Larissa rose to take it.

As soon as she touched it, a susurrus of whispers in tongues she didn't understand surrounded her head. She scanned the room. No one but the silent matriarch and herself were present, but she couldn't mistake the deep incantation of a woman's voice that culminated in a single noise.

The lonely howl of a wolf.

Larissa jerked her hand back, gaze darting to the grand matriarch. The old woman didn't move, holding the orb's chain loose in her grip, free for Larissa to tug away at any moment.

"You heard the echo?" Navus asked.

"Yes, a howl," Larissa said. "There was something else too, like...someone trying to tell me something important, but I don't know the language."

"Your great-grandmother was from Corserinth. The spells of this orb may have been done in her tongue. It was...*is* a dead language now."

She still waited, and after a moment Larissa tugged the chain from her grasp, opening her palm to study the orb. Its gold surface was wrought with the tiniest of carvings, delicate and beautiful.

"She crafted this?"

"Dothreal was a knight. Became matriarch of swords, like your mother." Navus swallowed, and her gaze darted back to the pool before returning to Larissa. "She was also...a darkkin."

"You mean she passed the Empirical and was a knight," Larissa said, "and then later joined the darkkins?"

"No." Navus drew the word out, as though she didn't wish to answer. "At one time, a knight could actively belong to both."

"But...the knights and the darkkins are different castes."

A smile spread over Navus's lips, her first genuine smile that Larissa had seen. The corners of Larissa's mouth tugged in response.

"Haven't you already learned today that not everything you were taught to believe is true?"

Larissa's mouth went dry. What was the grand matriarch saying, exactly?

Whatever the moment, it passed, and Navus's hand hovered for a moment over Larissa's open palm. But she drew back, clenching it in a fist.

"You must get that to your mother," she said, the coldness Larissa was all too familiar with returning. "It may be the only hope she has of slaying the evercry that destroyed your great-grandmother."

# Chapter 9

Larissa tugged at her wool cloak. It'd be easy to think she was removing the scratchy edge from her throat, but her irritation centered on her assigned company.

Valare. Atticus's chosen knight to escort her.

Knight-solaris, now, the title given to those who'd weathered direct conflict with an evercry and proved themselves in battle. Larissa grudgingly admitted the rank suited Valare. The last year had hardened the knight. Darkness tinged her eyes, and her movements wasted no time or purpose.

Everything else about her manner was all courtesy. Larissa didn't know if it was Valare's duty-bound nature or the presence of Matriarch Theras of the Darkkins that stayed any cruel taunts from her tongue, but whatever the reason, nothing of the kind seemed forthcoming.

"May I check your horse?"

It was the first thing Valare said to her after last year's insult and attack. Valare had saddled her own horse well before Larissa, with a deftness that spoke of much travel.

"Of course." Larissa stepped to the side, hiding a flinch when Valare approached.

She remembered how to ride, even if her last class in it was a year gone. But her familiarity was nothing like Valare's. She checked over Larissa's horse, tightened the girdle, and reaffixed the bit in the horse's mouth.

"Good job, Darkkin," Valare said as she finished. "But make the girdle tighter in future—it will loosen as we go. Be sure to put the bit full behind the horse's teeth, or she will take no directions from you."

"Yes, Knight-Solaris." Larissa fell on formality with all the saving grace of the Fair Lady. She had no idea how Valare became the best choice to accompany her south to the city of Espenel, but here they were.

A sword smaller than Valare favored—though not by much—was strapped across the knight's back. Twin daggers graced her hips. Her armor wasn't the rich cream of her family's lineage, but dark brown, hard worn and well-polished. The saddlebags, blades, armor—all of them well cared for but worn. They weren't the fanfare of a proud and arrogant warrior. They were the basic items needed to survive. As though she had less to prove now she'd become a knight-solaris.

Larissa wouldn't question Valare's lack of menace, but she wondered what had happened in the time they'd been apart. Valare's capacity to treat Larissa with all the respect due a darkkin was a relief. It appeared duty came before personal vendettas. But traveling a week with someone so frosty doused any potential excitement at the prospect of her first trip outside Lathore.

Dawn's dim glow filtered light through the mist of the mountains. Mist the same color as Larissa's dappled gray horse.

One of the saddlebags held several changes of clothes, thinner for the hotter coastal climate. The other contained a blank notebook to record her journey, several lengths of pencil lead, rations of food, soap, a sewing kit, and a few herbs. One of which Larissa wasn't ashamed to admit was the gorsen woe.

Over the horse's hindquarters lay Larissa's swag, and above it her bow and a quiver of arrows. She lashed her spear to the top too, but carried a thin sword at her side and several daggers about her person.

One of her blades was from Farrast. Rather than the standard folded steel and dual edges, it had four blades, a cross-shaped dagger. Runes were carved on the blade's facets, one for each element, acting as opposite. If Larissa stabbed anything made of fire, the blade would turn to ice. Speaking an element's name would also activate its rune.

Larissa knew enough from her lessons with Theras to only use magic when absolutely necessary, but it was comforting to still have it available as a last resort.

Along with her weapons, she wore armor—black leather pants and jerkin, metal shoulder pads and chest plate overlayed by a studded surcoat, belted in place. Less cumbersome than what she'd worn during the Empirical, and unadorned of family flare. Instead, her surcoat bore the crimson circles of the darkkins.

Over it all she wore a long, warm cloak, thick wool that in brighter light became darkest crimson. Underneath was the orb, obscured from view on its chain about her neck.

"*Keep it hidden,*" Navus had said. "*Never let it out of your sight, never let it leave your skin. Or it may leave you for good.*"

Larissa needed no more warning than that.

"Mount up," Valare told her.

The height of a nearby stand allowed her to sling a leg over the horse, then slide her feet in the stirrups, the horse steady beneath her. Taking up the reins, she held them tight in one leather-clad hand. Valare clicked her tongue and dug in her heels. Larissa's horse took this as an invitation and followed the other beast out of the overhang of rock that housed the stables.

Theras and Atticus waited for them by the gates to Lathore. Theras came to Larissa's side. Valare walked her horse to where her mother stood on the stairs to the barracks, an imperious tilt to her head as she surveyed them. Theras squeezed Larissa's knee, then slipped a ring off her finger. She held it out. Silver wrapped around a moonstone as large as Larissa's thumbnail, threaded with rainbow hues.

"It's blessed by the Lady," Theras said.

Larissa shook her head. She'd never seen Theras without the ring. "I can't take it."

Theras took Larissa's unresisting hand from the pommel of her saddle, tugged off her glove, and slipped the ring on her middle finger.

"You may need it." She wedged it on tight. "If you go to a sister city, show the darkkins this ring. They'll know to assist you in whatever you ask. Ride safe and remember what we've taught you."

Larissa pulled her glove back on. "I will," she promised, voice hitching. "I won't fail."

Something crossed Theras's face, a narrowing of her eyes and downturn of her mouth. But the emotion passed, and her friendly smile returned. "You'll do well, I'm sure of it."

Larissa took a deep breath and smiled, heart lightening at the confidence in Theras's voice. The matriarch let go of her leg, and both waited for Valare to finish what Larissa didn't doubt was a similar conversation with Matriarch Atticus. There was a distance to the pair—formal stances and the flicker of a frown on Valare's brow that was quick to smooth into indifference. Atticus tilted her head and said something that was snatched away on the wind. Valare's shoulders tensed, but she nodded and turned her attention to the road.

"Walk on," Valare called to her horse. "Darkkin, with me."

Larissa bid farewell to Theras and nudged her horse forward. Atticus didn't stay, heading back inside the walls of Lathore, no parting words for Larissa as she passed. Larissa glanced back to wave at Theras before they rounded the hill out of sight.

Their horses ambled down the mountain path into the

mist. For the first hour, Larissa did nothing but study Valare from behind, waiting for snide remarks now they were alone, but none came. The horses' hooves clopped over the gray stone road, wide enough to take a wagon and not much else. To one side, the mountain dropped away, disappearing down into the valley's fog. There wasn't a breath of wind, everything ominous and still. Larissa didn't mind the darker days of winter, but today there was something she found grim in the morning's dim glow.

She tried to remember the way down the mountain to Abbidon, a port town she'd only visited once, as a child, and their current destination.

Her mother had brought them to Lathore when Larissa was a few summers old. Raised within the walls of the Fair Lady's city, she'd never even thought of leaving until her latter years of school, when the responsibility grew to be too much. The idea of escape became an ever-present lure in those dark days before her graduation. She wanted to just run away from it all and never look back.

Now that the moment to leave was at hand, apprehension wormed its way into her stomach. She didn't dare ask Valare for her experiences of the plains below, lest she be mocked or ruin what had thus far been a courteous, if aloof, interaction.

After the second hour, Larissa got sick of the silence and nudged her horse to a faster trot so she could walk beside Valare. She'd practiced what she would say for a good half hour, but the words still stuttered from her mouth.

"I ap-appreciate your h-help, Valare."

Valare didn't even deign to look at her. "It is my responsibility, Darkkin."

Whatever spite might still lay within Valare's breast was absent in her words. Nothing but apathy. Larissa held back on her childish annoyance.

"What can we expect of the journey?" It was a well-rehearsed question, not about the past, focusing on what lay ahead.

"A horse and boat ride in silence." Valare gazed down the

mountain. "I don't owe you conversation too, Darkkin."

The repetition of her title sounded like a mockery, though there was no insinuation in Valare's tone.

"You could at least tell me what you know of the mission."

"To escort you to Espenel, and if required, on to Meggaloth."

"And that's all?"

Valare sent her a sidelong glance, as though the answer was obvious. Larissa couldn't believe it.

"You can't forgive me, can you?"

Valare turned on her saddle to stare at Larissa, and it wasn't hatred that pinched her eyes but disappointment.

"What's done is done, Westwyn," she said. "I'm not here for my ability to converse, just to fulfill my duty and make sure you arrive safely."

"I can defend myself." Larissa's raised voice made her horse dance a little and bump into Valare's steed.

"My commander has informed me of the importance of this mission," Valare said with a curtailed huff. "That we may run into trouble. I will keep you safe, and I'll do so at the expense of my life."

"I'm not asking you to risk your life for me, Valare." Larissa forwent a scowl when Valare raised her brow at Larissa's pointless remark, silently observing that, in fact, Valare was doing just that. Flushed, Larissa tried instead to reason with her. "We will be on the road for more than a few days, and I for one would like to have our first civil conversation since we were children!"

It wasn't rage so much as exasperation, but Larissa still shouted the last words, and Valare flinched.

"And what does the darkkin command?" There was a mild return of Valare's sneer, but any enthusiasm was lacking.

"What were you told about our assignment?" Larissa repeated, hazy on the details of the plan beyond taking the orb to her mother. The rest Atticus had relayed to Valare.

"I'm to take you to the resident knight at Espenel's garrison," she said. "I'm to be prepared that agents of the Evercry may seek an item on your person, and must ensure it stays with you at all costs. That's all."

Larissa wanted to groan into her hands, but she gripped the reins and eased the tension in her tone. "And the journey will take a week," she said. "Surely we can talk about things other than how much you hate me for failing the Empirical."

Valare snorted and took a deep breath, and Larissa readied for the tirade she'd expected all morning.

Shadows moved in the mist down the road. With a withering glare at Larissa, Valare trotted forward so they walked in single file, a more defensible position.

They needn't have worried. Out of the darkness rolled wagons loaded with goods. Barrels of wine, buckets of vegetables, pitchers of oil, and a dozen travelers come to see the sisters of the Fair Lady.

The city of Lathore wasn't made solely of those who followed her but also those who were willing to work. They were not worshippers; the Lady didn't ask for prayers, offerings, or adoration of any kind. Her purpose was to balance life against the darkness of magic. People sought shelter at her city after being tainted by the Evercry.

Those in the wagons were defeated. They had nowhere else to go.

Valare and Larissa exchanged nods with the brightly robed sisters who drove the wagons, but received only dull-eyed stares from the other passengers. Some of them bore severe injuries, burn marks or bandaged limbs. Larissa couldn't help herself and met one woman's eyes. The shadows within made her regret looking. Not all injuries were physical.

When the last cart passed, Larissa trotted her horse beside Valare's again, glancing back at the wagons fading into the fog.

"Is it always like this?" she asked.

"What did you expect? The world isn't the soft place you've known behind Lathore's walls."

Larissa's forehead wrinkled. "I'm not blind to the dangers that the outside world inflicts."

"No, Larissa," Valare said, the uncharacteristic use of her first name made condescending by her tone. "But it's one thing to read about it in a book and a different thing to experience it."

"Have you?" Larissa challenged, but curiosity softened the edginess of her question.

They rode a few minutes more in silence. The fog had lifted, craggy mountains casting monstrous shadows, but they shifted to rounder hills the further they descended. Larissa didn't think Valare would answer, until suddenly she spoke as though there had been no lull in the conversation.

"I was part of an escort," Valare said, almost under her breath. "We were transporting what the darkkin believed to be a potential evercry."

"A prisoner?"

"Yes. A rogue prince who attempted a coup faced judgment. The king charged us with presiding over the hearing to ensure it was safe. The darkkin warned the knight-solaris in charge that she should execute the prince that night. The knight didn't listen. His death would have brought the province to war. They *needed* him to stand trial."

"She did the right thing, though," Larissa said. "It's sometimes hard to see the danger until it's too late."

"Leastways you appear to have found your calling," Valare groused. It was Larissa's turn to lift a mocking brow. Valare cleared her throat, gaze settling once more on the road. "There was a valley pass we had to take him through, isolated because we were wary of fanatics coming to retrieve him. We didn't know the danger was in the king's guards that came with us as escort. One night, an agent freed the prince, allowing him to cast a spell over the king's men, goading them into false loyalty with magic. The king's men killed three sister knights before we knew what was happening. The knight-solaris in charge ordered me to protect the darkkin trying to disrupt the prince's spell, before they fell on us like beasts. Not human anymore, all they did was attack, even when mortally wounded. There was something wrong with their eyes..."

Larissa wracked her brain. A poison, perhaps, or even some magics of air to confound thoughts. Her mind spilled through the tomes she'd read, searching for a magic that would cause such an effect en masse.

"Whispering Will," she said after a moment. "An incantation to convince someone of your truth. But to a large group disinclined to be suggestible? The Evercry was hiding the prince's magical strength."

Valare nodded, a tilt to her lips. "That's what the darkkin called it after we were done slaughtering the king's men. It was only because of her it didn't affect us too. The knight-solaris removed the prince's tongue, and took him to the palace. I executed him when the king gave his verdict. The knight-solaris couldn't do it because they'd injured her. A sword through her leg that left her crippled."

Larissa could hear Valare's regret. Valare would only accept perfection, and whatever transpired that night had been far from what she expected, that much Larissa understood.

Keen to keep the communication flowing, she struggled to find something to add of her own experiences.

"You'd not like the darkkin halls, even if at times it may have made you laugh." She stared ahead at the road but saw in her peripheral vision as Valare's head tilted toward her.

"How so?" Genuine curiosity curled the question, and Larissa suspected it had to do with Valare's newfound respect of the caste.

"We go through regular trials to test our resilience to influential magics." Her cheeks flushed at the memory. "It's different from any other training. More...embarrassing." Larissa ducked her head, knowing her heated cheeks would give her away to Valare's astute gaze.

A grin flickered at the corner of Valare's mouth. "Confess,

Darkkin."

"You drink from a cup of wine imbued with suggestibility," Larissa said. "I suspect you'd like Darkkin Farrast, who was rather humorous in her sadistic enjoyment of my initial lack of resistance."

Valare leaned forward in her saddle. "What did she make you do?"

"Jump in an ice-cold pool, squawk like a chicken, and stick my finger up my nose."

There was a long silence as Valare stared at her. Then she chuckled. Her chuckle turned to a guffaw, and then a loud laugh that echoed over the mountain.

"I would have paid good coin to see that."

"But you never will," Larissa replied. "I mastered it within a day."

The humor faded and, in its place, Larissa saw a grudging respect, before Valare turned away in silence once more.

# Chapter 10

The Diophon river was a silver ribbon between the Lathorean mountains and the town of Abbidon. From a distance, the buildings with their red tiled roofs and cream walls were picturesque, promising a new world compared to the drab gray stone of Lathore.

As she and Valare descended the final hill, Larissa heard distant echoes, startling a memory. Her mother loading her onto a wagon, despite the late hour, to head up to Lathore. Larissa burrowing into the blankets and falling asleep with the rocking of the cart. Where they'd been traveling from, she couldn't recall, but the city had been bright with its lights at night, sounds of laughter in the streets.

Now it was her horse that rocked her as they made a steep decline before the road flattened out. They came up beside the frothing waves of the Diophon, where an arched bridge allowed passage to the docks and the main town. The bridge sat on stone, the other half made of wood that would lift to allow riverboats to pass. Right now the bridge was up to allow several stout tugs to struggle upstream.

Valare dismounted while they waited, and Larissa followed suit, shaking her numb feet and stretching her legs. She could ride, but the monotonous downhill plodding for hours wasn't what she was used to, and she was glad they were taking the boat later. She was careful to wriggle her sore rump on the far side of the horse from Valare.

"Don't forget to stretch your back," Valare called to her. "Grab the saddle horn and rear and arch your back downwards with your hips out."

Surprised, Larissa did as Valare suggested, and her back made a satisfying click. "That feels better. Thank you."

Valare didn't answer, and Larissa didn't push.

The bridge lowered, and they led their horses across the Diophon. They passed docks where ships waited to trade goods. It was a hive of activity, sights and scents that heightened Larissa's desire to travel. Merchants carrying tubs of spices haggled with farmers for bales of wheat. A woman ran her hands over reams of cloth, the lean salesman by her side wearing a self-assured smile. On the fuller boats, captains smoked pipes and gossiped over the brightly painted prows of their ships. Lighter boats yet to be loaded bumped against their moorings, as though jockeying for wares to carry. Some would truck upriver and round the mountain range to the far northern provinces. Others made ready for the easier journey down to the sea, and the trading port of Espenel.

Imports were stacked in wooden crates on the docks. Winding up the central street were tent tops and shop fronts of the long marketplace. People hurried to and from the docks, taking newly arrived goods into the market or departing on their boats.

Larissa expected Valare to seek out the dockmaster, but they walked their horses into town.

The street was broad, well paved, allowing the river trade access through town and to the farmland beyond. The markets held this morning's detritus of a rich winter harvest: potatoes, carrots, and all manner of root vegetable. Balconies overhead held red terracotta pots of herbs or the withered husks of summer's flowers. It would have been nice to have their scent to overpower the smell. The city of Lathore had a sewer system above reproach, thanks to the hot springs that ran through their depths.

Larissa could not say the same of Abbidon. The warm winter sun did not give the same heat as a turn of summer, but there was rankness in the air that wrinkled her nose. Valare looked back and laughed.

"Come down from your ivory tower, princess?"

Larissa wasn't about to burn the feeble bridge she'd built by taking offense. "Tell me you didn't do the same on your first visit."

"I've been here many a time," Valare said. "Towns smell, but cities are worse. You'll have to get used to it, Darkkin."

Larissa grimaced for Valare's amusement.

A few glances were shot their way as they wended through the crowds, most with a small smile or respectful nod Larissa did her best to return. Valare did the same, even calling out to some by name, until she brought their horses to a halt outside an inn.

The sign outside noted it as the Fat Pheasant. The building was not unlike its name, a hexagon with a peaked roof that speared up from the main structure. But it was clean, and some of the town's stench wafted away on a slight breeze.

"Why aren't we catching a boat?" Larissa asked as they took the horses to the stables around one side.

"We will," Valare said. "But we leave the horses here to take the next wagonload up the mountain. The afternoon boats won't leave for another hour or more. You have time to walk around the city."

Valare took off her saddlebags, and Larissa followed suit. They weren't too heavy, but finding the right way to carry her bow and spear, with the bags, wasn't easy when she didn't have them strapped onto her back.

"Give that to me," Valare said, taking the spear from Larissa.

"Thank you." Larissa slung her saddlebags over one shoulder, and the bow and quiver she held in her free hand. She followed Valare inside after a stable boy led their horses away.

Inside, shutters opened in the lofty top to let in sunlight. Balconies surrounded a central apex, where a large iron chandelier hung above the tables and chairs. Plain wooden furniture filled the tavern, accommodating a range of men and women in various stages of drink or midday's repast. The scent of ale, stew, and human sweat permeated the air, and she did her best not to react as she had done in the street.

Across the room, a bar half the size of the rotund inn offered patrons drinks of all sorts, from thick casks of wine and ale to the colored bottles on the shelves behind it.

"Hail, sisters," a large man called from behind the bar. "You have fellow travelers in your dining room."

"My thanks, Bruno," Valare said, heading through the tables of patrons to a side door.

"We have our own rooms?" Larissa asked.

"Only here. So many of us travel that it's a good meeting place before either the climb to Lathore or reassignment. If we don't have to return to Lathore, we stay here. It's close enough to home for many."

Valare led her to a darkened doorway, and without knocking, entered. The room beyond held a fireplace at the far end and a long table, windows slanting warm sunlight across its wooden surface.

At the table sat Jyan with another sister.

"Larissa?" Jyan leapt to her feet. There were marks of fatigue under her eyes, but otherwise she looked well. She wore a loose white shirt and leathers, as did the other woman. Jyan came around the table to embrace Larissa, who awkwardly returned the gesture, hampered by her luggage.

"What are you doing here?" Larissa asked.

"Finishing a tour," Jyan said, gaze darting between Larissa and Valare. "And you?"

"Darkkin delivery service," Valare said before Larissa could reply. "Escorted by yours truly."

"I'm surprised you both made it down the mountain without wounds," Jyan jeered, not at Larissa but at Valare, who shrugged.

"The duty must be done."

They exchanged a long stare, after which Jyan nodded.

Larissa watched in bemusement as Valare offered her arm, and Jyan grasped her forearm and held it for a moment. Not an embrace, but the gesture of greeting was made more meaningful by their locked gaze. No barbs, nothing but a mutual respect. It left Larissa feeling like an outsider.

"Where are you traveling from?" Valare asked.

"Desmordid," Jyan said. "Knight-Solaris Keladros and I met with the local fiefs regarding increased agent activity on their eastern borders."

The knight-solaris in question rested with her feet up on a chair, perusing her book during their conversation. At her name, she put it aside and stood, with a neutral smile at the newcomers.

"Knight-Solaris Keladros, this is Knight-Solaris Atticus and...Darkkin Westwyn," Jyan said, though she stumbled over Larissa's title. Keladros took Valare's forearm in another handshake.

"Well met, sister knight," she said, voice deep for such a tall, lithe woman, several heads over Larissa's height. She wasn't a hulk like Valare, far more slender, but her bare forearms were corded with muscle. White-blonde hair and darkly tanned skin gave her a contrasting coloring emphasized by her pale gray eyes.

Valare returned the greeting, then stepped aside for Larissa.

The knight-solaris didn't offer her hand, and Larissa was momentarily hurt. It must have shown on her face, for the arm that had fallen away rose to take Larissa's outstretched one after only a moment of hesitation.

"My apologies, Darkkin. Many of you dislike being touched."

"Not this one," Larissa said, quick to ease the knight-solaris. The knight's lip twitched, and Larissa realized her unintended invitation. Her cheeks flamed.

"Something to eat?" Keladros asked, kindly skirting past the comment.

"Please, thank you." Larissa put her things down with Valare's on the bench to one end of the dining room. There was a washbasin, and she stood back to let Valare use it, but Valare went straight to the table and poured herself a cup of water.

Larissa washed the dirt from her face and neck and undid the cloak about her shoulders. She couldn't place the sudden flutter of apprehension in her stomach until the thought struck her of when they'd all last sat and supped together. The last time she'd seen Valare. When their anger came to blows. Larissa flushed, scooping cool water from the sink to rub over the back of her neck.

Taking a deep breath, she made a point of sitting next to Valare, who only gave her a fleeting sidelong glance.

"Try the mulberries," Jyan said. "The days here have been warm enough for the first crops."

Larissa took a few and popped them in her mouth, before squinting over their bitter sweetness. She coughed. Jyan grinned, then poured water into a cup and placed it in front of her.

"Perhaps not quite ready yet." Larissa sipped the water before selecting a slice of bread from a bowl and surveying the lunch platter. Hard cheeses, a bowl of pickles, and cured meat that lay in thick slices. "How's life as a knight?"

"Intense." Jyan blew hair out of her eyes. "Much less dashing than we were led to believe, and my rear has calloused from all the traveling. My callouses have callouses. No man is ever going to want my arse by the time I make knight-solaris."

Jyan's interest in men was a surprise to Larissa, but she filled her mouth with food rather than ask questions that felt prudish and naïve. Valare sighed as she helped herself to the meat, and even Keladros's lip twitched. This sort of talk was a habit of Jyan's, it seemed.

"You've yet to see much combat, little one." Keladros licked her finger to turn the vellum page of the book she'd resumed reading. "In any form, be it in or outside a bedroom."

Jyan shrugged and dragged a plate of vegetables over to Larissa. "What about the darkkins?" she asked.

Valare's hand tightened on her cup, but her expression didn't change.

Larissa tried to focus on a neutral answer. "Interesting enough. Lots of books, different things to study. Trials I think vastly different from yours. But...I like it. I'm good at it."

Larissa stared down at her plate, waiting for Valare's censure, but the knight picked up a hunk of cheese and bread, then rose from the bench.

"I'm going down to the docks," she said, strapping her sword on her back. "I'll find a boat that will give us passage and come back for you." She strode out the door without a backward glance.

Larissa cringed. The work she'd done all morning appeared undone.

"I should catch up," she said, getting to her feet.

"Can I go with her, Keladros?" Jyan asked.

The knight-solaris didn't avert her gaze from her book. "Be back within the half hour. I want to make Lathore tonight, as soon as I have word we're not assigned elsewhere."

Larissa left her things and hurried out of the inn, Jyan not far behind.

"How by the Lady's hand did *you* end up with Valare?" Jyan said as soon as they were outside. There was no sign of Valare in the throng, but Larissa strolled down toward the docks, keeping an eye out for her.

"It's a long story, and I can't talk about it." *Literally*, she thought, as she remembered the binding placed on her tongue. Of all the people in the world, she most wanted to share it with Jyan, but it was her secret to hold no matter how tempted she was to test the seal. Everything about her resented the binding, a hidden magic she could still feel if she concentrated.

Rather than take offense, Jyan nodded, keeping pace beside her. "You're a mysterious bunch, I'll give you that much."

"Is it that different in the halls of the knights?" Larissa asked, glad she could drop her position's integrity for a moment to speak to her friend. It was nice too that it seemed not to matter they hadn't laid eyes on one another in a year.

"We see and do things no other sister has to face," Jyan said. "Being protected in Lathore makes many...uncomprehending of what knights go through. They know, but they don't *understand*. In her first tour, Valare executed a prince, and in her second she killed a sister knight enchanted by an evercry."

Larissa stopped, dumbfounded. "She did *what*?"

Jyan yanked her arm. "Don't shout. She was asked as an acting knight-solaris to finish the rest of her knight-solaris's tour in Thracia. But she was without a darkkin, as her sister darkkin had returned with the injured knight-solaris. It should have been a simple patrol, but the rest of the company fell into a trap. Bandits attacked them, under the control of an evercry none of them saw coming. A young mage, a girl, who lured sympathetic hearts to her cause. Valare was forced to kill a fellow knight— you'd remember her, Marelle."

The news struck Larissa mute.

She remembered the sullen girl with lanky, mousy hair and washed-out blue eyes, who was ever at Valare's side. Always laughing at her jokes at Larissa's expense. She hadn't liked Marelle, but that the girl was dead shocked her.

"Why did Valare kill her?"

"The mage took control of Marelle, used her body to attack the knights. Valare had a choice. Kill her sister and the mage, or let her other sisters die. She has a far greater respect for your calling now than you can imagine."

Jyan's shoulders hunched, and Larissa fought for something helpful to say. "I take it that both events led to her early promotion."

"Yes," Jyan confirmed. "But do you doubt she has earned it?"

Larissa shook her head as they threaded through marketplace stragglers, the day's heat fading as the sun touched the tips of Lathore's mountains. This time of year, sundown was quick to douse the town in coldness, and people shut their doors to keep in what little warmth the past-midday sun gave. An afternoon apathy clung to the streets as shops flicked over closed signs and shut their doors. Hawkers with little left to sell took their goods home, and the streets widened around them to showcase old sandstone buildings, yellow and warm.

They reached the docks, and Larissa scanned for a striking woman giving orders. The dock's chaos was much less than the bustling flurry they'd passed before, as most people had retreated for the afternoon's repast in nearby pubs. Distant music and shouting filtered over the docks, but otherwise it was quiet.

In the last of the streaming sunshine, Larissa walked on the hush of the world, enjoying a warm winter's day. Only a handful of boats remained, the captains dozing on their decks, hats over their faces, the lull of the river's passage as soothing as a rocking cradle. The pair steered between stacks of boxes in search of Valare and the dockmaster, but they saw few people, and no sign of the knight-solaris.

Larissa paused, the hairs on the back of her neck prickling. The sensation began as nothing more than a tingling awareness, but with every moment of silence it rose higher to a panic. She whirled around, looking for the danger.

"Where is Valare?"

Jyan looked about, unperturbed until she saw Larissa's face.

She drew her sword. "What is it, Darkkin?"

"I'm not sure..."

They were alone on the docks.

No, not alone. Three men walked toward them from a nearby pub, one the worse for drink being carried by the other two. They passed the sisters. Jyan lowered her sword but didn't sheath it.

It was the only thing that saved Larissa's life.

A shadow flittered over Larissa's face, and she glanced up. Startled by piercing sunlight, she didn't see the falling rope until it slapped down her face and tightened about her neck, dragging her back. She grasped the rough hemp as she fell against a tower of crates, the rope strangling her. She gasped for breath. Hands tight on the noose, she couldn't grab her sword. Jyan struck at the box. The sharp blow cut into the wood enough to sever the rope, and Larissa collapsed to her knees, yanking the rope off. Breath returned raw and harsh. Jyan jerked her blade free of the boxes. The supposed drunks ripped off ragged cloth to reveal studded leather and sharp swords underneath, which they aimed at Larissa. Jyan stood between her and the men.

"Keep an eye for whomever threw the rope!" she barked at Larissa as the three lunged at once.

Jyan brought her sword up in an arc, but these were no simple cutthroats or thieves. One blocked Jyan's sword, and the other two swept around her to come for Larissa. She drew her sword and backed away, wishing she had her spear. Two against one was no fair fight, and they moved on her with practiced ease. The first held a thick shortsword and had a shock of red hair. The other was a fatter fellow with a toothy grin. As though violence were a game.

He backed off as Larissa found an opening between the crates, but the redhead kept her attention diverted with tentative swipes of his sword. She defended easily, but they weren't seeking to kill, they were driving her to the river. She flicked a glance over her shoulder, catching sight of a boat at the end, an anxious captain glancing their way, preparing to make sail.

Beyond the docks was flat grassland that offered no hope if she ran, and when she turned, a woman stood between her and escape, swinging a rope. A scar bisected her face, giving her a lopsided smirk.

"Come on now, sister," she said. "Be good and get aboard."

Three, potentially four, against one, and no sign of Jyan.

She was trapped.

Her mind scrambled for spells but discarded every one as too dangerous. These weren't evercrys; they were ordinary people. She couldn't use magic against them.

A shadow slanted over the docks, a figure atop the crates behind her three assailants, vaulting through the air before they could turn.

Valare leapt on the back of the redheaded brigand, driving her sword down through the base of his neck. It cut through his armor, blood spilling from his mouth across the wooden beams, head almost severed from his body. The silent strike rendered the other two still, but only long enough for Valare to wrench her bloodied sword from the redhead's back. She charged the other man, his grin vanishing as their swords clashed together.

Larissa turned to her now single opponent, the woman, who held nothing but the rope. The woman flung the rope toward her head. A panicked Larissa batted it aside.

Hands wrapped around her from behind.

The burly man from the boat grappled her, trapping her arms by her sides. Dragged backward, she kicked for all she was worth, but to little effect. She tried to swing her sword, but to do so with the constraint risked cutting herself.

Larissa dropped the useless weapon, hand going to her waist and the spelled dagger.

The woman advanced on her, picking up the dropped sword. Larissa tugged the blade from her belt, but the man's brutish arms didn't leave her much room to make use of it. She turned it in, aiming for his inner arms.

"Watch out for her pigsticker!" the woman warned.

Larissa struggled, fought against the shrinking distance to the boat that would whisk her away. Over the woman's shoulder, though, a shadow slinked, silent as a cat. Jyan crept around the boxes directly behind the woman.

Larissa resumed her thrashing, tossing her hair in the man's face. Despite his barrel chest and arms, her weight and kicking caused him to grunt, struggling to hold her. He swore, and his grip loosened as her naked blade scraped over his arm. The woman lunged for Larissa's dagger.

Jyan's swift footsteps closed the distance, and she swung a thick wooden pole to crash into the woman's temple. The brigand collapsed onto the dock, dropping Larissa's sword.

Jyan hefted the pole, eyes on the man with his arms still about Larissa. "Let her go if you know what's good for you."

Valare advanced on him, leaving two corpses behind her. The two knights strode toward the boatman, dark scowls on their faccs  not anger, but a fierce protectiveness. They separated, forcing the boatman to split his gaze as he struggled just to keep Larissa in his grip.

Valare lifted her sword, her words pitched low, sending a shiver over Larissa's spine. "Let my sister go."

He glanced about at his fallen comrades. With a curse, he dropped Larissa to her feet and shoved her toward Valare. Valare snatched up her arm, helped her stand until the knight-solaris was between Larissa and the boatman.

His gaze flickered between them before he leapt aboard the boat, unlashed the last mooring line, and with a hard kick on the dock, propelled his vessel into the river's current.

Valare's stance didn't ease until he was past the docks. Then she turned to Larissa. "Are you hurt?"

Larissa shook her head.

"Who was that?" Valare said, voice heated with anger.

"I don't know."

Jyan came to her side, Larissa's sword in her hand. Larissa

winced as she took it, cursing herself for not being of more use. Had neither of her sisters been there, they would have taken her.

"And we can't ask them." Jyan gave a light kick to the prone woman on the dock, her blood dripping between the slats to plop into the river below. "They're all dead."

# Chapter 11

Hours later, Larissa's hands still held a tremor.

She was back at the inn, in the dining room reserved for the Fair Lady's travelers. She sat in front of the fire, blanket about her shoulders, a cup of cider in her hand. When night fell, the chill of winter returned, but Larissa didn't feel it. She was numb with fear.

Her fingers returned to the bruise on her throat, the raw mark left by the rope a grim reminder of the afternoon's events.

Valare sat by her side, a steadfast companion, offering unfamiliar platitudes, but Larissa felt more the burden with every one. The pair waited for Keladros and Jyan to return. They'd gone to send a report of the attack to the grand matriarch via the local aviary and were waiting there for a reply, the bird's flight up the mountain to Lathore and then back to Abbidon only a matter of hours.

"They wanted you alive," Valare said.

"Yes."

Earlier, alone in the water closet, Larissa had dragged the

chain out to check the orb still hung from her neck. It swung in the low lamplight, its magic smothered within the confinement of Dothreal's spell, and well hidden.

However, it appeared *she* was not.

They didn't even know who they were running from.

No, that was a lie. Their enemy, the one responsible for this attack, was whomever her mother was fighting. The Evervast. Larissa's palm went to her chest again, atop where the orb lay. This was more than a simple beast of darkness, she'd known that, but she'd been stupid not to be afraid or to believe this task would be simple. She'd just wrongfully assumed she would have time to reach her mother before her departure from Lathore was discovered.

But the Evervast already knew she'd left with the orb.

"They were waiting for you," Valare said. "They knew we were coming."

"Yes."

"What wasn't I told?"

"I thought you knew agents of the Evercry might try to steal it."

Valare grasped Larissa's shoulder, drawing her out of her paralytic contemplation.

"We aren't novices anymore." She twisted in her chair to better face Larissa. "They weren't just after whatever you carry—they wanted to take you with them. I don't think you comprehend the seriousness of the matter. We may have to return to the safety of Lathore."

"No," Larissa snapped, breaking from her reverie. "My mother's life is at stake."

The words tumbled out before she could stop them. Valare leaned forward to stare at her. "What do you mean?"

Larissa gritted her teeth, trying to work out what she could tell Valare. After today, it made no sense to keep any more secrets than the binding restricted on her.

"The darkkin my mother traveled with is dead." Larissa

watched Valare's fists clench. "She needs me to take her the orb so she can defeat—"

A hand settled about her throat, choking the words off. She reached to her neck, but there was nothing there except her own skin and the tightening of intangible fingers. Larissa panted through the torturous squeeze, dropping her cider cup as she reached for the strangling hold that wasn't there.

"Larissa, what is it?"

Valare's eyes widened as Larissa's face filled with blood, her pulse beating dully in her ears. The hands about her throat constricted until spots danced in her vision. On the tip of Larissa's tongue was the Evervast's name, the secret that evercrys could return. But Navus's spell would kill her if she tried to speak further. She didn't have the strength to challenge it. The binding's threat of death forced her to banish the confession to the farthest recesses of her mind. With every passing second, she thought less on the Evervast, and the constriction on her throat eased.

Panting, she slumped over the arm of her chair.

"What just happened?" Valare asked. Her hands hovered uncertain in the air as Larissa straightened. She retrieved Larissa's cup from the floor, placed a rag over the spilled drink, and poured her another.

"A binding," Larissa said, clearing her abused throat. She took the cup and sipped, swallowing past the rawness in her throat, the pain from the rope now doubled. "I can't speak of why I must get to my mother."

"Lady's grace... *Who* did this to you?"

Larissa stared into her cup and took another gulp before answering. "The grand matriarch."

Valare was silent for a time, brow furrowed in contemplation.

"If this was so very dangerous, why did they send me with you?" she said. "Shouldn't they have wanted a greater force? This isn't a matter for a single knight and darkkin."

Larissa shrugged, not about to relay what Valare's mother

thought. "We were to travel alone and without detection, so as not to draw attention. Atticus thought you the best choice."

"She's not so biased as to have picked me for preference," Valare said, catching Larissa's insinuation. She shook her head. "Commander Harker was returning from rest the night before we left. Lieutenants Lispeth and Dotson were free."

"Maybe they had other duties."

"It wouldn't have mattered." Valare waved away Larissa's guess. "There were dozens of far more experienced women who could have taken you."

"Maybe to draw less attention," Larissa said. "Two younger sisters, rather than a larger, more noticeable group."

"Is what you carry so dangerous?"

Though she fought to give Valare some measure of the truth, Larissa couldn't answer fully. She didn't want to feel that icy grip about her neck again, not after today.

"It's...critical to my mother's quest that I take this to her." She tapped the edge of the gold chain.

"May I see it?" Valare asked. "I want to be able to recognize it."

Larissa put her cup aside and tugged the chain out from under her clothes. The orb was harder to wrestle past the high ridge of her chest plate, but she wriggled it free. It glimmered in the low firelight, rings swinging as she held it aloft on its chain. Valare studied it without touching.

"It's spelled," she said.

"How can you tell?" Larissa asked, not with censure but genuine curiosity.

"You mean aside from the fact the grand matriarch gave it to you," Valare drawled, "placed a binding on you so you couldn't talk about it, and someone within spitting distance of the greatest of the Lady's strongholds just tried to kidnap you with it?"

Larissa raised her eyebrows and jiggled the necklace in her hand. Valare's gaze returned to the swinging orb.

"Something about it makes my skin itch."

That it irked Valare demonstrated she had at least some affinity to magic.

But Larissa wasn't given a chance to press. The door opened and Keladros came in. She glared when she saw what they were doing.

"Put that away *now*." She crossed to the window and closed the curtains. Jyan came in behind her, brow pinched and lips tight as she closed the door.

"What did you find out?" Valare rose from her chair. Larissa shoved the orb back beneath her clothes.

"The city guards have confiscated the bodies and will burn them."

Jyan's nose wrinkled in disgust. "One of them had... markings."

"Tattoos?" Valare asked. "A lot of agents ink their skin with their master's seal."

"No," Jyan said. "He had something beneath—"

"It doesn't matter," Keladros said, cutting her off. "He's dead, and the city guards are burning the bodies as we speak. The best way to be sure the evercry they served doesn't know what transpired."

"Are we safe?" Larissa asked.

"We aren't staying the night—we'll slip out when all are asleep." Keladros crossed to her bags and searched through them. "Jyan, get a week's worth of food, supplies, anything we've run out of or might need."

Jyan ducked out the door without a word, but her gaze darted to Larissa before she left.

"What do you mean 'we'?" Larissa said, standing by Valare.

Keladros looked between the pair. "The grand matriarch does not think it safe you travel with just one knight, but you cannot return. Get some sleep. We'll be riding in a few hours' time, and not stopping but to rest the horses."

"What about the river?" Valare said. Keladros shook her

head.

"The town's guard have given their report. They say the brigands came from downriver, were in town almost a week. If the boatman you saw has returned to their patron, then they'll be waiting for us. We need to make them think we've returned to Lathore. Matriarch Atticus will send down an escort, under the guise of taking us back home. We, however, will be long gone."

"More of us will draw attention," Valare said. "I can take her down through the farmland to Espenel on the eastern side of the river before we cross back over and head southwest."

"You aren't going there either. They'll be watching all the roads to Espenel. We take other untrod paths, and the darkkin cannot walk them without me. Don't argue with me, Knight-Solaris. I have my orders, and I'm giving you yours."

Valare's hands tightened by her side, the movement brushing Larissa's surcoat. "If we follow the forest road, we'll just end up back at the river—"

"Not necessarily." Keladros emptied the contents of her bag onto the table to check and repack them. "And anything is better than walking into their hands."

"But *whose* hands, Knight-Solaris?" Valare asked. "Agents are just mercenaries for hire. All we need is a show of force to ensure they back off, or to slip away before they can find us. They aren't infallible or magical in their own right."

"Don't be naïve, Atticus. One bore the taint of an evercry, and its agents were waiting for her, tried to take her. They knew of the darkkin's travel plans before she did, and they ambushed her on our home soil."

"They weren't just there for the object, were they?" Larissa said. "They tried to take me." Agents of the Evercry wanted the orb, and Larissa knew why, but that they wanted her too appeared to concern Keladros as much as it frightened Larissa.

"Yes, and we'll hope you never find out why," Keladros said. "Check your things. Only take what's necessary for hard riding."

Valare spun on her heel and went to her bags. After a moment,

Larissa followed suit. There wasn't much in her saddlebags, but she checked them over and got rid of what she could.

Jyan came back a while later, her satchel filled with rations and a few sundry items. She handed much of it to Keladros, then gave Larissa a bag of jerky, a handful of small hard winter apples, and a loaf of bread. No one spoke—there was only the sound of leather on leather as they packed, before weapons were cleaned, sharpened, and sheathed.

A knock came at the door.

Valare took her sword in hand, Jyan's going to the hilt of her own, and Larissa backed into a corner of the room. Keladros eased them with a gesture of her hand. She approached the door and slowly opened it. "What is it?"

There was a stuttering answer. "A complimentary supper."

"Mistress Hughs." Keladros drawled the title, her voice easy. "Who could fathom such a feast? Thank you for making it for us." Keladros parted the door wide enough for Mistress Hughs to come in. A white apron was snug about her waist, streaked with grease. She carried a tray heavy with food. The cook hesitated at their drawn swords for a moment, before slipping inside.

Scents wafted toward Larissa, the meal far more impressive than the fare at lunch. Lumps of freshly baked sourdough spread with butter, crockery brimming with creamy broth, and slices of roast beef still pink and steaming from the oven.

Valare and Jyan put away their weapons. The patter of Larissa's heart slowed down several skips, but she did not retreat from her corner.

"Thank you." Jyan took the tray and placed it on the table. "I'll bring it out to you when we're done."

"Just leave the tray outside the door, I'll take care of it," Mistress Hughs assured. "We don't want nothin' happening to our ladies. To think someone had a go at you on our docks... The town's guard has set out extra patrols. My boys are putting the shutters on outside your windows—you can lock them from the inside. My Bruno will stay up with our sons 'til the dawn. Ain't no one to say you came to any harm under the Fat Pheasant's roof!"

Fury turned the cook's cheeks scarlet the more she spoke. She wrung her hands on the apron of her dress, tinges of sweat gathered at her brow.

Keladros shut the door and leaned down to the shorter woman's stature, one hand on her shoulder.

"Our sisters are coming to act as an escort and take us away from here," she whispered. "If you could leave the room alone until they arrive, it would be most kind. I will open the door to them, but otherwise we will lock ourselves inside. Don't make your family stay awake for us, we'll be fine."

"Aye." Mistress Hughs nodded. "A good plan. I'll let my boys know they can get their rest, but to be up sharp when the other sisters arrive."

"Thank you so much."

Keladros ushered her out. They waited several moments, until the creaking floorboards beyond indicated the cook's departure.

"Won't they figure out we lied to them?" Larissa asked.

"Not if you keep your damn voice down," Keladros said with a scowl. "When our sisters arrive in the hours before dawn, they will act as though we're here. Anyone awake will be too tired to count the amount of people who enter, versus the amount who leave. Not if they're all wearing cloaks, and they will be—it's part of the ruse to fool anyone watching. Matriarch Atticus herself will be here, creating enough fuss all attention is drawn to her. We will be long gone by then." She sat at the table and dug into their supper. "Eat, it's the last hot meal we'll get for days."

Larissa did so, swallowing the hot soup with chunks of bread. It hurt her bruised throat going down but warmed the place inside that hadn't thawed since the attack.

"Where are we going?" she asked once the others had slowed down on their meal.

"Not here, Westwyn," Keladros said. "We'll discuss it later."

Completely chastised and feeling the fool, Larissa finished her meal in silence and then returned to her chair, notebook in hand. She wrote the day's journey per the custom of a darkkin, detailed but succinct, in neat hand.

At the table, Keladros picked up her book and used a vacant chair for her feet. Curiosity drove Larissa to tilt her head until she could read the cover. It wasn't unlike the one she held now. A darkkin's account. The name inscribed in ink on the front had faded. From the thin pages, Larissa knew it had to be a printed copy, and she felt keenly how far she would need to go to achieve the status for a reprinted book.

Larissa's fingers ghosted to her throat, to the sore flesh. She would have given a lot to talk to someone about the attack, even Valare, but she and Jyan played Longsword with cards, and Larissa didn't want to interrupt the tactical game. There was nothing to discuss anyways, she told herself; they already knew it was the work of an evercry, and Larissa couldn't share anything more.

Instead, she took care with her notes in the dim firelight, the precise lead marks sapping what energy she had left. Yawning loudly enough to crack her jaw, she didn't need to hear Keladros's admonishment to get some rest. She went to her swag rolled in a corner near the fire and laid down to sleep.

But it would not come. Despite her fatigue, the day's events kept replaying in her mind. The orb under her jerkin was so invisible to her senses that she frequently ran her hand to the chain to be sure it was there. And when her fingers left the chain, they drifted to her bruise.

Valare had been right all this time. She was weak.

But she'd sensed the danger today before it happened. She'd only ever had to pit her battle prowess against the other sisters, Valare the hardest. But something had warned her then that danger was afoot. She could only hope whatever instinct guided her did so again.

The fire crackled, and Larissa must have drifted off because the next thing she knew Valare was shaking her shoulder.

"Come, Darkkin," she said. "Time to go."

Larissa rose, still dressed. She hadn't even removed her boots, and her body ached from the hard surface of the floor. She did her best to ignore it, rolling up the swag and tying it to her saddlebags. She slung her bow across her shoulder with the quiver, her saddlebags over the other. Her spear became a walking stick. Keladros and the others shouldered their belongings as well, but rather than leave the swords in their scabbards, they drew them.

Jyan waited for Keladros to give the signal, then slowly unbolted the door.

In the room beyond were a few snoring men, but one, Bruno the barman, stood before the hearth warming his hands. His back to them, he was oblivious to their venture. Keladros crept soundlessly over the old wooden floorboards before she motioned the others onward.

Larissa was the last to leave. The door for the most part silent, it was the slow turning of metal on the lock that gave them away. The giant fireplace was far across the room, but the barman still turned at the sound.

She winced, Keladros glaring, but Bruno didn't appear startled. He scanned them, held Keladros's gaze, and nodded, then he faced the fire once more.

As though he hadn't seen them at all.

Larissa breathed a sigh of relief and followed the others out. Rather than the front door, Keladros led them through the kitchens and out back to the stables, where four horses stood saddled, bridled, and waiting.

No one else was about. Someone had readied them before the sisters arrived.

Larissa wondered on the discreet Bruno, who'd perhaps nodded not to Keladros but indicated the side door to the stables; he'd been waiting for them.

"Westwyn, take the mare." Keladros gestured to a yellow-coated horse with darkened mane and ears. Larissa attached her saddlebags, bow, and spear. With no need for direction, Valare, the bulkiest of the three knights, went to a brutish brown stallion. She ran a hand down its neck, and it ate something hidden in her palm, then let her climb on its back with nary a snort. Jyan held the other mare, its rich chestnut coat bright in the stable's single lamp. Keladros took the reins of a horse dark as midnight.

Rather than mount as the others had done, she led the horse to the barn doors.

"Head to the southern entrance," she whispered. "Take the old river road. A guard will have left the gates open, but cover your heads with your hoods."

Larissa did as she was bid, tugging her cloak over her emblazoned surcoat and pushing her braid under the hood too. The four became nothing but cloaked travelers, the dark browns of the knights' cloaks no different than Larissa's crimson in the night.

Keladros pushed open the doors, and Larissa followed Valare as she spurred her horse into a light trot.

Through midnight streets, they passed no one, no guards despite the late hour or the cook's promise of extra patrols. As though they knew to take no sight of the sisters' departure. The horses' hooves echoed across the dead quiet of the town, but they didn't linger to see any questioning lights as Valare led them to the southern side.

True to Keladros's word, the gates lay open—dangerous at this time of night, but again, there were no guards. Once past the gates, they bolted onto muddy flats and a long road by the river's side. Valare looked back, Larissa doing the same to be sure Keladros followed, and seeing the shadowy horse come close and catch up, the four stole away into the night.

High above them, an errant moon flitted between the ghostly haze of a cloud, its startling glow closer to noonday. A chill wind ate into Larissa's clothes, but the horse was hot beneath her, and her legs burned after the first hour's good canter.

Valare eased their pace when the city was a smudge of distant light behind them.

The river veered away from the road, and out of the darkness loomed large bare trees, long branches arching over the dirt road. The wind stirred, a susurrus whispering through their limbs like gossip at the sisters' flight. Valare dropped the horses into a walk once they were hidden by the tree line, and Keladros swung ahead of Jyan and Larissa to bring her horse beside Valare. Jyan drew alongside Larissa, who felt as weary as the poor beast beneath her.

"Do you think anyone noticed?" she asked, afraid and far tireder than she'd thought possible.

"Time will tell," Jyan said. "Keladros asked the captain's guard to leave the streets empty for her. But there are eyes everywhere. Still, they thought you were a pair, not four knights."

Larissa turned in her saddle. "Is that why you came with us?"

"That, and we couldn't leave you alone," Jyan said, eyes on the trees and the path behind them. "If they were waiting for you to arrive in Abbidon, they are spying on us...and whatever your quest, it's not for a mere darkkin."

Jyan didn't say it with any malice, but Larissa shivered.

# Chapter 12

Larissa was near falling off her horse. She bowed over the beast's neck, doing her best to stay upright, until Keladros called a halt to the intermittent sprints she'd demanded through the night and most of the morning. She led them off the road, deep in the woods to a pond where they let the horses drink.

Larissa slid down and took off the saddle, her mind almost numb as she brushed down the horse, laid the saddle on the ground as well as her swag, and then fell into a sleep that mimicked the dead.

It was a rude interruption when Keladros wakened her seemingly seconds later.

"When did you last sleep more than a kip, Darkkin?"

The sun's position told her Keladros had given her more than a moment, but not by much. The sun had moved past midday to early afternoon, but she knew from the winter season it wouldn't stay in the sky long.

She rubbed the sleep from her eyes. "Three days ago." Keladros frowned, and Larissa scrabbled to explain. "They woke me yester eve and charged me with my duty. I didn't sleep that night nor last."

"Eat this." Keladros held out a steaming bowl. "It will get you through the day. We do not stop again until we make the Falls of Scythia."

Warmth singed Larissa's palm before she changed the bowl to the other hand. "Scythia? It isn't on the way to Espenel."

Keladros stirred the stew. "But it's safe, and we can gather resources. Better than being out here in the open. Eat, you'll need your strength."

In due diligence, Larissa focused on her meal while she searched her memory for what she remembered of the sister city. Hidden behind a waterfall, Scythia was a place of healing, home to cool mineral springs that became part of the Tehnir river.

The fat smell of roasting meat drew her attention back to the bowl. The thick stew held more grease than meat, but it masked the herbs within. She took a tentative taste. Hawk's grove for heightened senses, calsthaw root for strength, and some other herbs that weren't as easy to identify. Larissa gobbled it down.

With every bite she felt herself returning. Aware of the herbal concoction, and that it wouldn't last indefinitely, she devoured it all, licking the bowl clean. When all had eaten, they packed up camp and resaddled the horses.

As Larissa sat in the saddle, her sores of the day before were their own little claws of pain in her rump and hips. She'd never ridden so much in her life, and she wasn't about to be given any relief soon.

Keladros took them back out to the road, and they cantered along its length again. Sunbeams flashed between the trees of the narrow wood, light, dark, light, dark.

The picturesque afternoon brought a memory so suddenly that only the horse's gait carried Larissa onward. The same avenue of trees, the same stretch of forest, but from long ago. Staring at the treetops from a view when she was much smaller, and rather than bare branches, there were the wide leaves of spring. A horse walked through the forest, jolting her a little as she sat in front of her mother.

*"Will it be cold in the mountain?"*

*"Colder than you've ever known before."* Her mother was taking her to Lathore. That journey was slow, filled with sunlight, the smell of horse sweat, and pieces of apple peeled with her mother's blade.

The memory vanished as quickly as it had come, and Larissa focused on the horse beneath her and keeping up with the others.

They rode hard.

Keladros slowed them when the horses began to toss their heads in tiredness, and watered them a little at a stream, before they were flying again.

Only when the sun's light grew obscured under the hush of an approaching storm did the horses tremble with fatigue. As they reached the forest's edge, the darkness of rainfall aided the burgeoning night, pattering over rolling hills. In the distance over the lowlands, the road met the river again, a much smaller village than Abbidon sulking on the waterfront.

And on the docks, a single vessel.

"The boatman." Larissa peered through a spyglass, recognizing the boat. "That's him, the one who tried to grab me."

People surrounded the docks, eyes on the water, even in the gloom. There was a tower by the river, its occupant facing upstream: a lookout for boats coming downriver. They were waiting for her. She suppressed a shiver.

"And he's found others to help him." Keladros took the spyglass from Larissa, sealing it back in the pouch at her waist. "I'll get what we need to make it to Scythia. Valare, do what you can with the horses' hooves."

Valare turned on Keladros, scowl creasing her brow as she came to the knight's side, standing under the eaves of the tree line. "I know you're in charge, Knight-Solaris, but we can't take that road."

"I'll get leather and rope and we will make the best of it, because there is no other choice." Keladros stood before Valare, narrower than the other warrior but taller. "We cannot stay in the open. They will be waiting for her at Espenel. We must get to the safety of Scythia."

"That path is too great a risk," Valare said. "I say we take our chances below with a few boatmen. Perhaps the others will be warned off once they see who we are."

Larissa glanced at Jyan, at a loss as to what the two knights meant. Jyan didn't meet her gaze, winding her horse's reins through her fingers. Larissa wanted to ask what was wrong, but Keladros's and Valare's argument hardly let her.

"Do you think they'll care that we're sisters?" Keladros said. "There is a *village* of them down there—cutthroats, plunderers, pirates, thieves, brigands. If an evercry has sent agents against your charge, then they won't stop there. Or did you not see the boats on the far side of the river?"

Larissa spun to scan the dark. The falling rain obscured her vision, but Keladros was right. Smudges of black lay on the far side, and now that night was coming, flickers of torchlight showed a greater presence.

Valare didn't stop. "Then we *steal* a boat, later at night."

"They waited for you in Abbidon, they'll be waiting for you *everywhere*." Keladros wiped the water from her face. "It isn't ideal, but it's the quickest way."

"We don't have the equipment or force we need to make the journey. Even the way to navigate it!"

Keladros snatched Valare's collar, yanking her closer. "We must get the darkkin to the safety of Scythia."

Valare shook her head, bowed in disappointment.

"As you wish." She brushed past Keladros. "I will see to the horses."

Keladros slung off her cloak to remove her surcoat identifying her as a knight of the Fair Lady, before covering herself again.

She slipped down the hillside, the rain giving her cover as she headed for the distant village.

"What is she doing?" Larissa hissed to Jyan, whose eyes followed her knight-solaris into the gloom.

"She's gone to steal scrap leather and rope." Jyan turned to her horse, fiddling with straps, her movements jerky, and Larissa was not blind to her fear.

"Where are we going?" She touched Jyan's arm, but Jyan turned back to her horse, checking over all its baggage, numb and unresponsive.

"Come help me, Westwyn." Valare drew Larissa from Jyan's side. She thrust tools into Larissa's hands. A hoof pick for rocks and a rasp to smooth iron edges of horse shoes. Larissa held the tools, at a loss as to why they needed them now. Valare crossed to her horse. Big brute that he was, he still snuffled her hand as friendly as a foal, looking for his treat. She gave him an easy word, stroked his flank, gave his knee a tap. The horse lifted his hoof, and Valare held out her hand. "The rasp, Larissa."

Larissa held out the tools to Valare, who filed the edges of her horse's hooves, before digging out stones.

Jyan took out similar tools, working on her horse and Keladros's, but neither spoke, their lips thinned, and the efficiency with which they took to their task spoke of other concerns. Larissa wanted to ask again what was wrong, but she didn't want to make matters worse.

Except she was about to swallow her own tongue, her pulse rising in her throat, the grating rasp of the file scraping across her last nerve.

"What is it you're afraid of?" she asked when Valare put down the last hoof.

Valare didn't bother to deny her fear. "We need to get to Scythia, and the only way to do so is to cross Still Water."

Larissa dropped the tools. They clattered to the ground, restarting her skipping heart.

"You can't be serious."

"It's the only place we can get you to safety and replan the route." Valare opened her saddlebag to grab jerky and apples. "Eat, rest, wait for Keladros's return."

Valare put the foodstuffs into Larissa's hand. She fought the urge to fling them down beside the tools.

"That is ridiculous," she hissed, gripping the apple hard enough to bruise. "The Writhing Dark live in Still Water. We can't go there at night, let alone on horseback."

"Keladros has gone to get leather to tie about their hooves," Jyan whispered, her voice carrying over the rainfall. "If we're lucky, they'll never know we were there at all."

"If? I've never left Lathore before, but even I know how dangerous a place it is. This can't be the only path."

"But it is," Valare said, "and we *must* get you to safety."

Larissa turned away. She steeled her spine and began to do as Jyan and Valare did, cutting thin strips of cloth to weave through anything that would make a sound. Over the metal pieces of the bridle, she threaded scraps from a thin shirt, to stop the jingling of the harness. In her bags she made sure everything was muffled. Lastly, she took out the soap to grease any creaking leather. There could be no noise when they crossed Still Water.

Venturing into Still Water was a fool's journey. Merchants and travelers used the river route, sailing around the coast from Espenel to Meggaloth; but this path was barred from them, and farther to the south was nothing but uninhabitable marshland. They had no other choice if they wanted to reach the Scythian falls.

None but the mad or truly desperate would venture into Still Water.

Stretching for miles between the Diophon and Tehnir rivers, it was a landscape of shimmering stone, turned smooth after eons of passing water that left a matrix of caverns beneath the surface. Above, carved from the heavy mineral content of the water and flash floods, stone arches sat over darkened pools that led to the cavern's depths.

And within the open mouths of Still Water lurked the Writhing Dark, mindless beings whose tentacles pulled victims down into the waterlogged caves to die. Devoured after drowning.

But in order to catch their prey, sound had to vibrate over the pools' surfaces. If the sisters could pass through without a sound, they'd be fine, but the metal of horses' hooves on the stone would echo, and they would have to get close to the pools to traverse Still Water.

Larissa shuddered. Shaking off her fatigue, she ate the meager meal Valare gave her before sitting under a tree and trying to doze while they waited for Keladros.

It was to no avail. Water dripped on her damp clothes, chilling her with the growing storm's presence. An iciness in her hands wouldn't abate, no matter that her leather gloves were lined with wool, and when she took them off, her fingers were edged in blue. She thrust them under her armpits and drew her cowl over her head, hunching over to keep warm. To stop the shaking that had nothing to do with the cold.

After a while, Jyan and Valare stood, focusing on a shadow at the base of the hill. Larissa joined them. The figure sneaking out of the town, their arms full, was Keladros.

"Mount up," she said when she joined them near the tree line. "We'll put these on once we're closer."

Valare got on her horse. "I did as you bid. All hooves filed, all metal made soft with cloth."

"We should be safer crossing during this rain," Larissa said, dragging up what little memory she had of the Writhing Dark. "The sound of the water splashing confuses them."

"That's only if it keeps falling," Keladros said.

"Should we wait until morning, then?"

"No." Keladros mounted her horse. "They've roused a scouting party in the village below. It appears they know we didn't take the river. A bird arrived while I was there. We must go before they figure out we didn't return to Lathore."

Sitting astride their tired horses, they skirted the outer village, down the hills and out of sight, following a hedgerow of farmland until neat fences gave way to trees again. They slogged through in the dark, the floor filled with autumn's rotting detritus, bare branches overhead alleviating none of the downpour. Larissa, sodden to the bone, pressed herself to her horse's back, the big animal's heat soaking into her.

The ground turned from rich mud to rockier pebbles, and their horses' footsteps changed from the swish of wet leaves to a sharper thud against stone.

"Stop," Keladros called, and they brought their horses to a halt. "We need to put the slips on now."

Valare lit a lantern and hung it from her saddle's pommel. The curtain of water about them shone golden in the dark night.

"How are we to find our way without the sun or stars to navigate?" Larissa kept her voice low as she dismounted with the others, though they were still far back from Still Water.

"There are markers," Keladros said, before her mouth twisted in a grim line. "I've passed this way before."

She gave Larissa four squares of leather, and rope to tie them on. Fumbling, Larissa picked up her horse's hooves one by one and tied the scraps around each of its legs. Soothing words helped, but her mare was unhappy, prancing at the strange bindings. One fell loose, and Valare came to her aid.

"Make sure they're all tight," Keladros admonished. "We cannot have any sounds. No talking either—if you must draw attention to yourself, wave your light."

Valare checked Larissa's horse, ensuring all the bindings were well fastened. She didn't mock Larissa's trembling hands. Jyan took out lanterns and passed them about, waiting until Larissa mounted her horse again before handing one to her. Larissa hooked the lantern's metal loop over the end of her spear, laying the weapon in readiness over her knees.

"The storm's almost passed," Jyan said. "What if water has

collected on the stone, won't it splash?"

"We shouldn't get that close to the pools, but steer clear where you can," Keladros said. "You will all follow me, and we go in single file—Mahcenae, the darkkin, then Atticus."

Larissa tightened her hands on the reins as they plodded their now silent horses across the rocks, each dull thud of their hooves carving another groove into her trepidation.

Out of the darkness ahead, the trees opened onto Still Water.

Her mind returned to images she'd seen in books, what she knew of the landscape and the Writhing Dark. Monsters in the deep with long arms, not unlike an octopus, but humans were their prey. Not evil, but with all the chaotic intent of hungry predators. There was no known way to rid the world of the creatures.

Keladros halted, gesturing for each of them to move into position before she turned back to the gray arches. Their shadows loomed in the lamplight, and a distant reflection illuminated rock waves as large as trees. Others only came up to the horses' knees. Along the stony forest floor were inky pools that marked entrances to the caves, some no more than puddles, and others as wide as ponds. Larissa's ears fair ached as she waited for Keladros to take the first steps out onto the wet surface.

Keladros's horse stepped forward, and there was barely a noise over the falling rain.

She gestured for the others to follow and rode further among the spires of stone. Each walked their horse onto Still Water, and each breathed a little easier as nothing leapt out at them. Keladros navigated the way through, though how she knew where to go was lost on Larissa, who could only ensure her horse stayed on Jyan's tail.

The rocks rose above them like Larissa imagined the waves at sea would, crests that never fell to stony beaches, forever frozen by their materials. Whatever allure the stone's visage might hold was obscured in the eve's darkness, and the storm's torment.

But with every second the rain fell softer, dissipating to a fine mist that cast long shadows.

Larissa thought her heartbeat alone might summon the beasts lurking below. Her hands locked tightly on the reins, and when the numbness spread to her wrists, she pried her fingers from their grip, flexing them to regain feeling. Her legs weren't much better. Tensing was making them tremble, but she feared what would happen should she so much as arch her foot.

Even the noise of creaking leather might bring the Writhing Dark.

Her body ached to move, but she remained rigid, focused on their goal, the waving glow of the lanterns casting curling shadows almost designed to deceive. Ahead, Keladros took a sharp turn, and Larissa craned her head to see what had subverted their path. A pool lay between two spires, blocking their western heading. Its surface shimmered with the lingering gossamer brush of rain, its inky depths enough of a warning to give it a wide berth.

Keladros stopped well back from its surface, drawing their party to a halt. In a nearby pool, Larissa studied their reflection, waiting for the bobbing lights to become the eyes of a Writhing Dark.

Sword in hand, Keladros motioned them to stay but urged her horse forward. She was far closer to the pool than they'd gone before, riding a narrow ledge between rock wave and water's verge. One misstep would send ripples over the surface.

Larissa choked back her indrawn breath, stifling the noise before it could begin. She stared into the water's depths, wide eyes watering with strain. Too terrified to blink.

Nothing moved.

Keladros's horse passed, and Larissa loosened her grip on her spear. Once Keladros was well beyond, the knight turned her horse in a circle and gestured for Jyan to cross. Jyan nudged her horse forward, silently drawing her sword as Keladros had done. The horse slipped by the water with nary a movement from within.

Larissa swallowed against the sour taste of apple and jerky. Taking the lantern off her spear and lifting it above her head, she squeezed her legs about the mare.

Each tremor of the mare's legs vibrated into Larissa, echoing as dully as the heartbeats in her chest, compounding fear with every step. The water's surface absorbed the glow of their lights, and she thought if she stared too long, it would suck her down too...

Until she passed the narrowest part, and joined Jyan and Keladros on the other side. She lowered her spear but kept it in hand, not breathing easy until she stood beside Jyan.

The last one left, Valare drew her sword in readiness. Its broad blade scraped the scabbard's side.

The hollow ring was a chiming bell over the rocks, growing in volume, its echo causing the horses to whinny and flatten their ears. Valare closed her eyes with a wince. Her expression turned to a scowl, and she opened her eyes, moving her horse forward before the last vestiges of sound could die away. Her crossing was quick, faster than the others, and they all watched the pool as the horse trotted by.

Larissa held her breath as Valare's stallion reached the narrowest part, hooves almost brushing the water. She made a silent plea to the Fair Lady. Then Valare was past, and the pool remained still.

Valare joined them, breathing deep, and Larissa smiled in relief, though Valare was scowling. Keladros's shoulders slumped as she lay her sword across her knees.

Then the water rippled.

# Chapter 13

Terror thudded within Larissa's chest.

There was no other warning before a black tentacle lashed out of the dark and smashed the light on Valare's horse. The horse shrieked, rearing as another arm lashed about its foreleg.

Valare's blade came singing down to slice through an arm seeking a grasp on her pommel. The monster's suckered length slithered to the ground, spilling dark viscous blood, but from her saddle, Valare couldn't reach the tentacle about her horse's leg to free them. Keladros swung at the monster and it jerked back, gripping the horse's leg in its retreat. Yanked off balance, the horse stumbled to the ground. Valare went down with it.

"Valare!" Larissa called, but Keladros was there, leaning off the side of her horse to bring her sword across the black arm on Valare's stallion. Her blade sliced through the meaty tentacle, easily as a carving knife through a roast, but the movement put her within reach of the beast.

There was a great sucking noise, and a wave of water spilled out onto the ground as a Writhing Dark burst from the pool.

True to its name, the unspeakable mass of black limbs were near indistinguishable in the night. The monster flung itself upon the party, a darkness that squirmed and glistened, as water appeared to stick to its slicked flesh. Several appendages sought to keep its victim, while the rest arched overhead to grab the other horses.

Valare left her mount behind, sliding with a grunt from beneath its flailing form. Keladros chopped the arms that tried to seize her, spreading thick ooze on the rocks. Her horse danced in fear, but she used each motion to make wide arcs of her sword. It wasn't enough. Larissa brought her horse to Keladros's weakened flank, spear aloft and looking for the best place to strike the creature.

Valare rolled away from the slimy limbs as they dragged her horse to the pool. Unable to kick away from the Writhing Dark's grip about its legs, the horse tossed its head and screamed, until the water cut it off with a splash. Jyan held her hand out to Valare, tugging the knight up to mount behind her.

Larissa kept a firm handle of the reins on her skipping mare, slicing through the air with her spear at the arms headed for Keladros. The point pierced flesh. A muscle-wreathed arm quivered, spattering her with its foul ichor. She wanted to run, but Keladros struggled to draw back when another attack demanded her action. Larissa forgot the arms and looked for its body instead, hoping to strike somewhere that would hurt. The darkness sucked away all chances of spotting a weakness. A surge of magic rose within her, longing to be used. Honed now with training, she brought it forward, completely in her control.

"Cover your eyes!" she yelled. She dove for the magic within, called upon the elements of air and fire, wrapped them on her tongue. "*Afithrios!*"

The magic ripped from her tongue and left ash in its wake. Despite her intent, panic twisted it, goaded it, her will unfurling on the tide of desperation. The night sky lit up as though it were day. Magic surged within her, fueling a sonic boom that echoed over Still Water. Monsters screeched in protest, slithering back into their pools. Except the one before them, who would not let go of its prize.

Her sight blurred, a kaleidoscope of images burning in her vision, but the magic surged within her, dilating her eyes despite the piercing glare, spikes of agony lancing her skull. But she could see the monster. With all her strength, she flung her spear at its mass as hard as she could.

The spear tore through tentacles and pierced into the Writhing Dark's body, sinking into unarmored flesh. Its arms reared back as it clawed at the haft of wood embedded in its side, and what might have been a face emerged from the water, white eyes and a gray beak snapping at the fading light.

It didn't retreat.

The Writhing Dark yanked the spear out and flung it into the darkness, but Keladros had taken the chance she needed to back out of range.

"Go!" she commanded. "Now, before the others return!"

They tossed caution aside as they brought the horses to a canter, their swift passing noisy, but there was no purpose in silence now. They darted by pools whose depths seethed, the Writhing Dark emerging now that the light had faded, more than one wrathful and hungry beast flailing at them. Larissa couldn't stop to retrieve her bow, and her spear was gone, so she took out the sword at her waist and hacked at any thrashing limbs that came too close.

Keladros rushed them through the waves. Their panicked horses needed no urging. Larissa nearly wept with relief as the rocks thinned, waves sinking to a stone floor, pools vanishing to nothing but mud puddles, until only flat rock remained and the edge of another forest was in sight.

Then Keladros brought her horse to a halt.

Ahead, a long pool blocked their path to the forest, its surface rippling in anticipation. In its depths lay a creature far larger than any of the others, two white eyes luminous as the moon, and it did not reach for them but waited, as if aware they couldn't pass but would try.

Larissa could make out trees beyond, but here on the edge, Still Water stretched in all directions, pools behind and to either side. They had no choice but to pass this last narrow pool. Behind them, the slick sound of flesh on stone grew. The Writhing Dark wouldn't be confined to their pools much longer, their need for the water overwhelmed by hunger to seek out the trespassers and stuff them in their wide gaping maws.

Out of reach of any grasping arms, but surrounded, they were trapped.

"Valare, Jyan," Keladros said after a moment. "You'll go after me. Our horses can make that jump, but we must give the Writhing Dark a distraction. Larissa, you follow last. It will give you the best chance to cross."

"You can't feed yourself to that thing," Larissa shouted, caution forgotten. "I can cast another spell—"

"Don't tell a knight-solaris what to do, Darkkin." Keladros didn't turn, but eyed the beast ahead. "Any more magic and the agents will know *exactly* where we are, if they don't already. I will leap from my horse's back to the far side. Hopefully it will take the horse and allow us to pass, but we must cross now, or we will die here."

Keladros gave a bloody war cry that echoed over the night. Goading her horse to a gallop, she rose out of the saddle, blade over her head. She bolted to the creature, her horse hammering blindly toward its death.

Jyan dug her heels into the sides of her mare, who grunted but leapt after Keladros's horse. Before Larissa could let fear consume her, she did the same, the tan horse beneath her streaking after the others.

Whole body shaking, she didn't know if she or the horse was more afraid as they charged the beast. Tentacles shot out of the long pool, seeking the oncoming prey.

Keladros's horse came to a shuddering halt by the water's edge, rearing up in the air, forelegs batting at the tentacles. The Writhing Dark fell on it with thick limbs, tentacles engulfing the horse. The horse squealed. Keladros launched from the horse's back, diving over the beast to splash into the shallows at the far side of the pool.

Though they'd not been more than a fraction of a second behind her, the Writhing Dark beneath the water was greater than Larissa had guessed, a single horse not enough of a distraction. More arms loomed out of the dark to strike at the oncoming horses. Larissa couldn't slow down, seized by terror's yawning pit as Jyan and Valare cut a bloody path through the limbs, their horse taking a nimble and dire lunge at the far shore.

The horse fell short. Its front legs landed on the soft dirt, but its back legs splashed into the water. Jyan was thrown to the safety of sodden earth, but Valare toppled off its back and into the pool.

Larissa's horse headed straight for where Jyan had fallen.

In sudden terror, Larissa yanked the reins, turning closer to the beast's jaws as her horse leapt. Waving tentacles reached out for her. Desperation brought magic to her tongue.

Across the splashing and shrieks of the horses came the lone cry of a wolf. All magic was struck from her senses, rendering the rest of the world silent. But the howl echoed on. Heat blossomed against her chest, and the echo of the Evervast called to the beast through the orb, willed the dark creature to retreat from her. She sensed its command as the limbs beneath her recoiled, drawing back as though stung.

Larissa landed on the far side. The world came crashing back.

Her teeth clacked together, biting her tongue. Her mouth filled with blood. The impact shuddered through her body, shook her down to fingers and toes. She almost lost her grip as her horse tried to run into the dark, but she jerked the reins and brought it back under control. It took a few dancing steps before she yanked hard, whirling back to help the others.

A human scream ripped through the night. Larissa's head twisted toward Valare, who was dragging herself on the pool's edge, hand clutching her leg. Their eyes met.

"Help me!" Valare cried.

Magic unfurled within Larissa, fierce and directionless as a hurricane. She couldn't risk hurting Valare.

Closer, Jyan lunged for Valare. Clasping forearm to forearm, she heaved back to free Valare from the water. Tentacles wound up Valare's legs. Larissa fought with her horse, intent on using the beast's strength to drag Valare clear, but it bucked her off, lantern flung aside as she fell.

Goverin's training saved her. Agility learned through daily training turned her tumble into a roll, and she dropped the sword so she didn't impale herself. She let the horse bolt, snatching up her sword.

Jyan's mare thrashed in the water, attracting more limbs, giving Jyan a chance to get Valare free. Keladros shredded tentacles flailing at Valare. Larissa ran to their side, sword at the ready, but the thin blade wasn't dexterous enough to cut through the muscular limbs. She flung it aside in favor of the magical dagger.

"*Firitos!*" The command heated her tongue, and the blade burned hot red, casting crimson light. A magically imbued weapon, the spell extended beyond the short blade to create a sword made of fire. Not a showy display that would attract attention, but *something* she could do to help. Without pause at the magic flowing through her, she hacked at the bindings, while above her Keladros fended off the remaining arms. The creature's skin turned white beneath her blade, and a screech cut through the air. The Writhing Dark dropped the horses to ravage those on shore. Keladros was knocked from her feet, sword lost as she landed face first in the mud.

"Keladros!" Jyan screamed, Valare in her arms, out of the water but favoring one leg. The Writhing Dark rose from the water, eyes thin slits of white, daggers in the night, full of poison. This close, the thickest parts of its arms were as wide as Larissa's body, and it fell on Keladros in malevolent anger.

Keladros cried out. Unable to dodge the creature's grasp, she was soon cocooned in writhing darkness, tentacles tight as a snake squeezing the life from its prey.

Larissa called to the knight, a scream tearing from her throat as she ran forward, plunging her fiery blade into the thickest arm about Keladros's middle. The Writhing Dark squealed in fury at the brand. She didn't stop, stabbing again as Keladros screamed, the arms constricting tighter.

There was a wrenching noise, a wet snap, and the cries stopped.

Larissa stared up into Keladros's face, her tortured expression now blank, gray eyes vacant as Larissa kept stabbing the creature. The tentacles yanked Keladros into the pool, Larissa's futile attack ignored. The Writhing Dark left only ripples in its wake.

With its absence, the night filled with a thousand despairing sighs. The wolf from Larissa's dreams called once more, mournful as her gasping cries.

"Larissa," Jyan called. "I need you."

She turned back to where Jyan's much smaller frame struggled to support Valare. Larissa ran forward, extinguishing the blade's power before sheathing it. She slipped under Valare's arm and took the greater weight.

"I've got you," she said, as they hobbled toward the forest.

"Keladros," Valare grunted. Larissa shook her head.

"She's dead." Jyan wiped her nose on her sleeve and gritted her teeth. She left Valare's side to retrieve their fallen swords and sheath them.

"We need to get farther away," Valare said. "Before it comes back."

Larissa nodded and, all their lanterns lost or broken, they slowly stumbled into the gloom.

They crossed the stretch of muddy ground before the safety of the forest wall, the dense undergrowth a welcome change to the rocks of Still Water. The day's rain rendered the leaves slippery. With no lights, and footing uncertain, they slithered over the foliage. All that mattered was their retreat from the foe they'd left behind, so Keladros's sacrifice was not in vain. Larissa stumbled many a time, and Valare grunted in pain, but she made no complaint.

Once out of sight of Still Water, Jyan and Larissa searched in the forest's twilight for shelter. A large tree on a hilltop offered meager protection, but they had little other choice. Valare fell against the tree's base with a groan, and Larissa knelt to give what aid she could. Fumbling in the dark, she felt Valare's leg. There was nothing broken—or at least not that she could tell, but she wanted to be sure. Valare hissed in pain at Larissa's wandering hands.

Larissa flashed back to the wet crunching noise that was Keladros's end.

"We need to make a splint," Larissa said. "Keep it straight as possible."

Jyan stared into the dark, sword in hand. "We only have the one horse, which has bolted, and no supplies," she said, anger tinging her voice. "Do what you can for Valare, Darkkin. I will fetch the horse."

She trotted off into the forest, and Larissa watched her go, feeling the sting in the comment. She was at fault for Keladros's death. A cry of hopelessness swept up her throat, but she bit it back.

"Don't do that to yourself, Westwyn," Valare said, reading Larissa's worry even in the dark. "You can't blame yourself for what happened. I started it."

There was no self-deprecating pity in the statement, but Larissa was familiar with the tone of Valare's condemnation. Except this time Valare used it against herself.

"We should never have come this way." Larissa scrambled

to her feet, putting her back to Valare as she searched the forest floor for two appropriate pieces of wood for a splint.

"It was a risk Keladros was willing to take. There were no other alternatives, and she deemed it worth it. I'm...glad it didn't take me too."

"It broke her spine." Larissa flung aside useless branches. "Snapped it before the Dark could drown her. I made it angry, and it killed her."

Hot tears scalded her cheeks. She wasn't worth Keladros's death. No price met the loss of the brave knight-solaris. For all her spellcraft and lessons, it had all amounted to nothing. She'd been helpless, not a sister of the Fair Lady but a weakling who'd let others sacrifice themselves for her.

"Larissa," Valare called, and then louder when Larissa ignored her. "If it's anyone's fault, it's mine. If I'd made no sound when I drew my sword, we may have come out of it without harm. But we can't change what's passed, and when Jyan gets back, she will not need to tend to your perpetual sulking."

That brought Larissa about, striding back to the tree's base, hand tightening on the one suitable stick she'd found.

"Perpetual sulking?" she yelled. "Is that what you think of me?"

"You aren't exactly a bundle of joy." Valare shuffled, hands on her injured leg. "Jyan made few friends in school bar you, and not for lack of humor. She's made many more since joining the knights."

And they were back to the oldest argument the pair had ever had. Larissa's worth.

"What do you want from me, Valare? Because I'll be *damned* if I apologize for never meeting expectations that I didn't make for myself. I'm done with it and with your attitude. I've found something I'm good at, and I won't be cowed by your bullying anymore. And in case you didn't notice, *without* my magic we would have been far worse off."

She snarled the last down at Valare, and was surprised to

find a smile break through Valare's grimace. Larissa was quick to realize what she'd done—goaded Larissa to anger rather than guilt. Quick, clever, and nothing like what she remembered of Valare. Larissa wished she couldn't see Valare's teeth gleaming in the dim light. Huffing in annoyance, she lay the stick down and went to hunt up another.

A thought occurred to her, and rather than throw away sticks that wouldn't work well, she collected as many dry branches as she could, then returned to Valare's side. Picking two of the straightest sticks, she set them down next to the knight until Jyan returned with something she could use to tie them to Valare's legs, and set about making a fire in the meantime. She placed the driest twigs in a small depression and drew the elemental dagger. Her hand tightened. She'd have to use magic again, but they were far from Still Water and few would dare cross it at night. Anyone who'd seen the magic would need to go around, and that would take days. She could risk a small spell.

"*Firilos.*" Her whisper caused the blade to spark, heat growing on its end, then lessening as she shoved the point in the heart of the branches. When it threatened to fade away altogether, she goaded the blade with her will, pouring magic through her hand until a small fire fought the odds of the wet sticks.

"It will at least tell Jyan where we are," she said, plonking down beside the glowing embers. Valare grunted, head tilted back against the tree trunk.

Larissa kept the fire going, building its strength against the cool night until it crackled well on its own. Pleased, she sheathed the blade and carefully propped more kindling on its sides to catch the flickering flame.

Night's darkness abated, and she sat back to see Valare hadn't moved, unconscious against the tree trunk. A fine sheen of sweat lay on her brow, skin pale under her eyes. Larissa leaned over and rested her palm against Valare's forehead.

She was too warm, the damp there not from the rain but a

growing sweat.

Larissa looked down at Valare's leg in the firelight, and twitched aside the torn leather of Valare's pants. Purple welts marked Valare's shin, edged in angry red, the skin surrounding it white despite Valare's bronzed olive skin. Larissa could see no wound, but there must have been some other cause for her sudden sickness than a mere bruise.

Larissa took out a knife and shredded the material to examine Valare's skin. There was something wrong with the discoloration. Larissa dragged the limb as close to the fire as she dared, and beneath the top layer of skin she saw the pinpricks of a poisoned barb.

"What is it?" Jyan's voice called from the dark, and Larissa started.

Jyan came up the slope, the sorry horse in her wake, its expression no less dour than Jyan's own. Larissa paid the frown on her friend's face no mind, running to the horse's side and reaching for her saddlebags.

"The Writhing Dark poisoned her," she said. "I need to remove the barbs, make a compress. What do you know of forest moss?"

"Moss?" Jyan asked, staring at the wound on Valare's leg. "Little enough."

"I'll go, then." Larissa took out a lantern and lit it. "Splint her legs first, and then make a moldy bread poultice. Can you do that?"

"Yes," Jyan snapped.

Larissa held back any complaint. "Thank you."

"I need not your thanks for helping my sister, Darkkin."

Jyan yanked a rope from the saddle and cut off a length, using the rest to tie up the horse. Larissa stood stunned at Jyan's tone, watching the knight wind the rope and wood about Valare's leg.

"Go, Larissa," Jyan said with an exaggerated sigh. "I can do it."

Larissa slunk into the shadows without a word, using the magic dagger as a torch.

A part of her looked along the sides of fallen logs for the feathery white moss she hoped would soothe the burning of Valare's flesh, while another part reeled at Jyan's sudden anger. Grief she could understand in the wake of what happened, but Jyan had never lashed out. At least not at her.

It was to be expected—neither knight had asked for this or knew her purpose, and Larissa had cost Jyan her mentor. Larissa wondered if it had been the same for Valare when her commander fell.

Finding a good handful of the moss, she returned to the camp. Jyan sat by Valare's side, splint tight on the knight's leg and the poultice applied.

Larissa fetched a square of leather and attached three corners to a series of sticks. The result she pitched over the fire, pouring water from a sack onto the leather to stop it burning. Within the water she placed the moss, ensuring the feathery tufts were covered. While she waited for it to simmer, she took out a smaller blade and removed the purple-tinged barbs in Valare's wound. The knight didn't stir. It wasn't a good sign. Once done, Larissa plucked out the wilted moss to coat the purple lines stretching beneath Valare's skin.

Valare started to shiver, and Jyan slipped behind her, using her body to cradle Valare's. Larissa took her swag off the horse and placed the blanket over them both.

"Build up the fire again," Jyan instructed.

Larissa shook her head. "The fire needs to be kept low or it'll burn the leather. I have to keep applying the moss, it'll slow the inflammation." She stared into the night. "Dawn is a few hours off. Rest a while. I'll stay awake—Valare will need more moss when that dries out."

Jyan dragged the blankets tighter around them. Larissa sat by the fire and watched the flames dance, high enough to heat the leather, low enough so it didn't burn. Her need to heal Valare gave her a focus that kept exhaustion at bay.

But Valare's condition did not improve.

# Chapter 14

Larissa used dawn's glow to pack up and douse the fire. She was feeding an apple to the horse when Jyan first stirred.

"We need to get to Scythia."

"Tell me something I wasn't aware of," Jyan bit out.

"If you wish." Larissa left the horse to stand over her old friend. "Valare will die if we don't get her to a healer in the next few hours."

Jyan studied Valare, who was as pale as a ghost. The stain under her skin had spread up her calf to turn the whole appendage a bruised purple. Larissa had stopped cutting the pants leg when the bruise climbed Valare's thigh to her hip. She'd slowed its progress, but that was all.

"Help me get her on the horse," she said.

Jyan winced as she slipped behind Valare's back. The knight was oblivious to them, slumped against a tree root. Larissa knelt in front of Valare and took her arms, but she couldn't hoist the broad woman onto her back.

"Give her a push," she told Jyan. The knight helped lift

Valare onto Larissa's back. Larissa grunted at the weight, not small herself but without Valare's muscles. She hauled Valare over her shoulder but couldn't rise. Grasping her elbows, Jyan gave her the leverage to stand, and with unsteady feet Larissa turned to the mare.

She struggled under the weight, short hard gasps escaping her chest when she tried to heave Valare over the saddle. "I can't...lift her."

"Fling her arms over." Jyan scurried to the horse's other side. "I'll pull her over the rest of the way."

Larissa didn't know where the strength came from, but as her knees threatened to buckle, she forced them to straighten, shoving Valare across the mare's back. Her relief was temporary, Jyan catching Valare's wrists but unable to get her torso across the horse. Larissa pushed Valare's feet until she lay over the saddle.

Jyan took the rope lead and untied the horse. "Which way?" she said, more to herself than Larissa as she glanced about.

"West," said Larissa. She'd memorized the map in the darkkin halls. "This forest isn't large. We should be able to reach the Tehnir in a matter of hours and head north, even find a riverboat to take us to Scythia."

"What about those bandits, or even agents? They are on the lookout for you."

"Do you think we look like three sisters of the Fair Lady right now?" Larissa laughed, humor burbling into her throat until she had to cover her mouth to muffle the giddiness.

Jyan scowled. "Westwyn, keep it together."

But Larissa shook her head, unable to stop the mirth. Shock, fatigue, and hopelessness settled on her shoulders, as heavy as the armor and wet cloak that wanted to drag her to the forest floor where she could sleep forever.

Her chuckles trickled to a stop. "Why are you angry, Jyan?"

Looking away, Jyan checked the direction of the rising sun and headed west. Larissa walked after her. They crossed the forest in silence.

All too soon, mirth was traded for an unsettling depression that dragged at her footsteps. Jyan stopped several times to wait for her.

"Keep up, Darkkin," she called from a rise Larissa struggled to climb.

"I'm sorry, Jyan," Larissa said, unsure of what else to say, but once she apologized she couldn't stop. "I'm sorry your mentor died saving me."

"She died trying to free Valare," Jyan snapped. "Whose stupidly large sword got us into trouble. But that doesn't seem to matter, not when you could have passed Still Water and the Writhing Dark yourself without getting a scratch."

The latter statement echoed in a whip crack tone that tossed the mare's head. Valare started to slip off, and Larissa rushed forward to steady her at the same time Jyan brought the horse under control.

"What are you saying?" Larissa asked, one hand on Valare's back.

"Twice, at the first pool when you were beside Keladros, and then at the end of Still Water. The Writhing Dark pulled back from striking you. I thought at first it didn't notice you, but when it reached out, something made it recoil."

Larissa's hand betrayed her as it drifted to the orb under her armor. Her gaze fell as she stepped back. "I didn't know that would happen."

"Did you suspect? Maybe you should have gone first. We could've used you to distract it to get across."

Larissa's indrawn breath hardened Jyan's eyes. "It wasn't me. I think...it's what I carry."

Jyan said nothing, but she glanced down at where Larissa's hand lay over her armor.

"It heard it," Larissa whispered. "I don't know how...but the Writhing Dark heard the call of the Ever—"

An icy grip clenched around Larissa's windpipe. It squeezed

tight and she scrabbled at her throat, unable to feel the hand stealing her breath. She struck back against it, keeping the orb in her mind, shoving against the binding's restraint. Spots danced in her vision. The forest spun as she tried to cough past the constriction. Jyan called her name, but her pulse pounded in her ears.

Falling to the forest floor, she bent over and gave in to the compulsion to banish all thoughts of the orb from her mind. The binding released her. But for the smallest moment, she'd fought the spell, and she realized that with time and the right tools, she could break it.

"What happened?" Jyan knelt nearby, one hand held out to Larissa.

"A binding," she croaked. "About the item I carry. I can't speak of it." She scrambled to a rock, relearning how to breathe.

Jyan stared at her throat. Larissa's hand rose to stroke the injured flesh.

"What is it?"

"Blue lines. A water spell." Jyan's gaze flickered between the mark and Larissa's face. "It doesn't explain why the Writhing Dark wouldn't attack you."

Larissa massaged her neck, covering it from Jyan's speculation. "I can't answer."

Jyan's frown grew. "Obviously, so don't try again. The horse can't take you and Valare."

She rose from her crouch and helped Larissa do the same. There was still something angry in her jerky movements, but Larissa ignored it.

They trudged downhill. Soon the forest gave way to larger trees, and in the distance, the rush of a river.

"The Tehnir," Larissa said, and for a moment the pair found energy to hasten their pace to the hill's bottom, sliding on the rotting debris. Larissa kept Valare steady on the horse's back; the mare did not like the awkward descent through shifting dead leaves and whinnied in protest until Jyan slowed down.

Less thick with trees, the ground opened to a grassy slope, until they could see the dappled sunlight banks of the river Tehnir through the shadows.

Better still, the roar they'd heard wasn't that of the river's currents but the great pounding of the Falls of Scythia.

Mighty waterfalls spilled rainbow hues into the afternoon air, tumbling from a towering cliffside dotted with holes that contained the Fair Lady's stronghold of Scythia. On the banks of the Tehnir, boats drifted downstream, carrying cargo out to the distant sea.

Further upstream was the city, and a bridge over the river. A well-traveled road swept from the bridge up and above the falls, but the three sisters crossed the bridge and headed for the entrance beneath the falls.

A white curtain of water covered the cave's mouth, but to one side was a pathway wide enough for a wagon. Beside it, the stone was wreathed in carvings of great water plumes and animals of the river: fish, eels, otters, beavers, deer, and bears. Two knights of the Fair Lady stood at the gates, letting travelers through. Sister knights of their order who would protect them.

A bounce returned to Larissa's step as Jyan hurried toward them.

"Hail, sisters," Jyan called. "We need to get to your hospital ward. A Writhing Dark attacked our friend."

The knights stared at them. Larissa echoed Jyan's statement. "She needs urgent care, or she'll die."

"What did you say attacked her?" a guard asked with suspicion. "And where did this happen?"

"Still Water," Larissa said. "We need shelter and protection, but foremost, help. Valare is the daughter of the matriarch of shields, and she needs a healer *now*."

Recognition drove the guards to haste. They called for a wagon, one knight taking the mare's bridle from Jyan.

Larissa hovered over Valare as the sisters loaded the prone knight into the back of the wagon. She climbed in beside her and

Jyan joined them, stumbling in her fatigue. Larissa caught her arm before she fell. They exchanged grateful smiles, a fleeting moment that said more than words.

One of the knights hitched a horse to the wagon, then trotted them under the waterfalls of Scythia. They passed a pool of deep water. The pair shuddered, despite knowing there was no danger.

Through caves and into the heart of an underground city, Larissa tried to keep track of their path. They were going uphill, unnatural openings carved into the rock to allow sunlight in. Any heat was diminished by overhanging vines, wide leaves casting shadows and keeping out the worst of the weather. White signs painted on smooth walls gave directions, but all Larissa cared about was the way to the ward.

Unlike the ward in Lathore with its narrow stone windows, Scythia's hospital ward had great arches that led to a balcony overlooking the river. Leafy vines and ferns crawled over the cliffside, creeping to the edge of patients' feet where they lounged in reclining chairs, embracing the morning sun. Columns flanked a long passageway to the treatment rooms, where green-robed sisters stopped in their tracks at their arrival, before rushing to Valare's side.

"What happened?" a woman asked, red braid bouncing on her back. Larissa yanked aside the scraps of Valare's pants.

"A Writhing Dark grabbed her," she said. "There are spines—I removed the ones I could, but they have some kind of poison. I put on a poultice of moldy bread and Fair Lady's hair moss, but it only slowed down whatever's happening."

The woman examined the wound. "You did as much as you were able. Leave her with us."

They whisked Valare away on a stretcher. Jyan and Larissa made to follow, but the nurses pushed them back.

"There's no purpose to you hovering," one said. "Come with me. We have chambers nearby you can have to yourselves. Rest and wash, you look exhausted."

"I need to see the matriarch of Scythia," Larissa said. "I also have urgent news to send to Lathore."

"And I," Jyan said. "We lost a sister knight on our journey."

The nurse scanned them, then called a nearby guard. "Take them to Matriarch Yaris."

The knight nodded, leading them away. Larissa and Jyan trudged after her.

Their arrival at Scythia brought relief, but so too did weariness loom worse than a storm, threatening to sink Larissa down into the depths of unconsciousness with every step. Her legs trembled, her arms were about to drop off, and her head spun in a cloud of fog as she tried to focus on where they were and what she'd tell the matriarch of Scythia.

They were led to an archway and left with two other guards. The new knights scowled at them, taking in their disheveled appearance.

"You couldn't find a uniform?" one sneered.

"We've just survived a walk through Still Water," Larissa said, her voice light, friendly, and full of scathing sarcasm. Jyan's hand on her arm didn't stop her. "Our friend lies dying in the ward above, a knight-solaris is also dead, and someone is trying to kidnap me. I think a dip of hot water and dabbing oil behind the ears is a little lower on my list of priorities than you might at first assume."

Her bright smile didn't smooth over her delivery, but the knight's scorn faded. The guard knocked on the doors.

"Matriarch," she called, "there is…" She turned back and raised an eyebrow at Larissa.

"Darkkin Westwyn," Larissa said. "And Knight Mahcenae, from Lathore."

The knight repeated their titles through the door, and a voice bid them enter.

Mirrors hung from polished stone walls all around the room, reflecting the light above them back and forth, creating a nimbus glow. A long table dominated the space, its shape molded to resemble a river. At the end of the table sat a woman, her pale skin and mousy hair rendered golden in the light. Piercing blue eyes took them in.

"I am Matriarch Yaris of Scythia." She gestured they sit. Larissa stumbled as she took one of the chairs. Carved of smooth twists of wood, as though made from water's passing rather than handcrafted, its hard surface cradled her weary form. Far more comfortable than it looked, but even a rock would have been a luxury.

"My apologies, Matriarch," Larissa began, words starting to slur. "We bring a sister in need of desperate medical attention, and news of the death of Knight-Solaris Keladros."

"Knight-Solaris Keladros?" Yaris gestured to a nearby sister, who brought over wine and food for the table. "You both look worn out, but I must know what's happened."

Larissa glanced about. At the guards by the entrance who watched with interest, the yellow-robed sister who placed a plate of cold fish and fruit before her, and at Matriarch Yaris dressed in white. On her shoulders sat the golden shoulder plates of one who'd slain an evercry.

Though she longed to taste the food, Larissa bowed her head instead.

"I beg pardon, Matriarch," she said. "But while I must ask for your protection, I also must be careful as to whom I speak, as per the grand matriarch's orders."

The matriarch's eyes narrowed, no doubt wondering what two slips of exhausted nothing had to do with Grand Matriarch Navus.

"Leave us." She waved a hand, getting to her feet to come down the table. The yellow-robed sister was the first to scurry out. The guards followed reluctantly. Though they were all sisters, Jyan and Larissa were still strangers.

Yaris poured a drink Larissa didn't touch, placed another goblet before Jyan, and sat herself beside Larissa. "Tell me what you can, and we'll do what we can to help."

Larissa wanted to weep at the easy way the matriarch treated them, wondered if it would continue when she imparted what had transpired.

"I'm carrying a dangerous...item," she said, careful of the binding. "We were due to take a riverboat for Espenel, but after being set upon by bandits, my knight-solaris, Valare Atticus, defended me, as did Knight Mahcenae. Her knight-solaris, Keladros, thought to take me to Scythia, but we ran into the same bandits and had to cross Still Water to get here."

The matriarch leaned forward. "Keladros knew the way through, as all knights of Scythia learn."

"That's how?" Jyan burst out, and then dropped her head at the matriarch's sharp gaze.

"Keladros hails from the south but grew up here, in the caverns of Scythia." Yaris sat back with a small smile. "All our students learn the codes in case they need to take Still Water's path. It is a sure way of escaping an unknown enemy, but one that comes with high risk."

Larissa swallowed against her next words, every one hard to speak. "Matriarch Atticus ordered her to stay by my side and get me here. Keladros died crossing the waves."

Keladros's empty eyes ghosted in her vision. She picked up the cup, drank thirstily, and then set it down.

"How did you escape, Darkkin?" Yaris asked, refilling her cup.

"Magic. Enough to send most of them crawling back beneath the waves."

Her flat answer caused the matriarch's hand to quaver, sloshing wine over the rim. Larissa rushed to explain herself.

"There was no other choice—it was either that or we all died."

Yaris stared at her, lips parted, and Larissa feared her fatigue had made her flippant toward the power she'd used. To admit not only her use of magic, but its strength.

"It was only enough to get them to back off," Jyan supported.

"Along with the elemental blade you used when you tried to free Keladros—"

She broke off, her eyes wide, unblinking and focused on the table. Larissa ignored the glint within, rage warring with grief. There was a long silence, Yaris studying them both.

"A knight of her caliber will be missed," she said. "But what item do you carry that warrants such a risk?"

Larissa wanted to speak of it but had no strength to fight the binding.

"This." She reached beneath her muddy armor to retrieve the orb. When she brought it out into the light, she thought for a moment she heard it whispering as the rings turned, but the sound soon faded.

Yaris studied the orb. "That is a perilous object. Though I know not what it is, I sense what is...within."

It may have been Larissa's exhaustion or a nuance of the light, but Yaris's eyes appeared to tighten, crow's feet flashing on the otherwise perfect face.

A sliver of doubt crawled inside Larissa, and she watched the matriarch with caution.

"You're on a very difficult quest, Darkkin." Yaris rose from her chair, picked up a quill and spare parchment from the end of the table, and scribbled a note. She took it to the doorway and handed it to one of the waiting guards.

"I invite you to rest and heal," she said, after she'd closed the door. "This is an awful turn of events, but things may appear better in tomorrow's light."

"What did you send?" Larissa asked, struggling to her feet.

"A message to Lathore. Assuring Grand Matriarch Navus you are here and safe, and I asked what she wishes me to do."

"We must travel onwards," Larissa said. "As soon as we're rested. There are agents of the Everv-cry looking for me." She barely changed the name of her foe in time, and was pleased when the icy fingers of the binding were only a fleeting warning about her throat.

"People come for miles for the healing spring water of our falls," the matriarch said. "You should sample them while we wait for a response. If that is what the grand matriarch thinks best, then that is what I will ensure happens. But rest here first—it should only be a few days before we receive a response."

Soothed by the words, Larissa nodded and allowed herself to be led out, Jyan by her side. They were taken deep into the mountainside, but rather than return to the ward or go to their respective knights' and darkkins' halls, they were given a private apartment for visiting dignitaries and sisters of high rank.

Sunlight dappled in from a hole in the ceiling of the cavelike room, which was edged in hanging vines. A hatch with chain lay to one side to cover the skylight in bad weather. The floor was polished to a high gloss, thick carpets in shades of green spread over its surface. A central pool steamed with heat, shallow and crystal clear. To one side was a table and chairs, and farther back a fireplace. Three doors gave way to stone platforms padded with rich furs.

"Please take your ease," their escort said. "I'll bring food and wine and leave it on the table."

"Thank you," Jyan said. "That would be very kind."

The guard nodded and shut the door behind her.

Larissa crossed to the table, taking off her things. The cloak went first, unsalvageable, ripped and muddy as it was. Next her armor, surcoat heavy with moisture. Shrugging it off eased the strain on her shoulders, though grit scraped against her skin. Her boots were harder, coming off with a sucking pop. She almost swooned at the ache that rushed to her feet. Lastly she shed her pants and underthings, rolling all off in one sluggish movement.

Now holding a ball of damp, sweaty clothes, she wondered how she would recover them all. Everything was wet, grimy, ripped, and stained.

She didn't even have a clean shirt to wear as a bathing shift. Her new habit of bathing clothed—thanks to the darkkins—was odd, especially given that Jyan stripped to her skin with no hesitation. But as Larissa stared down at the orb about her neck, the instinct to cover it was strong.

"Forget it, Larissa." Jyan sank naked into the steamy depths of the pool. "Those clothes are only fit to burn."

Larissa agreed, but she still put them to the side to be washed and mended. Forgetting her desire to hide the orb, she padded to the round stones that bordered the pool. Delightfully smooth under her feet, she was glad their glittering gray was not the same as the stones at Still Water.

Taking the steps one at a time, she grimaced as hot water lapped at every scrape and bruise. She sank into the heat, finding it pleasant but odd to have warm water and yet none of the smell she remembered from the halls of the darkkins.

"Do you think she'll make it?" Larissa asked, moments after settling her back against the pool's side.

"Valare's one tough old sow." Jyan rested her head back, eyes sliding shut. "She'll make it and go on cursing you. Either way, we can't help her now."

Larissa stared into the water, lost as to where to go from here. Even if Valare survived, she might not be fit to travel, and Larissa couldn't ask Jyan to go with her. She'd have to await other orders from Navus.

She also had a sinking suspicion that Navus would be most displeased at what had happened. Perhaps even blame her for it, after such a trial was placed before her and it went awry from the outset. She'd only ever wanted to find her mother, but now she wondered if the cost to see her would be too high.

A hand shook her shoulder.

"Larissa, wake up." Jyan was by the pool's side, wrapped in beige cloth. "Get out of the water before you drown, you idiot."

Larissa had lost time soaking in the warm water, oblivious to all about her. Someone had delivered her saddlebags in the meantime, and a tray of roast fish, fresh greens, and a flagon of wine waited on the table.

Picking up a nearby pumice stone, she rubbed away the remains of dirt that still marked her skin. From her feet and ankles to her waist and hands, from her chest up to her neck, where the orb still hung, and from the base of her skull through her thick hair. She let the long ends trail through the water, rinsing them clean.

Jyan held out an identical beige robe for Larissa, who crossed the pool and took it, stepping out onto the wet stone. Jyan tugged a lever on the wall and a stone hatch rose, allowing the water to wash down a drain.

Larissa sat at the table, barely feeling the chair beneath her and wanting nothing more than to crawl into the furs of her bed and rest her head. But she set about placing two servings of the fish and greens. She handed a plate to Jyan as her friend sat across from her, and they ate in silence.

The same fatigue had sunk into Jyan's face, twin bluish crescent moons beneath her eyes. Larissa wanted to ask if all was well, but her jaw could only chew the food—no words would come.

The fish's white flesh melted on her tongue. The greens had a satisfying crunch. But all of it meant nothing to her as she ate, lost in her haze.

"Sleep, Larissa," Jyan said. "You look like the dead."

Larissa rose to head to her bedchamber. "I think I am."

She didn't remember getting to the bed, lying in the furs, or that Jyan lifted them to cover her, but as she fell onto the mattress, the orb tumbled out of her shirt front. Her exhaustion was so heavy that she cried out but couldn't lift her arms.

Then Jyan was there, not touching but taking up the chain and slipping it back inside. Away. Safe. Hidden.

For now.

# Chapter 15

Larissa woke with a wolf's cry in her ears and a snowy chill on her skin, so tangible she shivered. She had to go, she had to run, to follow, to find the wolf...

She shot upright, the near dark confusing her for a moment, before she heard the distant rushing water. Scythia. They'd made it.

Hand over her heart, she stared about, the howl dying to be replaced by Jyan's voice, talking to someone in the antechamber.

Even sitting, Larissa's whole body ached, like a too taut bow ready to snap at the wrong movement. She ached. Her hesitant steps out of bed better suited an old woman. In nothing but a shift, she searched the room for something to cover herself and found a beige robe as well as her saddlebags.

She retrieved clean leather pants and a shirt. The orb swung about her neck, and she tucked it back beneath her clothes before leaving the room.

Jyan sat at the table, the matriarch of Scythia beside her. The matriarch's blonde hair, crystalline eyes, and benevolence were a far cry from the distant head of their sisterhood. However, despite being miles apart, they carried a similar coolness.

"Ah, Darkkin Westwyn, you're awake." Matriarch Yaris rose from her seat. "How do you feel?"

"Sore," Larissa answered succinctly. "How fares Valare?"

"Knight-Solaris Atticus is stable." The matriarch gripped her chair. Jyan's gaze darted to her, and Larissa did not like the way it narrowed.

"What does that mean?" she pushed. "Is the poison still in her?"

"No. But it sapped her of her vitality. We're waiting to see if it will pass or be permanent."

Larissa turned her troubled gaze to Jyan, who bit her lip.

"She's unconscious, Larissa. She won't wake up."

"I need to see her." Larissa headed to the door, but the matriarch stood in her path.

"I think you two need rest." She placed a hand on Larissa's shoulder. Comforting as the gesture was, Larissa almost groaned at the weight of a palm on her aching limb. "You've been through much, and the grand matriarch has already sent word that she needs to consider how we progress from here. You are to await her instructions, which should give you ample time to recover."

She sounded caring. But a pit of fear built in Larissa's gut, twisting like a venomous snake.

"That's good to hear." Larissa spoke the words, but she didn't feel them. "I think we'd like to see Valare now."

The crow's feet about the matriarch's eyes tightened. "I'm sure if she was awake, she'd like that."

"We'd still like to see her," Larissa pressed, unsure why they were being dissuaded.

"Of course. The guard outside will direct you." Yaris rose and left their chambers without another word. Larissa stared at her friend.

Jyan shrugged. "They've been posted out there since last night."

"Why? Do they think the orb—"

Jyan's flat stare made her stop.

"Me." Larissa's chin dropped to her chest. "They're there for me, aren't they?"

"You used magic." Jyan's soft voice didn't allay Larissa's guilt. "It doesn't matter to them that you saved our lives—you broke a cardinal rule. Even darkkins don't use magic the way you do."

A deep foreboding grew within Larissa. The howl she'd awoken with echoed again, rising with every octave of Jyan's gentle truth. "I wouldn't have done it if it wasn't called for."

Jyan shut her eyes and took a breath deep enough to lift her shoulders, before her eyes snapped open. "I know that now, and I'm sorry I didn't then—but I don't like how much I still don't know."

Larissa swallowed, the lump in her throat refusing to be dislodged. "Thank you. I can't explain yet, but I will. I just... There's something I must do, and I'm not sure the sisters here will help me."

It was a hidden fear, one Larissa only grasped as she said it aloud. Her deep misgiving since she'd first set out had solidified. If she couldn't talk about the orb's purpose, she couldn't explain to anyone how important it was; the grand matriarch's binding was both a safety measure and a gag. She needed to be free of it, to explain how important it was she get to her mother. Even if it meant foregoing her oath.

And even if it would take magic to unmake it.

Jyan stared at her, and for a moment Larissa feared her refusal to help.

"I don't need to be a darkkin to know when I hear lies." Jyan shrugged on a coat, covering the twin blades at her hips. "Something about Yaris doesn't sit well with me."

Larissa's shoulders dropped in relief, but she had to be sure. "You don't think we can trust our fellow sisters?"

Jyan grimaced. "Not when they set guards on us. And I'm

only here until my time is served. You well know I have other duties beyond the sisterhood of the Fair Lady."

Larissa paused. "But you risk much to aid me, and you don't know what I intend."

"I know the difference between right and wrong, and I learned it long before joining the sisterhood." Jyan waited by the door. "I don't like the way they talk to us. Like we're naïve children. In my experience, that only means they're hiding what they don't want us to know."

Larissa took a deep breath, speaking with care in every word. "I understand their caution, but that isn't going to help my mother. And if I don't get this to her, something much worse may very well happen."

Her voice quavered, and she hated the way it sounded. But it was true; Navus's secrets sat ill with her, now more than ever.

Stone entered Jyan's voice. Hard, uncompromising, unflinching. "You are bound by magics I don't understand. But that isn't my fight, it's yours. At Still Water, you saved us. You could have used magic at the docks against the brigands too, I'd wager, but I'd pay a higher bet still you warranted it was too dangerous. You only did it when you had to, and we'd be dead without it."

The guilt compressing Larissa's chest eased under Jyan's words. "I could only use it when I *knew* it was safe."

"Then you made the right call." Jyan's hands settled on her shoulders. "And you need to stop questioning that. We need to get you to your mother. *That's* the quest."

Renewed determination filled her, and Larissa went to her own saddlebags. She dug through her things and found one knife, but not the one she sought.

The elemental dagger was gone.

She tied her one remaining dagger under her cloak, along with her thin sword.

"They took my dagger," she said as she returned to the main room. "The one the darkkins gave to me."

"The fire one?"

"It's more than fire. It's all the elements, and it was by my belt that I left on the table out here. Someone has taken it."

Jyan's eyes slid to the door. "We need to be very careful."

"We need to check on Valare," Larissa answered.

They collected their coats and made their way to the hospital. Neither were unaware of the subtle eye of guards as they passed through the halls. They were being monitored; not because of the orb or its power, but because Larissa had done the unforgivable. She'd used magic.

It was one thing to use the tools of the darkkin to grant escape, another to use it as an active weapon. Larissa crossed that line, one she'd wandered the edge of too often, and her previous exhaustion gave way to her confession.

Yaris must fear what easy aptitude one so young exerted over their enemy's power. And Larissa, once convinced she needed it, hadn't thought twice about her easy use of a forbidden gift.

But in Valare's sickbed there was hope.

"Where have you two been?" Valare grumbled from her prone position, glaring at every nurse that came within snarling distance. "They made me eat *gruel*."

Sickness had reduced the bronzed knight to an ashen paleness, but in her eyes glimmered her usual tenacity. Larissa held herself still. If Valare wasn't in danger, why had Yaris warned them to stay away? Told them she was in a coma, when here she was, whole, hearty, and infinitely herself?

"You're awake." Jyan's relief was met with a frown, but Larissa understood her confusion.

"I am glad you are well, Knight-Solaris Atticus." Larissa hoped her formal tone would warn Valare of eavesdroppers.

There was a sardonic lift to Valare's brow before she answered with a weary sigh. "And I you, Darkkin Westwyn."

"We are to rest and await the grand matriarch's instruction."

The brow rose further. "Are we, now..."

Her gaze swept over the other sickbeds, some divided by

curtains of yellow. There was a breakfast hour bustle in the ward. Valare sneered in disgust before she flung back her covers, and though she shuddered, she got to her feet.

"I'll recover best with a decent meal, a hot bath, and just a few more hours' sleep."

Larissa almost sighed in relief. "That, at least, we can arrange."

Valare trembled on shaky legs, waving away offers of assistance but accepting the coat Larissa flung about her shoulders.

"Jyan." Valare gestured toward the end of the bed and Jyan obliged, grabbing Valare's sword and handing it to her.

Using it as a cane, Valare walked out of the ward, Larissa and Jyan flanking her sides. Only a slight limp and sheen to Valare's skin betrayed the fact that she'd almost died of poison. There were a few sisters about, and though one hesitated, her mouth open, they backed off under the trio's glare.

"You recover fast," Larissa murmured as they entered the corridor beyond. She kept one hand beneath Valare's elbow, ready to support her if she needed it.

"Good constitution." Valare's sidelong glance at the guards was as sharp as ever. "Is there something I should be aware of?"

"They think me a danger."

Valare stopped, and Jyan nearly ran into her. She gave Valare's hip a swat.

"If you need me to carry your fat ass, you'll have to let me find a trolley first."

Valare swiped at the other knight, who danced out of reach. But Valare took the hint, uttering no more questions until they'd sat with food in one of Scythia's eating halls. The same long tables were found at Lathore, but here the view displayed an underground waterfall into a river, where laundry was processed. The soft scents of elusive florals mixed with citrus from the kitchen's baked fish. Larissa joined Jyan in a respite of fish and sautéed spinach, whilst Valare wolfed down eggs, bacon, and at special request, a steak.

"That," she announced after her plate was clear, "was exactly what I needed."

True to her word, a healthy glow had returned to Valare's skin. Her voice softened as she scanned Larissa's face. "Now tell me why you're both armed in what should be a safe haven."

"I told Matriarch Yaris how we escaped Still Water," Larissa said. "That I used magic. They have guards outside our room now."

Valare wiped her hands with a napkin. "We're among our sisters, Westwyn. We're safe here."

"Is that why they stole the elemental dagger from me?" Larissa whispered.

Valare scowled at her. "You could have dropped it during the battle—"

"I used it to make the fire that saved your life."

Valare paused at that, hand clenching on the wooden table. "Have we word from Lathore?"

Larissa glanced at Jyan, who shrugged and said, "The grand matriarch told us to await further instructions here."

"I don't think we can wait." Larissa rubbed her brow. "My mother is running out of time. If we don't end this evercry with her, it may become much worse than we can fear, worse than I can tell you."

Valare's gaze dropped to Larissa's throat, the place where Navus's spell kept Larissa bound. "That appears a perilous path."

"Not after you know what I know." The howls of Larissa's nightmares still echoed inside her skull. "I can prove that this is what needs to be done, but not without breaking this...curse, and finding out where my mother has gone."

"Don't do anything foolish," Valare said. "As your knight, I cannot let any harm befall you. You must not do this alone."

"I'm not leaving you." No one was more surprised by Larissa's vehemence than herself. She ignored their astonishment,

Valare's fading frown and Jyan's widened eyes. "We set out together, we'll finish this together. That is...if you want."

She held Valare's gaze, jaw tight, a host of excuses, apologies, and hard-learned lessons on the tip of her tongue, but she kept silent. She wouldn't fall into any petulant sulk. The corner of Valare's mouth tugged into a smile, and she held out her hand across the table.

"I'm with you, Westwyn. Until it is done."

She took Larissa's arm, shaking as she would a sister-in-arms. Jyan stretched out, her hand over their grip on one another.

"Me too. To uphold our friendship, and Keladros's promise to protect you."

"So," Valare said. "What's our plan?"

Larissa let go. "I need to see the darkkins."

"Why? For magic?"

Larissa scowled at the distaste in Valare's voice. "I can't find my mother without help, and I can't talk to anyone about it with this binding. I have to break it."

It was more than a desire to sever the bondage of Navus's spell. Last eve's nightmares compelled her to travel. Not to the south, where the body of the darkkin lay and possibly a trail leading to her mother. The wolf's subtle call had grown, urging her north with no reason or purpose—all, she suspected, from the orb. North may be where she'd find her mother, and certainly the Evervast.

But she needed a reason greater than the echo of the Evervast to determine her course. Only the darkkins could tell Larissa what might be waiting for her there, and not while she couldn't speak of it.

"I'll be back soon." She rose from the table. "But you more than most understand duty, Valare, and right now I'm doing mine."

Larissa left the dining hall without waiting for Valare's answer. Spying the ever-watchful guards, she pulled the hood over her hair to blend in with the crowd of sisters partaking in breakfast and other daily tasks. She didn't want them to inform Matriarch Yaris of her whereabouts.

She'd seen a few darkkins about in their crimson robes, but she didn't know where their halls lay. If they were anything like the ones at Lathore, they'd be deep underground. Larissa found a secluded corner and, once sure the guards were not on her heels, stretched one hand to the floor, seeking magic.

A tell-tale sensation trickled over her. Scanning the corridor and spotting a set of stairs, she followed it. Magic grew stronger with each level of the caves she descended. Like the city of Lathore, Scythia was a network of tunnels and wings, stone polished from eons of passing feet. Windows were carved to the outside, many an opening hidden by waterfalls or verdant growth that shrouded the halls in coolness.

Larissa turned down corridors on instinct, following the distant tug in her mind.

Down a spiraling staircase she found a set of doors, and from the nuanced spell work in their architraves, she knew she'd found the right place. Rather than knock, she shoved the heavy doors apart. Like an overeager lover she had yet to experience, the magic of the darkkins ghosted her lips with a kiss, welcomed her with open arms, and filled her with a sense of purpose as she crossed the threshold.

She was where she belonged, and she remained untainted.

A domed roof towered above, shafts of sunlight filtering through cracks like an illuminated spider's web. They shone on a pale limestone athenaeum—circular, unlike the square one at Lathore. A ring surrounded the sunken study area, curtained doorways on its upper edge hiding what lay beyond. Two narrow waterfalls cascaded down the end of the seated rows to reach a deep pool in the center, flowing around a map.

A wide circle made of colored sand, the map was far more real than the simple leather one at Lathore. Patches of black marked places the Evercry might be. Her eyes trailed to the northwest, but there was nothing.

That didn't mean the Evervast wasn't there.

Larissa closed the doors behind her and swept the hood from her head. All turned to her, and she recognized the look.

Scarred. Hard. Keeping secrets no other sister knew.

"Darkkins," she said with a bow, relishing their name as she would a candied apple, "I need your help."

"And who are you?" One woman came forward, dressed as a knight but with the surcoat of a darkkin-thane.

"Darkkin Westwyn," she said. "I wish to speak to the darkkins' matriarch of Scythia, as she is the voice of Matriarch Theras, and thus I seek her counsel."

An older woman came from behind a curtain. Her dark eyes studied Larissa. Long brown hair threaded gray, she wore the heavy mantle of silver—one who had assisted in the slaying of an evercry.

Larissa crossed to her, shoving aside the sleeve of her robe to proffer the ring, the blessing of the Fair Lady that Theras had given her.

"Matriarch Theras bequeathed this to me." She lifted her eyes and stared at the matriarch. "It has not fallen from my hands."

Hidden in her words was a message, one she hoped the darkkin matriarch understood. She wasn't tainted, she hadn't fallen, she was still one of them. Between the ring and entering the halls, she had proven it beyond question, but she wanted to be sure.

The matriarch looked at the ring, the moonstone within, and though the sister beside her sighed at the sight of it, she did not move.

"Theras sent word you might end up here," she said. "And said I was to offer you what help I could."

Larissa's shoulders slumped in relief. "I would speak privately."

The matriarch nodded and gestured for Larissa to go with

her.

She was ushered down one of the curtain-lined corridors to the matriarch's private study, a pale marble room with the smooth wooden furniture of Scythia. Light reflected from bronze plates behind candles, flickering over texts that lined three walls.

"I know who you are, Darkkin Westwyn," the matriarch said. "Please call me Matriarch Leovyn."

"I need your help," Larissa said, foregoing pleasantries.

"Ask."

"I'm trapped by a binding," she said. "I need to break it. I must find out a truth that I can't on my own. Not while agents of the Evercry seek me out, and the Writhing Dark doesn't strike me down."

At this, Leovyn's hand fluttered to her chest, and she stared at Larissa with apprehension.

"What is it you carry beneath your shirt?" she asked, astute as any darkkin.

Larissa reached for the chain but stopped at the last moment. "I promise to show you, but first you must promise to help me, so I can find my mother."

For the longest moment, Leovyn gazed at her, and Larissa feared she would refuse. If Matriarch Yaris wanted her to stay here, then the matriarch of the darkkins might not help her. But if the ring was as true as Theras had promised, then she should be able to count on Leovyn's aid.

Leovyn slumped behind her desk. As though she carried a weight Larissa couldn't see. "I accept, though I hope you know what you ask...and what it may cost."

Larissa thought on her night terrors, growing stronger every day. On her fear that she was falling under the Evervast's sway.

"I do."

# Chapter 16

"This isn't right."

Larissa cursed Valare for the third time in as many minutes as the knight hesitated once more.

"I don't give a Lady's lock what you damn well think, Valare," she snapped, free to speak her mind in the safety of their apartment. "This is about my mother, it's about the Fair Lady, and it's *important*."

"Going against the grand matriarch's wishes is *not* the way," Valare said.

"I'm not asking you for permission." Larissa scowled, crossing her arms. "I'm asking for your help."

"That's right, Darkkin," Jyan said. "Raise your voice so all of Scythia can hear your secret plan."

Larissa ran a hand through her hair.

It took a day, but Leovyn had found a spell to break the binding. However, Larissa would need to share the burden of the spell's passing. Leovyn's instructions told Larissa to meet her later that evening, even volunteering a fellow darkkin for the ritual. Larissa almost accepted, and yet...

She could only ask someone willing to risk their life for her. And with Jyan's familial obligations, that left Valare.

"I swore I would help you," Valare hissed. "But this isn't the same, and you know it."

"I'd be happy to take your place, Valare," Jyan said, "but you're the one who was assigned to escort her."

"It's one thing to adhere to the mission and another to use magic for no good reason. That way lies the Evercry."

Larissa snorted. "And without doing this I can't prove to you *why* it's vital to break the binding. Don't you *want* to know?"

Valare's gaze dropped to Larissa's shirtfront, before she turned away. "Maybe we aren't meant to."

Larissa crossed to the window, glaring out at the rain. A storm had settled over the valley, and it doused any hope Larissa had of leaving. The roads were washed out, the river flooding. Many of Scythia's sacred pools were unusable due to an overabundance of water. Even so, the biggest impediment of all wasn't the Tehnir bursting its banks but Valare's stubbornness.

Larissa needed to see this done, sooner rather than later.

The wolf inside would not wait.

She went to Valare's side and dropped onto a stool, head hanging, unable to look Valare in the eye. "Do you remember the day you almost killed me?"

Jyan took a quick indrawn breath. Valare's body became still as stone.

"The blade you buried inside me," Larissa choked out, hating the weakness of her voice she was powerless to stop. "From ribcage to hip bone. I still touch the scar sometimes. I have a confession for you...it was no accident."

The room fell deathly silent.

All three were there on the day. Larissa and Valare had been paired against each other yet again, and Larissa found there was no fight left, not even for defense.

"It *was* an accident." Valare's hands clenched on her knees.

"I was so angry, but I never meant to hurt—" She stopped, teeth grinding.

Larissa laughed, even as her vision blurred. Valare stopped, brow furrowing in confusion at Larissa's bitter cackle.

"Always the arrogance," Larissa whispered. "Valare, I let my guard down on purpose." Valare's chin jerked up, and Larissa gave her a cynical grin. "You *hated* me. I never blamed you for that, for all I couldn't be. I made a choice for us both." She shrugged, the confession stealing a weight from her chest.

Valare bit her lip, looking anywhere but at Larissa. "No. Don't be stupid—"

"You know it's true," Larissa said. "I wasn't a swordswoman, I wasn't a knight, I would never be your blooded sister the way you wanted me to."

Valare sat back, chest rising and falling. "I never...I never wanted you to die."

Bile built on Larissa's tongue. The bitter irony had come too late. "And I never wanted to kill. But that doesn't make me weak. I might not be able to slay another, but I know magic. I've resisted it before." Larissa laid her hand on her robe, over the orb. "Yet with this, every night my resistance wanes."

Valare's eyes narrowed. "What spellcraft is this?"

"I can't tell you the circumstances." Larissa didn't flinch at Valare's hardening stare. "But my mother needs my help. She needs me and what I carry."

Valare scuffed her foot against the floor, then cleared her throat. "What do I need to do?"

"I need your trust."

Clasping her wounded leg, Valare rose from her chair. Her gaze darted over Larissa's face, but what she searched for, Larissa didn't know.

"You have it, Larissa."

Larissa fought not to close her eyes in relief. "Thank you."

"I'm going with you," Jyan said as they headed to the door. She exchanged a meaningful glance with Larissa. "Just to be sure."

The trio snuck through the midnight halls of the city and down into the heart of Scythia. When they arrived at the place Leovyn had chosen, Larissa knocked softly. The door opened. Leovyn huffed when she saw not two but three of them, though she didn't refuse them entry. She stood away from the storeroom's door to let them in. Supplies of linen and old furniture were pushed against the walls to allow a table in the center of the room, two chairs on either side.

"Why here?" Valare asked.

"They cannot disturb us here, and none will overhear." Leovyn ushered them in and checked the corridor before closing the door. Muttering under her breath, she drew a rune over it, one Larissa recognized. No one who listened through the door would hear anything, and no one could enter without breaking Leovyn's seal.

"I don't have to remind you how unorthodox this all is," Leovyn said, laying several candles on the table and pouring out a salt circle.

"No, you don't, but thank you." Larissa sat in a chair, arm outstretched.

Valare dropped herself down with a grimace into the seat across from Larissa.

"Your arm, Knight-Solaris," Larissa said, hoping the reminder of her title would overcome the knight's hesitation. Valare sighed and tugged the laces of her leather tunic to reveal her forearm.

Leovyn returned to the table carrying a thin dagger and a pestle of ground herbs, their scent aromatic and evocative of what was to come. "Are both of you ready and willing for the battle before you?"

"Yes," Larissa said, arm already bared.

Valare placed her wrist alongside Larissa's until their skin touched. Valare's skin hot against Larissa's cooler own, wrists level with each other's elbows, palms facing upward.

"For my sister," Valare said.

"Wait for the moment that you connect," Leovyn said, "and then think of the orb, Darkkin Westwyn. See before you not your ally and sister, but the grand matriarch, and your confessor. Remember the story, remember its truth, and your knight-solaris will see it through your eyes. Once shared, once weakened, the binding can be broken."

The blade in Leovyn's hands struck out and sliced down the inside of Larissa's exposed forearm. It hurt but she didn't move, blood welling out sluggishly to spill down her arm into the circle.

Leovyn painted the open wound with the pestle's concoction. It may as well have been lemons from the vicious sting, but Larissa focused on the scent. Moonslips and merryweather, thick herbs and a hallucinogen. It would give her the sight she needed to return to her memory of the binding. For Valare to share in her vision.

"Do you promise to take your sister's secret into your keeping?" Leovyn intoned to Valare.

"Yes." The blade flicked over Valare's wrist, and Leovyn coated the wound in herbs.

"Look to your darkkin. Trust in her, see her confession, so she can share the binding and break the bond not of her making."

Valare pressed her open wound onto Larissa's, forearm to forearm, and they clutched one another, blood and herbs intermingling across the dusty table's surface.

Dark stone walls spun in Larissa's vision, the herbs at work. Leovyn muttered an incantation. The magic expanded between her and Valare, opening a path between them—not a door, but a flower whose petals unfurled.

Valare was there, a sudden silent passenger in Larissa's mind. A tight ball of duty and honor that held secrets of its own.

Larissa ignored it to focus on her own path, swimming through her memories until she was once more inside Navus's chambers. The books on the wall, the map of the world, and the view to the Descent beyond. Navus sitting at her desk, telling

Larissa the secret she could not repeat.

But rather than focus on what Navus said, Larissa's head turned without her volition to the figure at the end of the desk.

To Matriarch Atticus.

Beyond the memories, Valare gasped. The vision shifted.

Spinning, Larissa was flung out of the study and into the darkness of a private room. Different from her mother's sparseness, or Jyan's luxury, the rooms were uncluttered but opulent in their furnishings.

Larissa grasped the edge of a wide desk. It was not her hands on the table, but the wide tanned hands of Valare, trembling where they clutched the wooden lip. These were Valare's memories, and Larissa didn't know the way out.

Behind her, there was a whispering softness in the air, before the crack of a lash.

It landed with such a snap that Larissa's breath left her, and she forgot everything but the pain.

"*What have you learned about hardship?*"

Larissa tasted blood on her tongue from a bitten lip, teeth clenched tight to keep from crying out. Her throat—Valare's throat—constricted.

"*You will never be ready for battle as long as you have never had to endure.*"

The lash stung, cracking across her bare back.

"*You are the shield of your order, and you* will *learn to bear the burden of that responsibility.*"

The whimper changed, became a roar, and Valare's voice echoed in the distance.

"Free me from this!"

But try as Larissa might, Valare had trapped her in the painful memory. Valare controlled the vision, swamped in magic she hadn't trained against, falling out of control from her fear.

Valare screamed. "This is wrong, this is the path of the Evercry!"

But she'd revealed the darkness inside of herself.

She was afraid.

"Valare!" Larissa shrieked, scrambling to bring the knight back to their purpose. "Focus on me."

"I can't!" Her wretched sob was nothing like the indomitable knight.

"You must." Larissa forgot the whip, ignored the pain, able to bear it for both of them. "We cannot fail in this."

"I can't do it..." The whip snapped again, and they both cried out.

"Please," Larissa begged, "trust me."

She fought to return to the room, the memory of the sacred pool, hoping to ignite Valare's devotion. But the sight of the holiest of their order was the last straw.

Valare severed the connection.

She let go of Larissa and fell to the floor, free hand pressed to her wound. Larissa was left to bleed on the table, arm outstretched to her knight.

"Valare," Larissa whispered, desperate, despite what she knew to be true.

Valare would not help her.

"No," Leovyn said, voice panicked, "this should not happen, the knight should protect her darkkin."

Larissa panted, trying to find the right vision, spinning between the Pool of Tears and the lash. If Valare wasn't there, she had to try to do it herself, or bleed to death.

Larissa gathered her will, took a steadying breath, and focused on the binding itself. Unaware of her intent until now, it rushed to the surface of her skin, ready to suffocate her as she thought of the orb's true symbolism.

The tight fingers about her neck rose, clenching her jaw and cheeks to cover her mouth, seeking entrance. Larissa cried out in pain, trying to close her teeth around the invisible intrusion that parted her lips. She bit down on the hand, but it only bloodied the fingers that shoved past her teeth and fed into her throat.

She shrieked for help. Leovyn yelled something Larissa couldn't hear over the pounding in her ears. Valare stared at her, jaw agape, backing away and shaking her head.

Larissa lay across the table, her mouth wide, lips splitting as the binding forced itself between her jaws and began pumping water into her, cutting off her breathing. Blood and water filled her stomach, a copper tang coating her throat as her free arm scrabbled at her mouth.

"You useless whore's spawn!" Jyan kicked Valare's chair out of the way and grabbed the blade from Leovyn's hand. She sliced her wrist open with barely a grunt. She snatched the pestle and poured the concoction over her arm, then slapped it down on Larissa's own, grasping forearm to forearm.

"I," Jyan's voice echoed, disembodied by magic, "*Jyan of Kahnirar, Kaur to the Kahniran throne, knight of the Fair Lady, take the darkkin's confession as my own.*"

Power surged from Larissa into Jyan. The hand down her throat vanished, and she vomited onto the table between them, coating their arms in blood and water.

Larissa thrust herself back into the vision before the hand could return, tucking the orb beneath her shirt as she felt it stir, responding to the magic. The bright flame of Jyan's mind was beside her as she sped to Navus's chambers. To her confession.

*There were evercrys that would not die.*

The whole story spilled out into Jyan, and so too did the binding. Jyan gasped, but the binding moved on. Across two people, it lost its strength. Larissa, to counter its water basis, called the element of fire into her mind, to burn the tail ends trying to sink into Jyan.

"*Areksis, arnos fritos!*" The spell flickered before it caught the binding. The pairing of blood acted as a conduit, and it burned the binding to nothing, becoming a physical manifestation as it reached their cuts.

Jyan cried out, but she held tight to Larissa's arm as they burned together. The spell sank into their exposed wounds, breaking their grip, sealing their cuts with a scar. Larissa slumped back in her chair and clutched her arm to her chest, panting through the agony.

Across from her, Jyan fell face first onto the table, before slipping off the edge. Larissa scattered candles as she lunged for Jyan, falling to the floor on hands and knees. She crawled over the stones, arms barely able to hold her weight. But Valare was already there, supporting Jyan to sit upright. Valare locked eyes with Larissa, the wrong secret shimmering between them.

Valare was the first to look away. Larissa ignored her to focus on the wide-eyed Jyan, who grasped for Larissa's hand with her unscarred arm. Larissa took it, held it tight.

"It's a lie," she whispered. "You were hiding the greatest lie they ever told."

Larissa took a deep breath. "I know, and this isn't over. But...thank you."

Jyan's eyes closed even as she gave a weak grin. Valare held her steady, so Larissa rose on shaky feet. She turned to Matriarch Leovyn.

"I can't thank you enough," she began.

"Go," Leovyn said. "I'll clean all this up. You must rest or you won't be strong enough to travel."

"This can't wait," Larissa insisted. "I'm not sure of our heading."

Leovyn paused, a hand raised to dismiss Larissa, but her weathered fingers curled into her palm. "Very well, tell me."

Larissa talked in hushed murmurs. She watched Leovyn's face change as she imparted her family's history, from pursed lips as Larissa divulged the darkest truths of the Evercry's nature, then to narrowed eyes of disavowal upon hearing of the existence of the Evervast. Larissa thought she might need to prove it, but then Leovyn closed her eyes.

When they reopened, they focused sharply on Larissa.

"I know what you need, and how to give it to you," she whispered. "It will guide you on your trip north."

Hope sparked in Larissa's chest. "How do you know I need to go north?"

Leovyn sighed, as though sorry for what she was about to do. "One of your great-grandmother's darkkins was from Scythia. I have her journal in my private library. I can give it to you."

Leovyn had the journal Navus had mentioned at the start of Larissa's journey. The one that told of Dothreal's quest.

"Thank you, for everything you've done—"

"You must leave tomorrow morning at the latest."

The fleeting blossom of hope in Larissa's breast withered. "Why?"

"Knights have been sent from Lathore. They come to escort the orb back to the safety of the city, where the grand matriarch has decreed it will be destroyed."

"But when—"

"Matriarch Yaris convened a council at lunch to warn us, but by then I'd already promised you my aid, and I couldn't take it back." Leovyn sighed. Guilt twisted within Larissa, but before she could apologize, Leovyn continued, "I think Theras sent a bird not long after the decision—it arrived shortly after the meeting. I did not know the details, only that the artifact you carried needed to be destroyed."

Larissa shook her head. "The orb is just a binding. If they break it, they release the echo. They will make the Evervast stronger."

"I agree with you." Leovyn grasped Larissa's shoulder. "I'll arrange for a boat to take you safely out of Scythia at dawn, so go, pack your things and rest. Meet me next morn at the far western docks."

Larissa embraced Leovyn. "I will. Thank you."

She crossed to Valare and Jyan, and though Valare didn't meet her gaze, the pair got Jyan to her feet. They stumbled back to their quarters, just an hour or so after they'd left. The guards gave them confused looks, and Larissa fought to think of a reason for their condition.

"This one." Valare poked Jyan. "Can't hold her wine."

One guard chuckled, and the other opened the door. Once they were inside, the door shut behind them.

Larissa went to the side cabinet to grab a goblet of wine for Jyan, along with a platter of fruit. After a moment, she snatched a goblet for herself and the jug for good measure.

"You read my mind," Jyan said, plopping herself down on a seat.

"No." Larissa grimaced. "Just your habits."

Valare stalked past them to the washbasin, where she scrubbed the potion from her wound.

Jyan tugged Larissa to sit beside her and held out her hand. Even without words, Larissa knew what she wanted. She took out the orb and handed it over, not letting go of the chain. The orb fell into Jyan's palm. She twisted it between nimble fingers.

"The echo of an evercry…"

Jyan only whispered it, but Valare turned as she finished a binding about her forearm. "Is that what that thing is?" she asked, glancing between them.

"It's part of a knight's song," Jyan explained, examining the orb. "Larissa's great-grandmother heard an evercry, but when she slayed it, the song remained. She bound it with magic to get it out of her head. Now Larissa's mother has heard the same evercry… It has a name, too. An evercry that's come again—the Evervast."

Valare's cheeks grew a shade closer to when she'd been poisoned by the Writhing Dark. "That's not possible."

"But it is." Larissa tugged the orb from Jyan's fingers, slipping it beneath her shirt. "The orb must be carried by a direct blood descendant to Dothreal, and so it falls to me, but so too does it call me. I hear it when I sleep now."

"An evercry is a possession from an old and dark god." Valare strode to the table and glared at Larissa. "A fragment of chaos—nothing more or less."

"What did you think this was about, Valare?" Fatigue and

irritation drove Larissa on. "Did you think it was for nothing that they bound me?"

"What you're saying goes against every credence of our order, and you expect me to believe you?"

"I already know how little to expect of you...Atticus."

Valare jerked back as though struck, hands curling into fists. "You wanted me to do something that goes against everything they've ever taught me," she snapped. "I'm not infallible, and I do not take kindly to your flippancy toward the grand matriarch's wishes."

"Damn Navus!" Larissa slapped her hand on the table. "I *needed* someone to help me. All I've ever done was push myself to my limits to match you. But where were you when I needed you? Stuff your honor, this was about your pride and fear, and you left me to *die* for it!"

Larissa got up with such a jerk that the cups toppled, wine spilling over the table, staining the cloth. A mark that would never come out, like the words they'd thrown at one another.

"If both of you could just stop for a moment," Jyan said, raising hands to each of them. "What's happening here *might* be more important than your egos. Larissa, you can't go by yourself, don't even consider it because the agents of the Evervast *will* find you, and you won't be able to fight them on your own."

Jyan stated what Larissa least wanted to hear. With her new plans to travel north, Larissa wanted company more than ever.

But not Valare's.

Larissa gathered a napkin to mop up the mess.

Jyan faced the other knight. "I understand that you hate magic, but this isn't about you. It's about the *matriarch of swords*." Every word enunciated slowly, dragged out until Valare's shoulders slumped. "She's trying to slay her evercry, a quest seven years in the making. She hasn't been able to because she needs this fragment of the song. And if our matriarch of swords can't kill it, then who will?"

Larissa cleared her throat. "I'm not going to leave my mother to face it alone. I *will* take the orb to her, as instructed by the grand matriarch. With or without you."

"Oh, so you'll obey her when it suits you, Darkkin? How convenient."

Larissa flung the sopping napkin aside. "You don't even care what happens if I fail, do you?"

"The grand matriarch has changed her mind, and disobeying her now that we know the threat is *wrong*. Perhaps my mother was right not to trust your magic."

A cold certainty settled on Larissa as she stared at Valare. She knew now why Atticus had chosen her daughter to escort Larissa. Understood after all these years the source of Valare's hatred, and who had fed it.

"Your mother was counting on this," she said. "She knew that if push came to shove, you'd let me die, or kill me yourself if you thought I'd succumb to magic. To the Evercry."

Her whispered words doused the heat of anger in Valare's cheeks to nothing but ash. When Valare didn't deny it, Larissa sat back, head reeling, so much of what had passed becoming all too clear to her.

"She didn't send me with a guard. She sent me with an executioner."

Staring at Valare's face, hearing the truth in her silence, Larissa's respect for her sisterhood vanished on the bitter tendrils of betrayal.

Larissa whirled away from the knight and went to her room. Valare followed her and stood in the open door.

"What are you doing?"

"Not staying here," Larissa said, ramming her things into the top of her pack.

"She's going to find her mother," Jyan said from the other room. "And she isn't going alone."

"What?" Valare looked over her shoulder at Jyan, and Larissa gave her friend a weak smile.

"My time as a knight is done," Jyan said. "I've serviced the

Fair Lady to the extent my law requires. Now I can go home, but I'm thinking some sightseeing might be in order first." Jyan went to her room and came out shortly afterward. She dropped a bag outside Larissa's door. Jyan had prepared for this, was ready to leave to join Larissa's cause before Larissa was sure of it herself. She steeled herself against tears of gratitude.

"You can't leave," Valare sputtered.

"Are you going to stop me?" Larissa took a step toward Valare. "Are you going to hinder me *again*?"

"I did what you asked. I went against everything I believed for you, and what did it get me? Nothing. It told you secrets I wasn't willing to share. You aren't the only one with scars, Westwyn. Get off your high fucking horse."

Valare spun on her heel, strode to her room, and slammed the door shut.

The space rang with her angry words, but Valare's speech didn't move Larissa. She'd been inside Valare's mind, and though the torment pained her, Larissa was wounded herself from Valare's betrayal.

"So," Jyan said. "Just you and me?"

"I trust you to keep me alive." Larissa studied Valare's door. "Leovyn's organizing a barge to sneak us out before dawn tomorrow. You know what's at stake, and you're right, I can't do this on my own."

"You say that now..." Jyan teased, but her eyes were fixed on the closed door. "All the same, I can't help feeling we would be better off with her at our side."

Larissa clenched her fist. She couldn't agree more. But she would never say so aloud.

# Chapter 17

Sleep riddled with nightmares, Larissa woke with crimson moons on her palms, covered in sweat, the howl of the wolf still echoing in her ears. She rolled to a sitting position, head in her hands. A glance out the narrow slit of her room showed it was still dark out. Larissa wasn't going back to sleep. Didn't want to with the fear of canines in her dreams. She slipped on her clothes, picked up the pack she'd prepared, and went into the main room.

Jyan waited there, silent. There was no noise from Valare's bedchamber, but Larissa didn't dare stay to find out if she would come.

They left without a word, slinking silently through the city's halls. Ghosting the few guards who strolled down corridors, and even a few drunk sisters, they hurried down to the western docks.

A rough and narrow stone passage opened onto a vast underground cavern, through which flowed part of the Tehlrended, a little-known river that branched from the Tehnir.

The Tehlrended led to the southern dry climes of grapes and olives on warmer coastlands. Though not their destination, it was the best way out of Scythia undetected.

The water was still as a lake. Boats tied to their moorings were ominous shapes in the dark, motionless as the water. The distant walls of the cavern could be mistaken for a starless night.

Larissa crept forward, keeping to the shadows, sneaking from rough stone pillar to pillar, Jyan close behind. They drew near to the wooden docks, Larissa scanning for Leovyn.

"Here," Leovyn whispered, from the gloomy doorway of the dockmaster's shed. She hurried over to them. "The last boat on the end of the pier. The boatmaster will take you to Ithica, far enough away to give you a headstart. Here is the book on your great-grandmother. It talks of going north from Janoir but not beyond—you'll have to work that out yourself. Last is a spear, my own from some time ago. I hear that is your weapon of choice."

"It is." Larissa wrapped one hand around the spear, and squeezed the small volume tight and slipped it in her pack. "Thank you, Matriarch. I owe you a great debt of gratitude."

"You owe me no favor. I was paying one back."

Larissa stilled. Leovyn stared at her, a slight chastisement in her eyes.

"You...you didn't know?" Leovyn said. "My help was never given for you. The ring was a sign of a debt I owed Matriarch Theras."

"I... But why?"

"Theras wouldn't have made such a gesture lightly. She believes what you do is important, and I must pay it the same respect." Leovyn's hands on her own squeezed far too tight for an older woman.

Larissa swallowed past the tightness in her throat. "Thank you even more so, Matriarch."

Leovyn embraced her, then vanished into the tunnels.

Larissa and Jyan crept over the sagging docks, past snoring boatmen on their vessels. Larissa winced at every creak of the old wood beneath her booted feet. But they woke none, crossing to a single lantern at the end of the pier where a vessel sat ready for launch. A young river boatmaster jumped to his feet and waved as he saw them.

"You are the knights with Her Lady Darkkin?" Dark eyes under a mop of long curls surveyed them in earnestness. "Get aboard, then. She said we should leave with great haste."

He left them to board, scurrying to his prow to hang the lantern, a quick and gangly spider with long limbs. He opened a hatch in the floor and gestured for them to hand over their packs.

"What about us?" Jyan said. "We won't fit in there."

"Under the canvas, both of you." He crossed to a stack of barrels and boxes and lifted the covering's edge. Jyan slunk beneath first, Larissa second, the pair scrunched as best they could against the wares. He flung the rough canvas over them and loosely tied it down.

"Wait," Larissa said. "What's your name?"

"Denobe." He secured the ropes.

"I'm Larissa, and this is Jyan."

"Pleased to meet you, but hush now until I say it's safe. I'll not have you risk my livelihood with jaw-flapping."

Chastised, Larissa fell silent as the boatmaster set to work.

They heard his bare feet slap against the deck, a small enough craft it only needed one master. The boat began to sway to the river's undertow as he ferried them out into the current. Larissa listened for any sound over the water, a task made more difficult by the soft noise of Jyan's breathing, her smaller frame cramped further between the boxes. The pace of her breaths quickened the longer they were confined to the tight quarters.

"Lady forsake us," Jyan cursed. "How much longer?"

"I don't know, it's only been a few minutes." Larissa nearly peeked, but there was a *thwack* on the canvas, and she jerked her hand back.

"Don't move," Denobe said. "We're coming past the guard

towers."

His feet appeared beside the canvas, and then his voice called out, melodious and plaintive. "Wake up," he trilled, singing the words. "Oh, sweet tower matron, open your gates for this eager traveler."

There was the noise of wood against wood, a doorway opening.

"I'll not have your nonsense this early in the morning," a woman grumbled at him, her voice older and none too amused. A gatekeeper and knight, Larissa guessed.

"I only wish my freedom to traverse your channel—"

"*That* is quite enough," the knight yelled, her volume increasing as the scrape of wood on stone echoed across the cavern. "I'm old enough to be your mother."

"A mother's milk encourages growth in lads like myself, would you come down and sample my...wine in return."

"I'll take my usual cask of whiskey on your return, Denobe," she chided. "And that is all, be off with you."

"Before it reaches your sister knights? My thanks, sister."

The boat drifted once more down the current, and Larissa watched sunlight creep under her corner of the canvas—weak and gray, it was still early yet, and she disobeyed Denobe to peek beneath the covering.

Square mirrors of water were laid out before her, giant stepping stones leading down to a lake. The river became a series of tiers, each one dropping to another level.

"Since you've done so anyway, you can lift the canvas now, sisters," Denobe said. "I can manage the weirs on my own, but sit at the front and don't move from behind the boxes. To look back is to stare into the Matriarch Yaris's private chambers, and believe you me, she doesn't like it when you do."

Larissa peeled the canvas back far enough she could see ahead, to the water that mirrored the sky, its surface bright with the rising sun.

Denobe leapt off the boat to a rock platform, hauling a great wooden wheel. After turning it, a gate locked into place behind the boat. Denobe ran to the other side and kicked the wedge out of a wheel, and the water drained into the next weir. Another jump and he was back aboard as the gate rose, the water equalizing with the next level. He used a pole to push them forward, and so they descended six more levels.

"This is a feat of engineering," Larissa said, studying the mechanisms.

"It's a nuisance," Denobe said. "But this is the fastest way to get from Scythia to Ithica, where you can take a farmer's road to Janoir."

"It can't be both." Jyan emerged from her cranny far enough to extend her legs. "It's either fast or slow, and we don't wish for slow."

"Aye, I know your urgency. The Matriarch Leovyn fares well by the goods I bring her, and I grow richer on the coin she gives me."

"What do you bring her?" Larissa asked, wary of yet another favor she could not return.

"I bring her olives stuffed with feta, and the sweet wines you sisters so love in place of a good cock."

Larissa's cheeks turned redder than the sun on the distant horizon, while Jyan burst out laughing.

"Who says we have to love something we only occasionally find useful?" she challenged Denobe. Larissa fought the urge to crawl back under the canvas and stuff her ears with cotton wool.

"Do you, Knight?" Denobe stood above the wheelhouse. Larissa looked back to study him properly. He was handsome enough, but he only had eyes for Jyan. "And I thought you only ever chose a man for the purpose of perpetuating your order."

"Tell me what other use he has," Jyan said, giving him her back as she stretched.

"Bringing you wine, peeling your grapes." Denobe's eyes roved over her. "Serving your desires."

"You are an incorrigible flirt. But not a very good one."

"I didn't realize the sister had words other than those of piety and good manners." Denobe clasped his chest. "Alas, the only songs of prose I sigh, are those that venture between maidens' thighs."

"I'm not a maiden," Jyan said, and Larissa looked at her sharply. "What? I won't choose a consort without first knowing what I like in bed sport. Heirs don't come about solely by rutting, or at least good ones."

Larissa began to think there was no blood left in her body for all the heat in her face, a blush spreading from her cheeks up to the tips of her ears.

"Can we..." She struggled for a moment. "...just not talk about this?"

For all his rakish charm, Denobe was silent in the face of Larissa's acute embarrassment. She sat cross-legged on the deck, arms wrapped about her knees, and stared at the horizon. As Denobe worked the weir, Jyan sat next to Larissa.

"You haven't..." Jyan's murmur drifted off.

"When on earth was there time?" Larissa said with exasperation. "What part of not leaving Lathore for the year, or ever, meant I...did that?"

Jyan rolled her lips, giving a slow nod. Her gaze fixed on the leering Denobe, hauling another water wheel. "Do you fancy him?"

Good-looking as he was, Larissa wasn't interested in someone who treated the matter with such sport. Her shoulders came about her ears, and she gave Jyan a slight shake of her head.

"You have other tastes?" Jyan gestured at her own body, more an indication of flavor than an offer, and Larissa's jaw hit the floor.

"That is *not* why I don't want him." She hunched in on herself. "I just...never *thought* about it."

"Not once?"

Larissa shook her head.

"My first time was with a mercenary."

"You paid him for sex?" Larissa said, aghast.

"Do I look like a damn piece of wood to you?" Jyan laughed. "He was a fighter for hire, all muscles and scars. Intense and sultry. I was at an inn with Keladros, and she said have at him, so I did."

It was said with a hint of sadness, and Larissa, sensing a light mood about to be brought low, leaned closer to whisper so the inquisitive ears of Denobe didn't hear her question.

"What...what was it like?"

Jyan looked over her shoulder to check on Denobe, called away by another turn of a weir's wheel, then leaned closer.

"You get...hot." Her fingers drifted to her lip, rubbing back and forth. "All over but especially *there*." Her hand drifted to her nethers for the briefest moment. "If he knows what he's doing." From her smirk, Larissa took it this had been the case with Jyan's mercenary.

Though a women-only order, sisters of the Fair Lady were at least taught the biological function of their womb, a dual purpose to explain their bodies' regulations but also to enforce the idea that a sister should bear daughters for the Fair Lady. They gave sons to whomever the father was, or the mother could leave the sisterhood with her progeny.

"Did it hurt?" Larissa asked.

"A little." Jyan squinted. "But...if you like him and he likes you, then not very much at all. It feels good, it *should* feel good. I think they tell you in school it feels like a dagger so you don't do it too hastily."

Larissa had heard the same stories, and a part of her was still apprehensive.

"If you like, we could find out, fair sister," a sultry voice whispered. Lounging over the roof of the wheelhouse, Denobe blinked his big eyes at her.

Larissa shot to her feet, swinging the bulbous end of her spear to smack him, but he dodged with cat-like reflexes. The spear thudded against the top of the wheelhouse. Denobe laughed, one arm wrapped around the mast, the other saluting her.

"You only had to say no." He leapt across to the stones to lift the last wheel, and then they were spilling out into a lake.

The sun had risen high enough that its golden rays painted the surface of the water liquid silver. Reeds were rendered gray in the early morning light, a fog wrapped about the bank like a lingering lover.

Still ashamed of her ignorance, Larissa went to the prow and sat down to watch as the boat crossed a mirror of the world. Over the prow, she looked down at her reflection, hair hanging in flaxen wreaths about her face. Her hand drifted up to her lips, and she wondered if anyone would ever kiss them. She met her own gaze, doubting what she could offer a man. What kind of man would she take...?

The orb spilled out of her shirt. Her hand shot out to catch it.

It wouldn't have fallen, but the thought sent her heart racing. Longing for the undefinable and the warmth of another's arms wasn't where her thoughts should lay. Stowing the necklace back under the safety of her clothes, she tugged the leather ties at her throat tighter and leaned her head against the figurehead on the prow, letting the smooth wood dig into her cheek, eyes closed against the dawn.

As it grew lighter, she went to her pack for the journal Leovyn had given her.

The thin pages of vellum offered story after story. Her fingers were light as she scanned the pages, searching until she found the account of where her great-grandmother fought the Evervast. Larissa buried her nose as far into the journal as she could, reading the darkkin's notes of her trek to the north.

The tale became frustrating when the darkkin noted their arrival at Janoir, the last trading hub that carried goods to the Western lands. It went against the code for a knight to travel without her darkkin, but she was left behind all the same. Dothreal's reasoning wasn't noted beyond her forbidding the darkkin to attend. Normally, the darkkin wouldn't have to obey a knight, but she did have to adhere to the wishes of the matriarch of swords. The darkkin waited a full week for Dothreal to return. When she did, Dothreal arrived wounded and distracted. Almost afraid. Any inquiry as to what had happened was rebuffed, but the darkkin mentioned a small instance of Dothreal shouting a name during a night terror.

Lisolel.

The word stirred a distant memory. Stories of a once-magic city to the far north. Lisolel was a tale of dark and tragic magic gone awry, a great and ancient chaos. But taken as tall tales, nothing but folklore. Another story to intimidate those tempted by magic.

Her fingers tightened on the book. What did she know of stories? Only that they didn't always tell the truth.

Larissa put the book away to take another from her pack, one with a foldout map. Jyan dropped down beside her.

"Did you find where we need to go?"

"Maybe," Larissa said. "Lisolel. But I thought it wasn't a real city. It was said to be a place of great magic undone by a terrible evercry. The last thing we want is…"

Her voice faded as she came to an awful realization: anywhere that held residual magic would be a tempting place for an evercry to make its home.

"How do we find it?" Jyan asked.

"I'm not sure. It's supposed to be in the north, but where for certain, the diary doesn't say."

"That's where we should go, though, isn't it?"

Larissa's gaze dragged to her right and over her shoulder, toward the north. Wind rippled over the reeds, a lonely tune in their fluted breath. It wasn't the cry of a wolf, but the pitch need only change slightly and it would be there, echoing in her ears, a howl of such longing and despair. The lure to seek its source ate at Larissa's resistance, tearing away chunks. They were headed the wrong way, she knew it in her gut, like she'd known right before the bandits struck. The boat trip would take them away from Scythia before they branched to the road further north to Janoir. Heading in even a slightly different direction left her heart palpitating and stomach queasy.

"Yes, we have to go north."

Jyan pulled the map closer. Her fingers traveled north through the rocky mountains to a distant shore. "There's nothing that way on here. Only high mountains and snow, impassable at this time of year. We could go to Janoir, and then head west for the ports of Eonin. They may have a boat we can take, but we'll need someone to sail it. Does the story say if the city was on the sea?"

"I don't know, but I think it's our best plan for the moment." Larissa lowered the map to stare at Jyan. "If you're sure you still wish to accompany me?"

"Of course." Jyan dropped her end of the map, broad grin in place. "I wouldn't have let you go with just Valare, much less completely alone."

At the reminder of her faithless knight, Larissa scowled. Jyan shook her head. She went to the canvas and stretched out to snooze under the watchful gaze of Denobe.

For much of the morning, their only companions were fog and the soft lapping of water on the prow, for the sun's glow had faded to nothing in the lowland's embrace. When she grew hungry, Larissa returned to her pack. Jyan cut an apple, handing pieces to Denobe, each slice given with an unsavory comment as the two barbed one another.

"How long before we reach Ithica?" Larissa asked as she retrieved her bag.

"Another half a day's journey. We'll be there before dawn tomorrow." Denobe crunched the apple. "But if you like, I could pull this boat over and show you another journey in your very own flora."

"We need to be there by nightfall," Larissa snapped. "And if you could take your genitals out of the equation for more than a few moments, it might garner you extra coin."

Denobe laughed but did as she asked and fetched his stick, rangy arms pushing them faster down the river.

Jyan's eyes roved over him. "Don't be too hasty to rob yourself of the chance to taste someone like Denobe. Men who love women above themselves are a rarity."

"I think if they are, then perhaps you were looking in the wrong places," Larissa huffed, retrieving an apple for herself and biting through the thick skin. Bitter juices filled her mouth.

"You are probably right, Darkkin." Jyan shrugged. "But I already have several princes to choose from when I return home."

Larissa sat back on her heels, unsure how much to ask about Jyan leaving. "Why now?"

"You knew I would one day. Ever since you figured out who I was, what I was hiding from everyone else. There are things in this world that fall outside of the Fair Lady's mandate, and I am one of those things. Just much sooner than I envisioned."

Gone was the manner of a jovial friend. Instead, the princess leaked through.

"You were always determined to tour with the knights for a few years before going home. What changed?" Larissa gently pried.

Jyan took a long time answering, the blade she'd used to carve the apple whittling away at the core. She no longer ate the slices but discarded them in the water.

"I had hoped for more time to become acquainted with the knights," she said, voice so soft and low Larissa kneeled closer to hear her better. "Knight-Solaris Keladros was a different kind of knight. She was a diplomat foremost, and I was stationed with her for a reason. But while I appreciate that some confidences cannot be shared with the people...it makes me angry, too angry, that such a secret was kept from us. Not from me as a knight, but from me as a queen."

Larissa sat back, perceiving the full measure of Jyan's wrath. "What will you do?"

Jyan tossed the core into the bog, eyeing its descent as her fingers curled into a fist. "I will return to Lathore once more, but only to prove I have stood my trials as a knight so I may return to my homeland. The walls of Lathore hold nothing more for me now. I need to go home, and take care of my people. Be sure that my family knows the deception of the Fair Lady's knights so that we move forward with greater hesitation. It isn't to say I distrust them—I only wonder what other secrets they're keeping from us."

There was no deviation in Jyan's path, merely an alteration in her plans.

"I envy you," Larissa said, voice thick with emotion after Jyan's speech. "That there's a place for you to go after this is all over."

Jyan's brow lifted, a curl to her lip banishing the cold countenance from her face. "I'll always need good counsel. And someone to keep me humble."

Larissa scoffed, glad for the lighter turn in conversation. "I'm not experienced enough to give counsel to anyone, let alone to a queen, and I don't believe you could ever be humble."

Jyan laughed. "Perhaps not, but we share something, you and I. And we have since the moment I first laid eyes on you. You were not merely a fellow sister of the Fair Lady. What you were was not only a friend, but an ally for the future. I don't know if finding your mother and giving her the echo is the right thing to do, but you do, which is enough for me."

Jyan extended her hand and Larissa grasped it, forearm to forearm, burn to burn.

"You see what others don't," Jyan said. "The way you used the chains to beat the Empirical hasn't left me, and it never will. You seek outside yourself to find solutions that don't involve violence. You've always thought your worldview a curse, and it's not. It is a blessing, especially for one called to rule."

"Whereas you, friend," Larissa said with a cynical chuckle, throat tight with an inability to accept Jyan's words, "need to learn to solve conflicts without a blade."

"When you deal with thugs like Valare..." Jyan grinned. "Who's to say that doesn't work?"

# Chapter 18

On their river journey, Larissa glanced back more than once toward the mountainside of Scythia, listening over the wind for any horns or bells that signaled her escape, but all was eerily silent. For most of the day she dozed on the deck, as did Jyan, knowing a full night of walking lay ahead of them. Denobe, despite his licentious nature, left them in peace.

Several times during the day, Larissa jerked upright, seeking out a wolf, its howl on the edge of her hearing. The summons was becoming worse; it called to her during the day now, not just in dreams.

Within sight of the evening lanterns of Ithica, Larissa and Jyan had Denobe stop before they reached the town. Made up of wooden walkways and houses on reed-woven rafts, Ithica was a common trading post on the river to Scythia. A huge inn dominated the waterlogged town, built on the only piece of solid land for miles. Though horses would be available, this would leave traces of their passage. Instead they pulled through the reeds to the riverbank, well before the town's lights.

The marshy swamps that surrounded Ithica were full of life. Monstrous crocodiles and large pythons. Fat water cows and bulbous dugong. And fish.

All the fish in the world.

The smell would have been appalling were it not for the round heads of river lotus in bloom, their thick green petals sticking up out of the water. Underneath their pervasively sweet scent was the raw and comforting stench of mud. Thick, and almost creamy with its pale tone, the mud coated Larissa all the way up to her thighs as she and Jyan jumped into the low water, intent on skirting the village.

Larissa hoped it was enough. Given their original goal was Meggaloth, anyone tracking them should believe they'd head further south along the river, and now they were going in the opposite direction.

"My thanks," Larissa said as Denobe handed down her pack.

"And to think, we could have been like this earlier," he said, his crotch almost level with their faces where he stood on the prow. He chortled at Larissa's scowl.

"I'd rather be in here with the crocodiles," Jyan said, adjusting the straps of her own pack.

"Liar."

Jyan returned his grin. "Take care, Denobe."

"And you, sisters."

Denobe pushed his boat back out into the current and headed downriver toward Ithica. Jyan waved as Larissa began the arduous task of slogging through the reeds.

Grimacing, Larissa was glad they'd rested all day. The swamp required hard wading through the muck, while also needing to keep an eye out for floating logs with teeth. Out of the dark came stinging insects, and the pair uttered curses as they trudged past the suffocating smell of the swamp.

Yet it wasn't long before their feet found the road, made of rough stone packed tight enough that the swamp couldn't consume it. Packs shouldered, they started their hike.

The winding road was dark against the pale mud and high reeds that lay to either side. Soon the swamp water and reeds faded to mossy trees that loomed out of the burgeoning fog. They followed the path as it rose into low hills. Near the top, they stopped, exhaustion and mud clinging to them.

"Fair Lady preserve us." Jyan found a thick tree trunk and slumped against it. "I could have finished today with a glass of wine and a bath."

"For the last time," Larissa said, joining her, "you didn't have to come."

"Oh? And let you, a darkkin who barely knows the pointy end of a sword, fall victim to agents of the Evercry? I am not some spineless shrew to sit on the sidelines and criticize when this all goes tits up."

"You know we face one of the darkest evercrys the world has ever known?" Larissa searched her pack and tugged out a wineskin. She tossed it to Jyan, who groaned in relief.

"Evercry or no," Jyan said, unstoppering the wine and taking a long draft, "we will make it to your mother. Between us three, we'll beat it for certain."

"You mean us four," a voice called.

Jyan leapt to her feet, sword drawn, and Larissa hefted her spear. Out of the darkness appeared a familiar face, riding a tall dark horse.

"I may not trust magic," Valare said, getting down from her mount, "but you were wrong on one particular point, Westwyn."

Larissa scanned the trees for the knights undoubtedly come to take them back to Scythia, but as the seconds drew on, she realized Valare was alone. She wasn't even wearing the knights' sigil. Larissa dropped her guard.

"And what point would that be?"

"I do trust *you*." Valare avoided Larissa's gaze. "It's not you that made me falter, it was the magic you stirred between us. I'm not here to bring you back, I'm here to take you to your mother, to fulfill my duty."

Jyan sheathed her sword but scowled. "You were happy to let her die for your fears."

"I was...*wrong*!" Valare said, loud enough her horse tossed its head. "Is that what you want to hear, you smug bitch? I was wrong." Valare's gaze left Jyan to focus on Larissa. Larissa's heart clenched at Valare twisting the reins between her hands, eyes wide and heartbroken. "You called on me for aid and I didn't answer. I will take the burden of failing my darkkin to my grave, and you were *not* the first. But you will be the last."

She came until she stood only an arm's length from Larissa.

"I will do better, Larissa," she said. "I will take you wherever you need to go. I may not agree with magic, but on my honor as a knight, which you know I hold sacred, I won't let you wander alone."

Larissa stared into Valare's midnight eyes, trying to see if this was a trap or a ploy to take them back to Scythia. A part of her didn't want to forgive, but then, Larissa was no less flawed. Valare hated Larissa once for the beatings Larissa never endured. As children, Valare hadn't become cruel until Larissa began to fail. And Larissa wasn't the only one with scars.

She held out her hand. Valare took it. The warmth of her palm eased the chill in Larissa's bones, tension melting at the firmness of Valare's grip, the reassurance. She hadn't known what relief Valare's presence and promise would bring.

"How did you find us?" Larissa asked.

"On foot. I followed the weirs down to the river, found a village, and bought a horse. You'd already said the orb directed you north. I figured the river was a ruse and rode cross-country to intercept you."

"You didn't let anyone know who you were?" Jyan said.

"You can't see it in this half-light," Valare said, "but I'm dressed as a mercenary. I may be honorable—that does not make me stupid."

There was silence for a long moment, before Larissa smiled. "What was it you were saying about mercenaries earlier today,

Jyan?" Her grin broadened with every word. "A fighter for hire, all muscles and scars."

"Fine," Jyan said. "Just don't ask me to sleep with her."

Larissa couldn't hold in her mirth at Jyan's expense, but Valare turned scarlet.

"Why on earth would I sleep with *you*?" she said after several moments, voice frosty and embarrassed. "You aren't even what I like in a woman."

Larissa stopped laughing. Jyan dropped the wine sack.

"What?" Valare held her chin high. "Are both of you too stupid to have realized?"

When neither of them answered, Valare sighed. "My mother doesn't care who I sleep with—all she ever wanted was heirs. As many as I would willingly birth. Who I chose to love was my own affair, as long as I gave her what she wanted. But I'm not about to change that much of myself for her ambition. We have far more in common than you know, Westwyn. I'm a disappointment to my mother too." Valare's voice drifted to softness, and Larissa couldn't find the words to make it better.

"I'm sorry," she said.

"The least you could do is light a fire," Valare grumbled. "It's still freezing, and I haven't eaten all day."

She took her horse through the trees, and after glancing at one another, Larissa and Jyan were quick to catch up. Trudging between the low branches of the forest, Valare found a low dell and tied her horse to a tree.

Larissa sought out firewood, and Jyan cleared a patch of earth for the fire, placing rocks around its edge. There was an odd compatriotism as they each did their tasks, and once done they sat about the fire together.

"Did anyone notice we'd left?" Larissa asked as she handed the wineskin to Valare.

"Yes." Valare took a good swig and passed it to Jyan. "It was what convinced me to leave. They did nothing. It was as though they didn't care."

"Matriarch Yaris didn't know all the details—"

"Except she came by our rooms with Leovyn, only hours after you left. The matriarch seemed...almost pleased at your escape. As though you'd done what they wanted."

That silenced Larissa, and Jyan, who was about to take another swig from the wineskin, put it to one side. "They must have known."

"How is it we could have done what she wanted?" Larissa said. "They were due to destroy the orb and take us back."

No one had an answer, the crackle of the fire filling the silence.

"Rest," Jyan said. "We have a long day ahead of us if we hope to make Janoir by nightfall tomorrow."

To Valare's credit, she didn't question their destination, which was good, as Larissa wasn't quite ready to share it with her yet. The diary was one thing, but it was vague at best. Larissa's conjecture that their destination was north because of the lure of magic might rescind Valare's trust again. Larissa couldn't afford to be caught up in Valare's second-guessing.

They rolled out their swags, Larissa and Jyan using their packs for pillows, Valare her saddle. The horse was hobbled nearby. With the fog of the marshes and the dense forest, no eyes would find them that night.

Somehow, with Valare there, and their heading northward, Larissa slept soundly.

—

She awoke with dew on her skin, a rock digging into her back, and a desperate need pressing on her bladder. The other two were awake, Jyan scuffing out the fire and Valare fixing a nosebag to the horse's head.

Larissa ducked behind a tree and squatted to relieve herself as she shivered in the morning's chill. Thick fog blanketed the forest, the sun's rays turning it to a nimbus glow that left her feeling eerily alone.

She returned to the party, and they packed up their makeshift camp, Valare strapping their packs on the saddle. They began the day's trek. Dawn trickled between the trees, a gray ghostly light, as the three walked along the abandoned road, Valare leading the horse behind them. The path was little more than two ruts for farmers' carts, but Larissa had chosen it with a purpose.

Valare passed out jerky for breakfast. "Where are we headed?"

"North," Larissa said between chewing. "We're headed for Janoir to start, and after that...I think I know the way."

"You aren't sure?"

Larissa spent some time on the mouthful of dried meat, as though it had stolen her words. Valare wasn't stupid, so Larissa spoke with caution.

"Leovyn gave me a journal describing the place Dothreal fought last, a city to the north called Lisolel. It's supposedly behind the Beverre Peaks. I think my mother has gone there too."

Valare frowned. "It shouldn't have taken her seven years to reach it."

"I know. I think it must have hidden from her somehow, and at the time she didn't know it was the same one Dothreal killed. Something must have changed recently, and I'm worried." As she spoke of it, the fear rose inside her, spilling out more words than she wanted. "If she's hunted it to Lisolel, she might have run into greater trouble. I think the Evervast has grown stronger, without the orb."

A gust of wind shook the treetops, the dense growth becoming sparser as the landscape tilted downhill. They all shuddered, looking about, but they were still alone.

"Can...can the Evervast hear you talking about it?" Jyan almost whispered. "Because that was just downright unsettling."

Valare shook her head. "Evercrys can't hear you coming. The Fair Lady lets you hunt them by hearing their song, not the other way around. We should be safe."

"But agents are still out there, looking for us." Larissa scanned the road, glad of the lack of pursuers aside from their plodding horse. "If we head for Janoir, we should be able to get horses and stay mostly undetected."

"Keladros was right to take the Still Water path," Jyan said, "rather than lead you on to Espenel where they were expecting you."

Jyan's sudden soft statement almost brought Larissa to a stop. She exchanged a glance with Valare, but the knight shrugged, silent as Jyan took one deep breath after another.

"She'd be proud of us," Jyan said, a little ahead of them now, rubbing one forearm across her face. "She'd cuff our ears for disobeying the grand matriarch, but...I think she'd be proud of us."

"Did your ears get boxed often?" Valare said, catching up to Jyan with a grin. Jyan's hand rose to rub an ear in response.

"What about you, Valare?" Larissa asked, glad of the change of topic. "I can't imagine you were anything but the perfect knight in your first two tours."

"Believe you me," Valare said, "none are harder to please than Knight-Solaris Hart. She had us up before dawn for practice, and none would sleep while work could still be done. We went to bed exhausted and rose tired. After three months of that, you could do anything. I remember not sleeping for seven days..."

Her voice drifted off, expression darkening.

Larissa took up the conversation's slack. "At least you're trained for it. I don't know how I made it those first few days of this quest. I haven't yet thanked you both for getting me through it."

"You're welcome," Valare said. "Though your thanks are unnecessary, it was my duty."

"Oh, for the Lady's sake, Valare," Jyan cried out. "Stuff an apple in that snout of yours and just take the damn praise."

The two traded insults, and companionable conversation carried them through the morning, until they came to the edge of the forest.

They all paused on the final rise, surveying the landscape beyond. Rolling green hills stretched onward to the horizon, and in the far distance, the highest hill was topped with plumes of smoke. A city.

"Janoir," Valare said, and Larissa nodded.

"We should be able to make it before sundown, and we can buy horses and supplies there for the journey north." She headed down the road again. "But we should enter the city before nightfall, and be gone by dawn."

They chased after her, the horse trotting to keep up. The sisters jogged along roads that became wider, passing small houses and large farms. Throngs of sheep dotted the grassy hills like low-flying clouds, and across the wind was the scent of manure.

Mud was thick as churned butter on the roads. By the time the trio arrived at the city's walls, Larissa was filthy from head to toe, darker earth layered over mud from the river the night before. Her hair was flecked with dirt, her clothes were chafing; she did not resemble a sister at all. She felt like a grimy coin against the yellow stone walls of Janoir, the city painted gold with the sun's departure.

All she wanted was a bath.

"We find an inn," she said. "Somewhere quiet and far from any of our sisters."

Valare and Jyan strode ahead, past the city guards lounging by the wall's gate, watching all who came and went with as little interest as the livestock in the fields.

"Our best chance is on the more disreputable side of town," Valare said.

Larissa let her take the lead, a little lost in the unfamiliar city, its high walls, tall buildings, and narrow twisting streets nothing like Abbidon. "So be it. We can't afford to have anyone know of our passing."

Valare's hand tightened on her sword at her hip. "But we are more likely to run into trouble."

"Let's do our best to avoid it, then," Jyan said. "Shall we?"

They slipped through a market selling sheep, pigs, and even a few cows, but Janoir itself was short on space. The buildings crowded to form tight alleys not even wagons could pass. As it was, their heavily laden horse pushed aside the evening throng, few others walking their mounts through the crowd. The three weaved through the city, more confusing than any maze and towering greater than trees overhead, as the occupants had built upward, confined by the city's walls.

One spire towered above the others: a ruler's palace, Larissa was sure, but she couldn't remember the lord's name.

Jyan led them further into the city, several times stopping at stalls tucked into alcoves between the awkward buildings. She'd make a small purchase and gossip with the stallholder. Valare would tug Larissa's arm, her other hand holding the horse's reins, and rather than be annoyed, Larissa stayed by her side. They wandered on until their packs were stuffed with new supplies and the closing shops forced them to seek out shelter.

"I've had three references to the Wriggly Pig on the far side of the city," Jyan said. "It's a travelers inn with horses and a reputation for being a tad unsavory."

Valare rolled her eyes. "How 'unsavory'?"

"Do they have baths?" Larissa wanted the clod of muck around her ankles gone.

"A few kitten washes won't kill you, Westwyn," Valare muttered.

Larissa was quick to grab her arm. "*Don't* say my name." The low hiss made Valare flinch.

Jyan gestured them on. "This way."

Jyan finally found the inn as the sun slipped its grasp on the day. Light shone from the five-story building, fattest at the ground floor, then narrowing in height as it climbed upward to overlook the city's walls. To one side sat a smelly stable, and Valare gave the boy there a coin to take her horse. Wearing their packs, they stood a moment outside the inn, wary of the raucous noise already spilling into the street. Larissa wondered if she'd get any sleep here.

Valare went in first, as fierce a mercenary as she was a knight, and the voices only died a little at her entry. Larissa was quick to follow.

Long low tables covered the tavern floor, predominantly men seated there, drinking from tankards of ale. Larissa tried not to inhale the pungent scent of stew, ale, and sweat. The men glanced at the trio of women, some looks lasting longer than others, and not all of them friendly.

"If any of these barbarians touch me, they'll lose a digit," Valare swore, but Jyan swanned in as though she owned the place.

"Smell that?" Jyan crowed. "This is why I like traveling."

Valare glanced at Larissa, who gave a one-shouldered shrug and followed Jyan. Valare stuck close to her, hissing at one man who raised his hand toward her.

"I'll give you a scar, and that's if I let you keep your fingers."

Any other hands dropped away, and they navigated their way across the tavern unmolested, conversation resuming now they were no longer a novelty.

"Barkeep," Jyan called to the rotund man behind the counter. "I'll take a room with three beds, and I need to know what you can do for me in the way of horses."

The barman scowled at Jyan through a ginger beard. "Room and board I can give you, but not horses."

"No matter," Jyan said, unphased. "Where can I get a few hardy horses?"

"There's a stable master just outside the walls. They take a highwayman's price, but they're good rides. Especially if you're heading north for the Bay of Eonin. I can recommend an inn I'm partnered with there."

The man was fishing for information, but Jyan paid it no mind.

"I have five years before I must marry a man I'm not interested in." She leaned over the bar as though confiding in him, but her voice wasn't soft. "I wish to see the Western lands, where they say gold runs aplenty, the wonders are marvelous, and the menfolk are handsome."

The barkeep's frown grew, bushy brows on his forehead wriggling like angry caterpillars. "You take a good look at our stock here," he told her. "That's Jakar Sumar over there. He's a brute of a man. Lysonese too, just like you."

Larissa glanced over at the man in the corner with a harlot on his knee, but his gaze fixed on Jyan, stare sizzling across the space. His muscles as well oiled as his leather jerkin, he flexed them for Jyan. Her lips curled even as the harlot glared daggers. His leer arrested Larissa's attention for a moment, before Valare shoved her shoulder from behind.

"Don't sully yourself," she whispered, less an insult than it was a warning.

"That man is not only rich," the barkeep whispered conspiratorially to Jyan, glancing at Valare and Larissa, "but he's a highwayman to boot, not that I'd advertise that. He's just paid off the bounty on his head to King Cylus."

That was the ruler's name, Larissa mused, remembering her studies. He wasn't fond of the sisters, so there wasn't an outpost here. It made the inn all the safer.

"And here I thought I might be over Lysonese men." Jyan lifted her chin at Sumar, and he raised his glass to her. The harlot on his knee stormed off in a huff, but he didn't stop her, eyes set on Jyan.

She tore her gaze from the burly man. "Now about that room..."

The barkeep nodded. "Mags," he called. A slim girl with mousy hair in a long braid came from the doorway to the kitchens, wiping her hands on a cloth. "Take them up top, the lady will like it better. Supper is already started—or do you want it sent up? We have a dumbwaiter, so it'll be quick, no need to wait."

"Oh no," Jyan said, surveying the tavern. "We'll eat down here."

She slid several coins across to the barkeep, whose brows rose until she laid down several more. The barmaid, Mags, stood waiting with a ready smile to show them to their room.

Larissa hefted the pack on her shoulder to follow Mags up the narrow staircase. There was barely enough space when patrons passed going down, some taking advantage of the small space to push against her, until they saw Valare over Larissa's shoulder and hurried on.

Larissa didn't need their sweat on her skin.

"Do you have baths here?" she asked.

"Oh yes, mistress," Mags told her. "We use the dumbwaiter for hot water. I'll set about sending some up to you."

Larissa didn't mask the groan she gave when Mags finally stopped at their landing. Her legs ached from the day's walk, feet numb as though they'd fallen off.

"Here we are, then." Mags opened the door onto a narrow room, high enough the windows looked beyond the city walls, sun setting in the far distance, the sea a blue smear on the horizon. But Larissa looked to the north and saw the gray blur of distant mountains. She walked away from the windows, intent on putting down her pack, and her troubles too, for a while.

To one side of the door were three beds. The other side held a small round table and two chairs, and in a corner sat a large tub near the hatch of a dumbwaiter. She dropped her bag, wondering how long it would take to get a wash.

"Who wants to go first?" she asked, as Mags handed Jyan a key and shut the door.

"I will see about those horses," Valare said. "I don't fancy our chances at the start of the day—I'd rather have them ready and waiting for us in the stables downstairs. We need only two, and I have coin enough for that."

She disappeared without another word, and Larissa gazed after her.

"She feels...bad, doesn't she?" Larissa said.

Jyan placed the key into Larissa's hand. "She's ashamed. She put her fears above her duty. You won't ever know what it cost her."

"I know what it cost *you*."

Jyan turned back to her with a smile.

"I'm going to speak to that Lysonese brute." Her grin broadened when Larissa rolled her eyes. "Not for that reason, though if it comes up, I promise not to bring him here. I want to know what bandits are on the road. If we'll encounter any when we head north. The agents that pursue you might use mercenaries, like they did in Abbidon. If Sumar's recently gained the favor of the king, then he won't mind selling out his previous brethren to a girl with a charming smile." Her leer would have done Denobe proud.

Larissa gestured at the empty tub. "Don't you want to clean up first?"

"Nothing a man like Sumar can't scrub off me."

Jyan winked and trotted downstairs. Larissa locked the door behind her, shoulders slumped. She was far tireder than she'd thought.

It wasn't just the travel; it was the nights, and the wolf howls that bothered her now during the day. The echo's pervasiveness drove her on, but so too did it flag her strength. Head hanging, neck too tired to support it, she only stirred at the sound of a bell.

It came from the dumbwaiter, and Larissa crossed to it, opening the hatch to see four steaming buckets.

"Thank you, Mags," she said with gratitude to the absent barmaid.

She emptied them into the tub after putting a plug in the bottom drain. When the buckets were empty, she rang the bell and closed the hatch. Another load of water should do it. She took off her jerkin and stripped off her muddy shoes and leather pants.

Standing in nothing but her underthings and a shirt, she opened the dumbwaiter a second time when the bell chimed. Only to find, not hot water, but a man.

# Chapter 19

He sprang out of the dumbwaiter and pounced on Larissa with the deftness of a cat. She stumbled back, weaponless, and fell as he crashed into her, pinning her to the floor with his wiry form. He pressed a blade against Larissa's throat, and she stilled under his grasp.

"I don't want to hurt you," the bright-eyed assailant informed her, breath hot on her face. "But you will not scream, or you'll find yourself the worse for it."

She didn't doubt him, but the instinct to call for help was hard to suppress.

Dressed as an ordinary merc, his face was vaguely familiar from downstairs, but now that he was close she sensed what she should have before. There was a taint about him, something that tingled her senses, sending her stomach rolling.

"You are making a grave mistake," Larissa panted, aware of the sharp pain on her neck. One twist and she'd die.

"What makes you say that?" he asked, looking her over with a favorable eye.

"I'm a darkkin of the Fair Lady. We do not travel alone."

"Thank you, but I don't see any knights here," the attacker whispered, his grin growing. "It wouldn't be Darkkin Westwyn, would it?"

Too late, she realized she'd given herself away. She gritted her teeth.

"How did you find me?"

"We heard the call…" The fingers of his free hand reached under the collar of her shirt, not to molest her but to pluck out the gold chain. "The echo of the Evercry."

The orb swung back and forth where he held it, and Larissa heard a distant cry through the city's spires, ringing on the wind. Only the knife on her throat stopped Larissa from snatching the orb back.

"That's impossible."

Her assailant dropped the orb and parted his own shirt to show a symbol carved over his chest. A rune she didn't recognize, but within its marking was the writhing magic of an evercry.

This was no mercenary but a true agent of the Evervast.

They'd found her.

Saliva coated her tongue, her heart hammering as inky tendrils slid under his skin. Like the tentacles of the Writhing Dark. She thrust her head away with a sickened gasp.

"This is not your fate, Darkkin Westwyn," the man said, lifting the blade from her neck, though he still held it at the ready. "Roll over and place your arms behind your back."

She fought for a reason not to do so, but he waved the knife inches from her face. He could hurt her if she resisted. She did as he asked. Slick rope, thinner than hemp, slipped over her wrists, snapping taut enough to cut off her circulation.

"Don't fret. The Evervast wants the last descendant of Dothreal alive," he whispered in her ear.

"My sisters will come for me," she said. Jyan was downstairs, right in the dining hall, and Valare was outside the city walls, but not far.

"You better hope they don't," he said, "because I don't need them as much as I need you."

His weight disappeared from her back, and he hoisted her to her feet. He shoved her toward the dumbwaiter.

"In you go."

With a dirty look at the man, she squished herself inside. Her legs didn't want to fold in after her. The agent shoved her leg before she could think about kicking him, then slammed the dumbwaiter's door to wedge her in. There was a rumbling noise, the sound of the dumbwaiter moving along its rails. Her muscles were all knotted, and she focused on flexing so they didn't cramp. There was light in the cracks between the doors, but any inclination to scream, she smothered. An agent with so much magic in him could hurt an innocent. She wouldn't be responsible for that. She had to think of something. The elevator jerked to a stop, the door opened, and she tumbled out backward onto the floor.

A pair of hands caught her.

It was the Lysonese man, Sumar.

"I hate the north," he said. "But for you it'll be worth it." When he grinned, a gold tooth flashed. He thumped the dumbwaiter, and it traveled skyward, on its way back to the agent.

Larissa glanced around the dimly lit cellar and caught sight of Jyan slumped in a corner. Though also bound, she was asleep, oblivious to her predicament.

"Worry not on her," Sumar said. "She goes south, back to her homeland. Her parents will pay me a fortune for her safe return—but you, you will give me something worth far more than gold."

"What?" Larissa spat.

Sumar picked her up and placed her on a nearby box. Hands to either side of her thighs, he eyed her legs.

"The Evercry will make me a weapon I'll use to slay any enemy," he said as he perused her. "It will be made of fire and darkness, and I will become a king. Might even marry a princess." He smirked over his shoulder at Jyan.

Larissa's eyes widened and he laughed. Legs free, she used the only option left to her. She kicked him in the crotch.

When he doubled over, he met her knee coming the other way. There was a wet crunch. Blood spurted from his nose, one hand clasping his groin, the other his face. She slid off the crate to kick him again. Sumar dodged, catching her ankle and tipping her over on her stomach.

She couldn't wriggle far enough away before his larger frame covered hers, forcing her onto her stomach, hands about her throat. The blood from his nose spattered over her shoulder as he snarled into her ear.

"You are *only* of use to me alive." One hand still squeezing her neck, he lowered the other one until it was sliding below her belly, down between her thighs, where he pinched hard enough to hurt. "I can't kill you, so the next time you try a stunt like that, this is where I will take my vengeance. Do you understand?"

She couldn't speak as the hands about her tightened, and she burned with shame and pain.

"Well?" he snarled, letting go of her throat enough for her to cough out an answer.

"Evercry take you!" Larissa hissed. Her fingers fumbled behind her back and found the hilt of a blade. Holding the handle tight, she jerked her head back, smashing again into his broken face.

He howled, rearing off her. His weight gone, Larissa rolled onto her back, knife in her hands, and sawed at the bindings, drawing what magic she could to her mind.

He struck her face, the backhanded slap stunning any spells from her tongue. Stars danced in her vision as she groaned, squinting against the agony rolling around her skull.

Oblivious to her newfound weapon, he lunged on her bare legs, tearing at her underclothes to enact his reprimand on the cellar floor. Fighting to keep her senses, she worked to sever the thin ropes binding her hands. Her jerking motion was masked as she kicked at him to no avail. He bashed aside her attempts and wedged himself between her thighs. Larissa cursed as the stolen blade cut more than rope, biting into her wrists.

With a sharp tug, he ripped off her drawers, and for the first time she was exposed to a man. She must have paled, for he laughed and reached into his own trouser front. A fount of nausea-inducing dread thrummed down her spine, distilling shock into desperate urgency, saturating her nerves with adrenaline like lightning, down to her numb and bleeding hands.

With a final cut, she broke the bonds with a snap and brought her arms in front of her. Her left arm continued its arc, and she slashed the knife across his exposed throat.

A crimson fountain sprayed over her. Sumar dropped his failing member to grasp his throat as his life force fled. He collapsed on his hands before her, and she drove the knife into his back. Once. Twice. Three times.

He fell, lying motionless on her bare legs.

Larissa scrambled back from the wet warmth that spilled over her thighs, sobs of relief escaping her that it was his life blood and not that of her virginity.

Crouched beside the growing dark pool of blood, Larissa drew her shirt about her body, clutching its thin material to her chest. She cringed at the blood's slickness as it soaked into the cotton. A scream built in her throat, and she bit her lip hard enough to bleed rather than let it pass. Inhaling lungful after lungful of air, her gaze fell on Jyan, and she crossed the floor to her friend.

"Some bodyguard you turned out to be," Larissa said with a semi-hysterical laugh. When it turned to a whimper, she swallowed the sound.

Through the sudden silence came the wheeling noise of the dumbwaiter. The agent was winding himself down, taking more time since he hauled his own weight, but on his way.

But he was trapped in a box, and this might be her only

chance at escape. Instinct drove her to race across the floor and stand to one side of the opening, trembling head to toe, back to the wall, stolen knife in hand. Sumar's body lay across the floor in plain sight. She hoped it would be enough of a shock.

The hatch slid open and she did not hesitate.

Her fist slammed blade first into the opening, and she was rewarded when it sank into flesh. She tore it out for another strike. A leg lashed out, kicking around to her middle, and with the wall at her back, she couldn't avoid it. The heel hit her in the solar plexus, and the breath thudded from her lungs. Winded, she let go of the knife, her hands going to her chest as she fought to inhale.

The agent stumbled out of the hatch. She'd wounded him, a gash to his thigh, bleeding enough he couldn't hold his own weight.

Larissa searched for her dropped knife, but he rushed her, weapon already in hand. She had to forego her knife to stop the hilt of his blade punching into her stomach, and she hit a stack of flour sacks. That he needed her alive didn't appear to matter anymore as he fell on her. Both her hands seized where he held the knife, and though she wasn't as injured, he was muscle-bound.

Droplets of heat sprinkled on her bare leg, and with a glance down, she saw his wounded thigh. She kneed it as hard as she could.

He cried out, one hand letting go of the knife to grasp his leg. She shoved upward with everything she had, twisting the blade around and ramming it into his midsection. He stopped, staring at her with wide eyes. She got her legs underneath her and rose, until the dominance shifted and she bore him down to the floor. She stabbed the knife as deep as it would go.

The blade scraped on the bone of his spine, his every breath shuddering the metal in her hand as the light faded from his eyes. She waited, watched to be sure he would move no more. Only after indeterminable minutes when his vacant eyes didn't blink did she ease.

Panting, she yanked the blade free and used a beam to climb to her feet, leaning against it for support. Her legs trembled. She uttered a platitude to the Fair Lady over the pitter-patter of her slowing heartbeat. For a moment, it was all she could do not to be sick all over the floor, nausea threatening to empty what little was in her stomach.

Until she heard a sound. There was a whisper, a faint susurrus that rippled over her, raising the hair on her neck. She rose to check the corpses, fearing they were still alive.

Sumar lay on his stomach, face turned to one side, wide eyes staring sightlessly. The agent lay on his back, not moving, yet the whisper drew her closer, and she crept forward until she stood over him. Blood stuck his shirt to his body, but through a rip she glimpsed the mark on his chest. The inky glyph called to her. She leaned down, careful not to touch it as she cut away the fabric. The black mark had faded somewhat, but she sensed the magic within.

So too the magic sensed her presence, the flesh wriggling. Whatever had called the agent of the Evervast to her was still there.

Fire. She needed fire now.

Panic goaded her to action. Words of fire formed on her tongue, building as she splayed her hand over the dead man's chest. "*Aras theris fiariltos!*"

He writhed, whole body quivering, shaking like a child's plaything. Limbs landed on her, grasping hands that wouldn't close. She shrieked, leaping back.

Despite the fire in her breath, the mark on his chest strengthened in form and color. She spoke the spell with greater ritual, channeling all her fear into burning the Evervast's presence to ash.

"*Aras clannest theris afirithos!*"

The mark came alight, lines of darkness sparking with her flame, burned from his flesh. Black smoke curled up from the body. The scent of foul meat roasting infused the air, wrinkled her nose. She dared not turn away. Hand outstretched, twisted into a gnarled grasp, she forced the fire magic throughout the writhing corpse. The stench became so strong she tasted it on her tongue, thick enough to bite. She wanted to choke, to vomit, but she held on until there was nothing but charred remains.

Her arm dropped, adrenaline slipping away. In its place came horror. Slicked in gore, bleeding and raw, the ever-present hollowness inside her filled instead with magic. With power. It rushed over the taste of defiled, charring meat to cling to her teeth. She should have been afraid, but the magic burned the terror to ash.

A door across the cellar opened, and Larissa shot a quick glance over her shoulder. It was the barkeep.

"I heard a noise..." His mouth fell wide at her appearance.

Larissa straightened, aware she was soaked in blood, so much that it ran in rivulets down her bare, bruised legs, but she didn't care. Magic flooded her system, curling out her mouth in long flaming trails that didn't burn her skin, her voice thick with it.

*"Your hospitality to my friends is...lackluster."*

He held his hands high in surrender. "I swear, I didn't know." He made to run, but she compelled him to stay, her hand raised to bend the magic to her will, lost in its haze. He froze, gaping, a fish out of water.

A glimmer pierced her vision—her ring had caught the lantern light, the moonstone red with blood. Seeing it, she took a shallow breath. Still on the brink, she inhaled one slow hesitant breath after another. A desperate attempt to focus on something other than the temptation to use the magic within.

"You came down here to get your payment?" She bent to Sumar's corpse, found his coin purse, and sliced it off. "Here. This should cover any bribe he promised. It should also cover our accommodation, more hot water for my bath, a large jug of wine, and your absolute promise that you will do everything in your power to ensure I have a good night's sleep."

Larissa walked across the room until she stood before him, the barkeep transfixed by the magic she wielded, and then she heard it.

The howl of a wolf.

Its lone cry echoed across the cellar and chilled her to her core. The ghost of something heard and not understood, the solitary sound chimed deep within her, plucking the chord of her loneliness.

It was no longer she that kept the barkeep transfixed—it was the necklace about her throat, spilled out into the open. The blood of her fallen enemies glowed against the burnished gold of the orb. The howl became louder, harkening back to all she'd lost, how isolated she'd become, until there was nothing else, nothing in this world for her but the sound echoing ever onward...

"Stop," she said, hands drawn up around her ears, knife fallen to the floor. "*Stop*!"

The eerie whine rose, wrapping her up in its solitude, telling her that she didn't just hear the sound, she *was* the sound, and she was alone.

"No!" she shrieked. She yanked free a stained dishrag at the barkeep's waist and used it to rub crimson off the necklace, polishing furiously as the noise threatened to consume her.

"Magic," he whispered. "Dark magic..."

He turned to run, and she lashed out. Her fingers dug into his arm, strong with magical taint, and he whimpered. The cry cut through to a part of her that warred with the orb and her need to punish those responsible. But the glistening ring on her finger was bright where she clutched the barkeep's shirt. Lit with blood.

"See the ring upon my hand," she said, grounding herself as she spoke. "It is blessed by the Fair Lady herself. I am a sister of her order, traveling in disguise. These men set on me to take me to my enemies, and you *helped* them."

The color drained from his face.

Retribution on any who harmed those of the sacred sisterhood was swift. The Fair Lady's followers were careful where they sent their knights and darkkins, and if any local lord or king didn't ensure they were treated with all due respect, they could find themselves plagued by an evercry for some time before the sisters would come help. For some who offended the Lady, it was years. Rulers did not look kindly on those that harmed the sisters.

But the true threat now was his imminent death at her hands, and Larissa wasn't sure she could stop herself.

"Sister...I didn't know." The barkeep fell to his knees. "I didn't know you were of the Fair Lady. I *swear*."

Larissa wanted nothing more than to crawl into her bath, and she made the desire everything she needed in that moment. Her longing for the simple comfort eased her wrath. Her thoughts were consumed by the desire to scrub the filth from her body until her skin was raw. Until the magic faded—unsatiated, but gone.

"Bring me a robe," she told him as she regained her senses. "And that's not all I'll be asking for. I'll need your silence too... Barkeep."

"My—My name is Santhos," he said.

"Hello, Santhos." Larissa sighed. "I am Darkkin Westwyn, and you've just forced me to kill my first man. Well, two. I can't imagine how my knight will react when she finds out. Best you help me sort this out so we can clear up the worst of it before she returns. She won't be pleased."

He scurried away with a whimper. When the door closed behind him, Larissa fell to the floor and covered her face with her hands, suppressing a nervous bubble of laughter that hiccupped into a sob.

She'd killed. Two people. In a space of minutes.

But rather than the nausea that had always threatened her at the sight of death, another churning of her stomach rose instead. *Hunger.* She scrubbed the tears from her eyes to look down at the orb. It still glowed. Taking the dishrag, she scrubbed off the rest of the blood, and after a time the light on its markings faded, along with the now distant sounds of a wolf.

Swaying to her feet, she crossed to Jyan. She slit the bonds at Jyan's ankles and wrists, but whatever Sumar had done to her had knocked her out stone cold. Bending over Jyan's frame, Larissa checked her over. No bruises or swelling—Sumar hadn't taken her by force. Her pupils were dilated, and when she checked Jyan's breath, there was a sweetness that was almost bitter. Maple vine, a harmless sleep aid, but the dose Jyan had imbibed wasn't small.

Larissa returned to the dead men. The agent was a charred smear on the floor, no magic there now. Sumar himself bore nothing to indicate he was anything other than a mercenary for hire. The same as their attackers in Abbidon.

Her examinations were done by the time Santhos returned. The barmaid Mags and an ox of a lad stood behind him.

"We'll take care of the bodies," Santhos assured her. "We won't tell the town guard. My lad Bran will carry your friend to her room. Up a back stairwell so no one will see."

Mags crossed to Larissa, holding out a forest green robe edged in pale yellow and made of crushed velvet. She allowed herself to be enfolded in the garment.

"Send food and drink to our rooms," she said. "And more hot water for my bath."

Santhos's head bounced in agreement. Larissa oversaw Bran pick up Jyan, then followed him up the stairs as he cradled the woman like a toddler asleep after a party. Larissa opened the door and Bran deposited Jyan on a bed, then left without a word.

She locked the door behind him, only to open it again a few moments later at a knock. Mags stood there, two other maids with her. They carried buckets of water and wasted no time depositing them in the cooling tub. Mags had also brought a new linen shift for Larissa and a bar of lemon-scented soap.

"I'll bring more buckets so you can have a soak after you've scrubbed clean," she said. "I've also sealed off the dumbwaiter. You can check it if you like, but just in case, I cut the rope." She handed over a bundle of hemp that could have been from any place, but there was a glint in her eye that gave Larissa the conviction that she was telling the truth.

"Thank you," she said, and Mags left with a nod.

More servants came with buckets, then a tray of roasted meat, a prime cut still pink in the middle, and an assortment of roasted vegetables. Larissa directed the meal to the small table down the far end of the room, its surface growing cramped with the abundance.

Several more maids brought flagons of wine, and behind them entered Valare.

"What is all this?" she said, staring at the laden table and Larissa's strange garb. "Where did you get that dress?"

"It's a robe," Larissa almost snapped. "And I borrowed it."

Mags raised her eyebrows, but her concern faded when Larissa nodded that she could leave. She passed Valare, before turning back to speak to Larissa.

"There are some dried fruits and cheeses I will bring up later with more wine, when I come to retrieve the dinner things."

"Thank you, and thank Santhos for me too."

"I understand your friend has brought horses to the yard," Mags said. "I'll check on them and ensure they're well fed. You'll find supplies already packed on them when you rise in the morning. Please, sleep well."

Larissa gave a half smile at the well wishes, knowing them for what they were: a request that they leave with all due haste. "I will."

Mags turned to go, then hesitated. "My father isn't a bad man. But this is not a cheap place to run."

With that parting comment, she left, leaving Valare staring between the shut door and Larissa.

Larissa crossed to the table and poured herself a cup of wine, watching with bemusement as Valare's confusion grew when she saw Jyan on the bed, snoring.

"I've been gone a half hour at most," she said. "Would you mind telling me what bloody well happened?"

Larissa drained her cup. "We were attacked."

She took off the robe, laying it with care to one side, revealing her torn and blood-stained clothes. Behind her, Valare gasped.

"Are you hurt?" She rushed over and spun Larissa around, yanking aside her shirt to check for wounds. Larissa waited while Valare studied the slick wounds at her wrists, clotted now but red and angry. Valare dropped to her knees, grabbing a cloth to wipe away the blood and be sure it wasn't further cuts. Larissa let her, too numb to do anything else.

Satisfied that Larissa wasn't too injured, Valare drew back, her hands fisted with rage. "What *happened*?"

"I'm fine, but I nearly wasn't." Larissa crossed to a bucket by the tub, tugged off the remains of her blood-soaked underthings, and used the hot water and soap to scrub the stains from her body. They were more than skin deep but required no stitches. She got in the tub and used the cold water to wash away as much of the muck as she could.

Valare checked on Jyan before picking up a wine cup for herself, giving Larissa as much privacy as the room afforded. Clean, Larissa emptied the tub. When she moved toward the remaining buckets, Valare waved her back into the tub and then poured the water in herself, even tipping the last one ever so gently over Larissa's head. Larissa sank into the bath's depths with a sigh.

Valare refilled Larissa's cup and brought it to her. She had to give Santhos credit for not scrimping. But then, he'd just been handed a purse full of riches and he owed a debt to those of the Fair Lady. She supposed he could afford to be generous now he'd been paid for more than mere betrayal.

Valare sat on the edge of the tub. "Care to tell me what

happened?"

Said with such kindness, so softly for someone like Valare. Larissa let the words out, numbness settling on her tone, lined with heat from the bath and forgetfulness from the wine.

"You left to get horses, Jyan to find out information from the Lysonese man."

"And?"

"I'd asked for hot water, but rather than buckets, a man burst out of the dumbwaiter. He forced me into it and took me to the cellar, where Sumar, the Lysonese man Jyan was intent on seducing, waited for me."

"To...rob you?"

It wasn't the word she'd been about to say.

"No." Larissa's hand trembled as she drained her second cup. "To take me to the Evervast and ransom Jyan back to her parents."

Valare jerked to her feet. "The Evervast knows we're here?"

Larissa shook her head. "I don't think so. One of them was close enough that he sensed the orb—got lucky, as it were. He was an agent, bore a mark of the Evervast on his chest. I burned the magic out of him after I killed him."

Larissa rubbed her eyes, itchy with tears, but she wanted to shout, to fling her cup at the wall, to drain another glass, lose herself in oblivion. The scene replayed in her mind, how they'd overpowered her, how she'd been forced from safety, how Sumar's hand had dug between her legs.

Shame burned like a brand, hot, scalding, and pervasive. With it, the confession came tumbling out.

"Sumar said he'd rape me if I tried to fight him off, and when he forced me to the ground, I got a knife off him. I...struck his throat as soon as I could. I killed him. And then the agent came down the dumbwaiter, and I stabbed him too, but he wasn't as badly wounded. We fought... I-I drove the dagger into him... I had to, and when the magic inside him, the marks carved by the Evervast, started moving, I burned the corpse with magic. I couldn't stop, I didn't *want* to stop."

Whatever numbness had kept her upright faded, and she bent over her knees to sob into the bathwater, dropping her empty cup over the tub's edge. "I used magic, I killed those men, I—"

"Larissa!" Valare grasped her arm, hand tight as she dropped to eye level. "You did what you *had* to in order to survive. And I don't blame you."

Larissa swallowed, blinking away tears. "Really?"

Valare picked up her cup and took it back to the table. She refilled it and brought Larissa a plate of roasted meat too.

"Have dinner." She handed the plate to Larissa, whose stomach did not want food. "I will keep watch over you, Darkkin. I won't leave your side again. If you want to get drunk, and I don't blame you, then at least eat or you'll be too sick to travel tomorrow."

"You don't care?" Larissa said, knowing it was irresponsible given what was before them.

"I drank two flagons in the space of an hour after I executed the prince. Knight-Solaris Hart let me drink to my heart's content, but only on a full stomach. Eat."

Larissa took the plate from Valare and chewed the meat. It was bloody, and a part of her was revolted, but the hunger that lingered within devoured the tender flesh, and she cleaned the plate, even had seconds when Valare brought it to her.

"What of Jyan?" Valare asked, finally handing Larissa a full wine cup, but Larissa sipped it rather than draining it.

"Tampered drink," she said. "There's maple vine on her breath. Nothing but a sleeping herb, just a very large dose of it."

Valare grimaced at their friend. "Then she will be sorrier than you tomorrow."

# Chapter 20

Jyan scowled at the rising sun. "You slit his throat?"

"Yes."

"And weren't sick?"

"No."

"By yourself?"

"*Yes.*" Larissa sighed, having already recounted the events for Jyan's benefit on their morning escape from Janoir. She wanted nothing more than to crawl beneath thick furs and sleep a week. "And I thought you were too ill to speak?"

"I am." Jyan winced with every step the horse took. "But I'm also impressed."

"Me too," Valare said on her other side. "Neither of you have thrown up."

"He drugged me." Jyan took a swipe at Valare, who steered her horse away.

"I'm fine," Larissa said, though it was untrue. The wine and the bath had gone to her head in very short order, and Valare had put her into bed. Now, her head pounded with every step of the horse's hooves, and it had worsened when Valare urged them into a canter for the first hour before dawn. Fleeing the city before any were awake. She wanted the roads to themselves, and Larissa understood why.

It didn't help her throbbing headache.

Here at least the roads weren't as muddy, earth lightening to whitish pebbles as they took the path north to the Bay of Eonin.

"So, what was with the mark on the man's chest?" Jyan asked. "Was it the same as Abbidon?"

"Without having seen it myself, I can't be sure, but I think so," Larissa said. "It was a sigil of sorts. Alive and moving, like a worm or snake, as though when it was carved into his flesh, something inserted itself under the skin."

Jyan gulped, hand on her stomach. "Oh...you shouldn't have told me that."

"And you wonder why I hate magic," Valare said.

"It's not normal magic, it's dark," Larissa said. The other two drew silent, staring at her. They wouldn't understand the details, but this mark was different to what she knew of runes, and very dangerous. "You don't put magic runes *in* people. An evercry will to their host, the body they possess, but it's a piece of their own magic—they're empowering themselves for specific abilities. And they don't share power. They don't give it to their agents. It's against the nature of an evercry to divide its strength."

"No agents I've seen or heard about have that," Valare agreed. "We're told what to look out for in acolytes, casual magic use in battle, but...nothing like a burn mark beneath the skin."

Larissa's hand ghosted over her lip, back and forth. "Though I could swear I've seen the rune before." Jyan reached across and shook her arm when she didn't go on. She shrugged. "I've been thinking on it all morning. I don't know why I think that."

"Could it be you ran across it in your great-grandmother's journal, or in your studies as a darkkin?" Jyan asked.

Larissa shook her head.

"Well," Valare said, shifting in her saddle, "we could at least hear how Jyan ended up in the cellar and next to damn useless."

There was a long-suffering groan. "I'll tell you on one condition, Atticus. That you never remind me of it again."

Valare cocked her eyebrow. Larissa turned in her saddle to better study Jyan, who faced the landscape.

"When I went to the bar, he came up to me and offered me a drink." Jyan gave yet another dramatic sigh. "And then I said we should find somewhere to..."

The rest disappeared on a mumble.

"What?" Valare said. "Those at the back can't hear you."

Jyan spun in her saddle. "I told him I'd fuck him, and we should go somewhere quiet!" she shouted. "I was hoping he'd tell me something of his fellow bandits and scratch a certain itch. You two might be prissy sisters, but not me."

"You succumbed to a single cup of wine and the promise of fornication." Valare tsked long and with much exaggeration, while Jyan glared daggers at her.

"Where were *you*, then?" she shot back.

Larissa let go of her knotted reins and held up her hands to each of them. "Don't start this. I swear, if any of us fight again, I won't take you with me."

"Because you going off on your own is a great idea," Valare scoffed.

"Is it time for another run?" Larissa interrupted. "I'd so hate for any remaining mercs to catch up."

She urged her horse into a canter, and the other two were quick to chase. Gone was the uncomfortable motion of the saddle. Instead, Larissa started to appreciate the cool wind on her face. The freedom of the run, the vitality surging through her as the horse thundered down the road, her companions' protests ringing in her ears as they raced to keep up. Her headache died on a rush of exhilaration as she just enjoyed the ride.

A subtle undercurrent wondered if that was because she was doing as the orb wanted and going north, but she ignored it.

After a while, Larissa spied a stream. She slowed her horse to a stop and leapt off to join the mount at the water. The other two brought their horses behind her, hooves loud on the dirt road until they became quiet thumps on the rich turf.

Her sisters joined her on the ground.

"A fire?" Jyan rubbed her temple. "I could use a cup of herbal tea."

Larissa retrieved some hare's bane from her pack. "Chew on this."

Jyan turned up her nose but took the herb.

"We shouldn't linger long," Larissa said. "I want to reach the Tharados forest line by nightfall. We must follow it along and look for the pass that will let us through the mountains to the sea on the far side. There should be a road, but it may not be there anymore."

"I thought you didn't know where we were going," Jyan said.

Larissa stilled.

"How do you know that, Darkkin?" Valare asked. Her expression was calm, but her hand dropped from the horse's bridle to her waist. Beside her sword. She waited for Larissa to explain herself.

"Because...because—" Larissa broke off and ducked her head, the old habit familiar before Valare's scrutiny, but the knight was having none of it.

"It's the orb. Isn't it?" Instead of her usual disgust toward magic, Valare's voice remained soothing, as though speaking to a wild animal.

"I'm..."

"It's okay." Valare came forward to take Larissa's shoulder. "I trust that you believe this is the right thing to do. But if I think the orb's influence is becoming too much or impairing your judgment, you know that we'll have to go back, don't you?"

Jyan bit her lip, gaze flickering between the two.

"I will," Larissa said, gazing north. "But I need to find my mother."

"I know," Valare said, and in an uncharacteristic gesture, embraced her. "And I'll do what I can to see that happen."

Larissa nodded, drawing away, rubbing her arms and wishing she could sense what the orb was doing to her. The information was just there, in her mind, sure as a path she'd walked dozens of times. But it was too dark to see.

After eating rations and refilling water bottles while the horses grazed, they walked along the road for a time, before mounting again and proceeding at a plodding pace.

Grassy knolls morphed into scrubby flatlands to the west, and away to the north the hills rose to mountains. Larissa listened for the cry of a wolf, but nothing came to her except the wind's lonely howl across the plains.

When the road swung west toward the scrubland, she knew she'd run out of time—they had to keep going north to reach the Beverre Peaks. But she'd had no sign that this was the right place. The earlier certainty was absent from her thoughts. And yet, the lure to turn from the path couldn't be ignored.

"Here," she said.

"Are you sure?" Valare asked. "There aren't any roads."

"I...think so."

"Cross country it is, then," Jyan said, nudging her horse out onto the grass.

Larissa paused, looking down the western road, and then to the southeast, back the way they'd come.

She'd relied on the echo to lead her to the Evervast, and hopefully her mother. That it was silent now, when it had lately only been growing in volume, made her hands sweat where they held the reins. Underneath her doubt slunk another certainty, that straying from the road was wrong. Dangerous.

"What is it, Darkkin?" Valare halted her horse. Larissa was unable to answer. Valare turned her horse around and came to Larissa's side. "What do you hear?"

"No wolves," Larissa reassured, "but the silence is somehow worse. As though if I heard that noise, I...I might be too frightened to go on."

"Do you sense anything else?"

Larissa shook her head. With a sigh, she dug her heels in, and the horse walked off the road. Its hooves cut into sodden earth, which turned from lush green to wild yellow, interspersed with bulbous shrubbery, tiny dark leaves with crimson buds ready for the oncoming spring.

Through wild terrain, they crossed the grassy plains until they reached the low hills above the road, at the edge of a pine forest. Clouds loomed above them. Wind from the mountains roared across the trees, the pines swaying, branches creaking. A tingle of apprehension ran over Larissa's skin.

The frozen wind turned their faces pink, causing the trio to pull their cloaks tighter. Beneath them, their patient mounts didn't even shudder from the harsh temperature.

Though well insulated against the cold, Larissa didn't think the shaggy horses were prepared for snowy weather.

"Do you think it will storm?" she asked Valare, who eyed the growing clouds with annoyance.

"I'd be a little more concerned by that," Jyan said, staring back down the hills behind them. Larissa turned.

A band of horses had left the road and was heading toward them. No shambling mountain ponies, these were a dozen good thoroughbreds, eating the distance between the road and the hillside where the trio stood. At a walk, it had taken them half an hour; with their gallop, the other party would be on them in minutes.

"Can we run?" Larissa asked, wondering if she hadn't burned the tainted magic out of the agent's body after all. She swallowed in dread that she'd have to use magic again, but with Jyan and Valare by her side, she'd burn magic through her veins rather than let them be taken.

Brow furrowed, Valare pulled a spyglass from her pocket and scanned their pursuers. She handed it to Larissa. "There's no need to run."

Larissa squinted through the glass. The oncoming riders cast long shadows across the ground, turning their mounts into messengers of night. White breastplates, crimson cloaks.

A contingent of the Fair Lady's knights. Three darkkins, and one senior knight—a knight-solaris, or possibly higher rank, but there was no mistaking the glint of gold on her shoulders.

"They're coming for us." Larissa gave the spyglass back to Valare.

"Yes." Valare studied them with narrowed eyes. "But we can't run, and we need to set up a camp now, before nightfall. We can take protection in the forest's cover, far enough back we can't be seen from the road."

Valare turned her horse toward the tree line and then dismounted. Larissa and Jyan followed suit.

"But...they're going to stop us," Larissa said. "We can't stay here—they're going to destroy the orb."

Valare didn't answer.

"Did you know?" Larissa snarled.

"And the purpose of me chasing after you would have then been...?" Valare said. "We failed. We got caught. I have no idea how, but I'm beginning to think the damn orb is cursed."

"We could lose them in the storm," Larissa ventured. Valare shook her head.

"You will not endanger our sisters like that. Let alone yourself. They may be sending support, rallying to your cause, you don't know. But we will stay and find out."

Larissa fumed, gaze darting between the thick woods and the oncoming riders.

Valare seized her forearm. "I know you want to go, but if we try to outrun them, we put them in danger. The weather's getting worse, and we're unprotected out here."

"And we can pinch first spot by the fire before they get here." Jyan gave a grin that withered under Larissa's stare.

Larissa wanted to keep resisting, but Valare squeezed tighter—not to hurt, but she wouldn't let go until Larissa's shoulders dropped in assent. Reins in hand, the trio nudged their horses under the whispering boughs.

Not far in, they found a small dell. The tree line would protect them from the worst of the wind. Larissa gathered wood for the fire, dropping it in piles next to the depression Valare was digging for a firepit. Jyan used a steep side of the dell to prop up a tent, rope and pegs hammered into the earth, large enough to accommodate three swags.

The thud of hooves on pine needles brought them from their tasks, and all three faced the pursuing sisters' arrival. The knight with gold at her shoulders leapt from her horse, took off her helmet, and crossed to them.

Broad-shouldered, the knight was still shorter than Valare. She had cropped white-blonde hair, dark eyes, and an unflatteringly pink complexion more to do with anger than unfitness.

"Knight-Solaris Atticus?" she barked, and Valare nodded. "I am Matriarch Aeleon of Dalanoir." Larissa recognized the city as being far to the south of Janoir. "I was touring my rounds in Janoir when I received word from the grand matriarch herself that you'd taken a leave of your senses and disobeyed orders to remain in Scythia."

Larissa opened her mouth, but Aeleon's hand cut through the air, silencing her.

"I came to escort my darkkin on her quest," Valare said. "As it is the duty of all who follow the Fair Lady—to slay the Evercry, until there are none."

"*Until there are none.*" The murmur around them from the still-mounted knights infuriated Larissa with the blind obedience.

Aeleon's scowl didn't falter, but she glanced toward Larissa.

"That would be Darkkin Westwyn, would it not?" she said, before she snapped at Jyan, "And you can only be Knight Mahcenae."

"On my way home via a circuitous route." Jyan looked

Aeleon over with no small amount of contempt. "Our focus should always be on the Evercry, and the grand matriarch charged Darkkin Westwyn with an item of great import to take to her mother."

"An item tainted by dark magic," Aeleon said. "Our darkkin sensed the orb last night and took most of the day to track its source and contain its effects, thanks to your blundering efforts. You left a dark taint on a body, what were you thinking?"

Larissa blanched. "I burned it out of the body. There was nothing left but ash."

"That's not what my darkkin told me." Aeleon gestured to a woman in dark robes. The woman slid off her horse, removing her crimson hood as she did so. Pale and lithe compared to the muscle-bound Aeleon, she looked up at Larissa through lowered lashes. The sting of betrayal burned hot within Larissa's breast that a fellow darkkin would betray her.

"There was...an echo of dark magic throughout that cellar," she confirmed. "Someone cast spells there. Ones involving forbidden magics. Whatever was done there would have been against the Fair Lady's wishes."

Breath escaped Larissa's wordless lips.

Aeleon gave them a triumphant smile.

Larissa glowered at what should have been her fellow darkkin, but the woman avoided her gaze. Aeleon paced before the trio, glaring at each in turn.

"You naïve girls have got it into your heads you are helping, when both of you are under a spell." She pointed at Larissa. "*Her* spell. She has gone against a sacred mission and binding of the grand matriarch."

Each word rose in indignation as she spoke. Larissa was aghast that this stranger knew of the binding, but also, that she had broken it.

"Thankfully..." Aeleon took control of her voice. "We have another who is suitable to safeguard the orb."

"You can't," Larissa said, stepping back. "It must stay with a

Westwyn. On that you cannot argue with the grand matriarch. It can only be carried by a descendant of Dothreal, or the Evervast—"

A smug smile spread over Aeleon's face, her glee evident.

Larissa had given herself away.

Now Aeleon knew for certain Larissa was no longer bound by the secret, that her accusation was true. It was why they hadn't cared if she left. Navus was exerting her right as judge, jury, and—Larissa feared—executioner.

Aeleon rested her hands on her hips, waiting for Larissa to further incriminate herself. Tired of the games they played, Larissa slashed her arm through the air.

"It doesn't matter if I broke her binding. If you give the orb to anyone not of Westwyn blood, the echo will break free and return to the Evervast. It must stay with the family line."

"And so it shall." Aeleon gestured to a cloaked figure on horseback, not a darkkin as Larissa had assumed, but a young girl, perhaps only twelve.

"Who is she?" Valare asked, confused.

"A distant relative who happened to be near Janoir."

A dim memory resurfaced, Navus's voice as she spoke of those who could carry the orb. Larissa stared at the wide-eyed girl, young and innocent, her blonde hair and brown eyes echoes of Dothreal's face. But she was young. Too young.

"You can't give it to her," she insisted. "It's grown stronger than Navus knows. The closer we are to the city of Lisolel, the more I hear the echo. Its magic is dangerous. If I give it to my mother, she will make this right."

"As anyone who dabbled in dark magic would think," Aeleon said, eyes searching Larissa's. "Or have you wandered so far down the path you don't even realize what you're doing is wrong?"

Around them, hands settled on swords, the knight's suspicion igniting the sisters' long-held intolerance of all who used magic.

"Not at all." Larissa squared her shoulders. "I've only done what they charged me with. Bringing the orb to my mother. *That* was my quest, and I have stayed true to it. But I don't know what will happen if you give it to an untried novice. She's just a girl—she hasn't even faced the Empirical!"

This was the wrong thing to say. Aeleon's smile grew.

"Yes, but you have, Westwyn. And were found wanting."

Familiar waves rushed over Larissa, an ocean tide of the order's strict rules, their judgment swamping her until she suffocated. She wanted to fight, but tight bands about her chest kept her still.

"Take off the orb," Aeleon demanded. "You are not a knight, and therefore have no business attempting to slay an evercry. You defied the grand matriarch's rules, and thus it is clear to all how far you've strayed from the Fair Lady's path. I pass on the grand matriarch's decree that you shall henceforth be banished from the Lady's grace."

Larissa's heart stilled in her chest.

Everything she'd ever fought to prove was for nothing. She was back on the walls of Lathore, useless, at the mercy of her perceived failings.

"The orb, Westwyn."

Larissa looked at Aeleon's knights, who had not sheathed their weapons.

At the young girl, her eyes wide with fright.

At her sisters. Jyan was scowling, but it was Valare that gave her pause.

For the moment their eyes met, she remembered why Valare hadn't wanted to run. These were her sisters, at least for this final moment, and she shouldn't fight them. Larissa would do what was right, not for any of them, but for Valare, who would be honor-bound to defend her.

She handed over the orb.

# Chapter 21

Larissa shivered, and it wasn't from the snowstorm bearing down on them.

Her focus had faded to the distant flakes falling on the plains beyond the tree line. Here in the forest, she was cocooned from the worst of the weather, but not from the general air of displeasure that had arisen from Matriarch Aeleon's knights.

Their fire was further down the dell. A clear distance from Larissa's camp. Valare was invited to share one of their tents, but she declined, with thanks. Jyan ignored the knights.

The trio sat round their own small fire, but Valare sat across from Larissa, keeping her distance. Her gaze lay on the flame, unfocused, but Larissa didn't miss her sidelong glance to the other knights. The first time Valare was an outsider among her own sisters was because of her vow to Larissa.

"The invitation still stands," Jyan mumbled. "You could always come with me."

"And do what?" Larissa said, in the same monotone she'd spoken with all evening.

"Travel the world." Jyan shrugged. "Visit all those places you read about and…what was it you said? Become a pirate queen of the desert sands."

Larissa was far from happy, but her lips tilted up all the same. "We've been here before. I told you I'd just get sunburnt."

"Wouldn't you rather find out? There's a library in the city, too many books for me to read in a lifetime, but you might. Has no one told you about the Great Library of Aongatha?"

Larissa sighed. "I've heard of it."

"That's settled, then. Come live at the palace, read books, advise me on how to rule…"

"That's really asking her to keep her fat head grounded." Valare poked at the fire, before dropping the burning remains of her stick and picking up another to do the same.

Jyan smiled. "Not that you'd know anything about having a fat head."

"I don't at the moment."

"You're fine, Atticus." Larissa used her surname as a reminder. "It's not like you haven't faced worse. You did your duty—it was far more than I could have expected of any other knight."

Valare's jaw flexed in the low light of the fire. She dropped the stick and wrapped her hands around the sword across her knees. "I know you don't mean that as an insult, but it sounds like one."

"Pardon my bitterness," Larissa said, the sincerity of her excuse lost in a rising wave of anger. "I don't feel particularly charitable towards the sisterhood I've known all my life throwing me out of my home and abandoning my mother."

She trembled, tugged her hood up high enough to cover her exposed ears. Unable to stop her hands shaking, she tucked them under her cloak.

Valare stalked across the dirt until she was inches away, resting her sword point first in the earth. "I won't abandon the quest, even if it doesn't see the end you wanted. I'll go back with them and at least ensure the orb's safe return to Lathore."

"They will destroy it," Larissa hissed at her, "which might ruin any chance my mother has of defeating the Evervast."

"She's chased it for seven years, and we've had no sign of her bar this letter, a dead darkkin, and the influence the orb has over you. The echo may very well strengthen the Evervast. We should have destroyed it all along."

"That's not how it works, and we don't know what—"

"We don't know a lot of things!" Valare snapped. "If Sword Matriarch Westwyn hasn't been able to defeat an evercry after all this time, how does she know for sure that releasing the echo will help her kill it? What if this is the Evervast using you, and the letter was never sent by your mother at all?"

This rendered Larissa mute. A protest bubbled on her lips, but Valare's words had dug into her with a blade, exposed the scabbed surface of fear hidden deep within her. She couldn't stop what Valare said next, no matter how much she wanted to.

"What if the matriarch of swords...is dead?"

Larissa stared into Valare's dark eyes, as though they were sucking the life out of her.

"You have to consider it, Larissa." Jyan sighed as she said it. "And there's more than that. You've been far freer with magic in our travels, and you cry out at night, as though the nightmare is winning."

Silence wrapped around their camp. Larissa didn't dare move, staring at the women she'd called friends.

"I'm...not evil," she said, voice fracturing. "I've walked the Hall of Songs, knelt before the Pool of Tears, was touched by the Fair Lady and not found *wanting*." She gasped the last word, an echo of the matriarch who was now eyeing them with suspicion from down the dell.

Jyan settled a hand on her shoulder. "That doesn't change how this looks. *I* believe you. But they don't, and none of us want to hurt them because they *aren't* our enemies, no matter how you feel right now. Yes, we broke the binding, and I would do it again—for me, that is a bond that will last all my life. But so too have I become afraid…for you."

Jyan embraced Larissa, squeezing her tight, and after a moment Larissa returned the hug.

"Do yourself a favor, Darkkin," Valare intoned. "Have something to eat and get a good night's sleep. Without the orb, you can at least do that, and tomorrow you should return with us. Hear from the grand matriarch herself rather than that pompous sow."

She muttered the last, and Larissa glared back at the other camp where Aeleon watched them, still in her armor, hands on hips. Larissa didn't know what else Aeleon wanted from her, but if she returned to Navus, she'd report Larissa was a threat, especially if she did anything contradictory to Aeleon's orders.

"You're right," she said. "I should go back. Be with the orb and argue my case to Navus. For all the good it will do."

"Then come with me?" Jyan asked.

"Why not? I've always wanted to travel the world."

The hollow future carved open the ever-present hole in her heart, and with muttered excuses, she crawled into her swag. She tried to sleep, tried to think of something to do, tried to ignore the trickle of warning that still managed to crawl into her dreams with the echo of a howl…

—

When Larissa awoke, feeling better than she had in weeks, it was to a world of white. Snow had built banks against the tree line, settling on the forest, thick enough it fell between the pines' brushy needles to coat the forest floor. The fire had sputtered to nothing, and a hush had fallen on the world. She scrubbed her eyes, crawled from the tent, and pushed dry twigs on the fading flame, lost in the quiet.

Aeleon's approach interrupted her thoughts.

"I sent a knight out to check the path." She walked past Larissa to the others, who were rousing. "Looks to me like we'll be stuck here another day until the storm passes. Do you need provisions or supplies?"

"No, thank you, Matriarch," Valare said. "We were supplied for our trip. We'll leave with you tomorrow."

Aeleon glanced at Larissa. "We?"

"I want to hear my dismissal from Navus herself," she said. "And should her verdict still stand, collect my and my mother's things. If the grand matriarch has deserted me, then so too has she abandoned my mother."

Aeleon sneered, then seemed to think better of any comment and walked back to her own camp. The crunch of her boots on the snow set Larissa's teeth on edge.

She stared after her for a time, before returning to their tent and her swag. Lying down, she searched her pack for the book in which she'd been lackluster in doing her duty as a darkkin to record her journey.

Going back to the last report, written several days ago in Scythia, she began to add the subsequent entries. She recounted in painstaking detail the journey thus far, until her hand cramped. When she surveyed the text before her, it read like she was trying to prove her innocence. Though she'd hand over the record to her sister darkkins, as was expected, it would be the first and last time she'd write for them. Tears splotched the lead-covered pages, and she took care to mop up the water droplets so they wouldn't show.

At some point she must have fallen asleep, as she woke blearily to deep twilight. The gray clouds had stopped sprinkling their bounty, and the air was crisp, freezing, and interrupted by the smell of stew.

She rose, ignoring the kinks in her back to take a log by the fireside, near Valare. The knight was busy scowling at Jyan.

"What's going on?" Larissa said, though a part of her didn't want to ask, too tired for any more disappointments.

"I'm convincing Valare to take a leave of absence." Jyan watched Valare stir the iron pot. From within wafted the smell of hot meat and vegetables, heartening at the end of a dismal day.

"More like telling me how to find a wife," Valare growled. "As if you'd know."

"My parents have already laid out a married life before me. Boring and predictable. I'll wed a prince my mother approves of, and my father will see it done. You two, on the other hand, could use some love in your lives."

Valare winced. Instead of answering, she served up stew.

"I didn't know you could cook," Larissa said, changing the topic of conversation.

"As Jyan says, at least it will make my future wife happy."

"Depending on how good it is." Jyan took her bowl and tasted the stew. "It *is* good!"

"Don't act so shocked," Valare said, settling back with her own bowl.

"For a piece of hock and some dried-up vegetables," Jyan added with a grin. Valare booted some snow at her, which flicked up and fell in her plate. Jyan tasted again and nodded. "Improved the flavor."

Larissa gave a weak chuckle at the scowl on Valare's face, and in the same moment, it hit her that this would be the last time the three traveled together. Perhaps be alone together.

A prickle curled on her nape, and she looked across to the other camp.

The young girl was staring at her. The one who carried the orb. Cheeks pale and shadows under her eyes, she sat bundled in cloth and close to the fireside. Larissa watched her shiver. She almost rose, but then Aeleon blocked her line of sight, her back to Larissa.

A sense of unending sorrow filled her. She'd known failure was what awaited her at the Empirical, but on this quest she'd never thought she wouldn't succeed. She had defied Navus's orders to see it done. For what?

The stew grew cold in Larissa's hands. She put it to one side, walking away from the camp.

"Where are you going?" Jyan asked.

"More firewood," Larissa said. "What we have won't last the night."

She strode off, her destination out past the camp and into the snowy forest.

Heading uphill, she walked until the camp was out of sight, her thoughts churning. She kicked her feet through the lower layer of snow, ignoring branches that stuck up like blackened ribs of a decrepit carcass against the pure white. She'd collect them on the way back. For now, she hiked, rising higher above the camps with every step, seeking some path through the trees and her life that wasn't about being rejected again and again.

She'd knelt before the sacred Pool of Tears and heard the Fair Lady's voice. If there was anything she was sure of, it was that the Fair Lady had tested her resolve and found that she wouldn't fall to the dark.

Had the echo of the Evervast corrupted her?

She wouldn't know until she stood before the pool once again.

But Navus wasn't about to let her return to the Hall of Songs. It would be better to leave Lathore and go south with Jyan. Do what she'd wanted from the very start. Retreat into a world of books and knowledge, and spend a lifetime satiating a curiosity that needed its thirst slaked somehow, if not with magic.

The tears trailing over her cheeks froze in chips against her skin, and she wiped them away. The wind had died, the storm blowing itself out, but as she scanned the forest, she was compelled to go on, keep walking, an unheard voice urging her forward. It drove her on past thinning trees, her footsteps grown quicker with unplaceable urgency.

Ahead of her, the pines parted, and she fell into a clearing.

Sweat broke out on her skin despite the cold, a shiver trembling through her that had nothing to do with the snow at her feet. Her soul was swept into a spinning vortex of horror.

A path led between the trees to an open sky, and at the end was the rock from her nightmares. The one from which she'd heard the echo of the Evervast.

Against a night sky full of stars, the rock pinnacle was a diamond of white snow, unblemished by footprints. Even as she comforted herself with the thought that this was not her dream, there was no wolf, a shadow leapt from the darkness onto the rock. The breeze ruffled pale white fur, black about its chest and back, framing its large head, ears pricked as it turned toward her.

The wolf of her nightmares.

Its vibrant blue eyes ringed with black spied her. She was transfixed. Dread and anticipation whirled inside her, a maelstrom without cease, and only when she could barely breathe did the wolf begin to howl.

The sound started long and low, the wolf's muzzle rising as its head tilted back, the noise high and keening across the snow-driven stretch. Larissa felt it strike her. Not a physical blow, but a deep gong inside her chest that vibrated into her ears, down her limbs, and reverberated outward back to the wolf. It echoed within, touched the desolate part of her that had cried so many times, surrounded by others yet utterly alone.

In its wake, a tremor started in her feet, a fear of the nightmare reaching its climax. It had haunted her night after night. Prowled after her in dreams and driven her to come here. Called on her to be in this place at this time, waiting for the moment when its howl would make sense to her.

She was awake, afraid, sure now of what fate she'd face when she turned around. Snow crunched under her boots, her eyes sliding closed as the wolf stopped howling. Once her back was to the wolf, she opened her eyes to the figure waiting for her.

"Hello, Mother."

# Chapter 22

Her eyes, fixed on Larissa, were not the caramel brown of Larissa's but a bright wolf blue. Dark blonde hair in braids, the breeze blew wisps across her mother's face, one that should have been familiar...and was not. Always stern, it was now gaunt. Black marks like veins writhed up her cheeks.

She was dressed in black furs and armor, sword in hand. Its blade glimmered with magic runes and blue fire. The sword was lowered, but the sight of a spelled and naked blade dried the words from Larissa's tongue.

Her mother had become an evercry.

Not the Evervast. Larissa's senses flared enough to recognize a difference in her mother; her taint was not of the same magic as the orb. Someone—no, some *thing* had done this to her, forced her down a path of dark magic. It was evident in the carvings on her cheeks and down her throat, the same as...

The agent at the inn.

"Larissa," her mother whispered, her name entangled in anger, "where is the orb?"

Disbelief assailed her, and without thought, Larissa stepped closer. "What happened to you?"

"The orb. Where is it?"

"Did the Evervast do this to you?"

The sword's point rose in her direction, and Larissa stopped. This was no longer her mother, but a creature of dangerous magical ability. Larissa was unarmed, and the orb lay only a few minutes down the hillside. She tried focusing on the woman who'd loved her, stroked her hair, taught her to use a sword.

"Where have you been?"

"Enduring..." her mother answered. Her voice was distant and unfocused, as though she listened to two conversations at once.

Larissa didn't doubt the hand of the Evervast in the runes carved into the flesh of her mother's face. In the cruelty of tainting her mother this way. The marks crawled down under her armor, would be all over her body. But Larissa had burned the marks free of the body in the cellar.

There might yet be a way to free her mother.

Magic came to her stronger than before, clear in her mind. Before she could speak a word of it, her mother's sword slashed down. Snow erupted beside Larissa, spurting up in the air, sizzling with the magic of the sword's strike.

"That will be your last warning, Larissa," her mother intoned, the same strict voice that had tutored her as a child. Larissa gritted her teeth; she knew better than to fight. The evercry's chaotic nature would soon not care for their bond, and that was placing too much faith in its tenuous connection as it stood.

"Where is the orb?"

Larissa shook her head. Her mother took a step toward her, and she took one back.

"Faithful to the end," her mother whispered, her eyes sliding closed. They snapped open again, pale as the moon and just as distant, and within their glowing orbs lay the Evercry. "Tell me *now!*"

The words rolled toward Larissa and wrapped around her throat, slipping over her tongue, a compulsion goading her to confess. Her hands reached up to grab something that wasn't there. But she'd fought a monster such as this before.

"No-o," she said in a strangled cry.

Her mother took another step, hand rising as she spoke words of dark magic, so garbled and monstrous they hurt Larissa's ears in her incomprehension. Shadows writhed toward her, invisible to the naked eye, but Larissa, trained to see magic, caught the tell-tale sparkle blurring over the snow. She retreated, but the tendrils twisted over the distance, faster than she could run. Magic wrapped around her body, squeezing her, a python enveloping its prey. She fell to her knees.

Her hands were too heavy to lift, as though encircled with lead. She panted at the effort, unable to fight both spells at once. She shut her eyes. Choking on the compulsion at her jaw, she fought not to say the words, not to even think of what the evercry asked, her sole focus on the magic binding her. She ground her teeth together. Forced the pressure coursing through her into her head, to keep her jaw shut, then into her arms to lift them. To combine the magical will tightening around her with her own magic, to break its hold. Trembling with the effort, she held her hands out toward her mother, and bringing the words she wanted to mind, burned them over her tongue before the compulsion to confess could take over.

"*Eifren firitos astorithos!*" The incantation echoed through her, touched the wellspring of power she'd fought to contain all her life.

Now, she let go.

Lightning crackled around her, her mother's dark power snapping like rope under the pressure of the magic she exerted. A wall of earth and fire rose around her, between her and the binding, to burst outward. The rush of magic beneath her hands struck the snow and lifted her to her feet as steam filled the air.

Larissa's mother's eyes widened. No, not her mother.

Maladel—one taken by the Evercry. Her feral grin did not belong to the woman Larissa had loved.

"The Evervast was right about you." Maladel tugged something beneath her cloak.

Larissa gasped, unsteady on her feet, trying to keep the magic bound to her will. Not by rune, ritual, or word; it floated within, and she couldn't remember the words to command it, already terrified of its eruption within her.

Maladel gathered long twists of leather in her hand, then flung them at Larissa. Power caught up the leather, and they cracked like whips over the snow. Though fire fell from Larissa's tongue, the insidious leather snakes split apart, becoming too many strands to count. Layers wrapped around Larissa before she could remove them, weaving unbreakable knots of dark magic that bound her wrists and feet, restricted her arms to her chest, folded her hands beneath her chin, and forced her jaw shut. The leather slipped over her mouth, silencing her.

Larissa drew breath through her nose, tried to wriggle free, but the bond sapped away the magic that had suddenly served her so well. She tottered on her feet and then tilted over, landing with a thud. Snow cooled her heated cheeks. She did not shiver from its touch but at the approach of Maladel.

The evercry crossed the snow and knelt before her. The iciness died from Maladel's gaze. One black gloved hand reached out to tuck aside a braid that had fallen over Larissa's face.

"Never forget, all I ever did was to make you strong," Maladel said, almost with pride. "Even knowing this will end soon enough, you served the Fair Lady well."

The hand stroked Larissa's temple, so familiar that its touch made her ache.

"Now you'll serve another mistress." The evercry waved her arm and dragged Larissa through the snow, as though an invisible rope were tied from Larissa's ankles to her hand.

Maladel stalked through the trees, toward the camp, and Larissa realized with horror that she was not alone. Others moved in the shadows, men and women, all clothed in white like snow-covered pines, hidden in the landscape. By comparison, her mother was the darkest tree, standing tall as she surveyed the camp below from the edge of the dell.

The knights sat by their fires, oblivious to what was about to befall them.

Maladel lifted her sword in the air, blue flame on its blade. Her arm dropped, and the agents of the Evercry rushed forward to take the camp.

Larissa screamed behind her bonds as agents fell on the unwary sisters. Silent arrows flew from the trees, felling the two knights on guard. The others jumped at the sound, grabbing their weapons, shouting warnings, but they were surrounded.

The two forces struck one another, the furious chaos of the agents against the orderly discipline of the knights, steel ringing on steel. Swords clashed and bows lashed. The sisters fought well, even beating the agents back when they took trained defensive positions. But the white-cloaked agents held the advantage of surprise and struck with unconventional weapons that burned with dark power. They outnumbered the knights two to one. Maladel strolled along the dell's wall, and she dropped Larissa on her side atop a slight overhang, where there was a perfect view of the carnage.

Larissa fought to summon her magic, anything that would help, but the endless fount had vanished under the binding. She could only watch. Larissa craned her head, looking for Jyan and Valare.

Closer to the end of the camp, Jyan and Valare stood back to back, swords in hand. Half a dozen attackers encircled them, and though Jyan spun on her heel, ready for battle, they did not fire the crossbows leveled at her.

Valare hefted her sword, scanning the battlefield until her gaze fell on Larissa, then the woman behind her. Valare's face turned to a snarl. Her gaze darted between Larissa, bound and gagged, and her sister knights. Hand tightening on her sword, she came for Larissa's prone form.

Maladel placed a boot on Larissa's shoulder, silencing her muted shouts to Valare. Her blade swung inches before Larissa's face. The flame on the sword's edge flickered brightly as it was lowered to rest on the exposed skin of her neck.

Icy agony speared her throat, the blade burning a brand on her skin with its cold fire and tainted magic. She thrashed against the torment, back arching, a scream trapped by the gag. But the boot on her shoulder held her in place as the blade dug in deeper. With it came fingers of dark magic, slipping beneath her skin and into her blood. Bile coated her tongue, choking her, and between the magic and pain, she thought she'd be sick.

Valare halted halfway across the dell, spitting a curse. "Fair Lady damn you, stop it!"

Jyan spun around at Valare's shout. Spotting them, she gripped her blades.

Maladel lifted the sword. "Don't move, Knight-Solaris, or the next one will do more permanent damage."

"Unhand her."

"If you think I won't harm her too badly, you'd be *wrong...*" Maladel lowered the blade again, this time to hover near Larissa's cheek. She pressed her face to the snow, but could not escape the blade.

"Fine," Valare shouted, dropping her sword. Behind her, Jyan threw her twin blades down, lips twisting as she muttered expletives.

"On your knees," Maladel commanded. Neither obeyed. "*Kneel!*"

Magic rolled through the clearing, pressure invisible as a storm bending the knights to her will. They both slumped to the forest floor, into a bow. Satisfied at their capitulation, Maladel shoved Larissa with her boot, letting Larissa fall on her stomach.

Larissa shoved her neck in the deep snow, cooling the burn there, weeping as a stain of dark magic seeped through the wound. It prickled under her skin, bringing revulsion in its wake, and when she tried to fight it, the binding wouldn't let her.

When she looked up, Valare and Jyan were bound, hands behind their backs. At the other end of the dell, all the knights were slain except Aeleon, who remained on her feet, Larissa's young cousin behind her.

"Stay back." Aeleon swung her blade between the approaching foes. "I warn you."

There was a true threat to that cautioning, the bodies of five agents at her feet. But she was the last knight standing, and at least a dozen agents remained untouched.

Maladel strode down into the clearing, sword in hand. Larissa watched in dread from the hillside as her mother's boots sank into blood-drenched snow.

"Aeleon," Maladel called, voice ringing over the remains of the battle. "How long has it been? Four years, I think. I find it amusing that you are here now, given you did nothing then."

"I came to stop it," Aeleon said. "I should have guessed then, Maladel, and all those years ago on the grounds of the Empirical. Too strong, too much, too great. It always corrupts, doesn't it? As you would well know."

The evercry stopped before Aeleon, her head tilted to one side. "Can you hear that?"

Aeleon's aggressive frown faded in confusion, but Larissa heard it too. The distant howl of a wolf, growing louder, a call that had to be answered. She rose to her knees despite her bindings.

This time the sound came from no wolf's maw but echoed from the depths of the forest.

From the mountains wrapped in snow.

From the stars peeking through the trees.

The sound bid Larissa to seek its source. The pain of her burn faded as she drew herself up, gaze falling to the girl behind Aeleon. The orb around her neck was spattered in blood, and it glowed, black light edged in white, darkest of magics. It sang to

Larissa.

Maladel glanced over her shoulder at Larissa, the eyes of an evercry piercing into Larissa's heart. She didn't know whether she ached for comfort, or shuddered in dread. The evercry gestured to her legs, and the binding rose from her ankles to her chest, snake-like leather wriggling, twisting about her, then hauling her one step at a time, until she stood by her mother's side.

"I knew you'd turn traitor," Aeleon hissed at her. "Just like your mother."

The evercry's sword thrust forward, piercing Aeleon's armor as though it were butter, driving through her chest with a wet thud.

All was frozen, the assault so swift even Aeleon was stunned, her mouth gasping like a fish. The evercry bared her teeth, skin stretching to macabre glee. Aeleon's ever pink face drained of color. Maladel withdrew the sword in a sharp jerk. Larissa tried to fall back, but the bindings held her in place as blood arced through the air and spattered droplets on her face.

Aeleon stood for several moments more, her blood spilling out onto already stained snow. She lifted her sword, but the evercry kicked it out of her weakened grip.

Falling to her knees, blood frothed at Aeleon's lips as she cursed.

"The Fair Lady will enact her vengeance on you," she gasped. "Your family's time is at hand. It is a truth I see—the Lady will not tolerate your treachery!"

Maladel's sword slashed down and struck Aeleon to the earth, where the battered remains of her skull leaked out, her face a crimson flower.

"Fools, one and all." The evercry turned her focus on Larissa's cousin. The girl crouched back, eyes wide at Aeleon's corpse, hard pants filling her cheeks, turning into puffs of cloud in the chill night air.

Maladel took a step toward her, and the girl scurried back

with a terrified squeal. The evercry snatched her arm, hauling her stumbling form close. Both mother and distant cousin faced Larissa, the girl's back to her mother's chest.

"For all her posturing, Aeleon was right about one thing," Maladel said. Her hand stroked the crying girl's locks. "Do you know how the orb works?"

Larissa shook her head. Drawing breath through her nose, she swallowed against the smell that wafted toward her, gore and blood sickening even in the frigid air.

"When Dothreal heard the song of the Evervast after she'd killed the human vessel it occupied, she sought a way to expunge it from her mind. Never sleeping, never eating, she was a husk by the time she found what she needed to do. I remember my mother telling me about her...how lost she became."

All the while she talked, she patted the trembling girl before her, voice faraway, as though telling a bedtime story. Larissa was reminded of many a night by the fireside, her mother teaching her the ways of a warrior and knight, what was noble and right.

Nothing before her now carried that virtue but the young girl.

"Dothreal called on dark magic as a last resort," her mother said. "And gave her life force to do so. After all the trouble you took to come here, and bring the orb safely to me, I do not have to watch you die. Not when one distant daughter of Dothreal will do."

With horror, Larissa realized what she meant.

It was the blood.

The reason the orb glowed in the cellar, why the darkkin sensed the dark magic of the Evercry. It hadn't been the blood of her enemies that spattered over the surface of the orb, it was Larissa's blood from where she'd cut her hands freeing her wrists. Just as it was the girl's blood now, from a wound on her hand where she must have fallen.

The Evervast's echo longed to be free, and Westwyn blood was the key.

But it would take more than blood. It would take a life.

Larissa yelled behind the binding on her mouth, but her mother ignored her pleas. She handed her sword to another agent, took from her waist a silver blade sharp as moonlight, and slit the girl's throat.

The girl gasped. Larissa tried to lunge forward, but the magical bonds held her back. Her cousin stared at her with open-mouthed shock as the evercry looked on, amused. When the girl started to fall, Maladel held her aloft, one gloved hand about her throat. Blood ran down her own arm, across the girl's chest, and drizzled onto the orb. Its glow brightened, the heart of a falling star, brilliant in its intensity, the rings about the orb spinning to create a vortex in the center.

The evercry lifted the chain high so the dark light fell on her face. The girl collapsed beside Aeleon, discarded now she was of no use.

Larissa wanted to drop to her knees, to weep at the girl's corpse, but the orb's unlocking captured her attention and she couldn't turn away. She held her breath as the whirling rings ground to a sudden halt.

Thunder erupted from the orb. It knocked Larissa on her back, even as Maladel stood untouched by the wave of power, freed from its confinement. Echoes carried through the forest, deafening all. Those that could clasped hands over their ears. But even after the initial wave passed, a sound followed in its wake: the long, lonesome howl of a wolf.

There had only ever been a single cry, but now it grew into the symphony of a pack. A dark, joyous cadence curled over the shadowed landscape, through the forest, over bodies, to the evercry's feet. When it reached the orb, dark magic shot out into the night. Larissa spun toward the sound, sensing its source beyond the mountains. From a city by the sea. Lisolel.

The Evervast was whole once more.

Larissa turned back to the evercry. Maladel studied the orb, now nothing but three rings of gold and an empty shell. She crossed to hang the chain about Larissa's neck.

"A reminder in the days to come," she said. "Of all you have accomplished."

Larissa looked up into the eyes of a monster and knew that whatever had been left of her mother was gone.

# Chapter 23

Larissa felt the palm of the evercry's hand on her back, pushing her through the forest.

It was not her mother.

When she stumbled, unable to see through the tears pouring down her face, the evercry steadied her.

It was not her mother.

When she leaned against a tree, the evercry took the binding from her mouth to give her water, before restraining her again.

It was not her mother.

The litany repeated itself in her head, with every step she took.

If she'd expected some sort of reunion with the thing masquerading as Maladel, the evercry made sure to disillusion her. She said nothing. Merely walked alongside her as they crossed the forest. Jyan and Valare followed behind, though why they'd been spared, she couldn't guess. What glances she could spare she shot over her shoulder, searching for them. A few glimpses gave her Jyan's scowl and Valare's lip bleeding from a backhanded slap.

Valare hadn't stood idle while the bodies of her sisters were ransacked for what little wealth or weapons they carried. Anything the agents didn't deem worth keeping was left to freeze. The horses they took as well, though none rode through the thick snow. Larissa's legs turned as numb as her feelings as she trudged along, the evercry's bindings a leash about her torso. Where she walked, she had no control.

Keladros's words rung in Larissa's ears; she wished now she'd never come to learn why the Evercry's agents wanted her alive. A cousin she'd never met had paid the price.

And Larissa didn't even know the name of the lamb that had taken her place for slaughter.

The evercry seemed to have no purpose in keeping her now, yet they trekked onward. Her eyes drifted to the runes on her mother's cheeks, like the ones she'd seen on the man at the inn. For all her best efforts, she couldn't recall a single text, artifact, or warning that had triggered her familiarity with them. She focused on keeping her feet, trying to think of a reason for appeal.

The next time they stopped to rest, Larissa gulped her fill of water and then took her chance.

"I'll do whatever you ask," she whispered for the evercry's ears alone. "Please, you want to take me to the Evervast, don't you? I see its mark on you."

The evercry lifted the binding to cover her mouth again.

"No," Larissa said, turning her head to the side. "I won't try anything, please, just hear me."

The flare of power within Maladel's eyes abated, and Larissa stared once more into her mother's face, drawn close enough Larissa saw the fine lines of strain about her eyes.

"What do you want?" Maladel intoned. The apathy Larissa heard there forced her to discard her intended plea to her mother, to the woman who'd birthed her. But she had another plan.

"Why not kill me now the echo is free?" She swallowed against the bile rising in her throat at the next thought. "If the Evervast wants me, I'll come willingly, do all it asks. All I want in return is that you free them."

"Why?" Maladel asked.

"You should know," she said. "Or remember. They are my sisters, and I don't wish to see them given to the Evervast."

The evercry studied them for several moments, and Larissa's pulse spiked.

"No." The evercry covered Larissa's mouth again. "They have a purpose. The daughter of the matriarch of shields, and the future queen of Lysonair? If it weren't personal, you would be of lesser value to the Evervast."

Larissa couldn't ask what she meant. How it could be personal when she herself had done nothing of note in her life.

Through the night and into the dawn they walked, past the forest to an old road between the mountains. Snow lay over it, but it didn't deter the hard-faced men and women of the Evercry, who went to several horses hobbled nearby and a wagon with supplies. They mounted the new horses and hitched a pair to the rickety old wagon. Canvas supply bags were pushed back, and the evercry helped Larissa on, placing her with her back against the headboard, right behind the driver, cushioned by the supplies.

Jyan and Valare were flung on their faces and made to crawl onto the wagon. The pair settled opposite one another, leaning back against the side walls, hands bound in front of them. Their guards left to mount horses, readying to move out. Maladel climbed into the driver's position, her hand held out for the reins.

Valare glared up at the evercry, body tensed to strike. Larissa shook her head, but Valare ignored her. Using the side of the wagon to stand, Valare bent over Larissa to snatch the evercry's sword.

Maladel's arm snapped back, catching Valare by the throat

before she could grab the weapon.

"That was dangerous, Knight-Solaris." She swiveled to look at Larissa, though she spoke to Valare. The ice blue irises were back, her mother's eyes glowing bright with the Evercry's power. "Anyone would think you wanted to have your blood spilled all over your darkkin's face. It would match the stains already there."

She tightened her grip on Valare's throat, leaning forward to brush the specks of dried blood from Larissa's skin. Larissa hadn't given any thought to the residue left there by the evercry's killing. Maladel's cold fingertips were gentle on her face. Valare writhed in her grasp, but she didn't seem to care as she stared down at Larissa.

"I...I w-will stop y-*you*," Valare grunted as the evercry's fingers dug into her throat. Her bound hands wrapped about the evercry's wrist, useless against Maladel's magically imbued strength. The agents didn't react, waiting for the evercry's orders.

"How?" Maladel turned her focus on Valare and twisted the knight's head from side to side, examining her with narrowed eyes. "You'd rather subject to my will than see her hurt. If I injure her body, it matters not—I could go so far as to remove a limb, as long as her mind remains intact." The fingers that had caressed Larissa's face drifted to her hair, tugged her braids, and brushed her ear. "I would cut quite a lot from her for your compliance."

Valare's eyes rolled to Larissa, who gave a minute shake of her head.

"What say you?" The evercry let go her grip, and Valare fell to the wagon's floor. At the soft pressure of Larissa's leg against her own, Valare bowed her head and resumed her seat. The evercry took the reins and flicked the horses on.

Larissa waited until Maladel faced away before she glared at Valare. Gag still in place, she tilted her head to the side and lifted her brows.

"I won't go quietly to my death," Valare said, glaring at the evercry's back.

The evercry paid the comment no mind, and the horses plodded along the abandoned road. Their wagon left grooves in the shallow snow. The agents followed on horseback, their eyes on Valare, who scowled in return. In two single file lines, anyone who bothered to come after them wouldn't know how many enemies they faced.

Not that Larissa thought they would come in time, or come at all. Aeleon's knights would be presumed caught in the storm, not expected to return to Janoir for another day or more. The Fair Lady's order might not send out a search party for weeks. A part of her wanted to laugh. If she hadn't hesitated, they'd have entered the tree line sooner. Aeleon wouldn't have seen them, wouldn't have diverted from the road. And Larissa would be dead.

It wouldn't have avoided Valare's and Jyan's capture, but it would have saved the others, spared her distant cousin from becoming an unwilling sacrifice.

She slumped against the side of the wagon, wishing she'd held the orb, that the evercry had come for her and her alone. She'd led them there, led them to their deaths.

Valare nudged Larissa's leg with her own. "You're sulking."

Larissa lifted her heavy head, glaring and unable to speak. Valare shrugged.

"What use did it serve last time? That's not the woman I want to see now."

Something in Larissa's eyes must have given away her morose thoughts, for the twist of Valare's lips melted back to her habitual scowl. Larissa's head dropped to her chest, and she squeezed her eyes shut, too tired for tears.

After a while, she studied her bindings. The thin black leather cords were twisted into runes, but she struggled to place them. When she finally deciphered their purpose, she cringed. They were a modification on the texts she'd studied. Symbols paired with purpose, with malicious intent. It sickened her. More than a mere restraint, the bindings absorbed her power. What little control she had over the elements fed into the ties. After a fashion, she worked out that while using magic would strengthen the bindings, not using magic wouldn't make them fail either.

She laid her head back against the side of the wagon.

Jyan gasped. Larissa's eyes snapped open. Her sisters stared not at her but her throat.

The burn. She'd attributed the pain at first to inflammation, but the magic she'd sensed when the blade touched her, coursing through her blood, now lingered there. Larissa swallowed the growing saliva in her mouth at the thought that it was *burrowing* into her, under her skin.

Just like the man she'd fought.

Just like her mother.

Her eyes must have said what her mouth could not. Jyan laid her bound hands on Larissa's knee, fingers outstretched to touch the wound.

"Leave her be," the evercry said, glowering. Jyan fell back without a word.

Hopelessness settled on the wagon, the emotion as useful as Larissa had come to be. She gave in to the rocking motion, head tilting to one side as she drifted off in a half sleep.

—

The wind ruffled her hair, and with it came the distant sound of wolves. A baying that could have been the wind, could have been her imagination—but it called to her. When she opened her eyes, the evercry stared down at her, eyes aglow, head canted as she studied Larissa.

Maladel turned back to the road as the wagon descended down the other side of the mountain pass. Ahead of them stretched a sandy plain, but rather than the yellow beaches of the sea, it was black. Sand glimmered beneath the sun like night inverted, with only daylight to prove they were not traversing a sky of stars. Out of the black sand loomed gray rock, chunks lying about, as a child's discarded playthings. The ruins of a once great city left abandoned. Far away, on the edge of the sea, a white castle stood against the azure sky.

Salt carried on the wind, and Larissa breathed in the cleansing scent. Again and again she drew it into her nose, and for the smallest moment, the itching burn on her skin abated.

Roads stretched in a spider's web from the castle. The buildings had turned smooth and hollow from centuries of blowing sands, and fine grains stung her face as they crossed the desolate wasteland. They passed a statue—a king, from the stone circle about his temple. His face had weathered into nothing.

Through the whirling eddies of sand came the breath of magic. Neither dark nor of a single element, it writhed over the landscape, almost visible on the winds that shifted sand between the pillared ruins of Lisolel.

Magic sank into the sightless eyes of the king, crawled over the stones of his forgotten city, and combed itself through the braids on Larissa's head. Welcome as the fingers of a hated lover. Though she could feel the magic stirring, none of it rose inside her, and every time she tried to mold it to her touch, it slipped between her fingers, like trying to hold the infinite grains around her.

Soon any magics she tried wouldn't matter, not with what was coming. Not if this was where the Evervast waited. Nausea settled in her gut.

"What happened here?" Valare whispered.

The evercry looked over her shoulder, not at Valare, but at Larissa. "A battle raged here between a grand matriarch and an evercry."

A grand matriarch? Dothreal's journal had mentioned someone fought the Evervast before her, but not who. Is that what became of Lisolel?

Larissa slumped down the side of the wagon, head thumping on the board. When she looked across at Jyan and Valare, she could only wonder what lay in store for them.

The rattle of wheels on sand changed to the clatter of cobbles as the wagon reached the castle. Its shadow fell over them. Arching her neck, Larissa caught sight of a figure standing atop the tower, garbed in black, stark against the white stone of the castle. A rumble ahead announced the lowering of a drawbridge, and the wagon trundled into a wide courtyard. A circular stone wall, half ruined, surrounded low buildings and the tower itself. It was manned by dull-eyed agents.

After the drawbridge was raised, the agents of Maladel's party dispersed but for a few, two of whom hauled Valare out by her hair and Jyan by her wrists. Maladel dismounted and came around the side of the wagon. She and Larissa stared at one another.

The evercry beckoned to her. Larissa sighed and walked on her knees until she was at the wagon's edge. She nearly slipped, but the evercry caught her shoulder and helped her off. Maladel's hand remained, and she guided Larissa into the tower.

Maladel urged her up a flight of stairs to a great door, the wood turned silver by the sea winds' timeless grace. The door creaked open on rusted hinges as Maladel approached, and Larissa was marched inside.

A large iron chandelier hung from the ceiling, lit with a hundred candles. The light did little to lift the air of gloom and neglect. Antique wooden furniture sat dusty and discarded, but made for seats for the relaxing agents. Tattered tapestries clung to the walls. Larissa was given no time to study further as she was taken to another staircase that wound up the side of the great hall. She glanced back at her sisters, but they were kept behind as Maladel drove her on.

Narrow slits in the walls showed both the hall below and the sea outside. She stole fleeting glimpses of the ocean. Upward they climbed, one stair after another, her legs burning, though the evercry didn't slow. Larissa's breath came in pants, the exertion a weak cover for her fear that surged with every step.

Above the whistling wind, a wolf's howl echoed through the tower, a sound she should no longer hear without the orb, but which was there all the same.

She swallowed past the dread, sweat growing cold on her skin as she took one shuddering breath after another. They climbed the final flight, and the staircase opened to the sky, a low wall stopping a tumble to the distant ground below. As Larissa reached the last step, she looked down at a great wave crashing hundreds of feet below. The castle was built on a cliff overlooking the sea.

On the tower's roof lay a wide stone circle, surrounded by unlit wrought iron torches. Across the tableau, a platform extended over the sea, the drop leading to death. A woman stood there, facing the ocean, her hand resting on the back of a stone throne. Larissa lost what remained of her breath.

The Evervast.

The creature before her writhed with an undercurrent of so much power Larissa wanted to be sick, but the salt wind kept her senses. Beyond the figure was an endless vista of ocean, painted gold by the setting sun. An orange orb, the sun lowered between the tines of the throne, the great seat carved with stone waves rising from the chair's back, intricate and beautiful but faded by wind and sea.

Larissa's gaze fell to the platform beneath her feet, and any desire to move closer faded.

Scrawled into the rock were dark runes, ancient in their marks, but the taint of blood was fresh, still sticky in the evening air. It called her. Larissa tried to step back, but Maladel's hand on her shoulder wouldn't allow her retreat.

They waited for the Evervast, who did not move until the sun sank below the distant horizon. Any shred of hope of surviving seemed to vanish with its light. The Evervast turned to greet her guests.

Larissa's world fell away.

The face was her mother's, yet she'd seen it somewhere else too. The longer Larissa stared at the Evervast, the more confused she became. With the binding in place, she could ask no questions, but she stepped away from Maladel. The matriarch of swords let her go, poisonous glare fixated on the Evervast.

The Evervast's caramel eyes glowed golden, her long pale hair—almost white blonde—was plaited in braids, and her skin was lighter too. But it was the soft bow of her lips, the long nose and wide eyes, that Larissa recognized from her own face. From all those stolen glances of her own reflection, looking for the features of the woman beside her, for her sternness and strength. For what was always missing.

The Evervast ignored Maladel, taking long barefoot steps toward Larissa. Her black cloak fluttered open to reveal a golden dress beneath. Larissa would have assumed she was a queen from the richness of her robes, and her skin fair, smooth, and lustrous. Devoid of dark marks.

When she spoke, there was a tone to her voice, a warmth Larissa had missed all her life that cast her back to a distant past.

"Hello, Daughter."

# Chapter 24

Larissa shook her head. Stared in disbelief.

In denial.

The Evervast flicked her wrist, and Larissa's bindings fell away.

"No..." she croaked. "No, you can't *be*!"

"You knew it when you saw me," the Evervast said. "I do not have to prove anything to you."

Larissa tried to back away, but the evercry's hand lashed out, catching her arm, dragging her back into the circle. Larissa didn't try to fight, staring at the face so similar to her own, the face of the woman who'd raised her.

"Who are you?"

Maladel turned her icy gaze on Larissa. "Your aunt."

"Tell her the rest, Maladel," the Evervast commanded.

Maladel's lips pressed together, but the Evervast wouldn't let her be silent. Larissa watched with horror as the marks under Maladel's skin began to twist, her jaw clenched, eyes blazing with wrath until the caramel brown succumbed to the biting tang of blue.

"I did what our ancestors had done," Maladel spat. "Stayed true to our allegiance with the Fair Lady. But your real mother did not. My sister chose a dark—"

"Ah!" The Evervast held up a finger, and Maladel's hands clenched by her side.

"Chose *another* path," she gritted out, stare locked on her twin. "I feared since we were girls her calling to magic. Watched as day after day the magic twisted inside her. Until the day of the Empirical. She was the last. She used magic to beat the test. And when the grand matriarch banished her, my fear only grew. That one day I'd hear the Evercry's call...and it would be for her."

"But...I don't understand." Pushed past all sense of self-preservation, Larissa's gaze darted between the two sisters: one an evercry, the other the Evervast. "How am I...your daughter?"

"Yes, Maladel, tell her what transpired." The Evervast walked toward Larissa, magic the color of sunlight crackling about her footsteps. The remaining sun's rays gave her golden hair a nimbus glow. Larissa struggled to keep her senses under the wave of power that rippled forth as the Evervast came within touching distance. Her skin tingled, hairs rising as the brush of magic sank into every pore, sliding its subtle fingers inside the wound on her neck.

It wasn't just the strength of the Evervast's magic, building within her, it was this place, overflowing with energy. The pressure was manageable, she'd lived her whole life controlling it, but a trickle of fear snaked up her spine at what might happen if she took in too much.

The Evervast twisted one hand into a claw, and Maladel's face flashed with pain.

Maladel glowered at the Evervast. "I *stole* you from her," she spat, the words seeming torn from her against her will.

All thoughts of her fate were swept aside by Maladel's confession. Larissa forgot Valare and Jyan waiting below, the danger of the dark forces sliding beneath her skin.

"You took me from my real mother, made me believe I had to follow in your footsteps. Why?" She took another step away from Maladel. The evercry's furious eyes flickered to her, and though they hardened, in their depths Larissa caught something else. Regret.

"I placed no expectations on you she wouldn't have," Maladel said. "But rather than proving your worth, you would have used magic as a crutch. And one day I would have had to come and kill you."

"She thought she could redeem you," the Evervast told Larissa, though she looked at Maladel. "That growing up in the embrace of the Fair Lady would keep you safe. Pure. When all it did was cage you." Her knowing gaze swung to Larissa. "Didn't it?"

A protest formed on Larissa's lips, the denial she'd shouted to herself for years.

But the Evervast's gaze pierced her heart, and pain and sadness burst from within her chest. Unbidden, she flashed back to every secret moment she'd wet the pillows with her tears. She'd learned everything she could to fit in, to be brighter and smarter and *good*. She'd tried to kill herself when she hadn't measured up. She had done everything in her power to prove herself to them, and all she ever remembered receiving in return was their censure.

As she stared at Maladel, at the aunt that had stolen her, Larissa struggled to fight the Evervast's truth.

"I..." Her voice faded on the wind, and she swallowed to find it again. "I still hold true to her."

"In your heart of hearts," the Evervast said gently, "do you believe that?"

She belonged with the Fair Lady, had knelt before the Pool of Tears in her sanctuary and known she was pure of purpose. She'd passed the doors of the darkkins, proof that she was not corrupt.

Whether that was true anymore, she wasn't sure. She was

afraid that Aeleon's accusation was right, that carrying the dark orb had tainted her in ways she hadn't realized, just as the evercry's brand was now doing to her flesh.

But the brand was more than merely an open wound seeping blood, letting in the magic about her. It was a towering wave in the recesses of her mind.

She didn't know what to do when it came crashing down on her, inevitable as the falling sun. If there was a path to the Evercry, then this was the start; she'd rush headlong into its embrace without the ability to stop, even if she claimed she wasn't drawn to its lure. Because that was fast becoming a lie.

As the magic stretched her senses further, it awakened something deep, beneath the hollowness she'd thought was endless. The fist of control she'd maintained all her life unclenched. The forbidden curiosity that drove her to experiment underneath the darkkins' noses—done not with any malice, but with longing to revel in her creations. The snippets of joy in the magic she'd kept secret.

This thought alone smashed against the foundation of all she'd been taught. Her head hung. Tears poured out from a bottomless well, even as she wished to sink so far down into its depths she drowned.

Pale hands entered her vision, then wrapped about her shoulders in a tentative grasp.

"I only wanted you back," the Evervast whispered. Except, to Larissa's ears, it was no longer the Evervast but the voice she'd always longed for, to tell her she was enough, that it was *proud* of everything she'd accomplished. The way no one else had ever told her.

When she looked up into those caramel eyes, so like her own, Larissa wept.

"I don't want to go on like this," she confessed. "I can't. I'm not...who I'm supposed to be."

Her mother, her real mother, brushed her hand down Larissa's cheek as they stared at one another. Eye to eye, the same color, the same height, everything the same.

She could bear no more.

Larissa fell to her knees, and the woman who should have guided her through life fell beside her.

"Who are you supposed to be?" the Evervast asked her, without irony, a simple and clear question no one had ever asked before.

"Not...this." Larissa shook her head, unable to lie even to herself. "Not someone who *hates* themselves for who they were told they should be and couldn't."

The Evervast settled her hands on Larissa's face. "No one should force a child down a path not meant for them."

Larissa wanted to abhor all the Evervast was, but she couldn't deny the Evervast's, her mother's, statement.

"The grand matriarch wanted you to kill in her name, did she not?"

Larissa nodded.

"The Fair Lady's knights said you must become like a woman who wasn't even your real mother, did they not?"

Again, Larissa nodded.

"But..." The Evervast held up a finger. "The Fair Lady didn't find you wanting, did she?"

Larissa paused, before her hands grasped the Evervast's arms. "H-how did you know?"

And when the Evervast smiled, she wasn't the tainted creature her mother had become, but something else, eyes aflame, the same color as the dying sun, and full of such joy as Larissa had never known.

"Because you want for nothing, Larissa. I know it. The Fair Lady knew it too. You are perfect, just the way you are, and there is nothing in the world you should fight for more than the person who exists inside you."

What reached inside Larissa now wasn't magic, or guile, or trickery.

It was love.

The Evervast loved her.

"You know there is always more to the story than they ever taught you in school."

"Tell me my truth." Larissa grasped her hand. "Tell me what really happened to me."

The Evervast's smile wilted. "I left the Fair Lady's halls and wandered the world. Years passed, and as I searched for purpose, I found your father at a library." The Evervast stroked her face. "But not long after you were born...knights came for us, *she* came, for the little magic we used, for what they feared we'd become."

Larissa turned to the evercry who still stood above her. "You killed my father?"

In Maladel's eyes, Larissa saw a truth that had always lingered there.

Those times by the fireside hadn't been about teaching goodness—they had been about keeping Larissa humble. Of teaching Larissa her place in the world. Under the yoke of the Fair Lady.

To stop her becoming like her parents.

With each new revelation, the deceptions of the past shred away, the ones Larissa had built her life upon, tearing her down to the foundations of her being. Her hands clenched against the rough stone platform. She felt the runes and their magic, and knew now what had been so familiar to her. It wasn't the symbols themselves; it was the magic that spoke of her true mother. Of her true self.

Larissa rose to stand in front of the woman who'd robbed her of a far different life, one she could have wanted, even thrived in. One where she could have been *loved*.

"That night by the fireside," she said, "you never heard the echo. But you knew she was out there...and that she would come for me."

"Yes," Maladel answered. "In our city she couldn't touch you, but I knew she'd wait. Until you were older. So I hunted her down, to stop her before she succumbed to the darkness." Maladel shrugged. "Now I belong to it too."

"What about *my* darkness, everything you, *they,* put me through?" Larissa's voice raised to a scream. "*How could you?*"

Maladel said nothing. There was nothing to say; she was convinced of her faith.

Larissa shut her eyes, swayed away. The Evervast enfolded her in her arms from behind, and Larissa leaned against her, used her as the support she'd always needed and never had.

A warning prickled in Larissa's mind as magic rose around them, but she didn't fight it. She let herself fall into the Evervast's power, not dark and twisted but golden, stunning as the summer sun and just as warm.

It sank through her skin, banishing the taint left behind by the evercry. The burn on her neck melted to nothing and left flawless skin in its wake. The power reached inside every ache, stretched down to the tips of her fingers, every bruise or scratch mended. Clarity entered her muddled thoughts.

Clarity and the metal ring around her finger pressed on her. Wild notions danced in her head. Instinct drove her to a sure conclusion that right and wrong were clearest with actions...and consequences. When she opened her eyes, magic filled her.

"And how do you propose to atone for such a sin?" Larissa's voice was fire, curling off her tongue, the power rolling down to drip lava from her lips that left her unburned and undefeated.

"Do you think it matters now?" Maladel replied. "Your mother has already done the worst."

Larissa stepped back beside her mother, her real one, and smiled. "Perhaps not. But I know a fitting end for you. From someone who mastered the Empirical in *three* strokes."

The evercry's power faded a moment, Maladel's irises darkening to brown again as her pride rose to the surface. "That's not possible."

"She's better than you," Larissa said with a laugh. "*Stronger* than you. That was who you tried to make me, *Mother*. Someone stronger than you."

"What are you suggesting?" the Evervast murmured.

"That we have true poetic irony in our grasp." Elation burgeoned in Larissa's throat. The Evervast's magic was swarming over her mind, and she couldn't stop it. "We have a knight of the Fair Lady slay the Evercry...*until there are none.*"

The last was spat with such venom Maladel's eyes narrowed.

"True to your credo, isn't it?" Larissa said.

The Evervast touched her arm. "This is your judgment, how you want her to die?"

"Yes!" she snapped, her gaze not leaving Maladel's. "I call on Knight-Solaris Atticus to enact her duty and slay this evercry."

The Evervast chuckled, deep-throated and spitting magic that was an echo of Larissa's jubilation.

"I had not envisioned the end of my twin this way," she said. "But I can't say I disagree." She clapped her hands, and about the stone circle, torches alit on the wrought iron stands. "Here now, let's do this straight away. Fetch her...Daughter."

As Larissa descended the staircase, she heard the laugh of the Evervast in her ears, but she was consumed with keeping her head. Thoughts rushed by almost too fast to keep track, but so too did a fragment of a plan she wasn't yet willing to count on. It spun gossamer fragile as a spider's yarn, glimmering within her, past the power that wanted to overwhelm her.

A chance she dared not think on lest the Evervast guess her intentions.

A truth she still held in a sliver of starlight.

A silver ring.

# Chapter 25

Larissa flew down the stairs as though they were nothing, magic filling her and spilling at her feet. Giddy with the power, she joined in her mother's laughter all the way down. She needed chaos in her mind, no thoughts on anything but the magic.

At the bottom, she tumbled out into the hall, and felt nothing. Not the impact of her hands on rough stone, nor the jarring through her knees—magic took it all away. Larissa couldn't stop the laughter, giggling at herself, guffawing at the idea magic could do this, chortling at the faces of Jyan and Valare.

Their eyes were wide, Jyan's hand raised to her lips, Valare's mouth a hard line. Their horror brought back Larissa's purpose, and she clutched to her sanity, not knowing how to stop her mother's power over her, but clinging to the weak semblance of a plan.

"Valare," she yelled as she scrambled to her feet. "Now is your time. Come do what you've always wanted."

She ran to where both sat on the floor. The agents guarding them parted for Larissa without question once they glanced into her face. Magic sparked from her fingertips and a golden hue emanated from her skin, and she knew her eyes would be the same. The same as her true mother.

"It can't be," Valare gritted out. "Larissa…"

"Valare," she mimicked.

This mockery instantly filled her with regret, and the doorway inside swept closed, holding back the flood of magic. She wanted to explain, but there was no time.

"Give me her blade," she shouted, and one of the agents scurried to serve her. None needed to ask if she came on the Evervast's orders; all could see the magic pouring from her body, uncontained, restless. Larissa had to set it free, feel the flow.

An agent darted to her, holding out the handle of Valare's sword. Instead, Larissa took a dagger from his waist.

"Get up." Larissa's harsh tone snapped with magic, and Valare rose, a puppet pulled on strings. Larissa regretted it, but kept the apology behind her teeth. She couldn't give herself away. Not yet.

"I never thought it would be like this." Valare widened her stance. "I don't blame you—the magic has corrupted you, but I know this isn't you, Larissa."

The sincerity in her voice stirred a despair in Larissa, but she couldn't give in to it, couldn't lose her fickle grasp on sanity by sliding across to sentimentality. It would break the façade. The Evervast would see.

No one was more surprised than Valare when Larissa split her bonds.

"Westwyn," Valare hissed, "are you *insane*?"

"Larissa, what's wrong with your eyes?" Jyan got to her feet, and Larissa snapped her bonds too.

"Don't want to talk about that, mustn't talk about that," Larissa babbled. Even though she'd left the Evervast's side, magic continued to pour into her, her true mother's elation a never-ending fount of power. The magic, finer than any wine, desired to be used, and Larissa could have gulped and gulped it down until she drowned. She held it back with everything she had left: the two women before her.

"Where is your sword, your sword, your sword?" she chimed, snatching it out of the agent's hand. When she unsheathed it, the sword sang, just as it had at Still Water.

But the blade was too dull. It would not do.

"Of *course,* it needs to be runed." She gave a high titter, and Valare eyed her with confusion and anger.

"What the Fair Lady's lock are you playing at, Larissa?"

Larissa slapped a hand over Valare's mouth.

"*Don't*...don't say her name," she choked out. Her thoughts were cobwebs caught on the wind, and it was taking all her self-control to keep the threads in her hands, to hold them all together. To balance between the magic filling her and her path.

*To walk in the dark between stars...*

Laughter burbled from her lips as liquid fire, and Jyan drew back, the horror Larissa had never wanted to see in her friend painted starkly on her face. Valare's scowl grew, and she grasped Larissa's arm tight.

"You are *losing,*" she growled. "Whatever they've done, you're becoming one of them."

Larissa's grin grew. She shook her head. "Not me, not now. Take the sword, hold it high."

Valare accepted the sword, and as she held it out, Larissa struck her own hand across the blade, turning it red with blood and heat, magic sparking from her hotter than a forge.

"*Adolebitque conbures, videt igne, igne luxuriate.*"

The sword in Valare's hand ignited with fiery magic. Light reflected in Valare's eyes, bright runes that would aid her not just in power but in her every movement—the tension of each muscle, the execution of each strike. To mask it all from Valare's senses, Larissa used the surplus magic within herself, releasing enough that she regained her sanity by an infinitesimal amount.

"Climb the stair," she said. "Slay the evercry."

"But…" Valare paused. "Your mother—"

"That *thing* is not my *mother*." Fire snapped through the air, Larissa's breath like a dragon's, and all about her flinched under the power of her words.

"As you wish…Darkkin."

Valare crossed the hall with sword in hand, and none of the agents stopped her as she began to climb. Larissa turned to Jyan.

"I need you to go."

"Don't be—"

"The evercry was right," Larissa said, rushing through her words as the wave rose within her again. "You are heir to a kingdom. Your future is too important to be lost to this cause."

Jyan's jaw clenched, her eyes sparking with an argument. Larissa shook her head.

"There's no *time*," she confessed, tone gushing with uncontrollable laughter. "Because I have nothing but a chance, nothing but a dance, nothing but a warrior's lance."

The mirth, the laughter, the chaos. She had to keep it all and keep it close.

Her hand tightened on the dagger, and she took one deep breath after another as Jyan watched and waited. How had the blade come to her hand? She forgot. Whatever insanity lay within the magic was everything Larissa had feared from the Evercry's possession. She wouldn't be her mother's daughter, she would be her puppet.

This thought goaded Larissa into thrusting the dagger's hilt at Jyan, and when she took it, Larissa pulled off the ring blessed by the Fair Lady. The moonstone glittered in the candlelight of the chandelier.

"Do you know what this is?"

"Yes," Jyan said. "But it belongs—"

"Don't say it." Larissa lowered her voice. "Wear it, give it to Matriarch Theras in Lathore, and tell her…tell her the ring was true. Stay back and out of sight—we both know you can't afford to die here."

After a moment Jyan took the ring, grasping Larissa's hand. "I hope you know what you're doing."

Larissa couldn't answer.

She ran after Valare, magic giving her unnatural speed so she was on the knight's heels in seconds. Valare turned, bringing down her flaming sword, but Larissa held her hands up and backed down the stair.

"Valare, listen," she pleaded, the magic fading now she'd spent some of it. "I don't know how much I can do, it's getting harder to think, but I need you to focus on one thing and one thing alone."

"What?" Valare asked. She came forward, ignoring the flames that leaked from Larissa's mouth. Larissa stumbled against the wall, head swimming. She dragged Valare close, hoped the Evervast couldn't hear.

"*Kill* the woman you know to be my mother. You must. You can't stop the Evervast, but you can stop the evercry. Remember your bond, Knight-Solaris. You are duty-bound to protect me, and I *need* you to slay the evercry."

Valare grasped Larissa's arm as she nodded. "Until there are none."

She sheathed her sword to help Larissa from where she'd fallen against the wall. Together they climbed the stairs, all the way to the rooftop, and the stone platform.

The evercry still stood in her place, and the Evervast had taken her throne. She held out her hand for Larissa, who crossed the platform to accept, molding to the Evervast's side when the creature drew her close. Valare stared between the two malicious forces.

"Is this what you want, Daughter?" the Evervast asked.

Larissa's laughter faded as the sea spray touched her face, sure as she could be of Valare's purpose, and her plan.

"What else would you have me do with such a woman?"

The Evervast smirked. "Your *niece* seems to think you

deserve to die by the hands of a knight-solaris. What say you, Maladel?"

Maladel unsheathed her sword, a slow smile spreading over her lips. The blade flashed an icy blue, runed in dark magic and power. "What hope does a novice have against me?"

Valare drew the sword Larissa had spelled, and along its length, flame-driven runes turned it red, alight with a power to burn the darkness.

When Maladel glared at Larissa, she shrugged. "I thought the odds should be fairer than you ever gave me."

"You have made a good choice, Daughter."

The Evervast's delight tickled Larissa, but she could pay it no mind. She had to watch her plan play out, feeble as it was. She had to focus on the wellspring of magic, and how much it fed from the Evervast's power. An abyss within she hadn't known existed, and she took in as much as she could, a bloated leech, hoping when the time came that it would be enough.

The narrow thread she'd held on to with the ring was cut. Now only one thing kept her from falling into the chasm of the Evervast forever.

The cry of a wolf only she could hear.

Valare and the evercry faced one another across the tableau, swords drawn, each prepared to die for what drove them. But amidst it all, Larissa saw the lie. This was not Valare's evercry. If Valare had any hope of winning, it was for the simple reason that she was a better knight.

And Larissa believed it.

The two knights raced across the platform, and the steel of their broadswords smashed together. Sparks rained across the stone. Again and again their blades swung, the knights matching one another in power, determination, and fearlessness.

For all Maladel's deft movements, Valare broke through her guard with brute force. Relentless in her attacks, she moved with precision and rage, raw strength shattering Maladel's defenses.

But it was a ruse. Maladel's form changed, and the blade

she'd swung at the same pace as Valare's attacks became swifter, surer of her strikes. One landed on Valare's armored side, and she grunted. Another clipped her leg, blood spattering on the runes.

With each arc of their swords, each metallic echo over the tower, their breaths came faster, their limbs trembling. They circled one another, sweat dotting their brows, and Larissa could feel the Evervast's growing dislike of the odds, magic rising from the runes in the platform.

"No," she said, reaching for her mother's hand. "This is my revenge. Don't you trust me?"

After the barest flicker, the Evervast nodded, drawing Larissa into her embrace. "Of course, Daughter."

Larissa let herself be enfolded, but she hadn't been looking at the Evervast when she spoke. Her gaze was fixed on Valare. Valare, who was bleeding in three places where Maladel had penetrated her defense. Valare, who didn't trust magic, but trusted Larissa.

The evercry attacked in wrathful, sweeping strikes, as though sensing victory, but a scream of frustration revealed the real woman beneath. Valare didn't succumb to weakness, keeping pace with the knight.

Desperation won out, and the evercry cut through Valare's defense, broad blade striking upward. Though Valare leaned back, the broadsword clipped her jaw to slide up her face and across her eye.

Valare screamed and fell to the floor, blood pouring out of her face onto the dais, but at the same time, Maladel dropped her sword to clutch the blade inside her belly. Valare had closed the distance, entering striking range to make her own thrust, even as she'd exposed herself. It was enough for her undercut to reach Maladel, slicing so far into her body that the sword came out the other side.

The evercry stared down at the weapon. She yanked the blade from her stomach and crimson spewed from her mouth.

Stumbling, she approached the Evervast, clutching her wound.

"Sister," the evercry hissed, eyes bright blue. "Help me."

The Evervast's grin was ecstatic. "I think you'll find that's up to *my* daughter."

Swallowing bile, Larissa extracted herself from her mother's arms and crossed the platform to collect Maladel's blade. A swift glance told her Valare wasn't dead, but it might be only a matter of time.

Larissa turned to her aunt.

"No!" Maladel swore. She lunged for the blade, but Larissa struck out with it, forcing her back.

"Was it worth it?" she whispered. "Did you think kidnapping me would turn out differently, or did you hope I'd die in servitude? Or save you the trouble and end myself?"

Maladel snarled at Larissa. Foregoing the sword, her hand curled, a warning sign of her intent to use magic instead. Larissa stood before her, unafraid.

Maladel struck out.

Dark tendrils reached for Larissa, but the Evervast wouldn't stand for it. Arcs of golden light created a dome around her. The black power of the evercry smashed into it, hammering at its shields, but the defense stood strong. The hair on Larissa's neck prickled as the Evervast sank itself into ensuring that Larissa could stand there, before the evercry's fury, untouched by Maladel's wrath.

All the while, Larissa layered magic over magic in her mind, brought forth all the knowledge both stolen from the library's texts and given at Theras's and the darkkins' hands. The fire she'd used to burn darkness at the inn melted into something else on her tongue.

Not fire. Not wind. Not earth. Not water.

Not darkness.

Light.

The Evervast's golden shield disappeared as the evercry's power died, Maladel collapsing to her knees with exhaustion.

"You failed," Larissa told her. "You could have left her, left me, alone. But you drove her down this path. You didn't just fail, you're at fault."

"Look what became of you anyway!" Maladel roared.

"It might not have come to this." Larissa bent down so she was at eye level. "But you were so certain of your righteousness. I should've seen it. In you. In Atticus. In Navus. All of you blind to your cause to the point of prejudice."

Maladel didn't answer her.

Larissa's shoulders slumped. "But it was more than that. You wanted me. Not from maternal love, but to carry on your legacy. A legacy that mattered beyond all other considerations... including me."

For a brief moment, the evercry faltered, and in her eyes shone the woman Larissa had known as a child, the woman who'd raised her with nothing but the best of intentions. Maladel reached out a bloodied hand, stroked Larissa's face, and whispered a single word.

"*Now.*"

Larissa lunged forward, driving the icy sword through the throat of the evercry.

A final assault of dark magic burst forth, and the Evervast rushed to Larissa's side, surrounding her in light when the darkness reached out to steal Larissa from the living. This wasn't Maladel, but the dark forces within her. Writhing limbs smashed down on the cocoon around Larissa, golden sparks like lightning burning ever brighter as the evercry, and the woman who had been Larissa's mother, died.

As the light faded from her aunt's eyes, Larissa couldn't help the sorrow that embraced her, as the dead woman never had. The long-held emptiness within her chest, which had filled up with magic, now overflowed with something greater than the power. Purpose.

"It is done..." The Evervast fell back to her throne, exhausted from the fight but elated. "My vengeance is complete. We are free."

Legs shaking, Larissa used the sword as a staff to help her rise, her vision whirling in the maelstrom of power she kept hidden behind clenched teeth. She held onto a single thought as she approached the Evervast.

"My daughter." The Evervast beamed. "We have done it."

Larissa smiled back, though it was done with thin lips, more of a grimace.

"Now all will be well."

"I..." Larissa coughed over the magic in her voice. "I want to see the ocean."

Her mother came over and took her arm. Still clutching the sword of her aunt, Larissa held on tight, unsteady on her feet, magic thundering louder than her pulse in her ears. She stood on a precipice, sensed the distant wave about to come crashing down on her, bury her in power until she forgot herself.

As though the Evervast knew, she assisted Larissa as they crossed to a great platform that hovered over the abyss below.

The Evervast stopped partway out, but Larissa walked on until her feet touched the edge of the stone platform hanging over the sea. She looked down into the depths of the ocean and was reminded of the Descent. The darkness she'd wished to throw herself into, to be lost forever.

"What is it, Daughter?"

"I'm not sure." Larissa stared at the water. Salt stung her face, soaking into her skin, and she breathed it into her lungs, let it bring clarity to her mind. "I once stood like this on the edge of the Descent and wanted to throw myself in."

Her legs wouldn't hold her up—the Evercry was there in her mind, close, too close, ready to consume her. She crumpled to her knees, her sword biting into stone, keeping her upright but weakening the ancient, weather-beaten platform.

The Evervast rushed to her side.

"It's all too much, I know," the Evervast whispered in her ear. "The truth, the power. But let it flow into you. It isn't a curse but a reward. You have done so well, better than I could ever have hoped for or expected, after what they did to you. I should have come for you sooner."

"Why?" Larissa cried in true regret. "Why didn't you come for me?"

The Evervast kissed her brow, held her face between her hands, and placed her forehead against Larissa's. "I wasn't strong enough to face the grand matriarch without the orb. I needed to draw you and it out—I needed to be whole again. Now that I have it, I know what I need to do."

A part of Larissa longed to stay, wanted nothing more than to stand at her mother's side, now that the false mother she'd known lay dead in the circle behind her. She collected the crumbling remains of her resolve.

"What shall we do, Mother?"

"We finish what we started," the Evervast said. "We have always been drawn to power, to this place. It's why we have come back again and again, and yet we've never triumphed. But you have reunited us, and together we can find true balance, not the persecution taught by those who rule the Fair Lady's acolytes. We are not enemies, only opposite sides of a coin."

Hot tears scalded Larissa's cheeks, but inside there was only ash.

"And the girl?" she whispered.

"What...girl?"

Larissa's hand clenched on her leg as the other tightened about the sword's hilt, bitterness coating her tongue until it was all. "The girl in the forest. Don't you remember?"

The Evervast shook her head.

A sob built within Larissa, greater than the magic, and she knew the time was at hand. She thrust upward, sharp and hard, burying the sword as far as she could into the Evervast.

"The girl in the forest that my *mother* slaughtered for *you*!" she screamed.

Uncontrollable power rushed through her hands into

the sword, burning through the body it pierced in an instant, turning it into a torch of human flesh. Magic lashed out at Larissa, the limbs of the Evervast, but they could not land, could not strike her. The very dome the Evervast used to protect her before, Larissa copied now, save for where the sword stuck in the Evervast. Larissa forced all the remaining magic she'd collected into the flames, both hands about the hilt. With a cry, she heaved the body over the edge, pitching it into the salt of the sea.

Down the Evervast fell, screaming, until she crashed into the black ocean. A plume of boiling air erupted. Larissa fell back. The entire world trembled as, below her, the Evervast died. Magic rippled outward. She scrambled for the safety of the tower as the coastline shook.

Rocks fell away beneath her feet, and she made a lunge for the castle walls. Her grip caught as the stonework beneath her crumbled down the cliff. Everything trembled, and her fingers began to slide. She closed her eyes, prepared to join her mother in her watery grave.

A vice grip wrapped around her wrists.

"Got you!"

Larissa looked up into Valare's eyes.

Eye. Her face was a mess on one side, but Valare's one good eye focused on Larissa.

"Don't folly, Westwyn," Valare growled. "Climb!"

Larissa scrabbled at the stone and the knight's arms. Beneath her, the tower shook, the explosion of the Evervast damaging the foundations of the castle, the earth in the cliffside itself. Scaling the rocks to safety, she fell into Valare's arms, heaving one breath after another, gasping as anguish washed over her. Valare grasped her shoulder.

"Come on, Larissa."

Larissa wanted nothing more than to fall with the tower. "I can't."

"You needed me," Valare said. "Now I need you to get

moving or we'll both die here."

Somehow Larissa found her feet, and upright they supported each other across the rooftop, every step shaky from wounds in flesh and soul. The castle's shudder grew with every step.

"Hurry," Valare cried, "the tower won't be standing for long."

The pair watched, too late, as the stairs fragmented away. Far below, the courtyard and escape beckoned, no sign of the Evervast's agents, but three horses pulled at their stays, panicking at the earthquake.

Beside them waited Jyan, who stared up at the tower, sword unsheathed. Larissa could barely discern her in the darkness of the tower, but she held the reins of a horse and the cart, ready to take them away. She hadn't run as Larissa told her, but prepared.

"We're trapped." Valare struggled with her impaired vision, head twisting about. "Look for a way to safety!"

"Do you trust me?" Larissa said, drawing Valare tighter to her side.

"At a time like this—yes, get us out of here."

Larissa looked over the edge. There was no other choice. "I'll use the last of the Evervast's magic to save our lives."

"I still hate this," Valare said, but she held on fast.

"Hate it all you like, but *jump*!"

Before they could, the tower shook, and their weight and exhaustion toppled them over the side. But not to their deaths. Larissa gathered the remains of the magic within and blew out her breath directly below them. Their plummet slowed, the air catching them up, floating them down to the stones of the courtyard like leaves on the wind.

They landed with a thud rather than the bone-crushing force of a true fall, but Larissa's strength had extended too far. Her knees buckled beneath her, and the world tilted.

"Larissa!" Valare cried, catching behind her knees. Larissa heard her voice as though it were far away. "Jyan, the wagon!"

Through bleary eyes, Larissa watched the wagon come

closer, the injured knight grunting with the effort of lifting her up. Larissa tried to rise, but Valare barked at her, "Don't move, Westwyn, damn you. You are no lithe wallflower."

"Did...did you just call me fat?" Larissa blurted, her brain addled.

Valare grunted. "Only where you're supposed to be."

Larissa wasn't given a chance to retort. Valare set her down on the rough wood of the wagon, Jyan's laugh echoing in her ears as she lay back. The wagon shuddered as Valare vaulted onto the back and kept shaking as Jyan yelled at the horses. Larissa gazed up at the tower from her prone position, watching the rubble fall, seeing the cold and distant heavens. In the night sky, Phaylinar, the bow-woman, cast a flurry of shooting stars. Whether they were the lingering magic of Lisolel, figments of Larissa's exhaustion, or the dying sparks of the Evervast, Larissa didn't care. She made a wish.

To never hear the howl of a wolf again.

# Chapter 26

A month after the tower's fall, Larissa sat cross-legged at the center of the Empirical stadium. She replayed the events in her mind, over and over, remembering them anew.

Three days Valare and Jyan waited with her as she wandered the beaches of Lisolel and the castle ruins, ears pitched for the howl's echo, eyes seeking others like her own rising from the surf. She told them they could leave, but they wouldn't go without her, despite Valare's wounds. Larissa had gathered what magic she dared to accelerate the healing, but she could do nothing for Valare's left eye. Whenever the need to attend Valare's fever wasn't great, Larissa scoured the coastline for any sign of the evercry or Evervast.

Not even their bodies washed up on the beach.

Larissa stalked the shores of the stormy sea until she was sure it was over. The agents of the Evervast had abandoned their mistress, but also abandoned enough supplies to sustain the trio long enough for Larissa to be convinced she had indeed slain the Evervast, and nothing remained of the evercry either.

The only howl she heard in Lisolel's sandy ruins was the wind, empty as Larissa was inside.

One thought returned her to Lathore. The morals that kept her head clear throughout the chaos. The call that guided her north. The echoes of the Evercry. She'd misunderstood it all, and now she knew what Navus feared.

Footsteps sounded on the stone of the Empirical stadium, distant but growing closer. Larissa didn't move; she knew who they belonged to. A simple invitation, this day and this time, yet the grand matriarch had made Larissa wait several days before confirming she'd meet with her.

Larissa used the time wisely.

Upon their return, Larissa stayed by Valare's side until she was sure that, while Valare was scarred and had lost the use of her eye, she was otherwise well. Larissa had then gone to the darkkins' halls. At the doorway, she'd hesitated, unsure she could pass, but if she didn't try then she wouldn't be able to test her theory.

She strode through unharmed. Her relief was caught on the wave of greetings from her fellow sisters. She embraced them all, but it was Theras she held tightest. In the quiet of the matriarch's study, over more than one glass of wine, Larissa relayed her story and gave Theras not only the ring but a promise of a debt she might not be able to repay.

Lastly, she went to Jyan's parents, who had arrived after word of their daughter's disappearance brought them to Lathore. Long into the previous night, Larissa had spoken to Jyan and her mother, and made certain arrangements with the queen of Lysonair for Larissa's future.

Everything was taken care of. Larissa only needed to face one last foe.

Navus's footsteps echoed across the stadium, and after a moment came the grinding of stone on stone—the lever that activated the bridge to the Empirical's platform. Larissa still sat, eyes closed, not bothering to stand in Navus's presence. Silence settled over the arena.

After a while, Navus's footsteps came toward her, her voice rebounding through the empty stadium.

"Why are you here, Darkkin Westwyn?"

The title sounded odd from her mouth, as though she'd tasted foreign food she didn't like. Larissa's lips twitched in amusement, but her voice was serene when she spoke.

"I remember that day," she said. "To think I'd never been so scared. Seems laughable now."

"All who face the Empirical should be afraid. They face their destiny."

"Yes." Larissa's eyes snapped open. "None so frightening as my own destiny, were there? Even for you, and you didn't have to bear that burden. You tied it around my neck like a noose."

When she met Navus's silver-eyed gaze, Larissa wasn't intimidated by its coolness, had stared into faces far more frightening. She gave Navus a slight smile. The grand matriarch stopped at Larissa's expression.

Without using her hands, Larissa rose in a fluid movement, swift and graceful, and the sudden gesture startled Navus. Her hand clutched her robe, a scowl growing on her face.

"Your actions at the trial were unheard of—"

"Except by those who'd witnessed a similar tactic decades before." Larissa's voice echoed over the arena, stronger than the grand matriarch's. She crossed to stand before Navus, only paces from the edge, taller than the aged, bent woman, before she whispered, "Is that not so?"

Any warmth she'd once seen in Navus's eyes was gone now, as though it had never existed. The fleeting kindness she'd so foolishly believed in when she'd endured the trial before the Pool of Tears had only been relief. Larissa had passed the test, and Navus could rest assured Larissa was untainted. With each second, Larissa became more certain that Navus was aware of her dark heritage and had feared she might one day turn to the Evercry. Just as her true mother had done.

"There is no point hiding the truth any longer," Navus said. "Your *aunt* brought you here. Your mother passed the Empirical by using the chains such as you did. When we would not grant her the title of knight for her efforts, she left. She met a mage, found out about her grandmother, and sought out the Evervast. Look what became of her!"

Larissa froze, staring at Navus, wondering if she knew what Maladel had said atop the tower, how similar their words. Seeing her for what she was—so rabid in her doctrine that she filled her acolytes not with devotion, but fear.

Fear of magic she so casually used herself.

Fear of magic users she could not control.

Fear of the Evercry.

And she fed that fear to all who came to stand here.

Larissa's hand settled on the sword at her hip, a gift from Theras. "I met the woman who birthed me, and I am *not* my mother."

Navus stilled.

"And now, the truth of my own test this time, if you please."

Navus didn't speak, and Larissa's lips thinned. She would never impress Navus, because no one ever could while she lived with such dread. Especially not Larissa.

"You may hate me," Larissa said, "but you cannot deny me, even though you denied my mother. It is you who are *beholden* to the Lady, and the lie you told won't suffice a second time."

"I owe you *nothing.*"

Navus drew back, retreating to the bridge, but Larissa advanced on, not seeing the noble lady that guided their order, but an old woman who fought for control as age took its toll on her mind. So firmly stuck in its groove of terror and hatred it had turned her blind.

"Tell me the truth," Larissa pressed. "What happened when I faced the Empirical?"

"You cannot make me do anything," Navus said, every word growing louder. "She may have passed as you did, but I never knighted your mother for her tricks, and I will not knight you!"

A protest echoed across the arena, and Larissa stopped her pursuit, smirking. The old woman's brows drew together, until she looked over Larissa's shoulder. Larissa didn't need to turn to know who stood there.

Valare, in the shadows of the Empirical's grandstands.

Dressed as a knight-thane, her cream armor was edged not in gold but in silver. Just like Darkkin-Thane Goverin. Valare insisted she never heard the call, only assisted Larissa with her duty, and therefore had earned the silver of assisting in slaying an evercry rather than the gold of slaying one herself. A black patch covered her left eye, her face bisected by a puckering wound from her brow to her jaw. By her side she carried the blade still imbued with Larissa's blood and runes. But the fire within the blade was no match for the fury in Valare's single eye as she took in the grand matriarch.

Beside her, her mother, the matriarch of shields, came forward, cheeks burning crimson. Her gaze was fixed on the old woman, and the intent within was clear: death before dishonor.

Footsteps rang from another of the stands, and there stood a future queen. Gold circled about her head and wreathed through her dark curls, an emerald at her throat and the forest green silk robes of Lysonair royalty falling from her shoulders. Jyan lifted her regal head and glared down her nose at Navus. Behind her, a couple came to stand on either side, one a noble man in elegant garb, the other a dark woman with a crown of her own, head tilted high. The queen of Lysonair and her consort. The trio stared down at Navus.

Yet another approached, from the third grandstand: Theras, the matriarch of the darkkins. Dressed in the crimson of their order, her ruby about her neck, she looked not on Navus but to Larissa, with pride.

Larissa bowed in honor to each of the three come to stand as her witnesses, before she turned to the grand matriarch.

"Knight me," she demanded. Navus backed away, and

Larissa stalked after her. Navus retreated up the stairs to her seat for the Empirical.

"I am not just a knight, I'm a bridge between the darkkins and the knights," Larissa said, her voice carrying across the stadium to all. "I am just as Dothreal was—a darkkin knight. One who can hear the song and wield magic without falling into the dark. A knight-somnus. You and your predecessors may have stricken it from the records, but that doesn't change what I am."

"Such a title does not exist."

"Would you like the proof? I've done the research." Larissa tugged her notes from a pocket. "These references may be in the restricted sections of the library, but you have no control over the darkkins' records." Larissa flung the notes at Navus's feet. The woman flinched as though they were vipers.

Larissa didn't wait for her denial. "My mother died draining the Evervast of its power, and then I killed it and cast it into the sea. Moreover, I ensured it will never come again. Is that not our credo, Grand Matriarch, to slay until there are none?"

The same lie Navus fed all of them, and every grand matriarch before her.

"That does *not* make you a knight," she hissed for Larissa's ears alone.

"You're right." Larissa came so close Navus abruptly sat down on her hollow throne. "The call of the Evercry makes me a knight, and I heard it in a lone wolf's howl. I heard it in nightmares well before this started, and you palmed it off as the growing influence of the orb. It wasn't the echo I heard—it was my birth mother, after the matriarch of swords's conversion to the Evercry was complete. The Evervast could do no worse evil than turn her own sister to the darkness. That was when I heard the call to slay my own blood mother, in the cry of a wolf. It was *never* the orb."

"That's impossible," Navus whispered.

"You know it isn't. And when my birth mother gave me all

the powers of the Evervast, I killed the woman who'd pretended to be my mother, who'd become an evercry. I slayed her with the assistance of Knight-Solaris Atticus, and then I killed the Evervast. Thus fulfilling a duty you never thought would be my mantle."

Silence echoed over the stadium. The witnesses to the evidence Larissa presented watched as she knelt before Navus, bowed her head, and waited. After a moment, Navus sighed. She retrieved the sword by the throne.

Head still bowed, Larissa felt the sword touch her shoulders.

"As Grand Matriarch of the Sisterhood of the Fair Lady," Navus said, her voice shaking, "I name you as one of our defenders, a knight of the Fair Lady. Arise."

Larissa lifted her head, but she did not stand. "Aren't you forgetting something?"

"What more could you want?"

"That blade isn't anointed with the Fair Lady's tears."

Navus's cheeks burned. Larissa rose.

"At every turn, you have sought to sway me," she said. "That day of the test, my foot on the bridge, I felt your magic..." When she had almost slipped and fallen to the pit below, before she could even face the trial. Now, looking into Navus's eyes, wide with fear at Larissa's knowledge, Larissa knew the depth of Navus's hatred. She would not leave without her prize.

"Take me to the pool," she said, "and afterwards I promise to go very far away. As a knight-somnus, I am allowed to follow a path of solitude and research, and I swear to you I will leave this place, no threat to you, or your position."

Navus's hand tightened on the hilt of her sword, and Larissa tensed, ready if the older woman thought to strike at her, but when her stony gaze turned to Larissa, Larissa said something she didn't know was there until it was spoken.

"We are not enemies, you and I," she said. "Just different sides of the same coin."

Navus's grip loosened, and after a deep breath, she got

wearily to her feet and led Larissa out of the stadium. Larissa turned back and, hand over her heart, bowed to the three corners that had supported her. Theras brushed away tears. Jyan waved, her mother placing a hand on her shoulder. Atticus dipped her head once, in approval.

Lingering, Larissa stared at Valare's single eye, wanted to close the distance between them. But the grand matriarch waited, so she turned away.

She followed Navus through the corridors and to her chambers. When she brought out the blindfold, Larissa closed her eyes, accepting its embrace.

"I know the way," she said, uncertain of the words' origins but knowing they were true. "And one day it will be my path."

"You presume too much," Navus snapped, some mettle returning to the fore.

"No. I see much clearer than before."

Navus took her hand. Down through the depths of Lathore they walked, and this time Larissa didn't falter. Not when Navus escorted her through darkness, not when she was told she couldn't remove the blindfold this time, not when she passed the pool of endless stars where the souls of past grand matriarchs rested.

Not when she found the edge of the Pool of Tears.

Still blindfolded, Larissa heard something that had been lost to her when she first came to the sacred place.

"She cries," Larissa said, moving with certainty to sink her hands into the water.

"She has much to cry about."

Larissa turned back to look at Navus with sightless eyes. "Not anymore."

She stepped into the Pool of Tears.

Navus gasped, but Larissa silenced her with a wave of her hand. Magic unfurled in her palm, snapping to seize Navus in the same way Maladel had bound Larissa. Navus shrieked, but Larissa ignored her. She stood, head canted back, senses strained as she waited for what had come before, the assessment of her worth. Now…there was nothing.

If the Lady disapproved of Larissa using magic, it didn't show, and if she would object anywhere, it would be here.

Larissa took this as an invitation and waded through the ankle-deep water. It rose to lap at her thighs, cool ripples chilling her flesh, and she strode out further still to the rock she knew was at its center.

Her skin tingled, a wave of magic rising around her, the Lady's essence crossing the pool like a subtle breeze. Once more she was enveloped, the Lady's regard like the caresses Larissa had always longed for. She fell in genuflection, water up to her shoulders, one hand resting against the eternally weeping rock face. Sorrow clogged her heart, sobs choked her, and she whispered an admission to the Fair Lady that Navus couldn't hear.

"I…" She lost her voice, and tried again. "I did it, but I'm sorry. I killed my mother and my aunt. I don't agree with them, but what they were doing wasn't entirely…wrong, for either side, was it?"

Nothing answered her, but Larissa's hair fell against her throat, braids brushed from her face by a passing wind.

"I will go away for a time," she said. "But I promise you this—I am true to you. That is the lesson I've learned through all this pain and anguish. I see you the way no one else does, because I know what it's like to be burdened with an expectation I never wanted. I believe in you, because I believe in me."

This time, when she cried, she heard the Fair Lady's sorrow. Kneeling in the water, her tears fell for the mother she'd never known, and the one she'd killed. For her lost life and what was yet to come. The truth of the Fair Lady…and the story behind the Evercry's existence. A burden of discovery she never asked to carry.

And yet, the Fair Lady's tears called on her to answer. To end her sorrow.

When her sobs subsided, she rose from the water—but no longer as Larissa, the darkkin scared of violence and bloodshed, but as a knight-somnus.

She trod the path between stars, but she was not made of darkness.

When she removed the binding about her face, all was as she remembered, the water-marked rock weeping evermore from an unknown fount. But even as she looked down on the pinnacle of rock, so too did she see the rivulets of water begin to slow.

Soon they would stop altogether.

Larissa kissed her fingers and laid them against the stone in the dying stream, stroking it as the two women she'd come to think of as Mother had stroked her cheek.

She stepped away. Navus waited by the edge of the pool, sword ready to knight her again, but Larissa pushed it to one side.

"I didn't need your acknowledgment," she said. "Only a reason for you to bring me here. I know who I am. The Lady has proved it herself." She took off the necklace about her throat, lifting the empty orb, and held it out to Navus. "But I will take my armor, gilt in silver and gold, for I have assisted in the slaying of an evercry, my aunt, and slayed the Evervast that called me, my mother."

Larissa stepped from the pool. Her own sorrow was no comparison for the tears eternally wept by the Fair Lady, ever spilling from the woe that decanted from her heart, but which could no longer fall from her face.

"I am a knight of the Fair Lady," Larissa said, "and you cannot take that away from me."

# Epilogue

Larissa gazed down at the Descent's heart.

It wasn't a strange, sullen, and forsaken place to her now. Between her real mother's ego, and her faux mother's determination, she'd tasted more of the Evercry's cup than she ever wanted.

The taint of the Evercry was a mark on her soul no good deed would ever remove.

Only the Fair Lady's blessing kept her from that desire for oblivion. This time, she would have done it out of duty to her sisters. She did not want to find herself one day in the embrace of the Evercry, and have her sisters hunt her down. But she wasn't contaminated. Wasn't evil. The magic didn't lure her any more than the temptation for a delicious dessert.

The absorption into all that magic was, could be, left her with more questions than answers. Like the first time she'd touched magic, what drove her now wasn't the lust for power but understanding.

The same determination led her here, onto the walls, to where she'd once thought to throw herself to her death. Now the concept was laughable. But Larissa was resolutely solemn, staring into those depths, wondering to what purpose the Evercry lingered in this realm, when the Lady stood so fast against it.

Larissa raised a hand over the lip of the Descent and opened herself to the magic below. Not an invitation—an observation, a chance to see for herself what lay in the heart of the Descent, just as she'd come to understand the Fair Lady's Pool of Tears.

Heat flicked her bare palm. She flinched but held steadfast, seeking what lay beneath, so aware of her it was quick to warn her off.

Or invite her in.

"Knight-Somnus Westwyn?" The voice stuttered over a title not heard in over a century.

Larissa dropped her hand. "Hello, Matriarch Nelasar."

Nelasar chuckled behind her. "Do you have time before your journey to sit with an old woman?"

Larissa turned from the shadowy depths of her curiosity. "Of course."

The matriarch was older. The grooves on her face deeper. Little more than a year had passed since their first meeting on the walls of the Descent, yet she had changed. She held a cane now, used it to help her sit. Larissa took off her traveling cloak and swept it about the older woman's shoulders.

"My, that's warm." Nelasar pulled the fur edges of the cloak to her face. "Won't it be hot in the desert?"

"It's a long way to the Naburi sands." Larissa didn't ask how the matriarch knew of her intentions. "And the nights there can be cold as the ones here."

"Lady forbid! Do you mean to go straight away?"

Larissa's belated knighthood took place just the day before, but there was no point to waiting. Navus wanted her gone, and truth be told, Larissa needed distance from the old woman's lies. Needed to see her sisterhood for its truth.

"When the sun hits the horizon." Larissa leaned back onto the rock beside Nelasar. "We'll take the river down to the docks and head via coastal routes. Truth be told, I'm looking forward to seeing an unfamiliar sea."

One crashed in her mind, the echo of her true mother falling into the depths of a midnight ocean, encased in gold, Larissa's sword in her stomach.

Her head dropped, hands clenching her knees, gritted teeth holding back a cry of absolute rage and despair. No matter her façade of calmness, at times the emotion washed over her still, an inexhaustible rage.

"It occurs to me," Nelasar said, taking a flask from her robes and unscrewing the cap, "that you'll walk through another night without knowing what or where the dawn might be."

Larissa twisted her head to study the old woman.

Nelasar sipped from the flask and handed it to Larissa. She sniffed the contents, a hot sweet tea, and took a swig. Honey coated her tongue and warmth sank into her chest.

"I didn't come here today to kill myself." Larissa passed the bottle back. "Not this time. I came to see the truth of what lies beneath. I came to know *why* we do what we do. What it is that makes the Evercry so evil. For I don't doubt its chaos, but I do doubt its malevolence."

"Oh? You think it doesn't mean to hurt? That doesn't change that it does."

Larissa shook her head. "But we hurt too—the sisterhood hurts. I've seen it. I've been hurt by it. How can we pretend that we're noble, when all the while, the virtues we hold dearest are a lie?"

Though her audience wasn't one she knew well, of all the places in the world that Larissa could have made such a confession, this felt like the time to be honest, to say her truth and see what it meant.

"Do you know they call us starseers liars?" The matriarch

gave a genteel shrug beneath the heavy cloak. "We consistently prove we are right, but we'll never not be fabricators of half truths to them. Fanciful, presumptuous, and ultimately wrong." Nelasar stared at the horizon, the dull haze of dawn reflected in her eyes. "I knew the grand matriarch when she was young. Became wary of her ambition years ago. But it is not her that you must fear, it is all those who came before, that made tradition out of what suits, rather than what is. A new dawn is coming, and they'll not feel it in their shadows until it consumes them."

Larissa tilted her head until her gaze met the old skyseer's. "You've seen the future."

Nelasar chuckled, sending Larissa a sidelong glance. "How do you think I found you in the first place?"

Larissa's suicide, the long ago thought of dying because she didn't belong.

"You came to stop me."

"There was no certainty."

Larissa took the flask from Nelasar's grasp and sipped it before handing it back. "There was enough to bring you here, not once but twice. I have no intention of killing myself now, so what is it you came for?"

Nelasar's fingers tightened about the metal cannister. "You want to start a war. You want to bring it back, what the Evercry once was, and we don't know yet if it will be for good...or greed."

Larissa blanched at her secret so suddenly revealed. "I don't want money or power—"

"No, but you want to prove them wrong." Nelasar sat up straight, pressing forward until Larissa felt her breath fanning over her face. "You want to show the grand matriarch how wrong she is. Even though you already did, it's not enough, not to you, not for all the harm she's done."

Resentment prickled Larissa's tongue. "If they lied about me passing the Empirical, and about ridding us of the Evercry permanently, what else have they lied about?"

"Some secrets are worth keeping. The Lady might have let

you hear her cry, but that doesn't mean you can do more than wipe away her tears."

Larissa flinched, but she had come too far to stop her quest now. "But I mean to. If the Lady balances the Evercry, but she doesn't exist on this plane anymore, then why does the Evercry linger? Why is she *still* crying?"

Nelasar sighed, long and heartfelt. "You are not the first to notice the growing imbalance. More evercrys are reported every day, even as our knights grow stronger. I wonder if in our attempts to eradicate it, we aren't making it worse."

Larissa stared at the horizon. Dawn's dim light filtered through the fog. "As long as people crave power, the Evercry will find a home."

"But...to what end?"

Nelasar's question voiced a concern Larissa hadn't yet been able to answer. But the answer wasn't here in Lathore, or in the heart of the Descent. She rose from her seat.

"I have to go."

"To the Library of Aongatha." Nelasar undid her cloak and handed it to Larissa. "I've never seen it, but I've heard it is endless in its knowledge."

"Not endless."

Nelasar grinned. "Do you think it holds the key to this riddle?"

"Perhaps." Larissa grimaced. "I...still don't know the right questions to ask."

"I think you'll find what you're looking for, in one form or another." Nelasar settled back against the stone. "Now leave me to my stars."

Larissa brushed the old woman's shoulder and then sank into the city of Lathore. There was nothing to collect—her bags were already packed with the Lysonese delegation's wagons. All she needed to do was saddle her horse.

In the stables, Valare was putting the final touches on the bridle for Larissa's horse. Farther down the road, the Lysonese queen stood beside her carriage, their entourage ready for the journey.

Jyan wasn't with them. She was in the stables, speaking with Valare, but she stopped as Larissa approached. With a quick glance at Larissa, she offered Valare her hand. "The invitation still stands."

Valare took her arm and brought Jyan into an embrace. "And I say again, no."

Jyan squeezed her and let go. She glanced over Valare's shoulder at Larissa. "I'll see you on the road."

Larissa nodded, puzzled at the behavior. Valare came to stand before her, not meeting her gaze.

"I've saddled your horse. You have supplies in case you get separated from the party, but you should stay with them at all costs—"

"Valare, I'm not hunting an evercry anymore."

Valare snorted. "You say that like you think personal safety is restricted to when you hear the song."

Larissa chuckled but stepped closer to Valare. "I don't have agents or an Evervast chasing me."

Valare's good eye sought Larissa's face, searched her eyes. "You underestimate the danger still out there."

"You aren't my knight anymore, Valare." Bile built on Larissa's tongue as she spoke, the idea of leaving without Valare now a disconcerting uncertainty, leaving her stomach in hard knots. "I'm a darkkin knight now, a knight-somnus. I don't need a bodyguard."

"Not that you would want this one." Valare turned away.

Larissa's hand snapped out, seized the other woman's arm. "Don't you *dare*."

Valare visibly swallowed. "I am not...fit to give you proper escort."

"I would always prefer to have you by my side," Larissa said, softening her grip. "Not just for your prowess, which I have no doubt will return once you adjust, but for your faithfulness, your determination, your counsel, and your courage."

The latter words were thickly said through the budding emotion in her throat.

"Are you choking up on me, Westwyn?" Valare taunted, but her tone was lackluster.

"I wouldn't give you the satisfaction, Atticus."

Valare raised her gaze, but there was a call behind her, the party readying to leave. Valare's hand tightened on Larissa.

"Don't go."

The sudden utterance was weak as a kitten's first breath. Larissa hesitated. She closed her eyes, took a deep breath, and drew away. "You know well enough why I can't stay."

Valare's fist fastened about her wrist, tugged her closer, brought Larissa within inches of her face. "Promise me you won't do anything foolish until I find you again, Westwyn."

Transfixed by Valare's sudden zeal, Larissa struggled for words. "I swear." Valare held her tighter still, and Larissa shook her head, finding a focus. "I won't do anything to jeopardize myself or anyone else, but you must know I go there to study the origins of the Evercry. But I would...wait for you. If I thought you would come."

Valare lifted her hand to brush her fingertips over Larissa's cheek, push a braid behind her ear. She dropped her head and sighed. "Would that you could keep out of trouble of one kind or another. Yes, I want you to wait for me, until I am certain I can fight by your side once more."

Larissa's heart thudded in her ribcage. Mouth dry, she nodded. "I promise."

Valare settled her hand about the back of Larissa's neck, as though to draw Larissa closer, but instead she squeezed and let go, before walking back toward Lathore. Larissa's palm ghosted over her face, already missing the warmth.

And when Valare glanced over her shoulder and gave a soft, sweet smile, it was as though she knew.

# Acknowledgments

None of this would be possible without my husband, Lucas, whose ceaseless support has given me happiness I didn't think I could possess. Even when things didn't work out the way I wanted, he was my rock, my port in every storm, my general in battle, my unshakeable foundation. I kept failing upward because of you.

To my other rocks:

Hart, I will always think of you when I ask myself how I ever made it here. You believed in me at the start when I didn't even think I had a chance. You will always be the first person I think of when I wonder at how I even started this journey. I love you, thank you.

Sarena, having you there, seeing the "day-in-day-out" side of me, gave me an outlet and understanding for so many stresses, heartaches, rejections, and publishing woes. But you were there to champion the good things when I didn't make much of it. Thank you for your belief.

Meg, you were there in the early days, and you said something that has stayed with me ever since: this story is not for everyone, but for those who read and love it, they'll remember it forever. Thank you, those words kept me going.

Jennica, my editor and the person who believed in this story as much, if not more, than me. I can't thank you enough for your comments, support, and patience. I didn't know how close this story was to my heart, and even as we cut it to make it readable, a herculean effort, you handled all the mental health triggers within this book with the utmost care, and for that I couldn't be more grateful.

And to every girl, teenager, and woman who felt like she didn't belong, who wore a mask to get through the day, who was left feeling alone. You aren't. There are so many of us. Reach out, and we will reach back to you.

# About the Author

Ejay started her author career in 2014 self-publishing a steampunk series called the Last Prophecy. In 2019 she wrote *Behind the Veil*, signing a contract with Literary Wanderlust, released on the October 1st 2021. She signed a second contract for *Echo of the Evercry*, a NA fantasy. She also released a scifi series, Queen of Spades, now an award-winning series. She has a short non-fiction story called *I Can't Hear the Sea with Gothic Seaside*. Judge for SPSFC, volunteer for Flights of Foundry 2022, panelist for Weekend Writers, member of RWA (Aus) and Sisters in Crime (Australia), and avid earl grey tea drinker, whose muse is a real pain.

You can find her on social media through the below links:

https://ejdawson.com/
https://www.instagram.com/ejdawsonauthor/
https://twitter.com/ejdawsonauthor
https://www.tiktok.com/@ejdawsonauthor

https://www.facebook.com/ejdawsonauthor
https://www.goodreads.com/author/
show/14845831.E_J_Dawson

www.ingramcontent.com/pod-product-compliance
Lightning Source LLC
Chambersburg PA
CBHW060859210726
48293CB00006B/1878